Generation One

PITTACUS LORE

MICHAEL JOSEPH
an imprint of
PENGUIN BOOKS

MICHAEL JOSEPH

UK | USA | Canada | Ireland | Australia
India | New Zealand | South Africa

Michael Joseph is part of the Penguin Random House group of companies
whose addresses can be found at global.penguinrandomhouse.com.

First published in the USA by Harper Collins Publishers 2017
First published in Great Britain by Michael Joseph 2017
001

Printed in Great Britain by Clays Ltd, St Ives plc

A CIP catalogue record for this book is available from the British Library

HARDBACK ISBN: 978–0–718–18876–4
TPB ISBN: 978–0–718–18879–5

www.greenpenguin.co.uk

MIX
Paper from
responsible sources
FSC
www.fsc.org   FSC® C018179

Penguin Random House is committed to a
sustainable future for our business, our readers
and our planet. This book is made from Forest
Stewardship Council® certified paper.

CHAPTER ONE

KOPANO OKEKE
LAGOS, NIGERIA

THE WEEK BEFORE THE INVASION, KOPANO'S father, Udo, sold their TV. Despite his mother's fervent prayers for his father to find a new job, Udo was unemployed, and they were three months behind on rent. Kopano didn't mind. He knew a new TV would manifest soon. Football season was coming and his father wouldn't miss it.

When the alien warships appeared, Kopano's whole family crowded into his uncle's apartment down the hall. Kopano's first reaction was to grin at his two younger brothers.

"Don't be stupid," Kopano declared. "This is some bad American movie."

"It's on every channel!" Obi shouted at him.

"Be quiet, all of you," Kopano's father snapped.

They watched footage of a middle-aged man, an alien

supposedly, giving a speech in front of the United Nations building in New York.

"See?" Kopano said. "I told you. That's an actor. What's his name?"

"Shh," his brothers complained in unison.

Soon, the scene descended into chaos. New York was under attack by pale humanoid creatures that bled black and turned to ash when they were killed. Then some teenagers wielding powers that looked like special effects showed up and began to fight the aliens. These teenagers were only a little older than Kopano and, despite the madness their arrival had created, Kopano found himself rooting them on. In the coming days, Kopano would learn the names of the two sides. The Loric versus the Mogadorians. John Smith and Setrákus Ra. There was no question who the good guys were.

"Amazing!" Kopano said.

Not everyone shared Kopano's enthusiasm. His mother knelt down and began to pray, feverishly muttering about Judgment Day until Kopano's father gently escorted her from the room.

His youngest brother, Dubem, was frightened and clung to Kopano's leg, so Kopano picked the boy up and held him. Kopano was short and stout like his father, but well muscled where his father was paunchy. He patted Dubem's back. "Nothing to worry about, Dubem. This is all far, far away."

They stayed glued to their uncle's TV day into night. Even

Kopano couldn't maintain his good cheer when the footage of New York's destruction was played. The broadcasters showed a map of the world, little red dots hovering over more than twenty different cities. Alien warships.

His father scoffed when he saw the map. "Cairo? Johannesburg? These places get aliens and not us?" He clapped his hands together. "Nigeria is the giant of Africa! Where is the respect?"

Kopano shook his head. "You don't make any sense, old man. What would you do if the Mogadorians showed up here? Hide under the bed, probably."

Udo raised his hand like he would slap his son, but Kopano didn't even flinch. They stared at each other until Udo snorted and turned back to the TV.

"I would kill many of them," Udo muttered.

Kopano knew his father to be a boastful man and an unrepentant schemer. It had been years since Kopano responded to Udo's big talk with anything but scornful laughter. However, Kopano didn't so much as chuckle when his father talked about killing Mogadorians. He felt it, too. Kopano itched to do something, to save the world like the guys he'd seen fighting at the UN. He wondered what happened to them. He hoped they were still out there, fighting, turning maggot-aliens to dust.

The Loric. How badass.

The second night of the invasion, Kopano stood outside on his uncle's veranda. Never had Lagos been this quiet.

3

Everyone was holding their breath, waiting for something terrible to happen.

Kopano went inside. His brothers and uncle were still blearily staring at the TV screen, watching horrific reports of a failed Chinese assault on a Mogadorian warship. His father slouched in an armchair, snoring. Exhausted, Kopano collapsed onto the futon.

He dreamed of the planet Lorien. Actually, it was more like a vision than a dream, the whole thing unfolding like a movie. He saw the origin of the war that had traveled to Earth, learned about the Mogadorian leader Setrákus Ra, and about the brave Garde who opposed him. The saga was like something out of Greek mythology.

And then, suddenly, he awoke. But Kopano wasn't on his uncle's futon in Lagos. He sat in a massive amphitheater alongside other young people from many different countries. Some of them were talking to each other, many were frightened, all were confused. They'd all experienced the same vision. Kopano overheard one boy say that a moment ago he was home eating dinner, he'd felt a strange sensation come over him and now here he was.

"What a bizarre dream this is," Kopano remarked aloud. Some of the nearby kids murmured agreement. A Japanese girl seated next to him turned to regard Kopano.

"But is this my dream, or your dream?" she asked.

Then new people appeared out of thin air, all of them seated at the ornate table in the room's center. Everyone in the audience recognized John Smith and the other Loric from TV and YouTube. Questions were shouted—What's going on? Why did you bring us here? Are you going to save our planet? Kopano stayed quiet. He was too in awe and he wanted to know what his new heroes had to say.

John Smith spoke to them. He was confident in a humble way. Kopano liked him immediately. He told them—the humans sitting in the gallery—that they all had Legacies.

"I know this seems crazy," John Smith said. "It also probably doesn't seem fair. A few days ago, you were leading normal lives. Now, without warning, there are aliens on your planet and you can move objects with your minds. Right? I mean . . . how many of you have discovered your telekinesis?"

A lot of hands went up, including the Japanese girl's. Kopano looked around, jealous and disappointed in himself. These other kids were learning telekinesis while he was sitting around watching TV.

A glowing Loric girl at the table with a strangely echoing voice displayed a map of Earth with locations marked. Loralite, a stone native to Lorien, now grew in these places. Those with Legacies—Human Garde, like Kopano was supposedly—could use these stones to teleport across the planet. They could join the fight.

"I obviously can't make you join us," John Smith said. "In a few minutes, you'll wake up from this meeting back wherever you were before. Where it's safe, hopefully. And maybe those of us who do fight, maybe the armies of the world, all of us . . . maybe that will be enough. Maybe we can fight off the Mogadorians and save Earth. But if we fail, even if you stay on the sidelines for this battle . . . they *will* come for you. So I'm asking you all, even though you don't know me, even though we've royally shaken up your lives—stand with us. Help us save the world."

Kopano cheered. He clenched and unclenched his fists. He was ready!

Suddenly, the evil Setrákus Ra was shouting threats, his black eyes scanning the room, his gaze boring into everyone. People started to disappear, blinking out of the dream. Kopano woke with a start, sweaty, his head aching.

Little Dubem was the only one still awake and he was staring at him. "Kopano," Dubem whispered. "You were glowing!"

The next day, with his family once again gathered around the television, Kopano made his announcement.

"The Loric visited me in my sleep. John Smith himself asked me to come join them in the defense of Earth. They showed me a map of the world with the locations of stones that I may use to teleport to them. One of them is located at Zuma Rock. I must go there immediately to meet my destiny."

Dubem nodded along solemnly while the rest of Kopano's family stared at him. Then his father and uncle broke into laughter, soon joined by his brother Obi.

"Listen to this one!" his father shouted. "Meet his destiny! Shut up now, we can't hear the news."

"But I saw him," Dubem said, his small voice shaky. "Kopano glowed!"

Their mother made the sign of the cross. "A devil has invaded our house."

Udo regarded his son through eyes narrowed to slits. Kopano stood tall, chest puffed out, hoping to cut a striking figure.

"Okay, Mr. Superhero," said Udo measuredly. "If you are an alien now, please show us your powers."

Kopano took a deep breath. He looked down at his hands. He didn't feel any different than he had yesterday, but that didn't necessarily mean the great powers of the Loric weren't lurking within him, right?

With a flourish worthy of a martial arts movie, Kopano thrust his hands towards his father. He hoped that his telekinesis would come rushing forth and knock his old man out of his chair. But while Udo flinched at the sudden move, nothing else happened.

Kopano's uncle laughed again and slapped Udo on the back. "Your face! You looked like you might crap in your britches!"

Udo scowled, then snorted in Kopano's direction. "You see? Noth—" His father's face suddenly contorted in anguish. Udo clutched at his chest, feet kicking out in front of him in spasms. His eyes went wide in panic. "My insides!" he screamed. "My insides are boiling!"

Kopano's mother screamed.

Kopano and his brothers all rushed to their father's side. Their uncle took a frightened step back. Kopano grabbed his father's arm.

"Father, I'm sorry! I don't know what—"

His father slapped him on the side of the head and grinned. Just like that, he was miraculously recovered and already turning back to the television. A practical joke.

"You stupid boy, I'm fine. Or perhaps my alien powers are just greater than yours, hmm?" He waved Kopano away. "Go on. See to your mother. You scared her bad."

Kopano slunk away. Had it really all been a dream? What would he have done with Legacies, anyway? A boy from Lagos rushing off to save the world? Even Nollywood didn't make movies with premises so far-fetched.

Little Dubem clasped his hand.

"I believe you, Kopano," his youngest brother whispered. "You will show them all."

At least, for a few days after his embarrassing announcement, Kopano's family was too glued to the news to mock him. But then the invasion ended, suddenly and brutally, with the nations of Earth coming together to simultaneously attack every Mogadorian warship. Meanwhile, the Garde, the ones who had invaded Kopano's dreams and promised him bigger things than Lagos, went to the Mogadorians' secret base in West Virginia and killed Setrákus Ra. Kopano imagined being there, fighting alongside the Garde, and melting Setrákus Ra with his fire-breath.

Fire-breath, Kopano had decided, would be his Legacy.

When the news broke that Earth was saved, they celebrated in the streets. His father hugged him close as they danced down the road, fireworks going off overhead. Kopano couldn't remember the last time Udo had hugged him like that. Not since he was a boy.

But the next day, it started.

Alien son, go down to the market before school and pick up the items I am thinking about right now! Use your telepathy!

Alien son, did you finish your homework?

Alien son, use your telekinesis to get me a beer, eh?

Kopano grinned through it all, but inside he seethed. His unemployed father had nothing better to do than sit home all day and think up ways to humiliate him.

Worse still, his bigmouthed brother, Obi, had spread the word around school. Soon, Kopano's classmates were teasing him, too. A stall in the marketplace had started selling rubber Mogadorian masks, hideous gray things with empty black eyes and tiny yellow teeth. A group of his older classmates chased Kopano through the halls wearing these masks and, when they caught him, they used rolls of duct tape to bind him to one of the football goals. They took turns kicking balls at him.

Until one day, when Kopano stopped a football in midair. When that happened, they all ran away screaming.

"Finally," Kopano whispered to himself as he began wriggling free. "Finally."

It had been three months since the invasion. Kopano, it

turned out, was a late bloomer.

That evening, he strode into his family's apartment to find his father napping on the couch. With his little brothers watching, Kopano used his telekinesis to levitate the couch high above the floor. Then he screamed, "Fire! Fire! Father, get up!"

His father sprung upright, swung his legs off the couch, and fell five feet to the floor. As he groaned and picked himself up, staring aghast at the couch still floating above him, Obi and Dubem cackled with laughter. Kopano simply grinned at his father, squaring his shoulders in the same noble way he had on that humiliating morning months ago.

"You see, old man? What did I tell you?"

Udo stumbled over to his son, a smile slowly spreading on his face. He grabbed Kopano's cheeks and pinched. "My beautiful alien son, you are the answer to all of our problems."

Many months later, when Kopano finally made it to America, the psychologist Linda Matheson would ask him what life was like back in Lagos, before he came to the Human Garde Academy.

Kopano would think about his answer for a long moment before answering.

"Well," he said, "I guess for a little while I was a criminal."

CHAPTER TWO

THE PATIENCE CREEK SURVIVORS
AN UNDISCLOSED LOCATION

FOR THOSE FIRST HUMAN GARDE WHO DID ANSWER John Smith's call to arms right after their visions, the invasion wasn't as glorious as Kopano had enviously imagined.

The story of Patience Creek wasn't reported on the news networks. The battle there didn't make it into any of the retrospectives made after the invasion. It was kept secret. Remembered by only the survivors.

Patience Creek was a secret government facility in Michigan where the Loric hid out after the invasion, plotting their counterattack on the Mogadorians. They were joined by a host of military personnel and a handful of Human Garde, those who had answered John Smith's telepathic plea or who had otherwise crossed his path.

Daniela Morales. Stone-vision.

Nigel Rally. Sonic manipulation.

Caleb Crane. Duplication.

Ran Takeda. Kinetic detonation.

There were others, but they didn't survive the assault when the Mogadorians discovered Patience Creek. Most of the military didn't make it out alive either. John Smith himself was nearly killed. It was bloody and brutal and not at all heroic. The ordeal showed John Smith that maybe the humans he'd recruited weren't ready for a full-scale war. They needed training that the Loric didn't have time to give them. Not then, at least. The humans needed protecting.

So, John Smith sent them away.

"Bloody Guantanamo Bay," Nigel groused.

Daniela rolled her eyes. "This isn't Cuba, man."

Nigel bent down and gathered a handful of bright white sand. He opened his fingers and let the grains blow across the crystalline blue ocean. The sun beat down on him—skinny bordering on bony, pale, a sunburn growing around his bleached mohawk, his cheeks pocked by persistent splotches of acne. He wore a black Misfits tank top in defiance of the heat. He gestured from the waves to the austere military base two hundred yards away—their accommodations for the last few days—and looked back at Daniela.

"Ominous military base on a tropical island," Nigel countered. "Where do you think we are?"

"It isn't that ominous," Caleb said. He brushed a hand across his buzz cut and skipped a stone into the ocean. Biscuit, Daniela's Chimæra, the shape-shifting Loric animal who preferred the form of a golden retriever, bounded into the water after the rock. "There's a snack bar."

"Not ominous to you, mate," Nigel replied. "You grew up in one of these places, didn't ya? And besides, your uncle's running the show."

"Guantanamo's where they bring the bad guys and shit," Daniela told Nigel. "We aren't prisoners. This is just a stop-over." She looked at Caleb. "Right?"

Caleb's uncle was General Clarence Lawson. He'd been called out of retirement and put in charge of coordinating the armies of Earth with the Loric during the invasion. Since then, it had seemed to Caleb like his uncle was await-ing orders. Like he didn't know what would happen next.

Back at Patience Creek, Caleb had acted as his uncle's bodyguard. "In case any of these aliens get out of line, you're the ace up my sleeve," Lawson told his nephew. Caleb didn't think he could go toe to toe with John Smith or one of the Loric, but he didn't argue. It had been his uncle's idea for Caleb to pose as twins. He was having problems controlling his duplication Legacy—a second body would pop out of him without warning—so it was better for his clone to sim-ply hide in plain sight.

Since they arrived at the island, Caleb had dinner with his uncle every night in the man's windowless office. These meals were largely silent, especially after one of Caleb's duplicates manifested and hurled a plate of food into his uncle's face. Since Patience Creek, the dupes were becoming harder to control. Rowdier. With minds of their own.

Caleb didn't tell anyone this. He kept his mouth shut, like a good soldier.

To Daniela, he simply nodded. "You're probably right."

Nigel snorted. He didn't buy anything that Caleb said. He turned away, watching his own Chimæra, the raccoon-shaped Bandit, root around for seashells.

Daniela clapped her hands together. "I just want to get back to New York, man," she said. "Find my mom. Do something useful."

They all nodded in agreement, even the silent Ran Takeda, the Japanese girl sitting in the sand nearby with her turtle-shaped Chimæra, Gamora, lightly stroking the back of her hand across his craggy shell. This was their life— watching news feeds of the aftermath of the invasion, eating microwaved military base food and hanging around on the beach. Sometimes, they practiced their telekinesis, copying the rudimentary games Nine had hastily taught them during their brief training session with him. They looked ahead, hoping they could eventually be of some use. And they tried their best not to think about Patience Creek.

Eventually, Daniela and Caleb drifted away, leaving Nigel alone on the beach with Ran.

"So, what do you think, silent and violent?" he asked. "We princes and princesses or prisoners?"

Ran looked over at Nigel. "I don't think anyone knows what we are," she said after a long pause.

Nigel grinned. He still couldn't get over Ran speaking in her precise English. He thought she'd been mute when he first met her at the Niagara Falls Loralite stone and all the way through the ordeal at Patience Creek. Everyone assumed that she couldn't speak English.

She had saved his life back at Patience Creek, maybe more than once, and so he stuck close to her. He started to notice the keen way her eyes tracked conversations happening around her.

And then he caught her smiling during one of his colorful rants. He confronted her and she admitted that she could speak English. Why hadn't she said anything sooner? Because no one had bothered to ask. As far as Nigel knew, the others were still under the impression that she was either mute, couldn't understand them or both.

That was how their alliance started. In the days after her confession, with nothing to do but sit on the beach and wait for news, Nigel and Ran got to know each other better. He told her about his dreary past in London, and she told him about her shattered life in Tokyo. They found they had something in common.

Neither of them had lives to go back to.

Nigel crouched down next to Ran and scratched under Gamora's chin. "Of course they gave you the Chimæra named after a Godzilla monster, right? Bit stereotypical, innit? Thought the refugees of the advanced alien society would be better than that."

"I don't mind. I have always liked turtles." She looked at him evenly. "You do not need to complain about everything, Nigel."

Nigel sighed, glancing over his shoulder to where Daniela and Caleb had meandered down the beach. "You agree with me, though. That this situation we find ourselves in is bloody mental."

"Yes," Ran replied.

"So, you could speak up about it," Nigel pushed. "Get my back when soldier-boy tells me everything's peachy. I mean, you gotta start talking to the others eventually, yeah?"

Ran gazed out at the waves, thinking.

"I did not think I would survive the invasion," she said at last. "All I wanted to do was fight. There was no point to talking, to making friends." She paused. "After we came here, I kept it up so that General Lawson and those watching over us would speak freely around me. Our situation is a strange one, as you said. We need to know who we can trust, nakama."

The four of them spent weeks on that island in a weird limbo while the rest of the world shakily recovered from the invasion.

Then, finally, they watched from the beach as a squadron of black helicopters arrived at the base. The choppers carried military personnel and posh people in suits and bookish-looking types with crates of high-tech equipment.

"The unholy triumvirate," Nigel observed. "Soldiers, senators and scientists."

"Something's going to happen today," Caleb said.

"No shit," replied Daniela.

General Lawson spent his entire day in meetings with these new arrivals. The Garde twiddled their thumbs until almost sunset, when Lawson finally called them into one of the base's dull conference rooms. Arranged on the table were a bunch of glossy brochures, all of them depicting a beautiful blond teenager in the process of lifting a chunk of brick wall over her head, freeing a family that had been trapped underneath. The caption read: *OUR PLANET—OUR PROTECTORS—EARTH GARDE.*

"A delegation from the United Nations arrived today," General Lawson began without fanfare. "A decision has been made regarding—"

"Hold up," Daniela interrupted, tapping one of the brochures. "Why does this bougie girl look so familiar?"

"That's Melanie Jackson," Caleb answered.

Daniela stared at him blankly.

"The first daughter? You know, of our president?"

"Oh yeah," Daniela said. "She's strong, huh?"

Nigel squinted at his copy of the Earth Garde pamphlet. "Lotta makeup for a spontaneous act of heroism."

General Lawson pinched the bridge of his nose and pressed on. "Ms. Jackson is the first enrollee in the Earth Garde program, a UN-administered initiative to train and deploy you LANEs—excuse me, you Human Garde."

LANE was a term first coined by the US military, possibly by Lawson himself. Depending on who one asked, it meant either Legacy-Augmented Native Earthling or

17

Legacy-Afflicted Native Earthling.

Daniela smirked. "That what they're calling us now? Human Garde?"

Lawson sighed. "It's simple and less . . . offensive than LANE, apparently. There are PR gurus involved. Not my area of expertise."

"Oi," Nigel broke in. "Did you say deploy? As in, like, stormtroopers?"

Lawson began again. His patience for being interrupted had grown exponentially since he started working with Garde. "Participating countries, which include England and Japan—" He looked in Ran's direction. "Ah, damn. Forgot to get the interpreter in here for this."

"Not necessary," Ran said. "Please. Continue."

Everyone stared at her except for Nigel, who belted out a laugh. General Lawson puffed out his cheeks and shook his head, taking Ran's revelation in stride.

"As I was saying, the Earth Garde program has been agreed upon by most UN member nations. All Human Garde from participating nations will be required to register with Earth Garde and undergo training and observation at the Human Garde Academy, which is currently under construction in California." Lawson slid packets across the table, filled with forms and dense contracts. "The legal details are in here. If you want, we can have your parents flown in before you sign anything."

"Bollocks to that," Nigel said with a snort, thumbing through the pages.

Caleb exchanged a look with his uncle, then shook his head. "That's okay."

Ran and Daniela said nothing, both their families unaccounted for since the invasion.

"Once you've undergone training at the Academy and proven you won't be a danger to society, you'll be deployed to an Earth Garde unit. Not as stormtroopers," Lawson said, with a glance in Nigel's direction. "No one faces a combat situation until they're at least eighteen years old and hopefully by then the remaining Mogadorians are routed and the world's a goddamn utopia." The old military man smirked. "As outlined, your time with Earth Garde will be spent doing humanitarian work. Currently, Melanie Jackson is assisting with the cleanup efforts in New York. Daniela, I know you're from there and you've already demonstrated excellent control of your powers. I've arranged for you to skip the Academy and go straight to Earth Garde. Help rebuild your city."

Daniela's eyes widened. Although she didn't talk about it much, they all knew she was still holding out hope that her mom would be found somewhere in the rubble of Manhattan. The hospitals there were overwhelmed, many neighborhoods didn't yet have power restored and survivors were still being found. It was possible.

She looked at the other three Garde. Back at Patience Creek, she had promised John Smith she would protect them. But the invasion was over. She'd kept her word. Nigel grinned at her, and Ran nodded once.

Daniela reached across the table for a pen. "Where do I sign?"

Nigel leaned back in his chair and studied Lawson. "Right, then. Who's going to be in charge of this Academy thing? You?"

Lawson shook his head. "No. My job was the war, and the war is over. The UN has appointed someone better suited to training people of your unique abilities."

"Yeah? Who's that?"

The Americans lobbied hard to host the Academy. With everything the United States had done to coordinate the counterattack against the Mogadorian warships, none of the other world leaders were in a position to push back. The Academy would technically be on international soil, the entire thing UN-funded, with Peacekeepers handling the security.

Fifty miles north of San Francisco, the secluded Point Reyes was chosen as the location for the Academy, the people of California and the National Park Service generously gifting the land to the United Nations. With a promise to be as eco-friendly as possible, building began immediately on the coastal cliffs of the former nature preserve.

"Damn, dude. Place is going to be huge," said the young man as he surveyed the construction, hundreds of workers already clearing earth and laying foundations, bulldozers and cranes rumbling across the landscape. "How many students we expecting?"

The older man standing next to him glanced up from his tablet. He pushed his glasses up his nose. "Last count they'd registered more than one hundred Human Garde. Finding new ones every day."

The young man whistled. His long black hair was tied back in a sloppy man-bun. It was windy here and he kept having to push rebellious strands of hair out of his eyes. He'd seen the blueprints and now, looking at the land, he tried to picture what the Academy would look like. Two dormitories each capable of housing five hundred students, a cul-de-sac of town houses erected for faculty housing, a school building equipped with state-of-the-art computers and laboratories, a recreation center, a training complex designed by the military, a sports fieldhouse, solar power and a tide-power generator. All that nestled between the fir trees of the valley and the rocky cliffs of Drake's Bay. Not so unusual, a private school in the middle of nowhere, albeit this one would be surrounded by miles of electrified razor-wire fence, its perimeter patrolled by round-the-clock security.

"What are you thinking, Professor?" Dr. Malcolm Goode asked, emphasizing the title that his young friend had negotiated for, despite never actually finishing high school.

The young man rubbed the spot where his prosthetic arm joined his shoulder. The thing still itched him like crazy.

"It's no penthouse," Nine said. "But I guess it'll do."

CHAPTER THREE

TAYLOR COOK
TURNER COUNTY, SOUTH DAKOTA

THE CLOSEST THING TO ACTION TAYLOR COOK SAW during the invasion was when a pickup truck filled with local boys rumbled by her family's farm and asked her father if he wanted to go to war.

"We're headed to Chicago, see if the army needs our help," announced the driver, Dale, the manager of the local grocery store. "Kill some of these goddamn aliens."

"Uh-huh," Taylor's dad, Brian, replied. "That right?"

Brian stood on their porch, his arms crossed skeptically. He and Taylor had run this farm together ever since Taylor's mom had run off. She knew what her dad's stance meant—it was the same as when one of the farmhands did something stupid. Her dad had an abiding patience for foolishness that Taylor didn't exactly share.

From a few steps behind her father, Taylor assessed the contents of the pickup truck. There were three men stuffed in the cab and another four perched in the bed, all of them carrying rifles and dressed in hunting fatigues. There was something almost comical about this bunch going off to fight aliens with bright orange reflectors glued to their shoulders. This whole day—warships, invaders, superpowers—it felt like a crazy dream to Taylor. She was scared, sure, have to be insane not to be. But that didn't stop her from smirking at her neighbors' makeshift posse.

One of the boys in the back of the truck caught Taylor's eye. "See something funny?" he asked. She recognized Silas, her father's main farmhand. He was in his early twenties, dark hair slicked back by a gloss of gel, a cigarette dangling from his lips. Taylor tossed her blond hair over her shoulder and crossed her arms, unintentionally copying her dad's posture.

"Have you seen the size of those spaceships?" she asked, meeting Silas's gaze. "What're your hunting rifles going to do against that? Jesus, they've got guys who can fly."

"The flying guy's on our side," Silas responded.

"Whatever," Taylor said. "I'm sure he's waiting for you to come save him, Silas."

"Better than sitting around doing nothing, anyway," he muttered.

"Running off to get killed, that's what you're doing," Taylor said. "You'll probably fall out of the back of that truck before you even hit the state line."

Some of the other boys in the back of the truck snickered. Silas seethed and fell silent.

"Folks on the news say we ought to stay in our homes," Brian stated coolly, sparing Taylor a glance over his shoulder. "Go home to your families for Pete's sake. It's a ten-hour drive to Chicago and who-knows-what. Safer to wait this out."

"It's the end of the world," Dale countered, his meaty arm hanging out the window. "We at least gotta go down swinging. Figured it wouldn't be neighborly if we didn't stop by and ask you to join us."

"Well," Brian replied with a sigh, "you asked. I'm staying right here, with my daughter. If you fellas insist on rushing off to do something dangerous, hell, you'll be in my prayers. I hope to see you again."

"Good knowing you, Brian," Dale said, throwing the truck into drive.

"I won't be in to work tomorrow, Mr. Cook," Silas yelled out as the truck started to pull away.

"Wouldn't expect you to be, son," Brian replied.

Taylor and her dad stood in silence, watching the truck careen up their dirt driveway and back the way it had come. When it was out of sight, their land was peaceful again. A butterfly floated by. The hogs squealed rambunctiously in the barn. To Taylor, it didn't look like the planet was in jeopardy.

"You don't think it's really the end of the world, do you?" she asked her dad.

"Don't know, sweetheart," Brian said calmly. Nothing shook her father, not even these so-called Mogadorians. "You want some ice cream? Might as well eat it, just in case the power goes out."

So, Taylor and her dad spent the invasion in front of their television, glued to news reports from the major cities. When the cable feeds occasionally cut out, they played tense games of Connect Four and Scrabble. Except for feeding the animals, they let their chores go and instead ate all the junk food in the house. Taylor tried to call and message some of her friends to see how they were doing, but the cellular networks were down. The farm started to feel like an island far removed from the battles taking place all over the world.

And then, just like that, it was over. The Mogadorian leader was killed, the warships went down and the Loric were hailed as heroes. The death toll was high, especially in the major cities, but those numbers seemed almost made-up to Taylor, like the entire invasion had taken place in a different universe. No one from Turner County died. When Silas slunk back to the farm a week after the invasion, she learned that he and the morons who took off to Chicago in their pickup truck had been turned back by the National Guard at a gas station on the Minnesota border. They spent the invasion getting drunk.

Within weeks, things were pretty much back to normal, at least in Taylor's part of the world. She saw the stories about human teenagers getting Legacies, about Mogadorians waging guerrilla warfare in Russia, about new laws that would apply to how extraterrestrials like the Loric would have to behave on Earth. None of this changed her daily grind. A war with her alarm clock, a few quick chores, school, dinner, homework, repeat.

At school, they called an assembly—all 158 students at the high school packed into the gymnasium—to talk about Earth Garde. It was a law now that anyone who developed Legacies needed to report them to their local authorities. Taylor had read about the Academy they were constructing for Human Garde in California. She didn't understand why the UN had to build that in America, or why the president and other politicians had pushed so hard to host. Anyone with Legacies was getting pulled out of their regular schools and sent there.

The guidance counselor asked if any of the students had experienced "visions" or "out-of-body experiences" because apparently those were things now. Taylor couldn't believe that the teachers were talking about this stuff so casually, like they'd just been plucked out of a comic book.

In the hall after, some boys joked about their "night visions" and Taylor groaned and rolled her eyes, secretly feeling relief that everyone at her school was normal.

"We're taking a road trip to Chicago this weekend to see the crashed warship," Taylor's friend Claire told her on the bus one day, a few months after the invasion.

"What?" Taylor replied. "Really?"

"I saw some girls on Insta, they got so close, that ugly-ass ship is like right behind them. So many likes," Claire

continued. "Maybe if I get close enough, I'll score some Legacies."

Taylor rolled her eyes. "I don't think that's how it works."

"They're alien powers! No one knows how it works!"
Claire laughed and nudged Taylor's ribs. "Come on. Like you
don't want telekinesis or whatever."

"And get sent away to their weird alien Academy?" Taylor
snorted. "No thanks."

"You'd probably get to meet John Smith," Claire replied.
"He's so hot."

"Really? He always looks like he's about to cry in all those
pictures."

"He's soulful! You're such a downer," Claire said without
any malice. "So, do you want to come with us this weekend
or what?"

Taylor didn't know how to explain to Claire that she liked
their peaceful bubble of Turner County without sounding
lame. So she lied about having too much work due and how
her dad needed her help. She didn't need an up-close-and-
personal view of an alien warship. Too real.

"It's like, everyone's already treating what happened like
it's totally normal," Taylor said to her dad over dinner that
night.

Her dad shrugged. "That's just people, hon. Given enough
time, they can adjust to damn near anything. A few hundred years ago, if you'd shown folks an airplane or a cell
phone, their heads would've exploded. I thought getting
wireless internet out here on the farm would be the most

awe-inspiring thing I saw in my lifetime. Pretty cool to be wrong."

"Wasn't so cool for all the people who died," Taylor said, pushing some corn around on her plate.

"No, that's true," her dad replied gently. "It can be a lot to wrap your head around. But we're safe here. You know that, right? Ain't nobody bothering little old Turner County."

Her dad was right. Taylor was comforted that Turner County remained pretty much unchanged in this brave new world. The articles she read about teenagers with Legacies speculated that everyone who was going to get the enhanced abilities had already gotten them—that it was a side effect of the war triggered by the Loric and that now it would stop.

They were wrong about that.

And eventually, her dad would be proved wrong about Turner County.

CHAPTER FOUR

TARGET #1
ARNHEM LAND, AUSTRALIA

THE CESSNA CAME IN LOW OVER THE TINY ABORIG-
inal village, sought the dusty runway and bounced through
a landing on the hard-packed ground. Nearby, a group of the
villagers huddled around a fire and prepared a freshly killed
sea turtle for dinner. They stuffed the spear-holes in the animal's shell with twigs and then buried it beneath coals so
that the meat inside the shell would cook. They paused in
their work to exchange glances as the plane's engine rumbled
to a stop. It was dusk and they weren't expecting visitors.

For this village, tiny was perhaps an understatement.
Only fifty aboriginals lived here, in the train-car-shaped
houses just a stone's throw from the Timor Sea. The walls
were made of corrugated steel, these all painted vividly with
images of stingrays and turtles and colorful dots and stripes.

Dogs that straddled the line between stray and domesticated weaved in and out of the mango and banana trees, barking at the plane.

Jedda, the village's matriarch, eyed the plane warily from the steps of her home, smoking a pipe. She was in possession of the village's lone satellite phone.

Even if she had called for help right then, it would not have arrived in time.

From inside the airplane, Einar watched the villagers shuffle about. He could tell they were uneasy. He was nervous, too. This was his first operation on behalf of the Foundation and he badly wanted it to go smoothly. Needed it to go smoothly. He wondered if this little village even knew that there had been an alien invasion, if they knew how much the world had changed in the last four months. He could see the glow of a TV set inside one of the houses. They weren't entirely cut off from society out here in the bush.

Still, he wondered if they even understood what they possessed.

Einar's gaze drifted away from the villagers and towards a tree where the fat leaves seemed to shift oddly on the wind. Not leaves. Those were bats. Dozens of them hanging upside down from the thinning branches.

He suppressed a shudder. It wouldn't be good to show weakness. Not considering his present company.

Sandwiched into the small plane with Einar were six very nasty-looking men. Mercenaries. All of them dressed in black body armor and carrying excessively large machine guns. Their leader was a Norwegian named Jarl, red-bearded with bulging neck muscles, a hooked scar that ran from his eye to the corner of his mouth. He and his men hadn't been much for conversation during the journey. The Blackstone Group weren't used to having a seventeen-year-old in charge of them. Einar wondered how much the Foundation was paying them.

Einar stood and delicately rolled up the sleeves of his shirt. He looked at Jarl. The men knew their orders; he didn't need to go over them again. Instead, he pointed at the serrated combat knife strapped to Jarl's belt.

"May I?" Einar asked.

Jarl handed him the knife handle first. Without hesitating, Einar gritted his teeth and dragged the blade across the inside of his forearm.

The villagers were taken by surprise when Einar stumbled off the plane. A young, pale-skinned boy, dressed in sharply pressed chinos and a white dress shirt, carrying a stylish attaché case, his brown hair parted from the side. Some rich gubba whose plane lost his way? An intern from one of the mining companies that were always trying to buy up their land?

Bleeding from a cut on his arm. Deep and getting all over his shirt. The guy held up his arm.

"Hello? I'm sorry. Can someone help?"

Only half the aboriginals spoke English, but they all got the gist. They exchanged looks. One of the boys tending to the turtle—no more than fourteen, dark-skinned, with a mane of curly black hair—started immediately toward Einar. Jedda barked something at him in Yolngu Matha, a warning, but the boy waved her off.

He couldn't explain it, but he felt an overwhelming urge to help this injured white boy. He felt like the stranger was an old friend.

"I'm Einar," he said. "Do you speak English?"

"Yeah. I'm Bunji," the aboriginal replied. He took Einar's arm in his hands, his touch gentle despite the calluses on his palms. "What ya doing way out here?"

"Lost," Einar replied. "Lost and hurt, as you can see."

"Not for long," Bunji declared, unable to keep the pride and excitement out of his voice.

Some of the other villagers had edged closer. They always wanted to watch Bunji use his gift, which he'd first discovered when his older brother had accidentally cut his hand on a fishing line.

Bunji pressed his hand onto Einar's arm, not mindful of the blood. He squinted, and Einar felt a wave of warm energy wash into him. The sensation that followed was like a pleasant tickle.

When Bunji took his hand away, Einar's cut was gone. His arm was healed.

"Remarkable," Einar said, smiling at Bunji. "My friend, can you do this?"

Einar held up his attaché, then let it go. The case floated there, suspended in midair by telekinesis. Some of the villagers gasped. Bunji grinned and laughed.

"You! You're like me!" The aboriginal reached out with his own telekinesis and levitated a handful of nearby stones. He floated them around the two of them like tiny meteors orbiting a planet.

"Indeed," Einar said, and opened his floating attaché, produced a tranquilizer gun and shot Bunji in the neck. All the rocks he was levitating fell out of the air.

By the time the stones hit the ground, Jarl and his men were stepping off the plane, their guns clicking as the safeties were flicked off. They took care of the villagers while Einar carried Bunji to the plane.

The Foundation would be pleased.

CHAPTER FIVE

THE PATIENCE CREEK SURVIVORS
AN UNDISCLOSED LOCATION

AFTER DANIELA LEFT FOR NEW YORK, THE REMAIN-
ing Human Garde spent three idle months at the island
military base, basically in limbo while they waited for construction of the Academy to finish. Ran and Nigel played
a lot of chess, using their telekinesis to move the pieces
around the board. Caleb started to grow his hair out and
kept to himself. Ran's room was right next to Caleb's and,
at night, she could hear him talking to himself—arguing
with one of his duplicates—but she never mentioned this
to anyone.

Nothing much happened at the base. Apparently, the only
job of the military personnel stationed there was to watch
over the three of them. Around the world, other newly discovered Human Garde endured similar holding patterns,

waiting for the Academy to officially open. The days blended together.

Until, two days before they were to depart for California, they came for the Chimærae.

"Colonel Ray Archibald has been assigned to lead security at this new Academy. He's a good man. Held down NORAD during the invasion. I briefed him on the three extraterrestrial creatures you and the others are in possession of. It's the colonel's opinion—and Earth Garde backs him up on this—that the animals pose a liability."

General Lawson stoically imparted all this to Caleb from behind his desk. Caleb sat opposite, perfectly at attention as usual. Regal, his hawk-shaped Chimæra, was perched on his forearm, his talons a gentle pressure. Idly, Caleb stroked his Chimæra's feathers.

Two scientists sent by the UN hovered at the edge of the room. One of them held a cage made of bulletproof glass, the airholes on the sides no bigger than pinpricks. The other wore latex gloves and brandished a syringe filled with some kind of sedative. They both watched Regal nervously, although the Chimæra paid them no attention whatsoever.

"Oh," was all Caleb managed to say to his uncle.

"Over the next six weeks, that Academy's going to be filling up with more than a hundred Human Garde, wild-ass teenagers all, from dozens of different countries. It's going to be a logistical nightmare keeping that place safe without adding shape-shifting monsters into the mix. You get me?"

Caleb nodded.

"Plus, we don't know what diseases these Chimærae could be carrying. They can transform into damn near anything. The Loric didn't think much of our environment when they set all this loose," Lawson continued.

Caleb looked into Regal's face. The bird cocked his head and flexed his beak. He didn't look sick to Caleb, but his uncle probably knew best.

"Okay," Caleb said, unable to keep some glumness out of his voice.

"It's just temporary," Lawson said. "Until the lab coats have a chance to check these beasts over, make sure they aren't a risk. You'll get Regal here back once he's been cleared."

"I understand," Caleb replied, swallowing. "I . . . have you told Ran and Nigel yet? They won't . . . I don't think they'll like this very much."

"I hoped that you'd help me convince them," Lawson said. "I know those two are . . . headstrong."

Caleb snorted. "They won't listen to me."

"Well, we aren't really having a discussion," Lawson said with a stiff shrug. "This is the way it's gonna be. They'll fall in line."

At a wave from Lawson, the two scientists approached Caleb and Regal. Caleb felt Regal's talons tighten on his arm, the Chimæra shifting uneasily. He held his free hand out towards the scientist with the injection.

"Better let me do it," he said. "He doesn't trust you guys."

The doctor seemed relieved to hand over the injection

to Caleb. Regal's dark eyes blinked, his head cocked, as he looked from Caleb to the needle.

"Sorry, buddy. I know this sucks," Caleb whispered to his Chimæra, hopeful that his uncle wouldn't overhear, or at least wouldn't judge him for being soft. "It's for the best, I guess."

Regal let out a squawk when the needle went in. Caleb thought it sounded more like sadness than it did pain, but he beat back this thought. Just like he beat back the duplicate that was trying to leap out of him, bundle up Regal and sprint as far away as possible.

Once Regal was peacefully asleep in his cage, they went in search of the other Garde and their Chimærae. Caleb had trouble keeping his shoulders from slumping on the way.

They found Nigel first, lounging in the hammock he'd hooked up in his room, listening to some screeching punk rock through a pair of oversized headphones. Bandit, surly-looking as his owner, rested on Nigel's belly with his furry legs up in the air.

"Mr. Rally, we need a moment—," Lawson began.

Nigel spotted the scientists—their gloves, the cage, the needle. He read the sullen look on the face of that goodie-two-shoes Caleb. He got the picture quickly.

"My arse! Run, Bandit! Escape the bloody fascists!"

Bandit listened. He dove off Nigel and transformed in the air, shrinking down to a mouse. He scurried toward the nearest air vent, the scientists too mesmerized by the transformation to react.

Not Caleb. He had orders. With a flick of his telekinesis, he shut the vent, cutting off Bandit's escape route. Then he plucked the fleeing Chimæra up, holding him telekinetically aloft, gently, his legs kicking. Bandit started to transform into a larger form—dark fur, claws and fangs. Before things could get any further out of hand, Lawson snatched the tranquilizer syringe from the frozen scientist and jabbed it into Bandit's morphing haunch.

"Young man, I appreciate your loyalty to this animal, but Earth Garde has determined—"

Lawson made it only that far through his lecture before Nigel punched him in the jaw.

Nigel was scrawny and hadn't thrown a lot of punches in his life, but what his punch lacked in power it made up for in passion. Not to mention the element of surprise. The blow caught Lawson off guard and sent the old man stumbling back. He ended up flopping right into Nigel's hammock, his legs kicked awkwardly up in the air.

Two duplicates sprung forth from Caleb and grabbed Nigel by the arms, pinning him up against the wall.

"You're just making things worse, Nigel!" Caleb yelled, the duplicates echoing his words.

"Shove it up your ass, ya sellout wanker," Nigel replied. Then he took a deep gulp of air and bellowed, his sonic manipulation Legacy making his next words loud enough to rattle the walls, not to mention make everyone in the room wince and stumble.

"RAN! THEY'RE STEALING THE CHIMÆRAE!"

Nigel's siren-like scream reached Ran all the way on the beach. She sat cross-legged, peaceful up until that point. Gamora basked in the sun next to her. At Nigel's scream, Gamora craned his stout neck to look up at Ran. She frowned thoughtfully, gently scratching Gamora under his chin.

"Better go into the water," she told him in Japanese. "Find me when it is safe, my friend."

Gamora seemed to understand. He trundled to the shoreline, glanced back once and then plunged gracefully into the ocean. Ran sighed.

Their departure for the Academy wasn't off to the best start.

CHAPTER SIX

KOPANO OKEKE
LAGOS, NIGERIA

WORD OF THE INCIDENT ON THE FOOTBALL PITCH traveled fast. Kopano was famous. Yesterday's tormenters were today's spokespeople, telling all their friends that Alien Boy Kopano was for real. Despite his mistreatment at their hands, Kopano didn't harbor any resentment towards those witnesses to his big day. In fact, he regarded them fondly, like a reluctant baby bird might view the cruel mother that launched him from the nest. Kopano didn't hold a grudge.

Everyone wanted to see what Kopano could do. "Prove it," they kept saying, the same challenge over and over. "Prove it."

By the end of the next school day, Kopano's face hurt from grinning. He'd spent much of the day doing tricks—levitating desks, juggling objects, even flying a couple of his screaming classmates through the lunchroom. His teachers were in awe, uncertain what the protocol was in matters of superpowered disruption. Kopano was one of their better students, usually quiet and courteous, so they let him have his day. After dismissal, the principal pulled him aside.

"What is happening to you is very good," the principal said. "You will be the pride of Nigeria. But please, Kopano, you must understand, this is a place of learning. You must try not to be so distracting to the other students."

"Not to worry," Kopano boasted. "Soon, I will be joining the Garde in America."

Kopano went home and told his family about what the principal said. His mother shook her head wearily. She'd spent the entire day at church. She told Kopano that she was praying for his safety, but Kopano was certain that meant she was trying to pray away his Legacies.

"Be careful, Kopano," his mother warned. "If you keep making a spectacle of yourself, they will come take you away. Or worse."

Kopano knew what his mother was talking about. Ever since the invasion, he'd been devouring every bit of news about the Loric and the changes they'd wrought. He had begged his father to drive him to Zuma Rock, where an outcropping of Loralite stone had grown, but Udo complained it would be a waste of time since the UN Security Council had set up a base there and weren't letting just anyone take tours. Also, Udo reasoned, the government might snatch him up if they got that close.

The prospect excited Kopano. The Americans had just finished building a school with the support of the UN that eventually all Human Garde from participating countries would be required to attend. It was only a matter of time before he would leave to begin his training with the other Garde.

That was what worried his mother.

"They will steal my child away to America and turn him into one of the aliens," she moaned.

"I want to go, Mom," Kopano said. "I'm not turning into an alien."

His parents ignored him, Udo dismissing his wife's concerns with a wave of his hand. He paced back and forth across their living room, a man possessed of a great idea.

"We have nothing to worry about," Udo said. "Kopano isn't going anywhere."

"You dumb man! You know how people in Lagos talk. Everyone already knows what he is . . ."

"Yes, they talk, that's true. But I know how to make it so that nobody important listens. The good people of Lagos will respect our family's privacy," Udo concluded. Kopano knew this meant his father would generously bribe as many people as necessary, although he wasn't sure where the old man would scrounge up the money. "And if this principal doesn't want our son in his school?" Udo stomped his foot. "Then we will give the man what he wants."

Kopano sighed, deciding not to argue. The Academy wasn't open yet, anyway. Let his parents have their way for now; eventually Earth Garde would come for him, no matter how many palms his father greased.

The next day, Udo made good on his promise. Instead of school, Kopano found himself sitting shotgun in his dad's old Hyundai, stuck in Lagos's bumper-to-bumper morning traffic. Already, the sun was hot overhead. The car's air conditioner needed fixing.

"Okay, I have come along," Kopano said with a sigh. "Now tell me what crazy scheme you have planned."

"It is not a scheme!" Udo yelled, pounding the horn as another driver cut him off. "You have a reputation now, Kopano. We would be stupid not to take advantage of that."

"What do I have to do?"

"Nothing! That is the beauty of reputations." Udo glanced in his son's direction. "Yes. That is good. Make that mean face just like that."

Kopano turned to look out the window. His gaze drifted to a roadside stall where a thin man with shifty eyes sold what he claimed were authentic alien artifacts. To Kopano, they looked like broken hunks of common electronics— toasters, TV parts, melted cellular phones—the kind of crap one would find in a dump. He shook his head again.

They drove across the bridge to Victoria Island, the slumped and crowded buildings of Kopano's neighborhood replaced by glittering skyscrapers, many of which were still under construction. A few of the wealthier kids Kopano went to school with lived on the island. Kopano also knew that this was where many of the foreign corporations set up—the banks and oil companies and real estate developers. A banner overhung the street reading *WELCOME TO AFRICA'S BIG APPLE.* Kopano rolled his eyes.

His father parked them in front of a fat hexagonal building. The windows were tinted gold, their glow reflecting onto the sidewalk and street. Udo told Kopano to wait, hopped out of the car and sauntered by the security guards at the door. He returned with a backpack slung over his shoulder, which he tossed into the backseat.

"What's in there?" Kopano asked, once they were driving again.

"None of our business," his father answered. "We are only deliverymen."

Kopano made to reach for the bag, but his father shouted and slapped his hand, accidentally swerving into the opposite lane. Kopano laughed. If he really wanted, he could wrestle the bag away from his father using telekinesis. But, he decided then, maybe it was better he didn't know. This work Udo had involved him in wasn't exactly battling Mogadorians for the fate of the world, but at least there was some excitement, a cloak-and-dagger feeling, like he was a spy. Kopano didn't want to ruin it by finding out they were ferrying bank contracts or something equally boring.

They drove halfway across the city, far away from Victoria Island, into an area where the roads were cluttered with potholes and the ramshackle buildings looked like they were jostling each other for room. Scrawny street vendors peered hungrily into their car. Kopano sat up a little straighter.

Udo parked them in front of a block where the buildings had collapsed in on each other, like a house of cards after a strong wind. The area was blocked off by police tape. A sign advertising the property developers who promised to revitalize the neighborhood was covered in graffiti.

Kopano spotted a group of men picking through the debris. Most of them looked like vagrants, sweaty from work, not much older than him. Supervising them was a chubby man in a hard hat who stood out all the more because of his wrinkled white suit.

Kopano turned to his father. "What now?"

Udo rolled down Kopano's window. "Give him the bag." He stopped Kopano from getting out of the car. "Use your powers!"

Kopano frowned. "Are you serious?"

"Just this one time," his father insisted. "Then they will know we're for real."

With shaky control—he was still mastering his telekinesis—Kopano lifted the bag from the backseat, floated it out the window and into the waiting hands of the man in the white suit. His whole crew had stopped to watch. Kopano got a kick out of how their mouths hung open in awe.

Days, and then weeks, went on like that. There were always more mysterious errands to run, an increasing volume of men in expensive suits and glittering sunglasses nodding their approval at Kopano's telekinetic deliveries. It got so that Kopano was going to school only a couple of days each week, and then only at the insistence of his mother.

He didn't show off anymore, so busy was he catching up on schoolwork. His teachers didn't make a fuss over his absences; they assumed it had to do with his training as a Human Garde, and Kopano suspected that Udo had played a role in that. He heard whispers about special treatment from his classmates, but no one had the guts to say anything to Kopano's face.

His father was, once again, an important man. All thanks to Kopano.

"Safest courier in Lagos!" he heard his father brag on the phone. "No one else will have their deliveries protected by a genuine superpowered Garde!"

They worked the banks, the oil companies, the developers. They delivered to hotels and hovels, to the slums and to resorts. Sometimes, they took duffel bags from policemen and delivered them to embassy employees. Kopano visited parts of Lagos he'd never seen before. He never looked in the bags, never asked what they were transporting. The family once again had a TV in their apartment. The rent was paid. Soon, his brothers would be transferred to better private schools. It was not America, it was not the Garde, but Kopano told himself he was doing good, at least for his family. He practiced a steely look on his deliveries but had a hard time keeping the grin off his face.

It was months before someone decided to test him.

Udo was navigating them to their drop-off, their sleek, newly purchased gray Lexus badly out of place in one of Lagos's more hardscrabble neighborhoods. Kopano had long ago gotten used to the slums. He didn't quite feel comfortable there but had begun to feel like their car was a bubble of protection.

Kopano noticed how suspiciously devoid of life this block was. He opened his mouth to say something. That was when a pickup truck accelerated out from the alley and slammed into the back of their car.

They were spun around. His father shouted. Kopano's ears rang.

When they came to a stop wedged against a street sign, Kopano saw them. Five men in bright red balaclavas. There were two in the truck and three on foot. They were all fit and Kopano thought they looked young but couldn't quite tell because of the masks.

"Bastards!" Udo shouted. "My car!"

The men descended on them. His father tried to drive away, but the Lexus sputtered. One of the men smashed through the driver-side window with a tire iron and began to punch Udo in the face. Another smashed through the back and grabbed the duffel bag they were transporting. Kopano watched all this in shocked disbelief.

Kopano's door was ripped open and two of the men dragged him into the street. One of them laughed; Kopano thought he sounded like a hyena. That was when he came to his senses.

He thrust his hands out and sent his two attackers flying with a burst of telekinesis. Their bodies looked like rag dolls as they hit a nearby wall.

The man punching his father stopped doing that and flung his tire iron at Kopano. The metal bar struck Kopano in the back of the head, caused him to stumble. He touched his scalp and found no blood. He was surprised by how little it hurt.

Kopano picked up the tire iron with his telekinesis and whipped it back at the man. He ducked out of the way and the tire iron crashed through the window of a vacant building across the street.

Another man jumped onto Kopano's back. Kopano ducked his shoulders low as if he were play-wrestling with his brothers, and threw the man off. He got back to his feet fast, but Kopano was ready, his fist cocked back.

Kopano was stout and had been in a few fights before, but he didn't expect the punch to knock the man fully off his feet. He didn't expect to hear the crunch of the man's jaw breaking. He looked down at his fist. It was as hard as a brick.

"Stop this!" Kopano shouted. "I will only keep hurting you if you force me to!"

One of the men he'd tossed into the wall rushed forward with a butterfly knife and stabbed Kopano in the stomach.

"Kopano!" yelled his father, spitting blood.

Kopano looked down. Where there should have been a wound, there was only a hole in his shirt. The knife's blade was folded up like it was made from paper.

His skin. It looked normal, but it was as durable as titanium.

Kopano backhanded the knife-fighter away from him, eyes wide with sudden fury. "You would have killed me! For what? For what?"

"Kopano!" his father shouted again, as Kopano loomed over his would-be murderer. "The bag! He's getting away with the bag!"

Kopano whipped around, spotted the man who'd taken the duffel bag sprinting down the street, laboring under the weight. The runner was already nearly a hundred yards away. Kopano squinted, tried to bring his telekinesis to bear. He'd never used his Legacy at this distance. He thrust out his hand, a telekinetic shove—and flattened the windshield of the car nearest the runner. The thief glanced over his shoulder, then hooked down an alley. Gone.

"I . . . I missed," Kopano said. The other thieves had used his distraction to scurry off, except for the two Kopano had knocked out.

"You let him get away!" his father barked. He came around the car, kicked one of their fallen assailants and tore off his mask. Neither of them recognized the guy. He was nobody. "Come on! We have to get out of here."

On the ride home, Kopano rubbed his knuckles and forearms. His skin didn't feel different. His sense of touch was unchanged. Yet, he knew, there was a new hardness lurking within him. He wondered if his new Legacy was a result of the jobs he'd been doing with his father.

"I do not think we should do this anymore," he said quietly.

"What!" his father bellowed. "Do you not understand what just happened, boy? We lost a delivery! The next job is the least of our worries. We will need to make amends and quickly."

Kopano didn't know what that meant. He shook his head and stared out the broken window, hot air rushing into the car. "This is not what I wanted," he said.

His father snorted, ignoring him. They rode home in silence.

That night, when he tried to sleep, Kopano could hear his father's pleading voice through the walls. Udo had been on the phone almost nonstop since they returned home, talking to whatever mysterious big man was in charge of the package they'd lost. He spoke in a meek voice that Kopano wouldn't have thought his father capable of. Kopano tossed and turned, Udo's wheedling apologies the worst kind of lullaby.

Kopano must have drifted off, because he did not hear the door to his room open, nor notice the shadow that padded across the floor. His eyes snapped open only when a cool hand pressed over his mouth.

"Kopano," a voice said. "It is time to go."

CHAPTER SEVEN

TAYLOR COOK
TURNER COUNTY, SOUTH DAKOTA

TAYLOR DISCOVERED THAT SHE WAS ONE OF THEM on the Wednesday morning when she reached for her buzzing alarm clock and accidentally sent the thing flying across her bedroom. The clock smashed against the wall, made a squawking sound like a dying goose and was silent. Taylor was 99 percent sure she hadn't laid a finger on it.

"Okay, get a grip," she told herself. "You were still half dreaming. It was an accident. You're freaking out over nothing."

Taylor held her hand out toward the broken alarm clock, gasping when it levitated and floated back to her.

"Dad!" she shouted.

Brian didn't hear her. He was already out of the house. Taylor threw open her bedroom window and gazed out over

their small farm. The barn doors were open, her dad probably in there feeding the hogs.

A dented pickup truck made its way up their dirt driveway. That would be Silas. He got out of his truck, hair slicked
back as usual, a pack of cigarettes rolled up in the sleeve of
his flannel shirt, like a dingy version of some old movie star.
Over the last few months, ever since she spoke up to him
during the invasion, he'd started looking at Taylor in a new
way, a creepy way. He always made a point of telling her how
much she'd grown. He saw her watching and waved.

Taylor shut her window. Took a step back.

"This isn't happening," she told herself.

It'd been almost a year since the world got crazy. Things
had been normal here, though, just like Taylor had hoped.
She'd even gotten comfortable with the idea of aliens and
superpowers in the world. But now . . .

"I . . . I can't be one of them."

But she was. Taylor realized she hadn't used her hands
to shut her window just then. She'd used her mind. She
went back to the glass, peering out, praying that Silas hadn't
noticed anything. Taylor watched him saunter into the barn
like nothing had happened and breathed a sigh of relief.

"Okay. Okay." She looked down at her hands. They were
shaking. "Nothing has to change."

Taylor decided then and there that she would act like
nothing happened. She got ready for school. Wiping steam
off the bathroom mirror after her shower, Taylor studied
her reflection. Blue eyes, wavy blond hair, a small nose and

rounded cheeks. She didn't look any different than yesterday. Granted, every day she looked more and more like her mother, a fact that annoyed Taylor. But there was no physical manifestation of her telekinesis.

Telekinesis. A year ago that word was strictly in the vocabulary of comic book readers and science fiction fans. Now it was everywhere. The telltale sign of a Garde developing their powers. There were PSAs on TV about what to do if you spotted someone using telekinesis. Taylor never thought she'd be one of them.

She would hide. There were fewer than ten thousand people in all of Turner County. Those government people she saw on TV would never come to South Dakota looking for one of their so-called Human Garde. Her dad had said no one would bother with their little town.

"Going to school!" she yelled into the barn as she half jogged down the driveway to where the bus waited. Usually, she'd never leave without giving her dad a hug and a kiss, but Silas was there, lingering in the barn's doorway waiting to take the tractor out, and even though Taylor knew he was just eyeballing her in his usual pervy way, she felt extra exposed that morning and couldn't bring herself to get too close.

Taylor zoned out in her history class, daydreaming about the fiery images she'd seen of the invasion, imagining herself there, clumsily floating around a broken alarm clock while pale aliens shot at her with lasers. She got scolded, her classmates giggling after the teacher called her name five times.

At lunch, her friends told her that she seemed distracted and Taylor brushed them off, making an excuse about not sleeping well. When the kid in front of her grabbed the last peach iced tea from the drink cooler, Taylor nearly used her telekinesis to snatch the bottle out from under his fingers, then immediately felt ashamed. Whenever she needed to reach for something, she could feel the telekinesis urging her to use it. Ignoring the ability was like not scratching an itch. It frightened her how much the telekinesis already felt like a part of her, an instinct she had to fight against.

"It'll get easier," she promised herself in the bathroom mirror as she washed her hands. Then she floated a paper towel to herself from the dispenser, screamed in frustration and stomped her feet.

Sooner or later, she would screw up and someone would see her. Unless she learned how to bury this power deep inside her, make like it never existed. But already that felt like keeping an arm tied behind her back.

On the bus ride home from school, Taylor stared mutely out the window while Claire rambled on about some boy. She watched Turner County glide by and then imagined the bus carrying her onwards, all the way to California and that bizarre Academy for Human Garde. If they caught her, that's where she'd end up.

She had promised herself that she would never leave Turner County.

Inevitably, this led Taylor to remembering the last time she'd seen her mom. She was nine years old and they were at the bus station in Ashburn. Her mom wore jeans that Taylor thought were too tight, a tied-off plaid shirt and a red bandanna in her hair. All the rest of her clothes were stuffed into the backpack she carried on her shoulder.

"You're coming back, right? This isn't forever," Taylor had said to her mom.

"Oh, honey," Taylor's mom said, and touched her gently on the cheek. "You can come visit me whenever you want. Minneapolis is only a couple of hours away."

Young Taylor glanced over her shoulder to where her father sat in their truck, watching them, a baseball cap pulled low to hide his eyes. She looked back to her mom.

"But how will I get there?" she asked. "I'm nine."

Her mom smiled. "You'll see one day, Tay. A person can't stay in Turner County forever. Even if it hurts now, you'll come to understand."

Minneapolis was just Taylor's mom's first stop in her flight from South Dakota. She kept going farther and farther east—after Minneapolis was Madison, then Chicago, and the last Taylor heard it was Philadelphia. Taylor never ended up visiting any of those places. Her mom promised that one day Taylor would understand, but she didn't want that day to come because it'd mean she was like her mother. She'd take over the farm from her daddy, just like he'd taken it over from his daddy.

Her dad made patty melts and French fries for dinner that night. She got the feeling that he had noticed her hasty departure that morning and thought maybe she was mad at him, so he cooked one of her favorite meals. Taylor hugged him while he was frying up the burgers.

"There's my girl," her dad said, sounding relieved.

Over dinner, Taylor studied her dad. He was a handsome man with his half day's growth of beard, brown hair graying at the temples, lean and tan from all the work around the farm. He'd never remarried after Taylor's mom, not even a girlfriend as far as Taylor knew, although the single ladies in the county still sent over cookies and pies on a regular basis. She got teary-eyed while picturing a scenario where she'd have to say good-bye and leave him here all by himself.

Brian caught Taylor looking at him and rubbed a hand across his cheek. "What is it? I got slop on me?"

She laughed. "No, you're all good, Daddy."

"If you say so." He kept looking at her. "What about you? You all good?"

She nodded. "Yeah. I'm fine. Just tired."

Then, Taylor reached for the salt and the little glass shaker slid across the table right into her waiting palm.

They looked at each other.

After a long silence, Brian said, "Well, I'll be damned." Finally, Taylor started to cry, big heaving panicked sobs, and her dad came around the table to hold her. "Come on, now. I always knew you were a special one and this just proves it."

"I don't—I don't want to be special!" Taylor replied through her tears. "I like our life here! I don't want anything else!"

Taylor's dad rubbed her back. "Come on, now," he said

quietly. "I saw them say on TV that the ones who get powers are the best among us. That they're destined to be important people."

"I saw that same show, Dad! The one lady said all that flowery bullcrap, and the other guy said it was all random. An alien lottery. And I didn't want to win!"

"Well," her dad said calmly, "I choose to believe the bit about destiny."

"Are you not listening? I don't want a great destiny. I like it here. With you I don't want to go to their dumb Academy."

"Then you won't have to." Her dad nodded once, like he'd just come to this decision. "You don't have to do anything you don't want to do."

"But it's a law now. You're supposed to . . ." She swallowed. "You're supposed to turn me in."

Brian shook his head. "Not in a million years."

"But someone else could see," Taylor said. "You don't know how hard it was today at school to control myself. All day, I wanted to use it. I'll slip up."

Brian considered this for a moment, studying Taylor, who was studying her hands like they'd suddenly become foreign.

"Just us and the hogs out here, most times," her dad said slowly. "Maybe if you practice doing your alien-thing around the house, it'll be easier when you're out in public."

"Ugh. Please don't call it my alien-thing."

"Sorry. Your Legacy."

Taylor frowned. All day, she'd been thinking about ways to suppress her telekinesis. Maybe her dad was onto something. Maybe instead of ignoring her power, she could exhaust it in the moments when it was safe to use, get it out of her system.

"It's worth a try," she admitted.

"Besides," her dad said, picking up the saltshaker and wiggling it through the air, "I think it's pretty cool to watch."

For a month, Brian's plan worked. Taylor used her telekinesis around the house—she floated her homework books out in front of her while she studied, poured herself glasses of water in the kitchen while standing in the living room and spooned sugar into her dad's morning coffee while flipping eggs. Her control began to get more precise, the tasks she could complete more complicated, the objects she could lift heavier. And while it felt like a part of her was asleep whenever she went to school or when Silas and the other farmhands were around, Taylor found it easier and easier to keep from slipping up in public.

But then came the day of the accident.

CHAPTER EIGHT

NIGEL BARNABY
THE HUMAN GARDE ACADEMY—POINT REYES, CALIFORNIA

SHE WAS PLAYING THE CLASSICAL MUSIC AGAIN. Nigel heard it as soon as he walked into Dr. Linda's office. Daintily plucked violin strings, whistling woodwinds . . . and was that a bloody oboe? Nigel couldn't tolerate that, so he reached out with his Legacy, grabbed hold of the sound waves rolling out of Dr. Linda's stereo and bent them until they were a jangling mess of out-of-tune squeals.

Dr. Linda narrowed her eyes at him and turned off her stereo. "Nigel, we've talked about this. If you don't like the music, you can ask me to change it."

"Where's the fun in that, love?" Nigel replied as he flopped down on Dr. Linda's comfortable couch, hugged a pillow to his chest and put his combat boots up on the armrest.

Dr. Linda's office was on the top floor of the administration building, the windows south-facing with a captivating view of the blue-glass bay. She kept the room open and bright, the walls covered in splotchy abstract paintings meant to evoke reactions from her patients. Her degrees, one each in psychiatry and developmental psychology, both from Stanford, hung over her neatly kept desk.

"We've also discussed respect for my space," Dr. Linda admonished, eyeing his boots. She was a short woman, barely five feet tall, with a cherubic face, graying brown hair cut in a bob and thick-framed lavender glasses that made her look like a naughty librarian. Nigel liked her, which was why he went out of his way to get on her nerves.

"What shall we talk about this week?" Nigel asked as he swung his feet to the floor. He slouched low, his long legs reaching across the space so he could almost play footsie with Dr. Linda. Not that he would. He idly flicked the barbell in his septum—his newest piercing, the thirteenth in his head alone. "Perhaps your love life for a change, eh, Doc? I'm bored talking about me, me, me, all the time."

Dr. Linda regarded him levelly. "You know I record these sessions, right, Nigel?"

"Sure. So you can keep it all straight for that bestseller you're gonna write, yeah?" Nigel used his Legacy, changing the pitch and timbre of his voice so that he sounded almost exactly like Dr. Linda. "I forced two hundred teenaged Garde to discuss their wet dreams. Here are my findings."

Dr. Linda was, as usual, unperturbed by his sonic manipulation. "I do not make you or any of the others discuss their quote-unquote wet dreams," she said dourly. "We could, though, if you'd like."

"Well, you certainly called my bluff," Nigel said, smirking as he worked a finger around the collar of his moth-eaten Suicide tank top.

"When I attempted to listen back to our session from last week, I couldn't hear anything on the recording," Dr. Linda pressed on as if he'd never interrupted. "Was that your doing, Nigel?"

Nigel tugged on his lip ring, not sure whether to fess up or lie. Eventually, he threw on his customary devil-may-care grin and nodded. "Sorry about that, Doc. Didn't realize my powers would flummox your recorder."

"What exactly did you do?"

"Neat bit of business, actually. I put us in a sound bubble." Nigel was unable to keep the pride out of his voice; this was a new application of his sonic manipulation Legacy. "Made it so nobody outside our little circle of trust could hear."

Dr. Linda tilted her head. "Are you worried people might be listening to our sessions? I assure you, these are kept completely confidential."

Nigel tucked his chin down and looked at the therapist skeptically. "If you say so, Doc. You live on campus, right? Over in the little faculty village?" He knew she did, so he kept going. "And you don't ever get the feeling you're being watched? Like every mirror's got a bloke with a clipboard hiding on the other side?"

"That's an interesting observation," Dr. Linda responded.

That was the token neutral statement she deployed whenever Nigel set off one of her therapy alarm bells. He kicked himself for giving her something to work with. "Do you think those feelings of paranoia might be rooted in your time at the boarding school?"

Nigel groaned. He'd been seeing Dr. Linda every week since he first arrived at the Human Garde Academy. You couldn't see a woman like Dr. Linda that often for almost a year and not let a few secrets slip.

So, much to his great regret, Nigel had told Dr. Linda about the Pepperpont Young Gentlemen's Preparatory Academy. "After that fuckin' helltrap, superhero training school is easy-peasy," he'd told her at the time. Nigel had recounted the details of his four years at Pepperpont grimly—the uniforms, the stiff professors, the chores, the very particular tie knots. "But you could get all that from Dickens, eh?" He went into the darker details. The rich boys with bad taste in music. The rich boys who wanted to get experimental with him, then pretended like it never happened, then beat the piss out of him every day for months. The endless teasing, name-calling, abuse. The time that they stripped him, shaved him and dropped him out of a second-story window.

"Like prison," he'd explained, "except instead of knowing how to fix up a shiv from a toothbrush, all these blokes knew the rules of cricket. Future barristers and brokers, the lot."

When the invasion happened and Nigel discovered he'd developed telekinesis, he released himself from the custody of Pepperpont. He found an open tattoo parlor to push clear the holes in his ears that had started to close, bought an updated wardrobe at a thrift store and pledged to live the rest of his days as the alien-fighting punk rocker that lived inside him, the same badass gorilla the nice people of Pepperpont had tried so hard to tame.

There was a warship over London. That's where his parents lived, although at the time they were in Zurich on a ski trip with his older sister and her stockbroker fiancé. If they tried to call him during the invasion—"Surely, they tried to locate you; you're their son," Dr. Linda had said—Nigel was long gone by the time they rang. He hadn't seen them since. There were visiting days at the Academy, but Nigel refused to add them to the list. He couldn't forgive them for Pepperpont.

"Perhaps you have lingering anxieties from your days there," Dr. Linda said in the present. Nigel had spaced out. "Even though you're safe here, perhaps you still feel the need to keep a part of yourself walled off."

"Yeah, you got it in one, Doc," Nigel replied. "Bloody breakthrough."

Dr. Linda raised an eyebrow. "How's it going with your roommate?"

A sudden change of topic. Nigel hated when she pulled that.

"Fine," he said. "The same. Whatever. Ask him yourself. Captain America's got his weekly head shrink scheduled right after me, doesn't he?"

"Have you reached out to him? Last week, you promised

you would visit the dining hall with him at least once a week."

Nigel folded his arms. Any chance of him becoming besties with Caleb went out the window that day on the island, when he helped turn their Chimæra over to the government. Nigel held a grudge, but Dr. Linda was persistent about trying to mend that relationship. "He apologized to you, didn't he?" Dr. Linda pressed when Nigel remained stubbornly silent.

Nigel grunted. "So?"

"So, I think forgiveness might be a good skill for you to work on, Nigel."

Nigel scowled. He thought about Caleb and their months spent rooming at the Academy together, surrounded by dozens of other Human Garde. Nigel was popular around campus—his classmates remembered him from the shared vision during the invasion, they knew he'd gone to fight the Mogs. The legend about how he and Ran had taken down a Mogadorian skimmer at Niagara Falls grew and grew—in every telling, they killed more Mogs, battled against greater odds. The other Garde who were there—Fleur and Bertrand, who had died at Patience Creek—were omitted from the story. Nigel didn't stop the tale from circulating. He liked having a reputation, even though it came at the expense of some real-life pain.

And maybe he'd let slip, when the other Human Garde were first getting to know each other, that Caleb was a government plant who would report their every action to the

Earth Garde administrators. So what? It was true, wasn't it? Caleb spent more and more time alone in his room rather than with his fellow Garde.

Well, alone wasn't exactly right. Caleb had the duplicates, after all.

"He doesn't have any friends. Still. After all this time," Nigel complained.

"Which is why you should reach out to him."

"What's that they say about a bloke, huh? A creep who can't make friends . . ."

"Do you think the boys at Pepperpont thought of you that way, Nigel?"

"Aw, that's a bloody low blow, Doc. Totally different scenario."

Dr. Linda regarded him evenly. "Is it?"

"I never did anything to those wankers as bad as what Caleb did to me," Nigel said defensively. As she stared at him, unspeaking, Nigel heard his tone of voice change. This wasn't his Legacy at work; this was the whiny boarding school aristocrat coming out. "This my therapy hour or Caleb's? I'm starting to wonder."

"What else would you like to talk about, Nigel?"

"How about me having to come see you every week?" he replied sharply. "Me and Ran, Caleb—we're the only ones on campus who see you all the time. People might start to think we're bloody abnormal."

"They will not."

"They definitely already think that about Caleb."

"You know very well why you're monitored more closely than the others. Precisely because you've been exposed to a life-and-death scenario."

"It wasn't even all that traumatic," Nigel muttered, thinking back to the brutal fight at Patience Creek. "I never think about it."

"No more nightmares?" Dr. Linda asked him.

Another little fact Nigel should have never let slip; he had a reccurring dream of being pursued down a smoky hallway by the mad Mogadorian woman who'd hunted them.

"No," he lied.

"Then I suppose you are cured," Dr. Linda replied. "See you next week."

In the posh waiting room outside Dr. Linda's office, Nigel found Caleb waiting for his appointment, seated next to one of his duplicates. The two were huddled close, apparently deep in a whispered conversation that cut off as soon as they noticed Nigel. It looked like Caleb had been scolding his clone.

"He wanted to eavesdrop," Caleb said sheepishly, gesturing to his duplicate.

"Uh-huh," Nigel replied, raising an eyebrow. "You're gonna want to cut that shit out, mate. It's not couples therapy. Wouldn't want the doc thinking you're a freak."

Caleb nodded in agreement. "Yeah, Linda says I shouldn't . . ." He trailed off, looking at his clone. "Never mind. He was just leaving."

The clone kept its gaze on Nigel, even as Caleb began

to absorb it. The process still made Nigel's skin crawl. The clone went transparent, like a ghost, and then slowly flowed back into Caleb. There was always a moment when they were back together but still overlapped slightly that would give Caleb a blurry four-eyed look, like a person coming apart. Nigel suppressed a shudder. He wasn't the only one on campus who Caleb unnerved, as evidenced by Dr. Linda pushing Nigel to be friends with the aloof duplicator.

When there was only one of him, Caleb stood up. He patted Nigel companionably on the shoulder—these Americans were always touching, high-fiving, back-patting—then brushed by him, into Dr. Linda's office. "See you back at home," Caleb said, as he closed the door.

Nigel wondered, not for the first time, if tonight would be the night that an army of Calebs held him down in bed and smothered him.

CHAPTER NINE

TAYLOR COOK
TURNER COUNTY, SOUTH DAKOTA

THE ACCIDENT HAPPENED ON A SATURDAY, THE DAY dry and sunny. "Got lucky with the rain," Taylor's dad reported. "Good baling weather."

The Cooks owned ten acres of hayfield, just enough to feed their own animals every year and maybe sell a few left-over bales to their neighbors. The weekend before, Brian and Silas had cut the field, raked the stalks into rows and left them out to dry. Today, Brian would attach the small baler to the tractor and ride over the rows, while Silas and a couple of other farmhands would trail behind, collecting the freshly made bales and lugging them to the barn. As usual, Taylor's job would be to direct traffic. Left to their own devices, Silas and the others would stack the bales nonsensically, like the year they'd piled the hay right where the tractor was always parked. Her dad hadn't realized until after the farmhands had left and he had to move every bale himself before he could get the tractor in the barn.

"You know," her father mused over breakfast, "we could do this whole thing just you and me. Probably only take us until noon. Nobody'd even break a sweat."

"Dad." Taylor rolled her eyes.

"My superpowered farmhand would be the envy of all our neighbors," he said with a laugh. Brian stroked his chin, suddenly deep in thought. "Probably save us a lot, actually. Could get to some of those projects I've been putting off. Well, you could, anyway, and I would supervise." He winked at Taylor. "This place might actually turn a profit."

"We do just fine," Taylor said. "Besides, if you cut Silas loose, how would he afford those butt-ugly tattoos?"

Brian chuckled. "Come on, now. Don't put that boy's 'art-work' on me. Making me think I oughta fire him for his own good."

"So, you had at least one smart idea this morning," Taylor replied with an easy smile.

Taylor had first noticed Silas's latest tattoo a few days earlier, when he made a show of sitting at their kitchen table, easing off the bandage and applying some salve to the raw, pink flesh of his forearm. The tattoo depicted a coiled serpent bursting forth from within a circle, its dripping fangs bared; as if in response to the snake's emergence, a scythe swung down for the reptile's throat. Taylor had eyed the tattoo skeptically. She imagined Silas walking around the fields, lopping the heads off of garter snakes for fun.

"You like it?" He'd caught her looking and immediately perked up.

"Not really," she said, and left the kitchen, but not before she caught the disappointed look on his face.

The farmhands showed up while Taylor was washing the dishes. There was Silas, of course, along with Brent and Teddy. Brent was around her father's age, plump, with a bushy brown beard. He was a distant cousin of hers, on her mom's side, although they weren't very close. He'd been helping out on the farm since before Taylor was born; Brent and her father had an easy camaraderie, even if her dad sometimes called Brent "shiftless" behind his back. Teddy, on the other hand, was a guy who'd gone to community college with Silas, muscular, quiet and sweet, a hard worker, basically Silas's complete opposite. Silas had gotten Teddy the gig on the Cook farm and Taylor always suspected it was because Silas knew he could pawn off some of his own work onto good-natured Teddy's broad shoulders.

That afternoon, Silas insisted on working without a shirt, even though the hay surely made his skin itchy. Taylor watched from the porch as he and the others hauled bales back to the barn. Once he worked up a good sweat, his ropey muscles caked with dirt and golden flecks of hay, Silas sauntered over to the porch for a drink of water. Taylor cringed.

"You hurt my feelings the other day," he said to her.

"How's that?" she replied with a sigh.

Silas held up the arm with the snake tattoo. "Making fun

70

of my tattoo. This one's important to me, y'know?"

"What is it? Some death metal band?"

"Naw, nothing like that—"

"Look, it's fine as far as tattoos go, all right?" Taylor said, hoping to end the conversation. "Just not my thing."

Silas leaned against the porch bannister. "You like a clean-cut type, that it? Like them boys you go to school with?"

Taylor's skin crawled, but she looked back at him steadily. In the past, she would have endured Silas's gross come-ons in silence. But now, even though she was keeping her power secret, the telekinesis made her feel safer. Bolder.

"Maybe you could get one of those Chinese characters next."

Silas perked up. "Oh yeah? You like those?"

"Yeah, maybe we could get an English-to-Chinese dictionary and see if they've got a symbol for 'creep.'"

Silas forced a laugh, then made a point of giving Taylor a once-over. "Come on, now. I ain't no creep. Nothing wrong with having an appreciation for the finer things in life."

Before Taylor could respond, they both heard shouts from the field.

"Help! Silas! Help!"

That was Teddy screaming. Taylor was off the porch in a flash, sprinting towards the field, Silas close on her heels.

The tractor had blown a tire and rolled over. Taylor's dad was either thrown or jumped clear. Either way, he lay a few yards away, not moving, facedown in the dirt. To make matters worse, Teddy had been too close to the baler when the tractor pitched and gotten his sleeve tangled in the machine. The baler could pull you in and strip your skin right off if you weren't careful, especially when it wasn't upright. Bloody welts were already forming on Teddy's arm where he struggled against the baler; Brent had his arms wrapped around Teddy's waist, doing all he could to keep him from getting shredded.

"Son of a bitch!" Silas yelled as he joined Brent in trying to free Teddy. "Turn that thing off!" he shouted at Taylor.

Without even thinking about it, Taylor used her telekinesis to throw the power lever on the baler. The machine wheezed to a stop. The three farmhands fell in a heap as Teddy's arm came free, Teddy crying tears of relief.

Luckily, in the chaos, the farmhands hadn't noticed Taylor use her Legacy. She rushed to her dad's side, fell to her knees beside him and rolled him over, her telekinesis helping with his weight. Taylor saw a gash on her dad's forehead from where he'd landed on a rock. There was a lot of blood— one side of her dad's face was caked in copper-tinged mud. Worse than just a few stitches. Taylor thought she could see a bit of bone peeking out through all the grime and gore.

A strange calm settled over her. She knew what to do.

Taylor pressed a hand to her dad's forehead, felt warm energy flow through her and into him and watched as his wound miraculously closed. Seconds later, his eyes fluttered open and she breathed a sigh of relief.

"Hell, what happened?" he asked blearily.

Taylor felt eyes upon her. She turned slowly, saw the three farmhands all standing there and staring at her. Their eyes were wide, their mouths agape. They'd seen what she did.

"You're . . . you're one of them!" Silas exclaimed.

"Hold on, I can explain," Taylor replied, her mind searching for a convincing lie.

Silas took off, running as fast as he could back towards the house. Taylor and the others watched, puzzled, as he sprinted to his truck and took off up the dirt road.

"That'll be trouble," her father said, sitting up. He touched the front of his shirt—nearly soaked through with blood—and shook his head in disbelief.

"Don't see what got into him. I didn't see nothing to be scared of," Brent said, her cousin turning to look meaningfully at Teddy. "You see anything, Ted?"

Teddy continued to stare at Taylor, his mouth open. Brent elbowed him.

"Yeah, uh, I mean, no," Teddy said. "Didn't see nothing."

"Double wages for today," her dad said to Teddy as he slowly climbed to his feet. "For the trouble."

Taylor stayed quiet through it all, her eyes on the dusty trail left by Silas's quick exit. She should've been amazed by what she'd done—healing a massive gash with just a touch!—except there was already a heavy seed of anxiety growing in her stomach. The way Silas had looked at her, not leering anymore but repulsed . . .

Well, the secret's out now, she thought, surprised to feel some small glimmer of relief. Whatever happens next, at least there's no more hiding.

Taylor snapped her attention to Teddy when he stepped forward and sheepishly held out his bloody arm. "Maybe I could also not see you doing your magic for me, Taylor?" He smiled shakily. "Please?"

For a week, Taylor and her dad waited for the other shoe to drop. Silas stopped showing up for work and wouldn't return phone calls. Taylor kept waiting for a battalion of soldiers to come and take her into custody, but after another week went by as if nothing had happened, she began to get hopeful.

"Maybe he didn't tell anyone," she told her dad over breakfast, although the words rang hollow.

Her dad's brow furrowed. He pushed his food around his plate, his appetite diminished since the accident.

"It ain't so much the telling that worries me," her dad said after a moment. "It's who he tells."

A few days later, Teddy showed up at the farm. He'd been picking up Silas's shifts since he disappeared, but it was Sunday, the day the Cooks didn't have help. Brian met him on the porch and Taylor eavesdropped at the door.

"I went out in Sioux Falls last night," Teddy explained. "Saw Silas. He was with a strange bunch of fellas, Mr. Cook. He saw me, came over, started asking about Taylor."

"Government types?" her dad asked.

"Nuh-uh," Teddy replied. "Y'know them Bible-thumping sort that go door-to-door sometimes, all intense and in your business? These guys looked like them but . . . meaner. Gave

74

me the heebie-jeebies, so I got outta there quick. Then, this morning, I seen some of them same guys driving around town. Figured it wouldn't be right if I didn't come out here and warn you."

After Teddy left, Mr. Cook got his shotgun out of storage. He sat out on the porch with the weapon across his lap and waited.

"Who do you think they are?" Taylor asked.

Her dad grimaced. "Don't know." He paused and she could tell he was debating how much to tell her. He touched the spot on his forehead where there should have been a scar from his fall off the tractor. "When all this first happened with you, I did some research into . . . you know, how things are now. There's some people out there, crazy people, with nasty ideas about kids with your gifts."

Taylor's hands shook. "Maybe we should call somebody. The police, at least."

"They'll take you away." He looked over his shoulder. "You want that, Tay?"

She shook her head. She didn't want that. But she didn't want her father to get hurt either.

"This is our family's land," her dad concluded resolutely. "Ain't nobody pushing me around on our land."

They came at nightfall.

Taylor's dad hustled her inside when the first set of headlights came into view. She didn't go far—she was the one with the Legacies, after all—her dad had only his shotgun and a single box of ammo. Taylor peeked out from behind the screen door, watching the vehicles come.

They made a show of driving up, coming in abreast of each other like they were in formation, riding roughshod over the fields. There were a couple of RVs, some pickup trucks, a handful of motorcycles and a big van like cops would use to haul prisoners. Spray-painted on the sides and hoods of some of the vehicles was that same snake-and-scythe symbol that Silas had tattooed on his forearm.

Her father stood on the porch with his gun ready as the men got out of their cars and formed a perimeter. Taylor assumed they were mostly men, anyway—she couldn't see their faces. Many of them wore gasmasks. Some of them opted simply for bandannas covering their mouths and noses like outlaws. Taylor didn't know what to make of the metallic headgear some of them sported. Looked almost like tinfoil hats. Taylor scanned the crowd but couldn't pick out Silas from their number. There were about thirty of them.

"You people are trespassing!" her father yelled. He made an effort to keep his voice steady, but Taylor could tell he was scared.

The men were armed. Pistols and machine guns and assault rifles. Her dad's shotgun was loaded with buckshot.

A man came forward from the crowd. He wore a black bandanna, a coal-colored duster and no silly headgear. His curly hair was salt-and-pepper. He held his hands up as if to keep things calm.

"Mr. Cook, isn't it? Brian Cook? Can I call you Brian?"

Her dad pumped his shotgun in response.

"Now now, Brian, don't go doing anything rash. We didn't come all the way out here to hurt you. On the contrary! We came to protect you."

"Protect me from what?"

"Why, from that thing living in your house," the man answered.

Taylor thought about the clips she'd seen of the Garde fighting during the invasion. They used their telekinesis to rip the weapons right out of the hands of their enemies. She could do that if she focused.

Except there were an awful lot of guns out there.

She looked down at herself and gasped. There was a red dot on her chest. Someone sighting her through the screen. She ducked behind the door frame, heart pounding.

"They always told us in Sunday school that the devils lived down below, but we know now that's not the case, don't we, Brian?" the man was saying. "They came from the stars. Descended just like Lucifer did. Seeded the world with their sin. Now that corruption's growing, manifesting in ways that defy the laws of nature. Satan, he wants you to see those powers as miracles. He wants you to worship these supposed guardian angels. But I know my Bible, I remember the words of Corinthians—"

"Jesus," Taylor's dad said. "Don't you ever shut up?"

The preacher sighed. "We're here to Harvest the sin, Mr. Cook. Your daughter, she didn't choose to have that filth possess her, and my heart goes out. It's a shameful and ugly business. But we got to do what God commands and Harvest these false prophets before they get a chance to grow. You go ahead and stand aside now, so we can do God's will."

While the man spoke, Taylor's dad half turned and hissed in her direction. "Taylor, you run out the back now."

"No, Dad."

"I love you, now you run—!"

Taylor's dad aimed his shotgun at the preacher.

He fired. And, at the same time, a dozen other guns fired back. *Pop-pop-pop.* Their peaceful farm, now a war zone.

And then, a moment later, the night sky filled with fire.

CHAPTER TEN

KOPANO OKEKE
ZUMA ROCK, NIGERIA

"DOES FATHER KNOW ABOUT THIS?"

Kopano's mom stared at him. "What do you think?"

She drove a car borrowed from one of her church friends, Kopano buckled in beside her. He could not remember the last time that he saw his mother drive. She hunched over the wheel, the color drained from her knuckles. She kept checking the rearview mirror, worried they were being followed.

It was Akuziem, his mother, whose cool hand had pressed over Kopano's mouth and awoken him in the middle of the night.

She had already packed a bag for him.

She led him past the living room, tiptoeing in a way Kopano found overly dramatic. His father was passed out in the armchair, a half-empty bottle of ogogoro in one hand, his cell phone clutched in the other. Finally done making apologies for their lost delivery, Udo had drunken himself into a stupor. When Kopano stopped to stare at his father, Akuziem grabbed his arm and yanked him down the hall.

"Say good-bye to your brothers," his mother whispered.

Kopano looked at her with alarm. "Are we in trouble, Mama?"

"I am sorting it out," she whispered back, then waved him forward impatiently. "We must be quick."

Kopano crept into the narrow bedroom that his little brothers shared. Obi stretched out on his back and snored relentlessly, while little Dubem huddled close to the wall with a pillow pushed over his head. Kopano kissed Obi on the forehead, the boy not even stirring. He couldn't reach Dubem's face, nestled as it was in his pillows, so he settled for squeezing his youngest brother's little arm. Dubem rolled over immediately, tired eyes trying to focus.

"Kopano? What's wrong?"

"Nothing," Kopano replied too quickly, his smile forced. "Just saying good night."

Dubem eyed him skeptically. He soon noticed the canvas pack slung over Kopano's shoulder. "Is this it? Are you going to America?"

Kopano sensed his mother's shadow watching from the doorway. Only then did it dawn on Kopano that spiriting him away to the Human Garde Academy was exactly his mother's plan. He had waited months for this day, but he never expected it to come so abruptly. He had imagined a going-away party with all their neighbors invited along with his friends from school, and then a tearful parting with his family at the airport. When would he see his parents again? His brothers? Would they be all right without him? Kopano wiped the back of his hand across his eyes.

"Yes," he told Dubem. "Don't tell Father until morning. He'll be mad."

"I will keep your secret," Dubem said, then sat up to hug him. "Good luck to you, brother. Write me letters."

The streets of Lagos were far less crowded after midnight, the bumper-to-bumper traffic and daredevil drivers of the daylight hours gone, although the cavernous potholes that needed careful navigation while the sun was up were even more dangerous now. Kopano found the deserted roads ominous. There were so few other cars that he wondered what sort of sinister people were hidden behind each set of passing headlights. In his mind, he concocted stories for them—criminals and vigilantes and fugitives like him. Was the boy who'd tried to gut him driving around out there, looking for vengeance?

"Father's gotten us in trouble, hasn't he?" Kopano said to break the silence.

"Not just Father, hmm?" his mother replied, then adjusted the rearview mirror. "Or did he force you to go along with his stupid scheme? You, with your powers . . ."

Kopano crossed his arms. "I thought . . . we needed the money. I didn't expect what happened to happen."

She tossed her head, dismissing Kopano's words. "Too late now, my son. You and your father angered some very bad people. Powerful people. And all your father can think to do is drink and cry on the phone and beg mercy. So, you and I will fix this. We know people more powerful than these so-called big men."

"Who? Who do we know?"

"The United Nations," his mother replied firmly. "Your friend John Smith."

Kopano stared at her like she'd gone mad. "They will take me to the Academy in America, Mama, not the rest of you."

"I know that. I also read the articles that say the families of your kind will be protected. So, you will go to America, and your new keepers will take the rest of us somewhere safe."

Kopano pretended not to notice the way his mother said "your kind," as if he was no longer Okeke, no longer Nigerian, no longer human.

It was more than a ten-hour drive north on the A22 to Zuma Rock, where the Loralite stone had grown and the United Nations had set up a headquarters. Kopano offered to take a turn behind the wheel, but his mother refused. She relaxed some once they left Lagos behind. They both did.

Kopano dozed off and awoke to the sound of hoofbeats. It was morning. A group of boys rode their horses on the side of the highway, racing their car, whooping and slapping riding crops against the flanks of their skinny mounts. Akuziem honked her horn in irritation and stepped on the gas until the jockeys fell behind them. They were in a rural part of the country that Kopano had never seen before. He had never even been out of Lagos. Once again, the reality of his situation dawned on him.

He was going to America.

They only stopped twice, both times for gas. His mother still wouldn't let him drive. She didn't take any food—Kopano bought a bag of potato chips and two large oranges from a stand when they passed through Auchi—but Akuziem only gulped deeply from the bottles of water she had the foresight to pack. His mother was hard-eyed, squinting into the sun. She'd remembered the water but forgotten her sunglasses. To Kopano, she looked like a woman on a mission. She drove fast.

"Are you so eager to get rid of me?" Kopano asked his mother, only half joking.

His mother's mouth tightened in a frown. "You are my son," she said, but Kopano could hear the doubt in her voice. Akuziem must have been aware of that, too, because she reached over to grab Kopano's hand and repeated herself with more conviction. "You are my son. I wish none of this had happened to you. But you are on a journey from God now. We must accept that."

By afternoon, they approached Abuja. The highway was crowded, although nothing like the traffic of Lagos, and Kopano felt comfortably anonymous. His stomach turned, however, when Zuma Rock came into view. For a long stretch, the road pointed right at the stone monolith,

Zuma Rock casting a shadow, its dull gray surface eating up the sun. Around Zuma Rock the land was green and hilly, not mountainous like one would expect, which made the 725-meter-high stone stick out all the more. To Kopano, Zuma Rock looked like God above had dropped a meteor in the middle of Africa and left it there. Zuma Rock made sense as a place where the aliens would choose to have their Loralite grow. It was as otherworldly a place as one could find on Earth.

As they drove closer, the newly built man-made feature of Zuma Rock caught Kopano's eye. A swath of the parkland around the giant rock had been recently converted into a military base camp. Scaffolding ran up and down the side of the rock face; even from this distance, he could see a small elevator going back and forth to the top of Zuma Rock. A helicopter circled overhead.

Akuziem's expression didn't change as they got closer. In fact, she looked even more determined than ever to see this through, her eyes locked on the checkpoints that loomed ahead.

There were detour signs. Large notifications in many languages that Zuma Rock was closed to the public. The traffic thinned around them, the other drivers following the curve around Zuma Rock and into the capital city of Abuja. Kopano's mom pressed onwards, ignoring the signs. Soon, they were the only car on the road.

They drove towards a group of Nigerian soldiers lounging in their Humvees, their vehicles arranged to create a loose roadblock. Kopano glanced at his mother. She slowed down but showed no sign of stopping.

"Did you tell them we were coming?" Kopano thought to ask.

"No," his mom replied.

Kopano stared at the soldiers, who were now paying attention to their little car. They were guarding a site of great power. Kopano was worried they would start shooting at any moment.

Kopano's mom rolled down her window and waved. The soldiers waved back, and she simply drove around them. Kopano nodded at one of them as they went by. The soldier lit a cigarette.

Kopano laughed in relief. "Just like Father says! If you act like you belong, you can get in anywhere."

"I packed your bag for you, Kopano," his mother replied stiffly. "I did not leave room for your father's wisdom."

The soldiers at the next checkpoint weren't so lackadaisical. They wore the light blue berets of UN Peacekeepers and manned a heavy iron gate that blocked the road to Zuma Rock. A very pale man with a bad sunburn and red eyebrows raised a gloved hand to stop them and approached their car.

"You have to turn around, lady," the soldier said with what Kopano thought was an Irish accent. "Place is closed to the public until further notice."

"My son is one of them," Akuziem countered stiffly. "He has the Legacies."

The soldier glanced at Kopano and then rolled his eyes.

Apparently, this happened a lot. "Sure he does. Look, there's no reward, you get me? You got a strapping young lad here, that's true, but the docs'll take one look at him and know you've wasted everyone's ti—"

Before the soldier could finish, Kopano used his telekinesis to float his beret into the air. The soldier took a step back, wide-eyed, and waved his hands above and below the beret, as if checking for strings.

"I could lift something bigger, if you want," Kopano offered with a smile.

"Not necessary," said the soldier, already getting on his walkie-talkie.

The soldiers ushered their car through the gate and allowed them to park in the shadow of Zuma Rock. A knot of men and women—some soldiers, but also some scientists in lab coats and a few people in business attire—speed-walked toward their car.

"I love you, Kopano, no matter what happens," his mother said.

"I love you too," Kopano replied.

Kopano would not speak to his mother again for some time. He was glad they had that moment, even if his mother's words were cut with the edge of doubt, as if she still wasn't entirely convinced Kopano was still Kopano.

What happened next was a whirlwind of activity. They were welcomed enthusiastically by the UN representatives and quickly separated. The people in the suits gravitated towards Kopano's mother. There were documents for her to sign on Kopano's behalf—visa applications, emancipation agreements, surveys of which vaccinations he'd received. The suits asked for her address in Lagos, the names of his father and brothers, and assured her that they'd all be brought somewhere safe.

"There will be a cure, yes?" Kopano heard his mother ask one of the men. "You do all this research with them so you can eventually find a cure."

Kopano's heart sank, but soon a barrage of questions from the scientists made him forget his mother's words.

How old are you? When did your powers first manifest? That long ago? All this time, right here, under our noses! Did you experience the vision of John Smith? Have you been practicing on your own? Why didn't you come sooner?

Kopano got the feeling that the science team stationed at Zuma Rock hadn't had much to do. They were thrilled to have him, nodding and smiling and writing down everything he said as if it were of the utmost importance. They showed him into their encampment, then brought him into a high-tech laboratory that was meticulously clean.

Any strange feelings or poor health? Depression? Anxiety? Have you used your Legacies in any hostile situations?

Kopano described yesterday's attack. The scientists didn't judge him for his year spent as a superpowered courier. One of them, the only Nigerian in the room besides Kopano, shook her head in sympathy. She understood.

A pair of doctors administered what seemed to be a very ordinary physical. The only speed bump occurred when they tried to take a sample of Kopano's blood. The needle pierced just the first layer of Kopano's skin when his Legacy kicked in. The syringe crunched and crumpled before it could reach his vein. Three times they tried with the same result.

"Is it possible for you to turn that off?" one of the doctors asked.

"I don't know," said Kopano. "It's brand-new."

"We've been told that when dealing with Legacies, it's helpful to visualize the desired result," one of the observing scientists suggested. "Perhaps imagine that you want to have your blood drawn."

"I do want to help," Kopano replied with a smile. "But who in this world has such a strong imagination that they can pretend to like needles?"

Everyone laughed. After a few more broken needles, the doctors gave up, settling instead for hair and skin samples, plus a few fingernail clippings. Apparently, his fingernails weren't made of the same stern stuff that lurked beneath his skin.

His physical complete, the initial ruckus of his arrival dying down, many of the scientists went off to quietly evaluate their data or video-chat with colleagues about the boy with impenetrable skin. Kopano was left alone with the Nigerian scientist.

"They're very excited," she said, gesturing after the other scientists. "You're the first Human Garde we've seen here."

Kopano puffed out his chest. "I am excited too."

Her name was Orisa, she was in her late twenties, with huge brown eyes and tightly arrayed braids. She was an employee of the World Health Organization who had volunteered to transfer to Zuma Rock when the "alien man- ifestation" occurred.

"Do you want to see it?" she asked.

They rode the elevator up the side of Zuma Rock, the little cage rattling in the wind. At the top, they were greeted by a pair of soldiers, both armed with automatic weapons and paperback novels.

"I guess guarding a rock on top of another rock doesn't take much attention," Kopano remarked.

Orisa smiled. "Honestly, until you came, this was the most boring assignment ever."

The outcropping of Loralite grew from the top of Zuma Rock like a tree of stone. Veins of the glittering cobalt-blue substance spread like roots beneath Kopano's feet. The Loralite growth was seven feet tall and reminded Kopano of a tidal wave in the way that it shot up sharply and then curved back over itself. He remembered what John Smith had said in the vision all those months ago—imagine another place with a stone, touch its glowing surface and the Loralite would teleport you across the globe.

Kopano couldn't help himself. He reached forward, hand outstretched.

Orisa pulled him back.

"Don't do that," she said. "You might teleport away on accident."

"I would come right back," Kopano promised with a crooked grin.

"Not all the Loralite growths are as secured as this one," she said. "Anyway, they say you Garde must be able to picture where you want to go."

"I can picture America. That's where I'm going, right?"

"Yes, but not by teleportation. You will be flown there." She caught Kopano's look of disappointment. "Old-fashioned, I know. But at least the plane is private."

"My father would be jealous," Kopano muttered with a smirk. He held out his hands towards the stone again, not to touch it, but like one would reach toward a campfire.

"Do you feel something?" Orisa asked, producing a notebook from her lab coat.

"Yes," Kopano replied, struggling at first to put the feeling into words. "It pulls me. I feel—I look at it, and I know it does not belong here. I should think of it as alien and strange." *Like the way my mother looks at me*, he thought but didn't add. "But instead, it feels natural. I know this stone like I know the sky."

There was a mountain of paperwork waiting for Kopano downstairs. They asked Kopano to read what he at first thought was a book but turned out to be a contract, the huge document stamped with the UN logo, written in a dense legalese and filled with subsection after subsection. He looked to Orisa for help.

"Basically, it says that you agree to enter the custody of the United Nations and that, after a period of training and once you turn eighteen, you will be conscripted to the Peacekeepers' Earth Garde division for a five-year term of service," the scientist summarized. "It also lays out the laws that Garde must abide by, that you agree to be held accountable for your actions and that you won't hold your home country or the United Nations responsible should anything happen to you."

Kopano nodded once, flipped to the last page of the mammoth contract and signed where indicated.

"Can I see my mother now?" he asked. "I'd like to say good-bye."

Orisa's brow furrowed. "Oh, I thought you already . . . she left, Kopano. The soldiers brought her to a hotel in Abuja. After she told us of your troubles; the rest of your family is being gathered as we speak." She glanced at her watch. "Your plane will be coming soon, but I could have her brought back . . ."

Kopano shook his head. "No worries," he said, and forced a smile.

She had left him. He would begin this great journey alone.

CHAPTER ELEVEN

TAYLOR COOK
POINTS IN BETWEEN

BEFORE THE SHOOTING STARTED, WHEN THE COS-tumed zealots with their snake-and-scythe tattoos were still making their way to the farm, while her dad was alone on the porch sitting watch with his shotgun in his lap, Taylor Cook decided to call the hotline.

"You have reached Earth Garde North America, how may I assist you?" a lady operator said, her voice kind but detached.

Taylor sat on the floor with her back against her bed, hands cupped around her cell phone, even though there was no chance her father could overhear. They advertised the hotline on TV and on billboards and all over the internet. The commercials featured young people practicing telekinesis, or accidentally setting trees on fire with Legacies. Any

Human Garde or extraterrestrial activity was supposed to be reported.

"I can hear you breathing," said the operator. "Hello?"

Taylor worked some moisture into her mouth, then finally spoke.

"I'm one of them," she said. "A Garde."

"Okay, honey," the operator replied briskly. "What makes you think that?"

"What—what makes me think that?" Taylor blinked. "I can move things with my mind. My dad, he got a cut on his head, and I healed it."

"How old are you?"

"Fifteen."

"I'm showing your location as South Dakota. Is that correct?"

"Yes, but listen, we need—"

"What you're going to want to do is get your parents to drive you on down to Denver. That's the evaluation center nearest to you. They'll take a look at you there, assuming what you say is true. We used to send out investigators, but we got too many pranks. If you've got video evidence of Legacies, you can upload it to our secure site. Let me give you that address . . ."

Taylor's mouth hung open, stunned by the woman's casual tone, the mundanity of it all. She raised her voice, hands shaking.

"You don't understand! There are people . . ." She got control, overcompensated and started to whisper. "There are people coming to hurt us. To hurt me."

There was a pause. When she spoke again, the operator wasn't so dismissive. She must have recognized the tautness in Taylor's voice.

"If you're in danger, honey, you should call nine-one-one."

"I know, I know. But . . . but my dad's worried you'll come take me away if we tell. It all started with this jerk with a weird tattoo—"

"Stay on the line, please. I'm contacting emergency services in your area."

"Wait—"

The line went quiet except for a series of clicks. Seconds stretched on. Taylor felt her palms getting sweaty.

"Okay, this is strange," the operator said, suddenly back in Taylor's ear. Her flippant tone was replaced with a gravity that rattled Taylor. "We can't get a response from the sheriff station in your area."

"Oh God."

"Help is on the way," the operator said. "If you can get to a safe place, you should do so."

An hour later, the Harvesters encircled their house. Taylor's father stood alone on the porch, rifle in hand, listening to a preacher dressed like an outlaw give an impromptu sermon on Taylor's "sinful" condition.

Help still hadn't arrived.

Guns went up. Her father got off one shot. Dozens of Harvesters fired back, the sound like a drumroll. Taylor dropped to the floor, huddled against the wall next to their front door. She expected shattering glass. She expected the *chunk-chunk-chunk* of bullets eating away at the wooden walls of her house. She expected not to make it through the next few seconds.

Instead, there was a sudden silence.

And a glow. A warm, orange glow, like fire. It was as if the sun had risen.

Taylor peeked out from behind the door frame. In the strange, fiery glow, Taylor noticed what she at first took for a swarm of gnats hanging a few inches from her father's rifle. His buckshot, she realized, suspended in midair, the heavier silver rounds fired by the Harvesters likewise stuck glittering over their front yard. Taylor glanced down at her hands—for a moment, she wondered if the stress had caused her Legacies to trigger, like the day her father rolled the tractor. But no, she realized, she wasn't capable of such a spectacular feat of telekinetic control.

The glowing young man floating over her driveway was.

Taylor heard the pitter-patter of rain. It was the bullets, falling harmlessly to the ground.

"Drop your weapons or I'll drop them for you," the glowing figure said.

Taylor recognized him immediately. The entire world knew John Smith's face. His sandy-blond hair had grown out from the picture they always used on the news and a patchy beard covered his cheeks. Seeing him there, floating fifteen feet in the air, his hands glowing with fire that spread up to his forearms, it was like a comic book come to life. Even the Harvesters, who moments ago had seemed so threatening, gawked up at the leader of the Loric. It was said that he possessed every possible Legacy, his powers near godlike, and that he'd single-handedly destroyed at least one Mogadorian warship during the invasion.

What in the hell was he doing in South Dakota?

Well, the operator had said she'd send help.

Brian dropped his gun as commanded, the clatter of his rifle against the porch breaking the stunned silence.

The Harvesters weren't so ready to comply.

"The devil himself is among us, brothers and sisters!" the preacher shouted through his outlaw bandanna. "The source of the infection that corrupts our young!"

The Harvesters trained their guns on John Smith. He didn't flinch. A second later, instead of a volley of gunfire, screams of surprise filled the air. With his telekinesis, John Smith had ripped the weapons away from the mob, a number of trigger fingers broken in the process. The disarmed Harvesters watched as each of their guns folded and twisted until they were nothing but useless metal rings.

"You aren't allowed to hurt us!" someone shouted. This was true. The UN had passed a resolution that any Garde— Loric or Human—couldn't use their Legacies against other humans, except in cases of self-defense.

With a demonstrative flick of his wrist, John Smith sent the crumpled guns flying towards the Harvesters' vehicles.

Antennas snapped, tires exploded, windshields shattered.

"I'm not hurting you, just your stuff," John Smith told the shaken Harvesters.

Even with their faces hidden, Taylor sensed fear from the Harvesters. Many began to back away towards their damaged vehicles. They'd completely forgotten about her and her father.

John Smith floated gently to the ground.

"Lie down," he commanded the Harvesters. "The authorities will be here soon."

They ran.

A tremor rumbled out from where John Smith stood. It was aimed away from their house, but Taylor could still feel the reverberations. The trucks and RVs flipped over like turtles. All of the Harvesters were knocked to the ground. Some of them stayed down like John Smith commanded, but others scrambled to their feet and sprinted towards the road. She noticed the preacher hobbling off her property, a Harvester under each arm half carrying him.

Taylor stood next to her father, watching the action from the porch. She reached out and grasped his hand.

"Wow," Brian said.

"I—I called them," she said. "I turned myself in."

"You saved our lives," Brian said.

"He saved our lives," Taylor replied. "He . . ."

Taylor trailed off when she realized John Smith was looking at her. He wasn't pursuing the fleeing Harvesters. At first, she thought he didn't want to leave her and her dad alone with the ones who had surrendered. But there was something about that look—he was stopped cold, staring at Taylor, almost like he'd seen a ghost.

Flashing police lights appeared in the distance, racing towards their house. The Harvesters wouldn't get far. She hoped.

"Um, hey," Taylor said, waving a hand to break John Smith's daze.

He shook his head, blinked away whatever memory had overtaken him and focused up.

"Sorry," he said after a moment. "You . . . remind me of someone. Are you all right?"

Taylor and her dad nodded in unison, both of them dumbfounded.

John Smith glanced at the overturned cars. "Sorry about the mess," he said. "I'll help clean this stuff off your property."

Brian laughed in disbelief at that.

"You saved our lives," Taylor said.

John Smith shrugged. "Earth Garde didn't have a team close enough and I was in the neighborhood."

"You were in South Dakota?" Taylor exclaimed.

"Canada, actually."

"Pretty big neighborhood."

He smiled. "Guess so."

Taylor kept an eye on the defeated Harvesters as she stepped cautiously off the porch. John Smith seemed kind and, in a way Taylor couldn't quite explain, deeply melancholy.

She had read an article about his time spent hiding out in a small town in Ohio before the invasion and how he tried to live a normal life. Maybe he would understand . . .

"Hey," she said, keeping her voice low so the Harvesters wouldn't overhear. "Is it possible to say . . . ? I don't know . . . that this was all a big misunderstanding? Could we tell the authorities that I don't actually have Legacies?"

John Smith raised an eyebrow. "But you do."

"Yeah, but . . . I don't want to go to the Academy." Taylor glanced over her shoulder. "I don't want to leave my dad alone."

John Smith studied Taylor for a moment, his mouth tightening, and then he looked down at his feet. He shook his head.

"I'm sorry," he replied. "That's beyond my power."

Taylor never got to see if John Smith made good on his word to clean the Harvester vehicles off their property. An armada of cops and FBI showed up—apparently, their local sheriff's station had been taken over by a second crew of Harvesters, so help had to come down from Sioux Falls— and they were soon joined by an unmarked government helicopter. A pair of Earth Garde representatives rode in on the chopper, local law enforcement immediately deferring to them. They instructed Taylor to pack a bag, which she did slowly and reluctantly and with a lot of help from her father. Then they were hustled onto the helicopter.

Taylor left the farm behind. As the chopper rose up, she looked over the remnants of the battle. She caught sight of

John Smith signing autographs for a group of local cops. She thought he glanced up in her direction, but she couldn't be sure.

Taylor and her dad were taken to the processing center in Denver. The building was located at the base of Pikes Peak, that location chosen because an outcropping of Loralite had grown at the mountain's top. They were greeted by a bunch of fast-talking lawyers, military brass and hypercurious scientists. They drew Taylor's blood and asked her to use her telekinesis to push on a piston as hard as she could in order to gauge her strength. She felt a strange mix of relief and disappointment when she caught a glimpse of a researcher checking the box for "average" next to "telekinetic strength." After that, there were the forms, an endless pile of them— pledges and agreements and waivers.

"Should we have a lawyer present for this stuff?" her dad asked, staring blearily at the latest document thrust before him. The two of them hadn't been given a chance to sleep and Taylor wasn't sure whether this was an oversight or on purpose.

"Mr. Cook, I am your lawyer," replied the middle-aged man sitting across from them in the bunker-like conference room.

"Oh," her dad said. Taylor could tell he was overwhelmed by everything that had happened. He was a trusting man, smart, but slow and considerate with his words. He was completely out of his element here. And Taylor—well, to her, the entire experience was like a waking nightmare. She thought about all the things left undone: her work around the farm, her essay on *Othello.* She hadn't even gotten to say good-bye to her friends.

"What if I refuse to sign this crap?" she asked their supposed lawyer. "Do I get to go home?"

The lawyer took off his glasses and cleaned them, an excuse not to look Taylor in the eyes. "By law, if you don't sign the agreements in full, your condition will necessitate a period of quarantine."

"Quarantine?" exclaimed her father. "But didn't you hear? She heals people!"

"Yes, but that may not be all she can do," the lawyer replied archly. "There's still so much we don't know about Taylor's condition. The health of the general public has to be taken into consideration."

"How long would I have to be in quarantine?" Taylor pressed on stubbornly.

"Indefinitely," the lawyer replied. "You would be the first, so the process would require some . . . figuring out. At the Academy, on the other hand, you will have a world-class education and receive the proper training for your Legacies. You won't be allowed off campus until you've turned eighteen, but your father will be allowed to visit once a month."

Taylor thought about using her telekinesis to slowly tighten the lawyer's tie. She could probably fight her way out of there. But what would be waiting for her? Years as a fugitive? Her father's life ruined? More Harvesters?

"Your family's farm will also be protected," the lawyer continued, as if reading her mind. "So another incident like last night's can be avoided."

With tears in her eyes, Taylor signed the paperwork. She was now property of the United Nations. An enrollee at the Human Garde Academy.

She was still massaging the pen indentation out of her signing hand when they whisked her off to a secluded military airfield on the outskirts of Denver. There was a private jet waiting for her. Taylor pressed her face into her father's shirt. She'd been fighting back tears during the entire process and now could feel them spilling over. He hugged her, whispering into her ear.

"Come on, now. Don't let these people see you cry. You gotta be strong, Tay."

"I don't want to go," she said, her words muffled into his chest. "I don't want to leave you all by yourself."

"Aw, I'll be just fine," he replied, although she detected a tremor in his voice. "Imagine all the good you can do, running around with that John Smith fella and his crew. You're gonna make me so proud."

And then it was time. They led her across the tarmac, up a set of roll-away steps. Taylor gazed back at her father, waved and then she was sealed inside. Minutes later, buckled into a plush leather chair, Taylor was off the ground, on her way to California in a private jet. Less than twenty-four hours had passed since Teddy had come by their farm to warn them about the Harvesters. To Taylor, it felt like days. She was exhausted, but too anxious to sleep.

There was one other person in the passenger section with her. He was black, built like a linebacker, handsome, with wide eyes that made him seem perpetually curious. She didn't feel so bad staring at him because he was staring at her, a big, doofy grin on his face.

"Hello," the boy said at last. His English was slightly accented, almost British.

"Hi," Taylor replied uncertainly, nearly too tired for socializing.

"I'm Kopano," the boy continued. "What's your name?"

"Taylor."

He switched to the seat right next to her and enthusiastically shook her hand.

"They told me we were making a detour to South Dakota to pick up another passenger—what a relief! I've been alone on here for half a day. Very boring." He held up his hands like he was taking her picture. "My first American friend. Just like the pretty girl they put on cereal boxes. Very classic."

Taylor felt herself blush, not really sure why. She couldn't think of any cereal boxes with girls her age. "And you're from . . . ?" she asked, changing the subject. "England?"

"Nigeria," the boy said proudly. "So, you are Garde, too, eh? I have never met anyone like myself."

"Me neither." Taylor paused. "Actually, I take that back. I met John Smith last night, but I guess that's a little different."

"John Smith!" Kopano shouted. "My hero! How tall was

he? Taller than me? You must tell me everything, Taylor. Right away."

So she told him, starting from the day she first discovered her Legacies. With Kopano's huge smile and enthusiastic nods, it was easy for Taylor to tell her story. It came pouring out of her. Taylor was amazed she managed to get through it without crying.

"I saw John Smith the one time, during the telepathic vision. His speech was amaz—"

"I'm sorry," Taylor interrupted. "The what?"

"During the invasion, when we were all called to action," Kopano said. Seeing Taylor's blank look, he slapped his knee. "Oh! You became Garde after the war. So, more of us are still being made, eh? Very interesting. Very cool. Let me tell you what happened!"

Kopano told her about what he'd seen during the invasion, how eager he'd been to help fight, but how his Legacies were slow to develop. He told her how he'd been roped into work- ing a shady job with his father until finally escaping for the Academy. Taylor thought she'd gotten her emotions in check, but when Kopano told her about the way his mother looked at him like he was something from another dimension, Tay- lor got choked up. She tried to hold it in, but a big guffawing sob escaped her and then she started crying again.

"What did I say? What did I say?" Kopano asked in a panic.

"Not you . . . ," Taylor said, wiping her face. "It's just all so much. We shouldn't have to go through this. I hate what's happened to us. I liked the life I had! I don't want to leave it all behind to go to this stupid Academy where I don't know anyone . . ."

"You will know me," Kopano declared. "We will be partners in carving out our great destiny as the stars have foretold it!"

"What stars?" She stared at him. "I don't want a great destiny."

Kopano smiled crookedly and Taylor realized he was kidding about the stars and destiny. Well, if not kidding, then not completely serious. Kopano locked eyes with her and made his face grave.

"A great destiny for me, then, and an ordinary and boring destiny for you. Together, I believe we can achieve this."

Taylor laughed in spite of herself. "You're nuts."

Kopano extended his hand. "Let us make this alliance official. Once we reach California, we will watch out for each other. You will make sure that I stay on the path to historic greatness, and I will make sure that your life is as unexciting as possible."

Taylor smirked. "So, what? If I find like a cat stuck in a tree or something, you want me to come find you right away?"

"Yes! Exactly! Damsels in distress, in particular." Kopano stroked his chin. "I would like them to become my specialty."

Taylor rolled her eyes.

"And in return," Kopano continued, "I will make sure you are assigned extra homework by our new teachers. I will remain constantly vigilant of the spectacular happening and make sure you are far, far away when it does."

"Okay, Kopano," Taylor said with another laugh. She shook his hand. "You've got a deal."

"Excellent!" he replied. "This, I believe, is the beginning of a great friendship!"

By the time they reached California, Taylor had fallen asleep with her head on the large boy's shoulder.

CHAPTER TWELVE

ISABELA SILVA
THE HUMAN GARDE ACADEMY—POINT REYES, CALIFORNIA

ONE OF THE BOYS ON THE SOCCER FIELD WHISTLED loudly when he spotted Isabela walking along the sideline. She paused and half turned, aimed a scornful glare in the whistle's general direction and shouted in Portuguese, "You will whistle much higher once I've cut off your balls!"

Simon walked beside Isabela, his short legs struggling to keep up with her long, purposeful strides. He was French, hairy for a fourteen-year-old, with a tousled mane of dark brown curls atop his overlarge head. Simon was in the process of learning Portuguese—it would be his fifth language after French, English, Spanish and Italian—which meant he'd been shadowing Isabela almost constantly these last few weeks. She tolerated Simon. Unlike most of the other males attending the Academy, he wasn't constantly trying to hit on her. Simon wasn't in her league and he knew that; Isabela admired his self-awareness.

"My obscenities aren't great yet," Simon said breathlessly. "What are 'colhões'?"

"Balls," Isabela replied in English.

"Ha," Simon said, then adjusted his belt. "And ouch."

"You should probably keep that stuff to a minimum when we meet the new recruits," Caleb said stiffly. He had been following a few steps behind Isabela and Simon. "We want to set a good example."

Isabela and Simon exchanged a look, then stifled laughter. Caleb noticed this, but said nothing. He was aware of his reputation—behind his back, the other students had nicknamed him "Hall Monitor."

"I heard one of these new kids is from Africa," Simon said excitedly. He rolled a crystal-blue pebble across his knuckles, the stone freshly charged with his Legacy. "I hope he doesn't speak English."

"Why must we all speak English, anyway?" Isabela complained. She tugged at the beaded bracelet that fit snugly around her wrist. One of the beads—the aquamarine one that emitted a slight glow when the sun hit it just right—was charged with Simon's Legacy. As long as she kept in contact with the bracelet—and the bead maintained its charge—she could speak and understand English. At least, Isabela consoled herself, the bracelet Simon had made for her wasn't a total fashion disaster.

"Because this is America," Caleb replied.

Isabela groaned in response.

The trio had drawn orientation duty for that day's two new arrivals. Simon was always one of the greeters—his Legacy made him particularly useful in that regard. Isabela and Caleb were chosen to give the tour because they both had empty rooms in their three-person suites.

"I don't understand why we even need roommates," Isabela huffed. "This campus is huge. There are entire floors in the dorms that we aren't even using! We could all have our own suites with two walk-in closets."

"I don't need that many closets," Simon replied with a shrug.

"No one needs that many closets, but wouldn't it be nice to have them?" Isabela asked. "Wouldn't it be nice to not share a bathroom?"

"Dr. Linda says it's good for us to socialize," Simon replied. "Chores are also healthy, apparently."

"Ugh, don't talk to me about that old cow," Isabela replied.

"I like Dr. Linda," Caleb said.

"You would," Isabela replied sharply.

Dr. Linda, the Academy's resident expert on mental health, was in charge of their room assignments. Isabela had asked her over and over again for reassignment, not because she disliked her roommate—Ran was about as quiet and respectful as one could hope for around here—but because Isabela valued her privacy more than most. The therapist always responded with the same psychobabble about support systems and bonding. Isabela didn't see how sharing a bathroom with two other girls would turn her into a better person, but whatever.

"This new girl better be as clean as Ran," Isabela said with an edge in her voice. "And quiet, too. We have a good arrangement, me and her. She keeps clean and meditates all the time, and I do whatever I want."

"Yeah. Sounds great," Caleb replied dryly.

A helicopter swooped overhead, circling around for a landing. Isabela sighed again. Now her hair was all out of place.

"We're late," Caleb said, walking faster.

"I'm sure Dr. Goode is already there," Simon replied. "He's got that thing about greeting all the new kids."

Dr. Malcolm Goode was one of their science instructors. When he wasn't teaching them chemistry and physics, Dr. Goode headed up the Academy's research staff. He studied their Legacies, helping the students better understand what they could do. He had a son of his own with Legacies, although he didn't attend the Academy. Isabela wondered how he'd gotten so lucky to avoid the monotony.

With Caleb now in the lead, the trio made their way down the path that led out to the helipad. The day was sunny and breezy, like it always seemed to be on these coastal cliffs. Sometimes, Isabela missed the sticky heat of Rio de Janeiro, parading around the Zona Sul in her bikini and sarong, looking for trouble. The wind here chilled her, made goose pimples on her light brown skin and forced her to wear more clothes than she would've liked. She shoved a curly tangle of dark hair out of her face.

The helipad was constructed in an open field to the east of the Academy. From here, Isabela could see the woodlands that created a buffer between the campus and the fence erected to protect them. When she was particularly bored, she liked to visit with the UN Peacekeepers who patrolled the perimeter. The soldiers were always sweet and stammer-prone—she was beautiful and possessed superpowers, a combination that drove ordinary men to speechlessness. The power to make even grown men nervous was intoxicating.

It was during one of those visits, casually flirting with a group of idle guards, that Isabela realized how easy it was for a person with her Legacy to escape from campus. She'd dipped down to San Francisco a half-dozen times since then, sometimes alone and sometimes in the company of Lofton, the handsome Canadian currently wrapped tightly around her little finger. His eighteenth birthday was quickly approaching and he'd recently been notified that the administration thought he was ready to graduate. They would have to make at least one more excursion to the city before he left the Academy to join Earth Garde.

Then, she'd need to find a replacement.

Ignoring Simon and Caleb, Isabela daydreamed about the little bar she and Lofton had found in Haight-Ashbury, the one that didn't bother checking IDs. She closed her eyes, let the sun heat her cheeks and imagined the boozy tang of margarita on her tongue.

The newbies waited for them next to the UN chopper, its propeller still making a slow rotation. Just as Simon predicted, Dr. Goode had arrived ahead of them.

"Kopano and Taylor," Dr. Goode introduced the new kids. "This is Simon, Isabela and Caleb. They'll show you around and get you settled in. You're in good hands."

Isabela quickly sized up the new recruits. The first was a sturdy African boy with a wide grin, the type that thought the Academy would be superhero camp. They got plenty of those. Next to him was a frightened-looking all-American girl. Isabela thought Taylor might almost be pretty if not for the huge bags under her eyes.

Caleb made sure to properly shake hands with the two new arrivals. Isabela didn't miss that he held Taylor's hand a little longer than necessary. The new girl smiled shyly. Caleb let go only when Isabela loudly cleared her throat. She gave Caleb a look of acidic amusement. These American boys. Always so obvious.

"So, you guys both speak English, huh?" Simon asked, sounding disappointed. He stuck the smooth pebble he'd been playing with back in his pocket.

"Simon's Legacy is quite unique," Dr. Goode explained to the blank-faced Kopano and Taylor. "He can charge objects with knowledge. Whoever touches an object thus charged can then access that information as if it were stored in their own neurons."

"Amazing!" Kopano stared down at Simon with reverence.

"It's especially useful considering Simon is a hyper-polyglot."

"Hyper-what?" Taylor asked.

"I learn languages easily," Simon explained. "Even before the Legacy."

"Isabela is using one of Simon's creations now," continued Dr. Goode. "She isn't a native English speaker, but the bracelet allows her to understand us as well as communicate seamlessly."

Isabela held out her arm so they could get a closer look at her bracelet.

"Pretty," Taylor said.

"Not so much when you need to wear it every day," Isabela said, adding dryly, "but it's worth it to understand all the interesting things you're saying."

"It lasts forever?" Kopano asked.

Simon shook his head. He was puffed up from all the attention. "I have to recharge them every week or so. Most people have me charge like a watch or a necklace."

"Sometimes he screws up and implants a memory along with the knowledge," Isabela said with a sly smile. "My last charge came loaded with a traumatic vision of young Simon wetting the bed."

Simon groaned and stared down at his shoes. "I'd had a lot of water when I was charging that one up," he complained. "Anyway, I'm getting better at filtering."

"May I try one?" Kopano asked.

Simon kicked around in the grass until he found a small gray rock. "Give me a second," he said, then closed his eyes and concentrated. Slowly, the stone changed colors, taking on an otherworldly glow that slowly faded to a barely perceptible twinkle. After a minute, Simon opened his eyes and offered Kopano the stone. "It's not my best work. Usually takes a lot longer . . ."

Kopano grabbed the stone and squeezed. "Now what?"

"Tu me comprends?" Simon asked.

"Oui!" shouted Kopano. "Je parle Francais!"

While the boys messed around, Dr. Goode excused himself. This was another of Dr. Linda's policies—after the UN orientation process that involved endless encounters with smelly bureaucrats and pushy scientists, the Academy's on-site headshrinker believed it important to get new arrivals among their peers as soon as possible. If Dr. Linda had her way, they'd spend the whole day playing icebreakers and doing trust-falls with these wide-eyed newbies. Isabela didn't know about Caleb and Simon, but she had better things to do.

She turned her attention to Taylor. The girl watched with tired amusement as Kopano and Simon had a rapid-fire dialogue in basic French. She didn't seem at all aware that Caleb was still staring at her. Isabela knew by the way his mouth worked in silence and the nervous movements of his hands that Caleb was getting ready to talk. Well, at least this might be amusing, she thought.

"Where are you from?" Caleb eventually managed to ask Taylor.

The question startled her. "South Dakota."

"Oh, cool. I'm from Nebraska." Caleb appeared puzzled about what to say next. "Our states touch."

"Yep," Taylor replied, an eyebrow raised. "They sure do."

"Cool," Caleb said. "So . . ."

The conversation was too painful, even for Isabela's dark sense of humor.

"Thrilling!" she said, gliding in to grab Taylor by the elbow. "Come now. Let's leave these drooling bobos to their silly games and get you settled in. You look completely exhausted."

Taylor glanced in Kopano's direction, like she was nervous to leave him behind. After a moment's hesitation, she allowed Isabela to whisk her towards campus. "Nice to meet you!" she called over her shoulder to Caleb.

"Yeah, you too," he said. He watched Isabela lean in close to Taylor and whisper in her ear, probably telling her something malicious about him.

"Our states touch. Real smooth talk, Casanova. That was embarrassing."

Caleb's shoulders tightened. He looked in Simon and Kopano's direction. They'd both fallen silent and were staring at him.

He turned in the opposite direction and found his own face mocking him. A duplicate. One had popped out without

Caleb even realizing.

"This is why we never had a girlfriend," the duplicate said, sneering at Caleb. "Because you're such a sad los—"

Caleb absorbed the duplicate. He took a deep breath and then turned to Kopano, pretending like nothing had happened.

"Should we get on with the tour?"

CHAPTER THIRTEEN

TWO WEEKS EARLIER, AN EARTHQUAKE STRUCK THE Philippines. A 6.2 on the Richter scale. The quake resulted in rough waters off the coast, waves just short of tsunami level. Five hundred died during the tremors and more during the subsequent floods, the casualties worse in the densely packed slums of Tondo and San Andres. Thousands were injured, many more than that displaced.

The world sent aid. The Red Cross, Doctors Without Borders, UNICEF, International Relief Team and others were on the scene, tending to the injured and helping the locals rebuild.

Earth Garde was there, too. Two of the young Human Garde along with thirty of their UN Peacekeeper handlers.

It was just the opportunity the Foundation had been waiting for.

Einar sat at an outdoor café amid Manila's bustling downtown. If not for the broken window behind him, one would never know there had been an earthquake there. The buildings in the wealthier parts of the city were reinforced, history teaching the inhabitants to prepare for the worst. Einar sipped his coffee and admired the patchwork architecture—colorful and glassy modern building competing with old Spanish and French architecture.

The air was humid and sticky, not Einar's preferred climate. He tugged at the neck of his powder-blue Habitat For Humanity T-shirt. Looking down at himself—the dumb shirt, his khaki cargo shorts, his brown flip-flops—Einar had to stifle a groan. He hated the outfit, but at least it kept him anonymous. Just another good-hearted young person here to volunteer.

He glanced over at the girl sitting at the table next to his. Another foreigner. Saudi Arabian. A zebra-print hijab framed her pretty face, her long-sleeved dress a matching black-and-silver. She daintily sipped from a cup of tea.

"This heat doesn't bother you," Einar said, pushing his own coffee away from him.

"I'm used to it," Rabiya replied lightly. She cringed as a man rushing down the sidewalk bumped into her table. "It's the crowds that get me."

"Won't be long now."

Einar much preferred working with Rabiya to the brutish Blackstone mercenaries. Their first mission on behalf of the Foundation had taken them to Shanghai. China didn't participate in the Earth Garde program, preferring instead to keep control of their own Garde. However, the invasion followed by the ongoing problems with Mogadorian insurgents on the Mongolian border had kept China from properly organizing and securing their Garde. Thanks to Rabiya's Legacy, they had easily accessed the Chinese research station and acquired their target—Jiao Lin, a healer. The mission was made even simpler when they discovered Jiao actually wanted to defect, the girl welcoming the lifestyle the Foundation could offer her.

It was always better when the targets saw reason, Einar thought, his mind drifting to Bunji and what had become of the Australian boy since Einar plucked him up from the outback.

He had a feeling today's target might prove uncooperative.

"Do you think this will be enough?" Rabiya asked him. "Enough . . . healing power?"

Einar glanced around. "Be careful what you say in public," Einar admonished gently. Her cousin was sick, dying slowly, and Einar knew this weighed heavily on Rabiya's mind. He smiled at her, using his Legacy to make sure Rabiya found his words and gestures properly reassuring. "This will be enough. I know it."

It had better be, Einar thought. Attacking Earth Garde

directly, even if their tracks were properly covered, would have consequences.

Einar's earpiece crackled to life. "Target incoming," said Jarl's gravelly voice. Einar gazed up at the nearby rooftops where he knew the mercenaries were positioned. He couldn't see them; they were too well hidden.

"Ready," Einar replied into the microphone hidden in his shirt collar. Rabiya, overhearing, set down her tea and pulled her bulky purse into her lap. She nodded to Einar.

From within one of his cargo pockets—he'd had to leave his attaché case at home for this mission, unfortunately—Einar produced a padded box. Inside was a small device, the size and shape of a large thumbtack. He pricked his thumb with the sharpened end, then bumped his fingernail across the barbed shaft that made the thing extra painful to remove. He knew what that felt like. He resisted the urge to touch his own temple and suppressed a shudder—Rabiya was watching him.

"You're going to chip him," she said.

Einar nodded. "Safest way."

Rabiya shook her head disapprovingly. "I don't like those things."

Einar said nothing. He traced his thumb across the device's flat head—the microchip and power source—and found himself thinking of Bunji again. They'd had to chip the aboriginal boy when they first brought him back to the Foundation. He was out of control. That was months ago, and there were . . . unfortunate side effects.

120

"Target at your location," Jarl said in his ear.

"I see them," Einar replied through his teeth.

The Earth Garde team was impossible to miss. A cavalcade of black SUVs drove up to the hotel across the street. A crowd was already amassing out there. It was the same thing as yesterday and the day before, for as long as Einar had been here, watching and waiting.

"They love the attention," he muttered.

Melanie Jackson hopped out of one of the trucks, smiling brightly for the camera-waving onlookers. There were smudges of dirt on her cheeks from work at the rebuilding sites, but her curly blond hair looked perfect. The quintessential poster girl for Earth Garde, never one to miss a photo op. She took selfies with the crowd, even lifting some of them up with her superstrength. The Foundation's research indicated that enhanced strength was one of the more common Legacies—common, but not desirable. Not like healing.

Melanie's partner, Vincent Iabruzzi, was slower exiting the truck and less enthusiastic about interacting with the crowd. The Italian looked exhausted, drained after a long day of healing the injured in the slums. The boy was barely eighteen, round-faced and a little pudgy, with a mane of kinky black hair and a shadow of beard. The Foundation's reports indicated that he'd been given the unfortunate nickname of "Vinnie Meatballs" by the so-called professor who ran the Academy. Einar supposed he could see the reason.

With his telekinesis, Einar floated the pronged microchip into the air. It was like a silver bug weaving through the air.

No one noticed it. Not until the little device bit into Vincent's temple.

He yelped and made to swat at his face, but that yelp quickly turned into a scream. His limbs jerked as the chip sent an electromagnetic shock into his brain, the signal specifically designed to disrupt the part of a Garde's brain that fired when they used their telekinesis. The chip induced seizures, loss of muscle control and sometimes temporary blindness.

"Vincent?" Melanie shouted, pushing away from her now-frightened fans. She reached out to her fellow Earth Garde but stopped short when three tranquilizer darts zipped into her neck and shoulders. That would be Jarl and his Blackstone snipers.

"Rooftops! Rooftops!" shouted one of the Peacekeepers. They drew firearms and tried to cover the dazed Garde, pushing them back to the safety of the cars.

A gas canister rocketed down from a rooftop, shattering a windshield. A second one soon followed, exploding in the middle of the street. The crowd was screaming now—panicked and choking from the tear gas, trampling each other, creating confusion for the Peacekeepers.

Everyone at the café was running for cover except Einar and Rabiya. She opened her purse, retrieved a gas mask and pulled it on. Then, she handed one to Einar and he did the same.

"Shall we?" Einar asked.

The two of them strode into the choking orange gas

towards where they'd seen Vincent drop. Any fleeing civilians who got in their way got roughly shoved aside by bursts of telekinesis. They found Vincent prone in the road, drooling, his body twitching. Two Peacekeepers stood over him protectively, tears streaming from eyes swollen by the gas. The two soldiers still managed to get their weapons raised in Einar's direction.

With his telekinesis, Einar twisted their arms around. The soldiers pointed their guns at each other's heads and fired before they even knew what was happening.

Einar knelt down and touched the back of Vincent's neck. The boy was sobbing. "Hush now," Einar said. "You're with friends."

Rabiya extended her hand, an eerie blue glow emanating from her palm, visible even through the thick blanket of gas.

Seconds later, they were gone.

CHAPTER FOURTEEN

ISABELA SILVA • TAYLOR COOK
THE HUMAN GARDE ACADEMY—POINT REYES, CALIFORNIA

ISABELA KEPT A TIGHT HOLD ON TAYLOR'S ARM, vaguely worried the fragile-looking girl would pass out. She didn't need that. On one hand, she wanted to be done with this tour so she could find Lofton and make plans for the night. On the other hand, Isabela rather enjoyed talking and was eager to get a read on her new roommate. Would she be cool? A tattletale? A nighttime crier? Isabela needed to know.

"So," Isabela started as they walked back towards campus. "What do you do?"

Taylor's tired mind worked slowly. "Do? I don't know what you mean . . ."

Isabela scoffed. "Get used to that question, my dear! Everyone will want to know. What is your Legacy?"

"Oh. I'm a healer, I guess. What about you?"

Before Isabela could answer, a golf cart zoomed across their path. The driver was a young UN Peacekeeper. The passenger was a middle-aged man with thinning hair gone gray at the temples. He wore a severely starched and medal-bedecked uniform and he looked, to Taylor, like a solid block of ice. He briefly glanced at the two girls as his cart sped by. Even though they were simply walking around, the man's look made both of them feel like they were about to get into trouble.

"Who was that?" Taylor asked.

"The warden," sniffed Isabela, snapping off a mocking salute. "Colonel Ray Archibald. UN Peacekeepers. Head of security. He makes sure no one gets in and none of us get out."

"He seems nice," Taylor said dryly, glancing after the colonel as they approached campus.

"Look, there," Isabela commanded, pointing at two large buildings on either side of the main walkway. "Boys' dorm and girls' dorm, okay? You'll be rooming with me and Ran. We're on the third floor. It's not bad. Good light. I hope you won't be dirty."

"I'm . . . no, I'm not," Taylor replied. "I won't be."

"Perfect."

Isabela pointed out the other important landmarks—the administration building where they took their classes and where the faculty held office hours, the student center where meals were served, the gym, the military-grade training center. She gestured towards the cul-de-sac-style clump of small cabins set a distance away from the dorms, explaining that the faculty lived there. Taylor's neck started to hurt from all the head-turning, Isabela's finger speeding around the grounds.

"How do classes work?" Taylor asked.

"They are boring," Isabela replied.

"Not really what I asked, but okay."

Isabela sighed. "They'll give you some tests. Sit you down with an academic adviser. Figure out if you are smart or dumb. Which is it, by the way?"

Taylor was taken aback. "Which . . . um? Smart? I guess."

"Hmpf. Arrogant," Isabela replied. Taylor couldn't tell if she was joking. The fast-talking Brazilian had already moved on, lowering her voice. "If you make it seem like you're uneducated, they will give you easier classes. I took algebra in Rio, now I'm taking it again. Very simple."

"Oh," Taylor said, nodding slowly. "I, um, I don't think I'll lie."

"Suit yourself," Isabela replied. "There is a lot of homework. They like keeping us busy. At first, I thought, why would I do this stupid shit, huh? What can they do? Suspend me? Call my parents? We are basically prisoners. What can they do to us?"

"What can they do?" she asked.

Isabela tossed her hair. She recalled her first few weeks at the Academy, when she had pushed the buttons of every authority in place, trying to find out how much she could get away with. Her experiments had paid off.

"First, they will take away privileges," Isabela said, ticking off her fingers. "Make the recreation center off-limits, exclude you from movie night, allow you to eat only the boring food in the dining hall. The chef here is very good, surprisingly, so that one hurt a little." Isabela watched Taylor, gauging her reaction.

"Okay . . . ," Taylor replied, slightly amused by how Isabela puffed up with pride at her tales of misbehavior.

"After all that, I still wouldn't do the work they asked of me," Isabela bragged. "I was ready to live like a monk. There's a decent beach here if you hike down the cliff. I figured I could spend my time down there until all the boring shit was over and they sent me off to be in Earth Garde. But then they started to punish my roommate and my classmates. Until Isabela does her work, they said, the student center will be off-limits to everyone."

"Oh, wow," Taylor said. "So you gave in?"

Isabela dramatically pressed the back of her hand to her forehead. "They found my weakness. I could not stand being unpopular."

Taylor's shoulders slumped when Isabela finished her story. She still held out hope that her new reality would dissolve like a bad dream and she'd find herself back on her farm in South Dakota. Isabela pinched her cheek as they approached the student center. Taylor flinched.

"Don't put on such a sad face," Isabela chided. "It makes you ugly."

Taylor blinked, startled. "Um, sorry."

"I shouldn't tell you these stories. I'm a bad influence. Anyway, life here is very boring, more boring than you'd expect considering the things we can do. Homework, at least, helps pass the time." She squinted at Taylor. "You don't want to be here, do you?"

Taylor met her gaze. "Is it that obvious?"

"Maybe you were thinking about getting yourself kicked out, hmm?" Isabela asked in a knowing singsong. "Don't bother. You're Earth Garde now."

Taylor noticed a tall woman emerging from the nearby administration building. She was probably in her thirties, although it was hard to tell with her wrinkle-free mahogany skin. The woman carried a tablet computer, her fingers dancing across the screen as she walked towards the faculty housing.

Isabela followed Taylor's gaze. "That's Lexa. She's in charge of cybersecurity or something. Later, you'll have to meet with her and give her access to all your social media accounts and emails."

"What? Why?"

Isabela rolled her eyes. "For our own good, they say," she replied, then lowered her voice. "I think she is secretly Professor Nine's sexy older girlfriend."

"Who's Professor Nine?"

"Ha! You will see."

Isabela led Taylor into the student center. The two-level atrium was clean and brightly lit. At one end of the room was an open kitchen, a few hot trays out for midday snacking. Long tables filled the room, with smaller booths on the balcony level. About thirty students were present, most of them a crowd of young men watching a soccer game on a wall-mounted flat-screen TV, although there were some students trying to study quietly on the second level.

"You said you came from South Dakota, yes?" Isabela prodded the quiet newbie, trying to wring some small talk out of her. "They made me learn all the states in geography. That's one of the boring middle ones, yes?"

Taylor's mouth tightened. "Some people think so."

"Lots of cows and stuff, right?" Isabela didn't wait for Taylor's defense of South Dakota, continuing on obliviously. "Did you have cliques in your little high school?"

"No," Taylor said with a tired roll of her eyes. "We Midwest barbarians haven't learned such complex social concepts yet."

Isabela picked out an orange from a fruit bowl, then raised an eyebrow at Taylor. She held up her arm, reminding Taylor of the bracelet charged with Simon's Legacy. "Sorry, the translator doesn't do well with sarcasm. Also, if I seem rude, please understand, it's just the language barrier."

"Oh. Oh no, you're fine," Taylor replied half truthfully. "I'm just exhausted."

Isabela smiled. There was nothing wrong with Simon's Legacy-powered translator. Isabela punctured the orange with her fingernail, peeled it and offered Taylor a slice. She gestured towards the group of boys watching soccer, noting with no small amount of satisfaction that a few of them had turned to subtly check her out.

"The boys here, they are probably the same as the boys where you're from. Dirty and stupid." Isabela waved at the group watching her and Taylor, then led her new roommate back towards the door. "They all gravitate together like smelly, immature meteors. But there are some differences. The Americans tend to hang out more with the Americans. We foreigners outnumber you here and it makes you all—" She slipped into a cartoonish southern accent. "Y'all, hmm? It makes y'all uncomfortable. Am I making you uncomfortable, pard'ner?"

"We don't all talk like that," Taylor replied with a raised eyebrow.

Isabela shrugged blithely. "Sounds like it to me. Anyway, the ones designated for combat—that means they have violent powers—they also tend to cling to each other, like the star athletes might, always trying to one-up each other. They are our jocks."

"Jocks I get," Taylor said.

"The ones who are close to graduating, they will pursue you the most, always flirting, because they think it's their last chance to get some before they go off to be Peacekeepers, you know? Pigs! Well, some aren't so bad." Isabela wrinkled her nose. "I am supposed to be showing you where the library is, but this is the stuff that really matters, yes?"

Taylor was surprised to find that she was smiling. Short of slapping the girl, there was no other way to respond to

Isabela's irrepressible bluntness. Also, it was good to talk about mundane things—like boys—instead of contemplating the stranger side of her new surroundings.

"You sound like you're making a nature documentary or something," Taylor said. "Like, the lady who went to live with gorillas."

"Sometimes it feels that way!" Isabela replied with a dazzling smile. "Observation is my hobby."

Isabela led Taylor out of the student center and took her down the walkway towards the training area.

"We girls, our cliques are much different. Many get tight with their roommates, whispering secrets long into the night." She flashed Taylor a sharp look to communicate that this would be out of the question. "There are the goody-goodies who do all their work. I thought maybe you were like this at first, but now I'm starting to think there's more to you. Maybe a secret rebel."

Taylor chuckled. "No. I'm definitely a goody-goody."

"That's okay. At least you aren't the brooding type. Like Ran. We get a lot of those, too. Boys and girls. Simon calls them little Bruce Waynes, but this is a reference I do not understand."

"That's Batman. His parents died and he became a superhero."

"Yes, yes, I know. I choose not to understand these silly pop culture phrases. Everything is like . . ." She shifted into a stoner accent. "Whoa, man, this is just like that movie or that TV show or who cares."

Isabela popped another orange slice in her mouth, tossed the peel away on the lawn and began ticking off fingers again.

"Then there are the artsy types, the hippies who want to use their Legacies to fix the world, the ones like me who don't give a shit and—oh, the tweebs."

"What's that?"

"A person who's only developed their telekinesis," Isabela explained. "They stick with each other, commiserating about what losers they are, waiting for their big moment. They are like virgins, but worse." She flashed Taylor a devilish look, her tone growing conspiratorial. "We had another healer before you. Vincent from Italy. He's off with Earth Garde now. You will be very popular. The idiot boys, they're always hurting each other. And you're much prettier than Vincent."

They entered the training center. In a huge grassy area cordoned off by a safety net, a handful of Garde practiced using their telekinesis to launch bricks at straw dummies carrying plastic machine guns. Low-tech, yes, but why waste the resources on gear the young Garde were just going to destroy? Everyone knew that Professor Nine had designed much of their training material himself. All the equipment—from the mundane straw dummies to a reprogrammable obstacle course with a vicious AI—had been inspired by Nine's own training methods when he was their age.

To Taylor, it was like stepping into another world. Her eyes darted from a girl shooting a torrent of frost from her hands that was cold enough to ice over a small pool to a boy who punched through the solid ice and lifted a massive chunk over his head. She jumped when a scrawny bleached-blond punk let out a piercing screech that exploded a pane of glass. Isabela smirked when the new girl shied back, half hiding behind her.

"Chaos, no?"

"It's . . . it's very intense."

"Eventually, you'll get used to the madness."

Nearby, a crowd had gathered around two boys. They stood twenty feet apart, hands outstretched towards each other, both of them sweating profusely despite not moving at all. One of them was small, barely thirteen, with dark hair and almond eyes. The other appeared to be almost eighteen, tanned, with fried-looking dreadlocks and a lean surfer body. Taylor watched them with her eyebrows furrowed. Isabela noted her interest with a sly smile.

"Checking out my boyfriend?" she asked.

"What? No." Taylor replied quickly.

"It's okay. He'll be graduating soon. Mentally, I'm already moving on."

Taylor tilted her head and made a show of examining the smaller boy. "Really? He looks young to be graduating," she said innocently.

"Not Miki!" Isabela replied with offense before she realized Taylor was joking. "Aha. So you are funny."

"I was just wondering what they're doing," Taylor said.

Isabela made a face. "A stupid game the boys here

invented. They call it Thrust. Probably because they aren't getting any." She waved her hand in the direction of Miki, the diminutive Inuit, and her boyfriend, Lofton. "They are pushing on each other with their telekinesis." She sighed. "Lofton is good-looking, but not very smart. Everyone knows Miki is strong for his size. Telekinesis is not about muscle, it is about willpower."

As soon as Isabela finished her sentence, there was a sound like dry wood breaking and Lofton was thrown across the room, overwhelmed by Miki's telekinesis. Some of the onlookers used their own Legacies to catch Lofton and set him down gently, but he came up cradling his wrist.

"Case in point," Isabela said with a dismissive wave of her hand. "Dummy probably sprained his wrist again."

"Oh. Should I . . . ?" Taylor started forward, but Isabela grabbed her shoulder.

"No, no. Once they know you'll heal them, they'll be hounding you nonstop. Are you ready for that today?"

Taylor rubbed her face. "Um, not at all."

Isabela dismissed Lofton with a wave, then dragged Taylor out of the training center. "Let him go see the nurse and then later he can lie to me and tell me he won his silly game while I rub ice on his muscles."

"You know, you never told me . . . ," Taylor began.

"What is my Legacy?" Isabela finished her question, leading her towards the dorms.

"Yeah," Taylor replied with a quick laugh. "Guess superpowers aren't one of my go-to conversation topics."

"That will change soon." She stopped, turned to Taylor and covered the other girl's eyes with her hand. "Close your eyes."

"Okay . . ."

"Now open them."

Isabela was gone.

In her place was Taylor.

"Howdy, I'm from South Dakota," Isabela said, her voice now Taylor's. "I like cheeseburgers and fireworks."

Taylor screamed. Then, she clapped both her hands over her mouth, embarrassed by the other students now peering in their direction.

Isabela grinned with Taylor's face. She knew how convincing her shape-shifting could be. She'd gotten Taylor perfect, right down to her threadbare hooded sweatshirt and ugly old sneakers.

Taylor finally managed to collect herself. "Wow," she said at last. "Do I seriously look that tired?"

In the blink of an eye, Isabela was back to her tanned and beautiful self. She still grinned. Most people, when she stole their shapes, tried to tell her that she wasn't getting it quite right. Not Taylor. She was chill enough to make a joke about it. Isabela liked that. She decided, much to her own chagrin, that she kind of liked this new girl. That was something of a personal milestone. With the exception of Ran, who she warily tolerated, Isabela didn't like any of the other girls on campus. Despised them, in fact. This half-clever, self-deprecating American, though—well, she might make a worthy apprentice. A project.

Isabela put her arm gently around Taylor's shoulders and guided her to the dorms.

"Yes. Let's get you a nap," she said, then leaned in close to Taylor and whispered, "And when you're ready to escape this place, I will show you how."

CHAPTER FIFTEEN

RAN TAKEDA
THE HUMAN GARDE ACADEMY—POINT REYES, CALIFORNIA

MONDAY MORNING FOUND RAN TAKEDA IN DR. SUSAN Chen's weekly Adjusting to the New World course. Dr. Chen was in her midthirties, pretty, with her hair always arranged in a fastidious braid. She was Chinese by way of Canada and, like most of the Academy's faculty, academically impressive; she held dual PhDs in world literature and behavioral science. Ran enjoyed Dr. Chen's literature class but liked these weekly New World meetings even more. The discussions were always freewheeling and wide-ranging— last week, they'd spent the entire session debating what to do about the Mogadorians in the Arctic internment camps. Ran wasn't much of a participator, but she liked listening to the debates, and especially the way Dr. Chen made complicated real-world problems of life and death seem like they could be solved right there in the classroom with rational debate.

This week, Dr. Chen had written "Constructive vs. Destructive Legacy Use" on the board. In the seat next to Ran, Nigel yawned dramatically.

"Look around at your classmates," Dr. Chen began. "What do most of you have in common?"

Ran pushed her overgrown black bangs out of her eyes and did as she was told.

She looked first at Nigel. Her nakama. The literally loud-mouthed punk who Ran knew was secretly fragile. Nigel did the talking, Ran did the listening. Nigel caught her staring at him and made an ugly face. Ran subtly raised an eyebrow. In their secret language of facial expressions, Nigel would interpret that correctly as amusement.

In the next seat over from Nigel was Lisbette. From Bolivia. Capable of creating and projecting ice.

Caleb Crane. America. The duplicator.

Omar Azoulay. Morocco. Immune to fire and capable of breathing it like a dragon.

Lofton St. Croix. Canada. His skin projected razor-sharp quills at will.

Nicolas Lambert. Belgium. Enhanced strength.

Maiken Megalos. Greece. Enhanced speed.

And on and on, around the room Ran went, until she arrived back at herself.

Ran Takeda. Japan. Girl who blows things up.

"Combat," Ran said under her breath.

Nigel raised his hand, getting Dr. Chen's attention.

"Oi, I got it, Susan," he said, and Ran's mouth tightened in disapproval. She didn't like the disrespectful way he insisted on addressing their instructors, but Nigel was Nigel. "We're all a bunch of considerable badasses, aren't we? Take over the bloody world with this bunch, couldn't you?"

Some laughter from the rest of the class. Dr. Chen nodded in patient agreement with Nigel's bluster.

"Exactly, Mr. Barnaby," she said. "These seminars weren't put together at random. This group, in particular, intentionally includes those with advanced control of Legacies that Earth Garde deems combat-oriented. One day soon, when your training here is completed, you'll be placed into a division of Earth Garde Peacekeepers and potentially be deployed into dangerous situations. War zones, riots, Mogadorian insurgents. That is your future."

"Heck, if that's the case, shouldn't we have this class in the training center?" Lofton spoke up in his lazy surfer drawl.

Ran felt her ears go red. Thanks to her roommate Isabela and the Academy's inadequate soundproofing, the mere sound of Lofton's voice made her blush with discomfort.

"Yeah. After your lecture on all the horrible things we'll be facing, most of us could probably use the extra training time," Lisbette said. She cast an envious look in Ran's direction. "Some of us haven't beaten Professor Nine's obstacle course yet."

"Correction. Only one of us has done that solo," Nigel

said, looking in Ran's direction as well, his face filled with pride. She pretended not to notice either of them.

"But that is exactly why we're here," Dr. Chen said. "Just because you're expected to be soldiers doesn't mean that has to be the sum total of your lives. As I've said before, you must remember that you are not weapons. You are people. And like all people, but especially Peacekeepers, you must aspire to be above violence. Today, I want us to think about how your violent Legacies might be used in unconventional ways, towards altruistic or beneficial purposes. Have any of you considered that?"

The room went silent. Ran looked down at her hands, both of them splayed on top of her desk.

"Approach it simply," Dr. Chen pressed. "What is one way that you could use your Legacies where no one would get hurt?"

"I can lift heavy things," Nicolas said at last, uncertainty in his voice. "Like, help build houses and stuff, right?"

"Good," Dr. Chen replied. "That's a start."

"We can all do that, brother," Nigel replied. "That's what the telekinesis is for, innit?" At a look from Nicolas, Nigel held up his hands. "Don't get me wrong. Unlike me, you're strong enough to be the beams in a skyscraper. Muscles from Brussels the sequel over here. But what can you lift with your hands that the rest of us couldn't lift with our minds? Nah, mate. That Legacy o' yours is good for punching. Strictly punching—"

"Thank you, Nigel," interrupted Dr. Chen. "Do you have

any thoughts on your own Legacies?"

"Oh, I'm easy-peasy. I can help the deaf to hear. I can shout tornado warnings across small towns. I can auto-tune rap songs."

"Ice sculptures," Lisbette said suddenly.

Dr. Chen turned in her direction. "What was that?"

"Um, I've been making ice sculptures in my spare time," Lisbette elaborated. "For fun. I can do that."

"Auto-tune? Ice sculptures? Dr. Chen's not asking about useless tricks," Maiken scoffed. "There's a water shortage in some countries, Lisbette. God. Ice melts. You can create water."

"Oh yeah," Lisbette said. "That too."

Dr. Chen held up a hand. "Now, hold on. Let's not discount artistic applications. One could argue that art is an altruistic use of one's Legacies, with intangible benefits to society."

"Hell yeah," Nigel said. "I'd rather have the Sweet than some bloody water, that's for sure. Follow your inner artist, Lizzy."

Caleb raised his hand. "Organ donation."

Dr. Chen turned to him. "Could you elaborate on that, Caleb?"

"Well, I can duplicate myself," Caleb explained. "So, a surgeon could perform an operation on one of my duplicates, take the organs and give them to someone in need."

Lofton made a face. "Do those clones of yours even have organs, dude?"

Caleb blinked. "I mean, I obviously haven't dissected one, if that's what you're asking."

Nigel gave Ran a look—the same slack-jawed and cross-eyed expression he broke out whenever his roommate did something weird. She gently tipped her head in response, reminding Nigel that he was supposed to be making an effort with Caleb. Unlike Nigel, she never blamed Caleb for the episode months ago with the Chimæra. He was just following orders.

"Mate," Nigel started in a gentler tone than the one he'd used with Nicolas. "Don't your duplicates disappear when you get too far away from them?"

"Yeah," Caleb replied. "But my range is getting farther . . ."

Nigel rubbed the back of his neck. "Right. But, uh, assuming them clones even have hearts and livers and whatever, wouldn't those organs just disappear when you absorbed them back up? You'd leave some poor sot with a hole in his belly."

Caleb nodded slowly. "I hadn't considered that."

"This is gross," complained Maiken.

"We might have to spend a little more time workshopping that particular idea," Dr. Chen diplomatically told Caleb. "However, Caleb's on the right track. That's exactly the kind of outside-the-box, nontraditional thinking that I hope to inspire in you." Dr. Chen's pacing brought her over to Ran's desk. "What about you, Ran? Any thoughts?"

Ran tensed up.

"No," she said quietly.

Dr. Chen smiled. "Come on, Ran. There're no wrong answers here. There's got to be something you can add to the discussion."

Ran felt the eyes of her classmates upon her. She racked her brain for something to say. With a touch, she could render an object's molecules unstable. When she released an object thus charged, it would explode with all the concussive force of a grenade. What were the altruistic and beneficial applications of that?

That's when the flash occurred. All of a sudden, Ran's mind went hot and she was back in Tokyo. Buried under a pile of rubble, the roof of what used to be her family's small apartment on top of her, her little brother crying somewhere close. Trapped. Suffocating. She shoved against the debris with all her might. The telekinesis that Ran hadn't even discovered yet triggered and the chunks of roof went sailing off her. Some of them—the ones she'd been touching— exploded. She staggered to her feet, blood in her eyes, not sure what she'd just done.

Ran was the only Garde known to have manifested her telekinesis and primary Legacy at the same time. Such a trivial fact meant nothing to Ran now and meant even less back in Tokyo.

"Ran?"

She couldn't hear her brother crying anymore.

"Ran?" Dr. Chen asked again.

The vision passed. She was back in the classroom, everyone staring at her. Her desk vibrated beneath her fingers.

Ran glanced down, saw that she had begun to charge the polished wood desktop. With a deep breath, she pulled that energy back inside her, narrowly averting an explosion.

"No," she said again, firmly, and this time Dr. Chen accepted that answer. Her teacher moved on, but not without a lingering look of concern for Ran.

After the seminar, Ran strode purposefully across the lawn towards the girls' dorms. It had been a few weeks since she last experienced a flashback like the one that overcame her in class. Foolishly, she'd begun to hope that they were fading, the visions of Tokyo during the invasion relegated to an occasional nightmare. Not so. Ran wished she were harder. More in control.

Nigel caught up to her. He looped his hand through her arm, matching her pace.

"All right, then," he said casually. "Nice day for a speed walk across campus, innit?"

Ran didn't respond. Nigel was adept at interpreting her silences, though. She didn't mind his presence.

"How's the new roommate?" he asked, each of them having gotten new additions to their suites over the weekend. "Mine's a real sweetheart. Excitable sort. Told me they're gonna write about us in history books. I can get behind that. A welcome change of pace from ol' Caleb, who I might very well find pulling guts out of a clone when I get back to our room."

"Mine seems kind," Ran replied. "Overwhelmed. Very tired."

"Getting the tour from Isabela would wear out a marathon runner."

"Yes," Ran responded noncommittally. "She is a healer. A good Legacy."

The atmosphere around them changed. It was subtle—the noises from other passing students became muffled and fuzzy, while their own soft footfalls in the grass sounded louder thanks to a lack of background noise. Nigel was using his sonic manipulation Legacy. He put them in a bubble so that no one would be able to hear them.

"We gonna talk about what happened in class, love? Or are we just gonna dance around it?"

Ran pressed her lips together. She knew Nigel got a kick out of it when she played up her own robotic nature.

"I do not dance," she replied stiffly.

Nigel snorted, but kept giving her that concerned look. "You had one of your episodes, didn't you?"

"Yes."

"You not taking those meds Dr. Linda prescribed?"

"No."

"Why not?"

Ran stopped. She turned to look at him. "Are you taking yours?"

After learning about what happened to them during the invasion, Dr. Linda had prescribed both Ran and Nigel the same antianxiety medication. Ran remembered how Nigel had clicked their two identical pill bottles together like they were cheers-ing. Now, he flashed her a sly smile.

"Nah. You know they made me tired. I gotta stay functional."

"As do I," Ran said.

"So we're both full Cuckoo's Nest," Nigel observed with a shrug. Then, his face got serious again, an expression Ran wasn't used to seeing on his pockmarked cheeks. "Look, you know I tell you all my shit . . ."

"Yes," Ran said.

"But if I'm ever talking too much, if you need to get something off your chest, you know I'm your man, right?"

Ran smiled. A rare thing. She put both her hands on Nigel's bony shoulders, carefully avoiding the spiky studs sewn onto his denim vest.

"You are my man," she said. "Do not worry about me."

Nigel laughed brusquely and looked away. "All right. We had our moment, didn't we? Let's go back to silently repressing our feelings, yeah?"

Ran let her hands drop away and they resumed their walk across campus. Nigel's words were stuck in her head, a couple of random phrases that hinted at some bigger inspiration.

Gotta stay functional.

Repressing our feelings.

Ran stopped walking.

"I have to go back and see Dr. Chen," she said suddenly.

"Huh? About what?"

But Ran was already jogging back towards the administration building. "I will see you at dinner!" she called over her shoulder.

Ran found Dr. Chen still in the seminar room, tidying up for the next class. The jog back hadn't come close to winding her and Ran had a habit of entering rooms quietly. When she finally spoke, her soft voice made Dr. Chen jump.

"I have an answer."

"Oh, wow—Ran. You scared me."

"I am sorry about class before," Ran said, believing Dr. Chen was referring to the near explosion at her desk.

"It's okay," Dr. Chen replied kindly. "So, you gave my question a little more thought?"

"Yes," Ran said, a tinge of excitement in her voice. "The best way for me to benefit society using my Legacy—the only way, I believe—is for me to stop using it entirely."

"Well, Ran, that's not exactly the point of the exercise—"

"Please inform the other administrators," Ran concluded. Her message delivered, she was already halfway out the door. "I will no longer blow anything up."

CHAPTER SIXTEEN

TAYLOR COOK
THE HUMAN GARDE ACADEMY—POINT REYES, CALIFORNIA

TAYLOR'S FIRST FEW WEEKS AT THE ACADEMY WERE so busy that she almost forgot to be homesick.

After a meeting with Dr. Chen to assess where she stood academically, Taylor was given a full schedule of classes. She started every day with the brutal back-to-back of organic chemistry and trigonometry, two classes where she immediately felt overwhelmed. The teachers at the academy were different from the ones back home—faster talkers, sharp and enthusiastic, demanding.

Once her brain was appropriately mushed, Taylor finished her school day with European history and then classic literature. Taylor got into the habit of sitting in the back during history, keeping her head down where it was safe. Sometimes, there were objects literally flying around the room. With such a diverse population, class discussions often boiled over into intense debates. On her second day, Taylor witnessed a girl freeze her neighbor's hands to his desk during a shouting match about socialism.

Literature class Taylor actually enjoyed. She'd always liked that class best, but back home her classmates weren't such enthusiastic participators. At the Academy, most of the other kids always had something to say, although their book discussions were thankfully much mellower than their history ones.

"I remember Mrs. Reynolds used to have to call on people to get them to talk about *The Scarlet Letter*," Taylor told her father over the phone, reminiscing about her ninth-grade English teacher. "It was like pulling teeth. I used to feel embarrassed raising my hand so much."

"Shoot," her dad replied, his smile audible. "I used to keep my head down, pretend to be asleep until the teacher moved on. Although, in those days, they'd smack you with a ruler . . ."

"It's so different here," Taylor said. She lowered her voice, even though the corner of the student union with the shared phones was completely empty. "These kids all have so much to say. They have so many opinions. This one guy got into an argument with our teacher because he doesn't think Shakespeare actually existed. Nobody would ever come up with a crazy theory like that back in Turner, much less go at it with a teacher over it."

"So, wait," her dad said. "Shakespeare is real or no?"

"It's like they're all so sure of themselves," Taylor contin-ued. "Like because they got Legacies, everything about them is suddenly marked for greatness."

"Well, you superpowered types are the chosen ones," her dad said. Taylor laughed. "Don't know why you're laughing, kiddo. You're one of 'em."

Taylor still couldn't believe that.

"You do know they record all those phone calls, yes?" Isabela scornfully said one night when Taylor returned from her nightly talk with her dad. "That is why we cannot have cell phones. There is no privacy. The internet, too. Think about the resources this Academy has, hmm? We should all have laptops. Two laptops! But we must go to the computer lab like third world people in the nineties. All so they can monitor us."

Throughout her rant, Isabela lounged on the couch in their common room, her legs draped across Lofton. During her few weeks at the Academy, Taylor had learned that he was something of a fixture around their suite. She'd begun to think of him as handsome furniture.

"Wait," Lofton said. "They keep track of our internet use?"

Isabela raised an eyebrow. "Why do you sound so con-cerned, hmm? What have you been looking at?"

"Nothing," he said quickly.

"Pervert," Isabela replied with a dismissive wave of her hand. "Do not touch me."

"Anyway," Taylor said, steering the conversation away from Lofton's browsing habits. "I'm just talking to my dad. I don't care if they listen in, if that's even true."

"Of course it is true!" Isbaela said. She quickly moved on. "Your dad's coming to visit soon, yes?"

"Next month," Taylor replied with a frown. The Academy allowed visits from family only once a month and she'd arrived just after the most recent Family Day. It'd been too long since she'd seen her dad face-to-face.

"Taylor's dad is a muscular farm man and a bachelor. I am very excited to meet him," Isabela explained to Lofton.

Taylor groaned. "You're disgusting. I've got homework."

And she did have homework. Essays and work sheets and lab reports, but also less mundane assignments. Every night, she was required to use her telekinesis to levitate grains of rice—not all at once, but one at a time—and keep count of how many she could manage before letting one drop. Telekinetic precision, Taylor soon learned, was much more difficult than blunt force. By the end of her second week, she was up to thirty-seven.

"Very good!" Kopano said enthusiastically when she told him. "I can only do twenty-nine. Rice! I would much rather cook and eat it."

Another day, another six hours of classes, followed by a few more hours of rigorous physical activity in the training center. Taylor and Kopano didn't have any classes together, so they often found each other during gym time. They trained their telekinesis by tossing objects back and forth, chatting about their days in this strange new place. Neither of them was allowed to run the obstacle course yet—a daunting gauntlet of ropes and barbed wire, pits and water traps, powered by a projectile-launching AI that adapted to their abilities. They watched from the sidelines as their classmates attempted the course and came back bruised and bloodied, never able to reach the off switch at the end of the run.

There was regular exercise, too, under the watchful eye of the Academy's staff of fitness professionals, who were all as impressively credentialed as the professors. Kopano chased Taylor around the track, huffing and puffing, unable to match her pace. In turn, Taylor looked on in awe as Kopano curled mammoth barbells.

Kopano winked at her. "My muscles are yawning," he told her as he effortlessly curled another 150-pound weight. "These weights, they must be broken. Or else I am the strongest boy here. That is probably it. They think my Legacy is Fortem, like Nicolas, but that mine is presenting in a much different way."

Taylor put her hands on her hips. "I saw Nicolas lifting way more than one fifty."

"I am just warming up!" Kopano replied. He switched hands and Taylor noticed the barbell remained suspended in the air.

She glared at him, catching on. "You're using your telekinesis, you cheater!"

"I am not," Kopano cried, offended. "Come see."

Taylor came over to put one of her hands on top of the dumbbell. She tried to force it down. Instead, she ended up rising off her feet along with the weight, lifted by Kopano's telekinesis.

"A new record from the mighty Kopano!" he shouted.

"Put me down!" Taylor laughed.

Another day, they had yoga class, but with a twist. Throughout the stretches, their instructor commanded that they keep an egg telekinetically hovering over their heads. Taylor found she was good at this exercise. She moved between stretches fluidly—from down dog to a back bend and then into a sustained tree pose. Her mind cleared and her gentle hold on the egg became second nature. She dropped her egg only when Kopano violently exploded his own during a bow pose—the fourth egg he'd broken—and she could no longer keep in the laughter.

"So, they still haven't figured out exactly how your Legacy works?" Taylor asked him after class. They'd been at the Academy more than a week.

Kopano scratched dried egg flakes out of his hair. "Not yet. They know that I am hard as steel when they try to poke me with their needles, but they do not know why it is so inconsistent or if I can control it." Kopano grinned. "Professor Nine wants to shoot me."

Taylor's eyes widened in alarm. "What? Kopano, that's insane!"

"I agree. Yet I am also strangely excited about it." He looked at her. "I kind of want to know what would happen."

Taylor squeezed his hand. "Kopano. Please. Don't let anyone shoot you, okay?"

Taylor had recently gotten firsthand experience with gunshot wounds. In order to train her healing Legacy, Taylor was allowed to leave campus one day per week. Accompanied by Dr. Goode and a team of stone-faced Peacekeepers with concealed weapons, she traveled to a hospital down in San Francisco. Under the guise of a "clinical study," Taylor saw a variety of patients with different types of injuries. When some of them realized what she was, they demanded a real doctor, but mostly the people she dealt with were sweet and eager to be well.

"I have some experience with Legacies like yours," Dr. Goode told her during their first visit, perhaps anticipating her nervousness. "I once sustained an extremely grievous wound that was healed by a Loric. The process does not hurt the patient and I've suffered no ill effects since. All that is to say—you can only do good here today, Taylor."

She looked down at her hands. "I'll . . . I'll do what I can, I guess."

"I also understand that your Legacy has limits, especially as a beginner. No one is expecting you to heal everyone in this hospital. Part of what we're trying to discover with these visits is just where your limits are and how far you can go beyond them," Dr. Goode continued. "As for the process itself, I believe it helps to visualize the body knitting and to . . . ah . . . push positive energy out of your body."

Taylor couldn't help but snort at "positive energy." The phrase sounded like something out of one of the New Age books her mom used to read before she bailed. However, when she focused on her first patient—a man in his twenties who had gashed his leg falling off a pier—she could feel the aura Dr. Goode spoke about come flowing out of her.

The cuts and bruises were the easiest to heal. She could visualize what the skin was supposed to look like, channel her warm energy through her hand and into the patient and the flesh would mend beneath her fingertips.

Broken bones were more difficult. The doctors observing her showed Taylor X-rays of where the fractures were. That helped a little. Taylor visualized filling in the shadowy crack in the bone and, slowly, her Legacy took over. It began to seem like Taylor could sense the injury. Visualization or not, her Legacy knew something was amiss and gave her the power to fix it. When a girl whose arm had been shattered in a car accident wrapped Taylor in a bear hug, she couldn't keep the giddy smile off her face.

Taylor met her match with a middle-aged cancer patient. The woman was frail, her head wrapped in colorful scarves, her eyes wet with hope. Lymphoma, the doctors said. The woman was no longer undergoing treatment; everything had failed. Taylor swallowed hard and pressed her palms against the woman's abdomen.

The healing energy poured out of Taylor, but was swallowed up by the sickness that grew inside the woman. Before, when she finished healing a person, Taylor felt a satisfying sense of reconnection—the patient's body was whole again, her Legacy snapped off in response. But now, with the cancer, her Legacy just asked for more and more energy, feeding it into the woman but making very little progress.

Dr. Goode stepped in. "Taylor, perhaps that is enough for today."

Taylor had gotten lost in the work. Five minutes had passed. She was sweaty, yet the back of her neck was cold. In fact, she was chilled all over.

"It's okay, sweetie," the woman said. She brushed a damp curl of hair out of Taylor's face. "I knew it was a long shot."

"I'll keep trying," she promised. "I'll get better. We'll both get better."

Later, Taylor sat in the dining hall and pored over an anatomy textbook. Maybe if she could better understand the human body, she could improve the potency of her healing.

"Look at this one, doing extra work," Kopano observed, sitting across from her. "Where is the girl of a few weeks ago who didn't even want to be here? Although, I suppose you did want boring and well—" Kopano squinted at a chart of the nervous system. "It appears you have found it."

"Don't make fun," Taylor replied. "This is serious. I felt like—like I really did some good today."

Kopano's expression immediately straightened out. "I did not mean to joke," he said. "You are a hero already in ways I have only dreamed of. You are changing lives. Isn't it amazing?"

"It's . . ." Taylor felt her face get hot. She couldn't help but agree. "It kind of was. Yes."

"Aha! At last, you admit it!" Kopano replied, his irrepressible grin breaking loose.

Taylor shook her head. "I just . . . I have to get better. It's hard to explain, but . . . I could feel the power inside me . . . and I could feel it start to weaken gradually, the more I used it."

"I know that feeling," Kopano said. "Like the headaches we get when we use too much telekinesis."

"I've never gotten one of those."

"No? Well, you have never floated your little brother around for eight hours."

"This feeling was different." Taylor searched for the right words. "My Legacy—it was like a sun existing inside me. And every time that I healed someone, it got a little dimmer, a little closer to setting. So, by the end of the day, I could still feel the warmth from my Legacy but . . . but it was like night, you know? I knew the sun would come back eventually, but I couldn't bring any more light. Does that make any sense?"

Kopano stared at her. "It does. It's like poetry."

"Yeah, yeah," Taylor said with a wave of her hand. "The point is, I need to figure out how to make that sun brighter."

"I have no doubt you will succeed," Kopano said firmly.

Lying in bed that night, Taylor realized that she was actually excited about the next morning. About her strange and sometimes unruly classes, her training, her friendships with Isabela and Kopano. She felt almost guilty when she thought about her father, because she was beginning to settle in.

So, of course, that was when the nightmares started.

In the dream, Taylor found herself back on her farm. The grass was overgrown and it swayed around her legs.

Something caught her eye—rivulets of blood on the emerald-green blades.

"Dad?" she called out.

Her farm looked decrepit. The walls were singed, the shutters hung crookedly from the windows, the roof sagged. There was something on the porch. In her father's rocking chair. Was that a body? A skeleton? Was that . . . ?

Someone behind her chuckled. Taylor whipped around. She saw the Harvester preacher in his vestments, a black bandanna covering the lower half of his face. He led something on a leash—a creature, gray-skinned and reptilian, but with the hulking appendages of a large gorilla. The thing salivated, licking its long, purple tongue across rows of razor-sharp teeth. It watched her hungrily through empty black eyes.

"Abomination!" the preacher shouted.

He dropped the leash. The beast charged her. Taylor tried to run, but . . .

Taylor woke with a barely stifled scream, out of breath, sweating.

Shaken, Taylor stumbled out of her room, still half asleep. In the common room, she padded over to their mini-fridge and grabbed a bottle of water. Her hands were shaking. She wanted to call her dad, but the student union would be closed at this time of night.

Instead, she knocked gently on Isabela's door. She remembered Isabela's policy on slumber party secret-sharing—we are not children!—but that wasn't what Taylor had in mind.

She needed the blustery Brazilian to tell her she was being stupid, to tell her to go back to her own bed. She needed to not be alone, just for a few minutes.

When Isabela didn't answer, Taylor gently nudged open her door. "Isabela? Are you awake?" she whispered.

Taylor managed to get the door open only about a foot before it knocked into something. A nightstand, pushed close to the door for some reason. And, when Taylor jostled it, a metal bell sitting atop it jingled sharply. It was as if Isabela had booby-trapped her room.

"Izz? What the hell?" Taylor whispered to herself, a moment before a dark shape lunged out of Isabela's bed.

For a moment, Taylor thought she was back in her nightmare. In the moonlight, through the narrowly cracked door, Taylor couldn't be sure exactly what she saw. The shape looked like Isabela—her slender body, her wild raven hair—but the face was twisted and wrong, scarred, like a horrible Halloween mask.

The apparition screamed at Taylor in a language she didn't understand. Was that Portuguese? With a violent telekinetic thrust, the door slammed in Taylor's face.

Taylor took a stunned step backwards.

"Is everything all right?"

Ran stood in the doorway to her room, hair tousled. In the weeks they'd been living together, Taylor hadn't interacted very much with Ran. The Japanese girl was polite and pleasant, but generally kept to herself and had little to say. Isabela told Taylor not to take it personally; Ran was like that with everyone. Well, everyone except for that rangy British boy Nigel.

Taylor glanced back at Isabela's closed door, uncertain what she just saw or how much to tell Ran. Eventually, she nodded, rubbing her eyes.

"Yeah, everything's fine. I just . . . had a bad dream. Sorry to wake you."

"I was already awake," Ran said.

"Okay. Well, good night."

Ran said nothing, but remained in her doorway. Feeling like she'd experienced enough weirdness for one night, Taylor trudged back to her room with her head down.

When Taylor was nearly at her door, Ran spoke quietly. "I also have nightmares."

Taylor turned back. "Really? You?"

Ran nodded. "Ever since the invasion. Why does that surprise you?"

"I don't know. You just seem so . . ." Taylor shrugged. "Tough, I guess."

Ran studied Taylor for a moment. Then, she stepped aside, gesturing into her room. "Would you like to talk about what you dreamed?"

"I . . ." The offer took Taylor aback, but after a moment's consideration she nodded. "Okay. Sure."

That night, huddled next to Ran on her bed, Taylor told her roommate about her farm, the Harvesters and the hideous creature that mauled her. Ran stayed quiet throughout the telling. At the end, Ran was still, her eyes closed. Taylor assumed she had fallen asleep. She yawned, her own eyes getting heavy.

"These dreams, they are creations of darkness," Ran whispered, without opening her eyes. "When we talk about them, we drag them into the light. We realize that they cannot hurt us anymore."

Taylor hoped that was true.

CHAPTER SEVENTEEN

RAN TAKEDA
THE HUMAN GARDE ACADEMY—POINT REYES, CALIFORNIA

THERE WERE NIGHTS WHEN THE ADVICE SHE'D given to Taylor rang hollow to Ran herself. Nights when no amount of meditation could quiet the echoes from her past— her brother's cries, the collapsing walls of her family's home, the explosions. Nights when, lying in bed, Ran felt pursued, like the Mogadorians who had nearly killed her at Patience Creek were still out there, chasing her.

On those nights, she ran.

Only a few nights after she'd consoled Taylor, Ran found herself jittery and anxious. She untangled herself from sweaty sheets and pulled on her workout clothes, slipping quietly out of her suite. The students had a midnight curfew, but it wasn't clear exactly when in the morning that was lifted. Anyway, it didn't matter to Ran. No one ever bothered her about her four a.m. runs. She wasn't sure anyone even noticed.

Ran first jogged around the dorms, picking up speed as she hit the path that led out to the woods. When she reached the tree line, she was in a full-on run. She turned—it was still too dark to go crashing through the woods—so she sped along the edge, her footfalls answering the steady buzz of crickets. In her uneasy state, she imagined the crooked shadows of tree branches as claws, reaching for her. She sprinted until her legs ached and her lungs burned, and then she pushed herself to go faster. If she went hard enough, maybe she could outrun the darkness at her back.

Eventually, her sweaty tank top cold against her spine, Ran doubled back for campus. The lights were on at the training center. That was unusual. Professor Nine sometimes held sessions before class, but not this early. Curious, Ran jogged in that direction.

As Ran drew close, she heard the clamor of the obstacle course in motion. Someone was making a run, which wasn't allowed without faculty and medical supervision.

That rule, obviously, didn't apply to Professor Nine.

Ran peeked into the gymnasium just as Nine stopped a burst of rubber shrapnel with his telekinesis and redirected the fragments so they would knock off course a sandbag swinging for his head. Nine wore only a pair of gym shorts and sneakers, so Ran could see where his prosthetic arm met the stump of his shoulder, the skin there red and upraised, run through with blackish scars.

As Ran watched, Nine leaped onto a balance beam and sprinted across it, dodging under a series of electrified wires. A piston-powered brick battering ram waited for Nine at the end of the beam. He put his shoulder into it, leaving cracks in the stone as he spun clear.

One of the course's wall-mounted cannons took aim at Nine, tracking his movement and firing bursts of rubber slugs faster than his telekinesis could work. Nine evaded them by running up the nearest wall, his antigravity Legacy kicking in. The computer adjusted and pieces of the wall began to leak grease under Nine's feet, making vertical progress difficult. He slowed down and the cannon fire began to catch up to him, so Nine leaped across the gym, towards the opposite wall, reaching out—

His fingers grazed the wall's surface, failed to stick and he fell. He landed in an awkward heap on the course's floor and was quickly peppered by rubber bullets. Ran grimaced.

Nine had tried to use his antigravity Legacy to go from wall to wall, but in the moment had forgotten about his prosthetic limb. His power didn't work through the metallic fingers.

Ran slipped away as Nine pounded the floor in frustration, not wanting to further invade the Loric's privacy.

Her stomach growled and so Ran headed for the dining hall. The doors were locked—the breakfast shift wouldn't begin for another couple of hours—but that posed no problem to Ran and her telekinesis. After popping the dead bolt, she paused briefly in front of the dining hall's bulletin board, reading the sign advertising the Academy's upcoming "Wargames" event. The students would be taking on the UN Peacekeepers in some sort of battle scenario with Earth Garde present to observe. She knew Nigel was excited about that, although also disappointed that they wouldn't be working as a team.

Ran tiptoed into the kitchen, liberated an egg from the refrigerator and headed out through the service exit. Cupping the egg in her hands, she walked down the path that led to the Academy's beach. It was cold by the water, but Ran didn't mind. She plopped down in the sand and waited for sunrise. She liked how the sun would come from behind her, heating the sand first and turning the water slowly purple.

Holding her egg, Ran used her Legacy. She'd sworn off exploding things, that was true, but no one needed to know about this silly trick, which wasn't even worth mentioning in Dr. Chen's seminar. She pushed just enough kinetic energy into the egg so that she could feel the molecules vibrating, let the egg sit in that agitated state for a few seconds and then sucked the energy back into herself. That process—retrieving the energy she produced—stung her palms and made Ran flinch.

The end result was a hardboiled egg. She cracked the shell with her fingernail and began to peel it away.

"Thought you'd given up your Legacy," said a voice from behind her.

Ran half turned. It was Professor Nine. She hadn't heard him hiking down—the big Loric was surprisingly stealthy.

Ran wondered if he knew she'd been watching him earlier. He sat down next to her, drying his sweat off with a towel.

"I had to file a report with Earth Garde about you," Nine continued when she didn't immediately respond. "Those dudes were pretty disappointed. I think they had a list of things for you to explode."

Ran popped a piece of egg into her mouth. "You may tell Earth Garde that I will use my Legacy for breakfast purposes only."

Nine snorted. He looked at Ran for a long moment and she could tell he wanted to say something. She waited in silence, looking out at the waves.

"Look, my job here is to make sure you and the others learn how to control your Legacies so you can go through life without hurting anybody. I mean, anybody you don't want to hurt." Nine paused. "After you graduate from here, you want to go be Earth Garde MVP, that's cool. You want to live some boring-ass life as a very specific chef, that's cool too."

"Hmm," Ran replied noncommittally.

"Point is, you don't want to use your Legacies for Earth Garde, that's fine with me. I don't know if those UN tools will be chill about it, but we'll cross that bridge when we get there. But what I gotta know, if I'm going to graduate you from the Academy, is that should push come to shove, if your life or someone else's life depends on it—I need to know you won't hesitate to drop all this pacifist horseshit and blow up some bad guys. Because whether you like it or not, you're a Garde, and situations like that tend to happen to us."

Ran considered Nine's words.

"I will not hesitate," she said quietly.

Nine nodded once, satisfied, and stood up. He laid his towel out in the sand and began the process of detaching his prosthetic limb. Ran realized he planned to go swimming.

"By the way," he said, "how's the new roommate?"

Ran tilted her head. "Taylor? She is fine. Adjusting, I think."

"Good," Nine replied, and set his arm down in the towel. "Keep an eye on her, yeah? You wouldn't think it, but healers got it worse than badass types like us. The whole savior thing, it can mess 'em up."

There was something in Nine's tone—almost like a warning, almost like he wasn't saying exactly what he meant. Before Ran could ask him any further questions, he jogged towards the water and dove into the waves.

CHAPTER EIGHTEEN

CALEB CRANE
THE HUMAN GARDE ACADEMY—POINT REYES, CALIFORNIA

"YOU KNOW WHAT YOUR PROBLEM IS, MAN?"

Caleb Crane shook his head. No. He did not know what his problem was.

"You don't have any balls. That's what your problem is."

Caleb's brow creased. He grew up with two older brothers and a drill instructor for a father. He was used to this kind of talk. That didn't mean he appreciated it.

"You like this Taylor girl, right? But it's been weeks and you haven't said anything to her. That's pathetic, man. I'm not even saying you should flirt with her. I'm not sure you're capable of that without embarrassing yourself."

Caleb rubbed the back of his neck. He sat on the foot of his bed, the door to his room closed. This lecture—on the topic of how huge a loser he was—had already been going on for some time.

"You could be like—'Hey, how are your classes going? What kind of music do you like? What are your favorite movies?' They call that small talk, you creep. I mean, if she asks you those questions back, you'll have to lie because your taste sucks and your life is lame, but whatever. Anyway, probably better to lie, just say you like what she likes. Always agree with her. That's a good strategy. How hard is that, dude?"

"It isn't really my style," Caleb replied. "To, um, be so manipulative."

"You don't have a style! Look, I know your confidence is shot because of, like, your brothers beating the shit out of you all the time and kids at school making fun of your big ears . . ."

This was true. Caleb had been mocked mercilessly in elementary school for his ears—which he had since grown into. His classmates would flop their arms in front of their faces like an elephant's trunk and make trumpet noises with their mouths. It had stuck with him.

". . . but you're good-looking now. I mean, you're okay. Your clothes suck. We can work on that. But listen, all you need to do is be nice, chat her up a little—and then, boom, you're her friend."

"The friend zone," Caleb said. "I heard that was bad."

"What? Did you read that in some ladies' magazine? Don't say 'friend zone.' Ever. Look, stupid, here's what a guy with your limited charms has to do. You get in tight. Buddy up. And then—well, school here is stressful. She's probably emotional. Most girls are. You wait for her to let her guard down, for her to need a good cry—and whose shoulder is she going to look for?"

"Mine?"

"Bingo!"

"But . . ." Caleb's brow furrowed. "The goal is to make her cry?"

"No! The goal is to take advantage of an emotional situation. God, you're a hopeless case. Why do I even bother?"

Caleb looked up at himself. A duplicate. Him . . . but different. A fast talker, mean, with highly questionable opinions about the opposite sex.

"I think it's time for you to go," Caleb said.

The duplicate held up his hands. "Whoa, hold on—"

Caleb stood up. He could reabsorb a duplicate without wrapping his hands around the duplicate's neck, but this one had really gotten on his nerves.

"Ack—! Stop!"

And then he was gone. The room was quiet. Caleb was alone.

Outside, in the common room, Caleb found Kopano watching a martial arts movie. The Nigerian smiled and waved.

"This part is good!" Kopano said. "You guys should come watch."

Caleb glanced over his shoulder. "It's just me."

"Oh," Kopano said, paying more attention to his movie than Caleb. "I thought I heard you talking to someone in there."

"No," Caleb said. He watched a few seconds of the movie, then headed for the door. "I've got Dr. Linda. See you later."

Dr. Linda pushed her reading glasses up her nose and peered down at Caleb's file, thumbing through notes on his recent training activities. "I see here you were able to create nine duplicates this morning," she said. "A new personal best."

Caleb sat opposite Dr. Linda on her couch, back straight, hands on his thighs. "Yes," he affirmed.

"And did you have any issues with control?"

"No, ma'am," Caleb answered, then frowned. "Well, not during the training, anyway."

Dr. Linda looked up from his file. "What happened, Caleb?"

"Afterwards, in my room, I duplicated without realizing it," Caleb confessed. "One minute I was thinking about . . . I don't know. Stuff. And the next minute he was there. He was a jerk. Really mean to me."

Dr. Linda tapped her pen against her chin. "Are you angry with yourself, Caleb?"

"What? No."

"We've talked about this before, haven't we?"

"We have?"

"The duplicates are completely in your control," Dr. Linda said, standing up. "When one of them talks to you, when you talk back—this is you having a conversation with yourself."

Caleb shook his head. "The stuff this guy was saying—I wouldn't say anything like that."

Dr. Linda went to her filing cabinet. "No. You wouldn't. But your subconscious? Able to communicate without a filter? One can only imagine what kind of truths might tumble out. It seems pushing your powers can exacerbate these incidents. Tiredness, stress, strain—these conditions create adverse behavioral reactions in regular people. In someone with your Legacy, the problem is—no pun intended—multiplied."

Caleb crossed his arms. "It's not just me being tired. Or, if it is, it's because I keep them in check and then lose my grip. I swear, Dr. Linda, they have minds of their own."

"They literally do not."

Dr. Linda handed Caleb a slim file. He already knew the contents; she had shown it to him during their last session. A few weeks ago—spurred on by Caleb's continued insistence that the duplicates were their own people as well as the discussion of anatomy in one of his classes—Dr. Goode and the Academy's medical staff had given one of Caleb's clones an MRI. Not only was no brain activity detected, but the duplicate appeared to be made from a substance that only approximated human flesh. There was something not quite right in the molecules, but samples proved hard to examine because they kept being reabsorbed into Caleb. At the same time, the researchers gave Caleb his own MRI. They found that his brain responded whenever a duplicate acted or was stimulated.

Last session, the results had given Caleb pause. He'd had a week to think about them, though. He set the file down without looking at it.

"All due respect, Dr. Linda, because I sure do appreciate all you guys have tried to do to help me, but . . ." Caleb looked down at the floor. "Since we're dealing with, y'know, alien powers and stuff? Couldn't the science here be wrong? Maybe my duplicates think in a way that's beyond what your machines can register."

Dr. Linda narrowed her eyes a fraction. Caleb knew that look. He had disappointed her.

"In my opinion, and in the unanimous opinion of the doctors and scientists who work here, that is simply not the case."

Caleb nodded stiffly. That was his habit whenever an adult said something authoritative, even if he didn't necessarily agree.

"Maybe," Dr. Linda continued once it was clear Caleb wouldn't say anything else. "Maybe you could bring one of your duplicates to our next session. Do you think that might help you better express yourself?"

Caleb shook his head. "Oh no, I don't think so. With another one of them here, I don't think I'd get a word in edgewise."

Back in his room, the duplicate wasn't happy with him.

"Talking shit about us to your therapist. That's real cool, bro."

It was the same duplicate as before—the aggressive one. He'd started to think of this one as Kyle, like his brother. The duplicate paced back and forth, agitated, while Caleb again sat on the foot of his bed.

"You've always been a tattletale," the duplicate growled. He shook his head in mock bewilderment. "Look. This is getting pathetic. You should let me take over for a while. Watch how much better I make your life. You'll love it."

"I don't know. I think Dr. Linda might be right," a second duplicate said. This one stood next to Caleb's bookshelves, perusing the small collection of paperback sci-fi novels he'd amassed. The reasonable one. He didn't show up too often. Caleb was glad for his presence.

"Dr. Linda's a goddamn quack," said Aggressive-Caleb, striding over to glare at his fellow duplicate.

"On the contrary," Reasonable-Caleb countered. "She seems like she knows what she's doing. I'd say there's a fair chance that we're simply figments of Caleb's imagination made manifest. Or aspects of his personality that he's repressed. You'll recall that his childhood—our childhood—didn't have a lot of room for expression." Reasonable-Caleb turned to smile gently at his counterpart. "Perhaps it would do you good, friend, to consider your own existence with a more open mind."

Aggressive-Caleb responded by punching the other

174

duplicate in the face.

And then they were brawling. The duplicates knocked over Caleb's books and went crashing into his desk. He couldn't tell which one was which anymore. Caleb sighed and stood up.

"Okay, enough," he said, concentrating briefly so that he could reabsorb the duplicates. "It's time for dinner."

Caleb preferred to eat early, before the dining hall got too crowded. As soon as he sat down at a table in the back with his tray, he noticed Taylor across the room. Normally, she would eat with Isabela or Kopano, but tonight she was alone except for the huge textbook spread out in front of her.

Here was the opportunity Caleb had been waiting for. They were both alone and in a casual, no-pressure setting. Why shouldn't they eat dinner together? He could ask her all the questions he'd been cataloging in his head—what music did she like? What movies? What was it like growing up in South Dakota? Caleb's heart fluttered at the possibilities.

And then, he was sitting down across from her. He was actually doing it! Taylor smiled up at him—casual, relaxed, happy to see him—and he could smell her shampoo from across the table. She was like an oasis in this desert of foreign weirdos and mutant teenagers; a girl just like the ones from back home. The ones he never got up the nerve to talk with. But this was a new Caleb.

"Hey there," he said.

"Hi," she replied. "How's it going? Caleb, right?"

"That's me."

Except it wasn't.

Caleb watched as his duplicate settled in across from Taylor. He could see from the duplicate's eyes and hear through the duplicate's ears. Doing so created a disorienting echo effect, but Caleb had long ago gotten used to that.

"How you making out so far?" the duplicate asked Taylor. "Pretty big change from back home, huh?"

"Oh, that's right. You said you're from . . ."

"Nebraska."

"Right, right." Taylor closed her textbook and smiled at Caleb. "It's pretty nuts. A lot different than home, that's for sure."

"No kidding," the duplicate replied with a casual good humor that Caleb envied. "I'd never even been to Canada before this and now we're in like the world's biggest exchange student program."

Taylor chuckled. "I was really intimidated at first. I didn't want to be here at all. But I'm starting to get used to it."

A dinner tray thunked on the table in front of Caleb, startling him. Nigel took a seat with his usual cocky smile. Caleb blinked at him.

"Evening, my good man," Nigel said. "Up for a bit of roommate bonding?"

Caleb had noticed how lately Nigel seemed more social. The Brit was making a point to invite Caleb to watch movies with him and Kopano, or to eat together, or walk to class. Caleb suspected this was Dr. Linda's doing. If she'd gotten Nigel to finally forgive him for what happened on the island—what his uncle made him do—then that was a relief. But this was really bad timing.

"Um, I'd like to be alone, actually."

Taylor raised a confused eyebrow. "Ha—but you sat with me?"

Caleb squinted. The duplicate had spoken the words he intended for Nigel. Through his clone's eyes, Caleb could see Taylor now wore one of those weirded-out looks he was familiar with from back in Nebraska.

"Now isn't a good time," he told Nigel through gritted teeth.

"Sorry, I spaced out there," the duplicate said to Taylor, talking fast. "My roommate is always blasting this crazy death metal in our suite. I was just thinking about that. I've got two older brothers, so I'm used to sharing a living space but man, our dad would've never allowed us to listen to music at that volume."

"Oh. Got it," Taylor replied with a benefit-of-the-doubt smile. She shrugged. "I'm an only child and I actually don't mind the roommates, they—"

Caleb didn't hear the rest of what Taylor said. Nigel distracted him.

"Not a good time?" Nigel asked with a laugh. "Looks to me like you're sitting here by yourself having a wank. Of course it's a good time." When Caleb responded with silence, Nigel began looking around the dining hall. "Unless you're expecting somebody else . . . ?"

It took Nigel only a moment to notice Taylor and the duplicate engaged in conversation across the room. Slowly, he turned back to Caleb with an openmouthed look of bewilderment.

"The hell are you up to, Caleb? This like one'a them old TV shows where the bloke hides in the bushes feeding his mate lines?"

"Please, Nigel, just be quiet," Caleb pleaded.

"Some kinda weird hetero courtship ritual?" Nigel continued, laughing now. "You got your bloody clone over there talking you up? Is that it? He asking that bird—have you met my mate Caleb?"

Across the room, Taylor screamed, "I can see through you!"

At first, Caleb interpreted these words metaphorically—she'd spotted him and Nigel, discovered that he wasn't man enough to talk to her on his own. But no, Taylor spoke literally—his clone had gone transparent, ghostlike, as Caleb's concentration floundered. A moment later, the clone simply winked out of existence. Taylor screamed again.

"Uh-oh," Nigel said.

Everyone in the student union stared in Taylor's direction. Taylor, however, stared at Caleb, at last noticing him at his back table. Nigel worked a finger under the collar of his T-shirt and slid his chair innocently away from Caleb's table.

"What the hell was that?" Taylor shouted at Caleb.

In response, Caleb got up from his seat and fled.

✧ ✧ ✧

After dinner, as Nigel crossed the quad headed back to the dorms, the duplicate caught up with him.

"Hey! You really screwed that up for me, asshole!"

Before Nigel could turn around, the duplicate shoved him in the back. Caught off guard, Nigel stumbled a few feet and fell, landing hard on his hands and knees. He rolled over, skinny arms extended in defense, blood trickling from a scrape on his elbow.

"Oy! What the hell, Caleb?"

"I'm not Caleb, mate," the duplicate responded, unblinking eyes staring down at Nigel. The duplicate's fists clenched as he loomed over the scrawny Brit. "You like running your mouth. Maybe I should teach you—"

From out of nowhere, Caleb raced across the lawn and shoulder-blocked the duplicate to the ground. The duplicate bellowed as Caleb dove on top of him. Caleb began to pummel his mirror image, raining down punch after punch. The duplicate didn't bleed; but Caleb's fists left indentations in the thing's head like he was slamming his knuckles into clay. Nigel watched all this wide-eyed, crab-walking backwards.

Caleb's final punch thudded into the dirt. The duplicate went transparent and disappeared. Out of breath, he turned towards Nigel.

"I'm sorry about that," he said. "I . . . they've been out of control lately."

Caleb stood, then reached down to help Nigel up. Nigel

slapped away his hand and got up on his own, brushing himself off.

"You've lost the plot, mate," Nigel growled. "I been trying to let bygones be bygones but you're bloody mad, aren't you? Got it out for me."

"I don't. I don't have a problem with you. That—that wasn't me."

Nigel snorted. "Dr. Linda, she wants me to buddy up with you, thinks you need a friend. But you got friends, don't ya?" Caleb flinched as Nigel tapped on his own forehead. "Your friends are all up here, eh? Bloody nutter. They should commit you."

"I do, though," Caleb replied softly. "Need a friend, I mean."

Nigel's lips were curled in a sneer that slowly faded in the face of Caleb's abject piteousness. "Oh, for shit's sake, Caleb . . ."

"Ever since this happened, ever since I got my Legacies . . ." Caleb ran his fingers across his bloodied knuckles. His eyes were getting watery. "The stronger I get, the longer I stay here—they keep getting harder to control. I don't know who I am anymore. And those—those things. They just pop out of me. I don't mean them."

After a moment of reluctance, Nigel put a hand on Caleb's shoulder.

"Listen, I changed too, when I got my Legacies. I . . ." Nigel shook his head, trailing off. "We're all going through it, mate. We're all bloody damaged. Your damage is just showing more on account of how your powers work."

"I don't know what to do," Caleb said quietly.

"Here's what you do," Nigel replied. "The next time that asshole duplicate pops out, you come and get me, your friend Nigel, and I'll give him a spanking he won't forget."

CHAPTER NINETEEN

ISABELA SILVA

THE HUMAN GARDE ACADEMY—POINT REYES, CALIFORNIA

ISABELA PRESSED HER EAR TO THE DOOR OF HER room. She could hear them out there. Gossiping without her. That stung. Gossiping was one of her favorite pastimes.

"And then it turned out it was one of his, like, duplicates the entire time," Taylor said. "How weird is that?"

"Very strange indeed," Ran responded.

"Why would he do something like that?"

"I do not know," Ran replied after a long moment of quiet reflection.

Because he likes you! Isabela wanted to shout through the door. Instead, she huffed out a breath and continued to eavesdrop.

Hiding out in her room like some kind of dorky shut-in wasn't Isabela's style, but she'd been doing a lot of that since the incident a few nights ago. After Taylor's breach of Isabela's sanctuary—barging into her room in the middle of the night, the nerve!—Isabela had decided their friendship needed a brief cooling-down period. If Taylor thought she could just come traipsing into her room at all hours . . . no. Just no. Not okay. There needed to be boundaries.

Isabela did have to give Taylor some credit; she hadn't pressed Isabela since their midnight encounter. She kept her distance, gave Isabela space. So many of these Americans were like Dr. Linda. They always wanted to "talk things out." Isabela was glad that her roommate wasn't one of them.

Also, Isabela's eavesdropping led her to believe that Taylor hadn't said anything about the other night to Ran, even though the two of them were suddenly best buddies. That was a relief. The girl could keep a secret.

Isabela decided she would let Taylor apologize to her tonight. Just as soon as Ran went to bed.

In the meantime, Isabela checked her face in the mirror to make sure everything was where it should be. She tucked a curl of dark hair behind her ear and stuck out her chin. Was that little upraised bump a pimple? She shape-shifted just a little, smoothing her chin. She tilted her head to the side, then decided to lengthen her eyelashes as well.

These Legacies had their uses.

Stuck to the corner of Isabela's mirror was a picture of her family at the beach. The shot was taken two years ago—her beautiful mother, her potbellied father, her little sister who tried so hard to ape Isabela's disaffected pose and Isabela herself. Pretty, Isabela thought, looking at her younger self, but not as pretty as now.

She smiled at herself in the mirror. Oh, how the boys had been checking her out the other day. She had liked that.

After the incident the other night, Isabela had made an unscheduled trip to San Francisco. They weren't allowed to have locks on their bedroom doors at the Academy, but Isabela decided that policy didn't apply to her. As usual, she was able to sneak off campus by shape-shifting into one of the soldiers and simply signing a car out of the motor pool. In the city, she bought a dead bolt. And an iced coffee. They didn't get an allowance at the Academy, so she'd had to spend a little time disguised as an alluringly dirty-faced homeless woman, collecting singles from tech guys as they rushed off the BART.

Not a bad day, all in all. Helped take her mind off things.

Isabela felt much more comfortable now that there was a sturdy lock on her door. She didn't need to push her nightstand underneath the doorknob anymore.

"Maybe you should just be honest with the people in your life," Dr. Linda had suggested during their last session. "Remove all this need for secrecy."

Isabela scoffed at that. She had told Dr. Linda about the incident with Taylor, but left out the trip into the city that followed.

"If you gave me my own suite like I asked for, we wouldn't even be having this conversation," Isabela replied.

"Mm-hmm." Dr. Linda glanced down at her notes. "You know, I received another call from your parents. They say you haven't been responding to their letters. They'd very much like you to put them on the visitors list."

Isabela crossed her arms and looked at the clock. "Are we almost done here?"

Isabela shook her head. She'd spaced out staring at that picture of her family. They were good people. They loved her. And Isabela loved them. She even missed them, especially her sister.

But they did not know her now. They knew only the old Isabela. If they came, there would be too many questions.

The common room sounded quiet. That meant Ran was probably off to bed. Isabela brushed wrinkles out of her shirt, straightened her skirt and exited her room with a flourish.

Just as she'd hoped, Taylor was by herself, studying her anatomy textbook on the couch. She looked up at Isabela with a tentative smile.

"Hey, stranger."

"Hello," Isabela said with a flip of her hair.

Taylor closed her textbook. "So, I kind of feel like you've been avoiding me . . ."

"No. Obviously not," Isabela replied. She glided over to the mini-fridge and got herself a bottle of orange juice. "I am very busy. Lots of classes. You know."

"Yeah, I know how much time you spend on schoolwork," Taylor said dryly. "Anyway, um, I don't know if I overstepped or something, but I didn't mean to. I was just having a rough night and thought . . . I'm sorry if I, like, violated your privacy."

Isabela smiled brightly. "All is forgiven," she said magnanimously. "In the future, if you need me to hold your hand after a bad dream, please wait until morning. I am not myself when woken up by an American rhinoceros bursting into my room."

Taylor chuckled, shaking her head in disbelief. "You're so good at accepting apologies, Isabela."

"I know." She paused. "Oh, by the way, I listened to your conversation earlier. Allow me to illuminate the ways of the male mind for you. Caleb has a crush on you, pretty girl."

"Hmm." Taylor leaned back on the couch. "He's got a weird way of showing it."

"Yes, well, he is a weird boy, isn't he? Handsome, though, if you like them all clean-cut. You would make a good-looking couple."

"I don't know about that."

"They will put you two on the brochures for the Academy. Look at these nonthreatening Garde with their blond hair and smiles! Of course, Caleb is a secret freak, I think, but still. Everyone who goes here is strange in some way."

"No kidding," Taylor replied. "But you can stop with the matchmaking. I'm not interested in him like that."

Isabela shrugged happily. "It doesn't have to be forever! Maybe just a little fun. Loosen you up. You can be like me.

There's no harm in sampling."

Taylor laughed and covered her face with her hands. "I don't think I could ever be like you, Izzy."

Izzy. Her little sister called her that. Isabela felt a warm rush of affection and flopped down on the couch beside Taylor.

"Something to aspire to," Isabela replied. "If you don't want to discuss your love life, we can discuss mine. I have been dating Lofton for six weeks now. Getting bored. He graduates next week—good timing. Lofton goes away, no messy breakup and I find someone new."

"Uh-huh. And you have a list of candidates, I'm sure."

"I was thinking about your boyfriend's roommate, actually. The Nigerian guy."

Taylor's eyebrows shot up. "Kopano?"

"Yes. Big muscles on that one. Nice smile."

Isabela watched as Taylor ran a hand through her hair, her cheeks flushed. She bit her lip. They'd been talking so easily a moment ago, but now Taylor seemed to be struggling to find the words.

"Uh, yeah . . . ," Taylor said at last, her expression clouded. "He is nice."

Isabela smiled. So, she had learned something about her roommate tonight. The girl did have an interest in boys after all.

Isabela stood up and dusted off her hands as if she was done with the matter. "Eh. Never mind. I will choose someone else." She noted the look of relief on Taylor's face with some satisfaction. "Now, I need my beauty sleep," Isabela declared.

Taylor stopped Isabela before she could return to her room. "Hey, um . . ." The American's voice was quiet. "One more thing?"

"Yes?"

"I don't know . . . I don't know if I should say anything. But if you . . . if you ever want to talk about what I saw the other night—"

Isabela turned around slowly, one of her eyebrows arched, her lips a cold line. "What did you see, Taylor? What are you talking about?"

Taylor hesitated. Recognizing the tension in Isabela's words, she wisely backed off. "Nothing. Never mind. Good night."

Isabela nodded sharply. "Good night."

Back in her room, Isabela slid her newly installed dead bolt into place. She exhaled slowly. Taylor was sweet and kind; she wouldn't say anything about what she had seen. She'd leave it alone.

Talk about it. Pah. What was there to talk about?

As always, this late in the day, Isabela's face had begun to ache. It was like that tense sensation one gets from smiling too much. Her stamina had vastly improved in the months that she'd been at the Academy, but the constant Legacy use still drained her by nightfall. She took one last look at herself in the mirror, touched her smooth cheek and smiled wistfully.

Then, she turned off the lights.

With a sigh of relief, Isabela let her true face slide back into place.

CHAPTER TWENTY

KOPANO OKEKE
THE HUMAN GARDE ACADEMY—POINT REYES, CALIFORNIA

SIX A.M. THE FIRST RAYS OF SUN SHONE RED
through the gym's wide windows. Kopano braced himself
as he brushed by a series of thick ropes that hung from the
ceiling. Cautiously, he made his way through the training
center's deserted obstacle course. The program wasn't active
at the moment—that meant no ball bearings or electric
shocks would come shooting out at him. But still, there was
danger. An attack would come. And soon.

Because Kopano was not alone.

"YAAAA!"

The scream alerted Kopano just seconds before Professor
Nine dropped from the ceiling and landed on top of him.
His knees crunched into Kopano's shoulders and knocked
the wind out of him. In his one metallic hand, Nine held a

savage combat knife. He plunged the blade down between Kopano's shoulder blades.

The weapon crumpled against Kopano's skin. With a grunt, Nine flung the ruined weapon away. Kopano rolled beneath him and socked Nine with a punch to the sternum. The older Garde went flying backwards.

Kopano's fists were as hard as bricks. Nine sucked in a breath as Kopano scrambled to his feet.

"Did I hurt you?" Kopano asked, grinning.

"Yeah," Nine replied. From the back waistband of his pants, Nine drew a pistol. "Same question."

Blam! Blam! Blam!

Kopano flung up his hands. One of the rubber bullets he managed to deflect with his telekinesis. The other two thudded into his chest. Kopano felt that now-familiar tightness in his skin as his flesh hardened to rebuff the impact. He wouldn't even be bruised.

"Painless!" he shouted at Nine gleefully. Then, he reached out with his telekinesis and yanked Nine's gun away.

Nine retreated. Kopano gave chase. His limbs always felt heavy right after his invincibility kicked in. Carefully, he hurdled a pile of logs, part of the obstacle course. His body got lighter, loosened up, and he picked up speed. These fights with Professor Nine had become part of his routine. Three times a week, bright and early. Nine pushed him, tried to hurt him and was rarely successful.

"Remember!" Nine shouted over his shoulder. "Control your Legacy! Think about what you're doing!"

Nine reached the sideline of the obstacle course, where a dented Dumpster usually served as cover for the projectile attacks launched by the system. With strength that still awed Kopano, Nine ripped a metal sheet off the side of the Dumpster and held it before him like a shield.

Kopano cocked his fist back, knowing his knuckles would harden as soon as he struck the metal. Sure enough—*wham!* He punched a dent into Nine's makeshift defense, nearly knocking the steel straight back into his professor's face.

Nine recovered quickly. He swung the metal at Kopano's head in a backhand motion. Kopano ducked, but the move was meant only to create space. Nine leaped on top of the Dumpster, escaping again. He held his hand up towards the catwalk that overlooked the training center.

"Weapon!" Nine called.

From above, something white fell down. Nine caught the object and sighed.

"Thanks a lot," he said dryly.

Kopano squinted as he climbed up after Nine, who now held out a pillow in front of him.

"Are you going back to bed, Professor?" Kopano asked with a grin as he squared up with Nine.

"Less talking, more hitting," Nine countered. He bounced from foot to foot on the Dumpster's creaky lid, swinging the pillow in front of him.

"As you wish," Kopano replied.

He should have known it was a trap.

Kopano swung a big right hook at Nine. The professor

raised the pillow to block. Kopano felt his knuckles strike the soft surface—and then his fingers cracked. He shouted in pain and surprise.

The pillow was filled with rocks. Worse yet, Kopano's Legacy hadn't kicked in to protect him.

"Hold! That's enough!" Dr. Goode called down from the catwalk.

Kopano thought a couple of his fingers were broken. He stomped down on the Dumpster, not so much in pain as frustration. This was the third time he'd been injured in practice, always because Professor Nine managed to somehow surprise him.

"You all right?" Nine asked. He tossed his loaded pillow away with a clatter.

"I'm fine," Kopano muttered, nursing his injured hand. He looked up at Nine with watery eyes. "Why doesn't it work? What good is being invincible only some of the time?"

"Clearly, you aren't invincible," Nine replied, and hopped down from the Dumpster. Kopano followed. "Or maybe you could be. But you're letting your instincts do the work for you instead of controlling the power."

"I have listened to all the lectures," Kopano replied, ashamed of the desperation in his voice. "About visualization and meditating on the energy within me. But there is nothing to visualize, Professor. And I do not feel any energy. It simply happens, or it does not."

"You aren't trying hard enough, kid," Nine responded brusquely.

Kopano frowned and began to pluck off the plastic sensors that Dr. Goode always affixed to his body before a session. Just then, the scientist made his way down from the catwalk, thumbing through results on his tablet.

"Anything to report, Malcolm?" Nine asked.

Dr. Goode stroked his chin and looked appraisingly at Kopano. "Actually, I did pick up an interesting reading," he said, and Kopano's heartbeat quickened. "When your Legacy successfully triggered, your weight momentarily increased. It went back to normal when you gave chase to Nine. Did you feel that, Kopano?"

Kopano nodded, remembering the heaviness in his bones when he first chased Nine. "Yes. That happens sometimes."

Nine snapped his fingers. "There you go, man. That's what I want you doing from now on. Thinking like you're fat."

Kopano frowned. Dr. Goode patted him on the shoulder.

"It'll come, Kopano," he said. "Go see Taylor about that hand."

As Kopano trudged off the obstacle course, Nine called after him, "Kopano! Show me something today, man. I'm counting on you."

Kopano nodded in response, then quickly turned away to hide his grin. Nine was counting on him! He didn't want the professor to see how giddy that made him. Had to be cool and macho, like Nine.

He'd show Nine something all right.

He'd win today's Wargames event even if he had to do it by himself.

"How'd you do this?"

"I punched some rocks."

"That was dumb."

"They were hidden inside a pillow."

"Even dumber."

Kopano chuckled. Taylor held his hand, letting her warm healing energy flow into his fractured fingers. In a matter of moments, the swelling was gone and Kopano was able to flex his digits without pain. He bowed dramatically to Taylor.

"Thank you," he said.

"Yeah, yeah," she replied, shaking her head as she let his hand drop.

The two of them were part of a larger group on their way to the wooded area south of campus. Although participation in the Wargames event was entirely voluntary, all of the Academy's students were required to attend so they could at least watch. Many of the instructors were making their way to the woods as well. Students chatted excitedly, all of them discussing the possible challenge Professor Nine had designed in concert with Colonel Archibald and the Peacekeepers. The Garde got plenty of training time with each other and at the obstacle course, but today would mark the first time any of them faced outside opponents. The atmosphere reminded Kopano of when his school would face a rival in sports.

"You're actually excited about this, aren't you?" Taylor said. He hadn't realized she was watching him.

"Yes! Aren't you?"

"Not really." Taylor lowered her voice. "Even if it's just pretend, doesn't it strike you as weird that the people who are supposed to be protecting us would want to fight us?"

"Professor Nine says it's all to help us train," Kopano replied with a shrug. "Perhaps such violence goes against your natural instinct as a healer. I would understand that." Kopano punched his open palm. "But my natural instinct is to be a warrior!"

Taylor laughed and shook her head. "You got beat up by a pillow today, warrior."

They spotted Nigel and Ran in the crowd and went to stand by them.

"All right, big boy," Nigel said in greeting and squeezed Kopano's bicep. "Ready to kick some ass?"

Kopano grinned. He liked his roommate—both his roommates, actually, even if Caleb was a little strange—and always felt encouraged by Nigel's sharp and boisterous words.

"Oh, Kopano the mighty is ready," Taylor answered Nigel with a roll of her eyes. She looked to Ran. "Surprised to see you here."

Ran tilted her head. "It is required."

"She might be Legacy celibate, but that don't mean she'd miss a class," Nigel said.

Kopano shook his head. He'd heard the rumors about Ran swearing off her Legacies, just like he'd heard about what a total badass she supposedly was. He'd never gotten a chance to see her in action.

"How're you going to get better if you don't use your powers?" he asked Ran, baffled.

"Why would I need to get better at something that I do not intend to use?" Ran replied.

Kopano blinked. "But come on! Don't you think you got Legacies for a reason? Lorien picked us!"

"And perhaps that reason is past."

"But what if it's not?"

"Then I shall wait for a new reason to present itself," Ran said coolly.

Nigel flung his arms around the both of them. "Don't let her rain on your parade, mate. Ran and I, we been around a bit. She wants to take a holiday, I don't blame her."

Kopano frowned. "I should have been there. I should have answered John Smith's call."

Nigel and Ran's expressions both darkened.

"Brother, I'm not sure if that's true," Nigel said.

Before they could say anything else, a shrill whistle called them to attention. With the hundred or so students finally all gathered, Nine stood before them. Colonel Archibald joined him, red-faced from a close shave, his uniform immaculate. Nearby stood a man Kopano had never seen before—middle-aged but baby-faced, with slicked-back brown hair and a dapper suit. The newcomer held a tablet computer, jotting frequent notes with a stylus.

"Listen up!" Professor Nine shouted. He waved to the well-dressed man. "We've got a special guest for today's festivities. This is Greger Karlsson, an evaluator from Earth Garde. He's one of the dudes who will decide what kind of missions you're sent on once I decide you're ready to graduate. Make a good impression! He's Swedish and I hear he really likes it when you do that Muppet voice, right, Greger?"

Greger smiled politely at Nine and inclined his head towards the students, his gaze already appraising them. Kopano puffed out his chest.

"Now listen, I'm required by some law to tell you guys that this is a joint exercise between Earth Garde Academy enrollees and the United Nations Peacekeepers. Participation is absolutely optional. For those who do choose to participate, every precaution will be taken to ensure your safety, but safety can't be guaranteed. Ominous shit, right?" He glanced over his shoulder at Colonel Archibald. "Satisfactory, boss?"

Archibald nodded. Kopano looked around—the expressions of his classmates ranged from trepidation to excitement. He nudged Taylor.

"You might be busy today," he whispered.

She gave him a stern look. "You promised me boring, Kopano."

"Here's the situation," Professor Nine continued, pointing into the woods. "About a half mile into the trees, there's a cabin being held down by Peacekeepers. Your mission is to gain access to that cabin and rescue the hostage trapped inside. Our own Dr. Goode has volunteered to play the role of hostage, so, you know, if you don't rescue him, science class is going to be rough."

"The soldiers in the woods and guarding the cabin are all armed with nonlethal weaponry," Colonel Archibald spoke up. "My men and women would greatly appreciate that you take the same care with your powers that we're taking with our armaments."

"Yeah. Don't hurt 'em too bad," Nine said. "The point of this exercise isn't just to fight some soldiers. It's also to assess your teamwork and strategy skills. I could tell you the best way to take out these chumps, but I'm not going to do that. I could also break you into the most efficient teams possible, but I'm not going to do that either. That's all going to be on you. Anyone who's successful earns . . . hmm . . . let's say twenty hours of recreation time. That's three skip days."

As soon as Nine finished his explanation, the dozens of young Garde began chattering among themselves and breaking into teams. Kopano looked around eagerly. Most of the students with noncombat Legacies and the tweebs who hadn't yet developed their primary powers were already gathering at the edge of the woods to spectate, while the bolder Garde with more violent Legacies divided themselves up.

"Of course Professor Nine would give away such a good prize for brute strength," Isabela complained as she sauntered over to their little group. Simon followed along behind her, waving to everyone.

"There's literally no way I can participate in this," Simon

said. "Maybe next time the competition won't be so agro."

Taylor smiled. "You're welcome to come join us conscientious objectors."

"I want those recreation hours," Isabela muttered. "It isn't fair."

"Yes. And I want to show this Earth Garde man what I can do," Kopano added, looking around.

"You even figure out what that is yet?" Nigel asked.

"Well, not exactly," Kopano answered. "But I would still like to do it!"

Taylor bumped her shoulder against Ran, nodding discreetly towards Greger. "He's watching you."

Ran had already noticed how the Earth Garde representative was keeping an eye on her. She shrugged loosely. "He will be disappointed."

"Look at this group of badasses!" Lofton St. Croix said excitedly as he approached. Following behind him was Caleb, the fire-breathing Omar Azoulay, Nicolas Lambert the Belgian strongman and the speedy Maiken Megalos. "Ran and Nigel, c'mon, join Team Lofton."

Nigel snorted. "Look at this. You're just cherry-picking everybody from Dr. Chen's class."

Kopano felt a momentary flash of disappointment that he hadn't been selected for that seminar.

"Hell yeah I am," Lofton answered Nigel. "You know, I already got my call up to Earth Garde. I'm gone in like a week. If I get those twenty rec hours, I can take it easy until then."

Nigel glanced at Ran. She shook her head.

"Sorry, mate, but we're a package deal," Nigel told Lofton. "Ran sits out, so do I."

Lofton rolled his eyes. "Dude, your, like, singing powers hardly make the dream team cut anyway. What we really need is the hard-core chick who explodes things and once brought down a Mogadorian warship."

"It was only a Skimmer," Ran corrected.

"Seriously?" Kopano asked.

Ran nodded. "And I am not playing. Good luck, though."

Lofton sighed. Before he could express his disappointment, Isabela sidled up next to him.

"Don't worry, boyfriend. I'll be on your team."

Lofton laughed. He gave Isabela's butt a squeeze and kissed her on the forehead.

"Yeah, thanks for the offer, babe, but we're going for a full-frontal assault here. You're not exactly what we've got in mind."

"Great plan," Taylor said. Isabela crossed her arms and silently fumed.

"These army tools have never faced anything like us," Lofton said dismissively. "We're going to go right at them. They won't be ready."

Caleb spoke up for the first time, having spent the start of the conversation awkwardly avoiding looking at Taylor. "Actually, uh, I have some ideas we might—"

Lofton clapped Caleb on the shoulder, cutting him off. "It's cool, bro. You just make as many decoys as possible and beat some ass."

"May I join you?" Kopano asked.

Lofton raised an eyebrow and looked him over. "You're supposed to be bulletproof, right?"

"I may be invincible," Kopano said. "I also hit very hard."

"He's solid," Caleb said.

Lofton shrugged. "Well, at least we didn't come over here for nothing. You're in."

Kopano grinned. He turned to Taylor as the rest of Team Lofton made their way to the edge of the woods. "Wish me luck."

"Do not wish these sexist lunkheads luck," Isabela snapped.

"Good luck, warrior," Taylor said with a smile, ignoring her roommate. "I've got a feeling you might need it."

◇ ◇ ◇

They lined up at the edge of the woods. Kopano stood between Nicolas and one of Caleb's duplicates. With all the clones, there were a dozen of them, ready for battle. They were the first team to make a run.

"We head straight for the cabin," Lofton said. "Take out anything in our way. Nothing to it."

They all nodded in agreement. Kopano rubbed his hands together and focused. He searched for that feeling of heaviness that Dr. Goode mentioned, the sense of being weighted down. Nothing. He felt tragically normal. But Kopano was sure his Legacy would come when needed; it always did.

Professor Nine blew a whistle and they were off.

Team Lofton ran into the woods. For the first few hundred

yards, they saw no sign of soldiers. The trees became clumped closer together and they had to weave through them. Kopano felt a rush flow through him—he was on a mission, charging towards a target! This was the kind of heroic experience he'd envisioned.

Soon, the cabin came into view, only partially visible through a veil of vibrant green foliage. Kopano sensed movement in the windows, but didn't have a chance to examine that more closely.

"Hostiles!" Caleb shouted, his six clones echoing his words a moment later.

Three soldiers stepped out from behind trees. Kopano's group skidded to a stop with a good bit of distance still between them and their opponents. Each of the soldiers carried what looked like a traditional shotgun.

"Take them out!" Lofton yelled. The sharpened spines that grew from his skin on command burst through his shirt. He plucked a few of them and flung them at the soldiers.

The soldiers bolted for cover as Lofton's darts whistled by them, but not before they each fired a round into the air. Kopano extended his hands and threw up a barrier of telekinesis. His nearby classmates all did the same. It's what they were trained to do. None of them could reliably stop bullets on their own—not quite yet, at least—but together they were strong enough to slow to a crawl any projectiles coming at them.

Kopano's brow furrowed. He expected buckshot or rubber shrapnel like the kind Professor Nine had used on him that morning, but what hung in the air was much different. Each of the shotguns had discharged a metallic round about the size of a beanbag. They glowed and beeped with increasing frequency.

A countdown.

"Explosives!" Caleb shouted. At that moment, Kopano recalled how his roommate was what the Americans called an "army brat." He probably had experience with military tactics and exercises like this one.

Perhaps they should have planned better, but Lofton's bravado had been infectious and now it was too late.

The orbs burst apart with a piercing hiss. Each discharged a thick cloud of orange-tinted gas. Immediately, Kopano's throat tightened and his eyes burned. The fiery aroma of cayenne filled his lungs.

Lofton gagged. "We need to pull back!"

"No!" Caleb shouted. "We're committed! Push through! Maiken, use your speed, get a funnel going."

Caleb's duplicates didn't need to breathe. They barreled through the smoke cloud and began to pummel the soldiers. Meanwhile, Maiken, coughing raggedly, began to speed around in a circle, creating enough wind to blow the gas away from them.

That's when the rest of the soldiers struck from behind. In their haste to reach the cabin, Team Lofton had passed right by this squadron in hiding. They were surrounded.

Kopano heard a metallic twang. He turned just in time to see a soldier holding what looked to be a high-tech crossbow.

The weapon fired a metal circlet attached to a length of tensile wire. Eyes burning, Kopano couldn't get his telekinesis working fast enough. The circlet hit him right in the neck, opened on impact and snapped around his throat like a collar.

A charge went through the collar. An electric shock that drove Kopano to his knees.

With his telekinesis, Kopano tried to rip the electrified weapon away from the soldier. But just then, another Peacekeeper discharged an oddly shaped gun. The weapon looked like an old-fashioned blunderbuss and filled the air with hundreds of tiny projectiles, the harmless chaff spinning and flashing. The effect wreaked havoc on Kopano's telekinetic control.

A trio of darts—tranquilizers, probably—thudded into Kopano's chest. His Legacy kicked in, prevented the ammo from piercing his chest. A small victory.

All around him, his teammates were suffering similar attacks. Omar was down already, peppered with darts, and Lofton and Maiken had both fallen victim to collars like Kopano. Meanwhile, Nicolas had been locked into shackles around his wrists and ankles, the bonds magnetized together so that even his enhanced strength couldn't keep him from folding over. Only Caleb and his clones were left standing, and they were steadily losing ground to the soldiers.

"Oh, this is bad," Kopano grunted. He wrapped his hands around the wire that bound him to the soldier's electric crossbow, but the voltage running through his body only increased. It was too much.

As Kopano fell face-first into the dirt, he spotted Professor Nine, Greger and Colonel Archibald at the edge of the fray. Archibald smirked, Greger jotted notes in his tablet and Nine scowled.

Team Lofton never even got close to the cabin.

Show me something, Professor Nine had said.

The only thing Kopano showed the administrators was how gracefully he could be knocked unconscious.

CHAPTER TWENTY-ONE

PROFESSOR NINE
THE HUMAN GARDE ACADEMY—POINT REYES, CALIFORNIA

PROFESSOR NINE STOMPED OUT OF THE WOODS, coming back to Colonel Archibald and Greger. Archibald's smile was infuriating. Greger, busy feeding notes and ratings into his tablet, glanced up.

"Where'd you go, Nine?" he asked.

"To take a leak," Nine grumbled. He glanced down and zipped up his fly.

"Are we about ready to wrap things up?" Archibald asked.

Nine glared at the military man. The day had not gone well for his students. After the first group of Garde had failed spectacularly to make it to the cabin—many of his most talented fighters among them—four more groups employing conservative tactics were similarly dismantled by Archibald's team of Peacekeepers and their high-tech weaponry. He'd made his disappointment with the Garde obvious, although his stream of insults had dried up about twenty minutes ago, morphing instead into stewing disappointment.

"I, for one, gathered some interesting insight," Greger said.

"Don't think of this as a failure, Nine," Colonel Archibald said smugly. "Think of it as a learning experience. Now you know how you can better hone your teaching methods."

Before Nine could respond, Nigel approached the edge of the woods. Behind him, the dejected student body sat in the grass, many of them nursing minor injuries. The scrawny Brit in his spiked-denim vest and combat boots didn't cut the most impressive figure, even as he cracked his knuckles and rolled his neck.

"Can I give it a go?" he asked.

Colonel Archibald raised an eyebrow. "Just you alone, son?"

"What can I say?" Nigel replied. "I believe in myself."

Nine crossed his arms and fixed Nigel with a stern look. "You're sure you can play by the rules, Nigel?"

"Aw, of course, boss."

"Nonlethal," Nine said firmly. "Remember. These soldiers have families. They're on our side. This is just a game."

Archibald and Greger both gave Nine a strange look. Nigel raised his hand in a solemn pledge.

"Swear I'll be gentle."

"All right," Nine said. "Let's see what you've got."

Without any sense of urgency, Nigel strolled into the forest. Like they'd done with all the other attempts on the cabin, Nine and the other observers followed behind at a safe distance. Out of the corner of his eye, Nine watched Greger pulling up the Earth Garde dossier on Nigel. He skimmed the file quickly, lips pursed.

"Pardon me, Professor," Greger began. "But why did you emphasize nonlethal activity with Mr. Barnaby? I have his powers down as sonic manipulation. I don't have any notes here about deadly applications."

Nine bit his lip. "Uh, well, it's something we just discovered. The kid reached a frequency the other day that caused aneurysms in rats."

Greger's mouth opened. "You're kidding."

"Nah," Nine replied. "Some of the research staff reported headaches afterwards, too. One of them had bleeding on the brain. Luckily, we caught it in time. Didn't Malcolm send out a memo on this?"

"No," Archibald said sharply. "He did not."

"Fascinating," Greger said, already making revisions to the file in his tablet.

"Yeah, well, it's not something he's been able to reproduce. Not that it's something we've been trying to reproduce, you know? Probably just a freak thing."

As Nigel continued into the forest, he fell into the same trap as all the other teams. He passed right by the first group of soldiers—camouflaged and hidden in trees—and they dropped down behind him. They could've picked him off then and there, but Archibald's men were under orders not to engage prematurely; they wanted the Garde boxed in. Soon, they formed an ever-tightening perimeter around him. Nigel didn't seem aware. Or, maybe more accurately, he didn't care.

When the cabin came into view, the group of soldiers guarding it stepped out to complete the trap. This was as far as anyone had made it.

Nigel held up his hands in surrender.

"All right, chaps, here's my strategy," he said. "I'm going to ask you nicely to release the hostage and let me win, yeah? Nobody's tried that yet. I'm thinking maybe this is one of those tests where we're supposed to fail, eh? Or look for a diplomatic and outside-the-box solution? What do ya say?"

Some of the soldiers exchanged glances and snickered.

Archibald was unamused. He spoke into his walkie-talkie. "Take him."

A soldier slightly behind Nigel fired a tranquilizer dart. Nigel managed to whip around just in time to deflect the projectile with his telekinesis. He wasn't able to turn back quickly enough to fend off another flanking soldier, this one launching one of those wire-attached shock collars. As soon as the collar was around Nigel's neck, the soldier depressed a button on his crossbow mechanism that sent a burst of high voltage cranking through Nigel.

Nigel's whole body contorted in pain. His head flew back and he let loose an eardrum-shattering howl.

Birds in the trees rose up in a squawking panic. Greger

dropped his tablet as he attempted too late to cover his ears. Colonel Archibald's chin went to his chest like he'd been struck, all his features tightening. Many of the soldiers cringed and tried to cover up. Some of them accidentally discharged their weapons into the dirt.

Despite the splitting pain in his own head, Nine charged forward. The scream rolled out of Nigel uncontrollably, loud as a tornado siren amplified by a megaphone. He lunged towards the boy and swiftly backhanded him with his metal hand. Nigel fell to the ground, the maddening scream at last cutting off.

"That was it, wasn't it?" Nine shouted, his ears ringing. "That was the frequency!"

Nigel stared up at Nine groggily, panic slowly creeping into his expression. "I don't know! I—the bloody prick was shocking me and—and I lost control!"

Greger took a halting step backwards. "Are we—were we exposed to something?"

"I don't know," growled Nine, looking around. Many of the soldiers had thrown off their helmets and were massaging their temples or pinching the bridges of their noses. Nine noticed one soldier who had been close to Nigel clean a bit of blood out of his ear.

"Christ," Archibald said, massaging the side of his head with the heel of his hand. "What's the protocol here?"

"Run back to the others," Nine snapped at one of the soldiers. "Get Taylor Cook up here. She's a healer." He looked up to the cabin, then back to Archibald. "Bring all your men in. Anyone who was in earshot needs to be checked." He surveyed the soldiers. "Anyone feeling dizzy? Nosebleeds?"

The soldiers, uneasy now and uncertain what to do, exchanged glances. One of them raised his hand. "I'm—uh, I'm feeling a little dizzy, sir."

"Me too," added another.

"Lads, I'm sure it's nothing," Nigel said pleadingly. "I, uh, the frequency only murdered some rodents the one time and I'm not even sure it was the same—"

"Stop talking," Nine snapped. "Shit. I knew this was a bad idea, Archibald."

"Don't put this on me because your students can't control themselves!" Archibald shouted back.

"What?" Greger asked, tilting his head to the side. "What? I literally can't hear what you two are saying."

Taylor jogged onto the scene along with the soldier who had gone to fetch her. Her eyes went wide when she saw Nigel on the ground, bleeding from the mouth, still attached to a shock collar. Nine snapped his fingers in her face.

"I need you to check all these men," he said.

"Check them? For what?"

"For, like, brain damage," Nine replied. "See if they need healing. Maybe we got lucky, but . . ." He urged her towards the soldiers. "Just put some healing into them. For safety."

"What's going on?" Dr. Goode asked as he ambled down from the cabin with the bored group of Peacekeepers who had spent their entire day guarding him without actually seeing any action. He glanced from the stricken Nigel to the busy Taylor, and finally to Nine. "Did something happen?"

"You didn't hear the shriek?" Nine asked.

"Of course we heard it, but—"

"That was the death frequency," Nine said grimly. "Nigel used his death frequency."

"Accidentally!" Nigel croaked. He rubbed his throat, freshly released from the shock collar.

"His—?" Dr. Goode stared blankly at Nine. "His what?"

Before Nine could answer, Taylor gasped and stepped back from one of the soldiers. He was a young guy—midtwenties with a baby face and a patchy red beard—and his eyes widened in alarm at Taylor's reaction.

"What—what's wrong?" the soldier asked.

Everyone went silent and stared. Taylor tentatively pressed her hands to the soldier's temples. Her eyes narrowed in concentration. She shook her head suddenly and spun to face Nine.

"He's—there's something wrong. His brain is—I don't know—it's like there's a darkness? A hemorrhage maybe? It's beyond what I can handle."

The soldier visibly paled. "But . . . but I feel okay. Ears are ringing a little."

"We need to get him back to campus," Nine said resolutely. "Everybody, let's go."

As a group, soldiers and Garde hustled back through the woods. Even though he was done screaming, everyone kept their distance from Nigel except for Taylor. She walked next to him, tending to the minor bruises he'd received during the skirmish. While the redheaded soldier seemed by all appearances to be fine, that didn't stop a couple of his buddies from hooking his arms over their shoulders and half carrying him out of the woods.

Dr. Goode quickly caught up with a speed-walking Nine.

"I'm sorry, Nine, but I don't understand what's happened," Malcolm said. "What is this business about a death frequency?"

"I'd like the healer to check me, if she's free . . ." Greger said nervously, glancing over his shoulder at Taylor.

"What is there to understand, Goode?" Archibald snapped. "You were supposed to send out a memo."

"A memo? Colonel, I have no idea what you're talking about," Malcolm protested. "Some kind of high-pitched noise capable of producing bleeding on the brain? It's—I hesitate to use the word 'preposterous,' but . . ." He looked again at the silent Nine. "Nine, what's going on?"

Slowly, a smirk spread across Nine's face.

Up ahead, the dejected student body came into view. Many of them stood up from the grass, surprised to see the Garde emerging from the woods with a full complement of shaken soldiers.

None of them were more surprised than Nine, who stood among the students, in the middle of giving Kopano a pep talk.

"What the hell!" Nine said in greeting. "You couldn't wait for me to finish pissing?" Nine was about to say more, but his mouth hung open in confusion. He was staring across the grass at himself.

Archibald, Greger, Goode and all the soldiers turned to stare at the Nine who had led them out of the woods. Only Nigel and Taylor didn't look surprised. In fact, they were grinning.

In a blur of motion, Nine's prosthetic arm turned back into flesh, the fingernails coated with bright pink polish. That hand closed around the handle of a tranquilizer pistol, yanked it free from a stunned soldier's belt and jammed the barrel under Colonel Archibald's chin. All this happened while her form was still transitioning—growing shorter, muscles diminishing, dark curls sprouting out of Nine's head.

Isabela stood with a gun on Archibald. Her other hand patted Malcolm on the shoulder.

"Hostage rescued," she declared. "And we also captured the enemy leader. I believe that should be worth an extra twenty hours of recreation time, yes?"

CHAPTER TWENTY-TWO

RAN KNEW THE BRAZILIAN WAS UP TO SOMETHING the minute Lofton rejected her from his team. Ran recognized the spark in Isabela's eyes—part mischief, part vengeance.

She approved.

The plot hatched while Team Lofton was being picked apart by the Peacekeepers. Isabela would impersonate Professor Nine. With Nigel's help, she would concoct a story about the deadliness of his sonic powers. Taylor would pop up at the end and sell the entire ruse with her healing.

"We will win without even having to fight anyone," Isabela declared.

Nigel snorted. "Yeah. Except for me, right? Taking one for the bloody team."

"Stop complaining and act like a man," Isabela replied

with a dismissive wave.

"It's kind of like cheating, though, isn't it?" Taylor asked.

"No!" Isabela replied sharply. "I did not hear any rules. So how can it be cheating?"

Ran stayed silent throughout the discussion, at least until Nigel looked questioningly in her direction. Out of solidarity with her, Nigel had announced that he wouldn't be participating in the competition. He didn't know what to make of her renouncement of her Legacy—Nigel was trying to support her, but he still loved using his own powers. For all his put-on cynicism, he really wanted to be a hero. Last year, he'd been the first to volunteer to join the original Garde in the fight against the Mogadorians. Her own vow against using her Legacy aside, Ran would never deny her friend the opportunity to participate in Wargames—something he clearly itched to do.

Ran bowed her head to Nigel. "It is a good plan. You should do it."

They all grinned, especially Isabela, at her approval.

Now, all they had to do was wait for Professor Nine to separate from Archibald and Greger.

When it became clear what Isabela and her team had pulled off, a cheer went up from the dejected student body, many of whom had spent the afternoon getting beaten down by the Peacekeepers. Colonel Archibald and his people loudly questioned the validity of the results.

"What were we supposed to do?" the soldier with the

red beard, the one who Taylor had convinced he was dying, complained. "Shoot at Professor Nine? He wasn't part of the exercise!"

Greger, the Earth Garde liaison, watched Isabela with new admiration. "I must say, it was an excellent ploy. True outside-the-box thinking is not easy to teach."

Professor Nine beamed, an entire day of losses forgotten. "I taught her that."

Isabela smirked, but didn't say anything in response to Nine taking the credit.

Archibald shook his head. "That would have never worked in a true battlefield scenario."

"Indeed?" Greger cocked his head. "In the chaos of a true battlefield, I think her technique would have been even more successful. She could have slipped in and out, undetected, as one of your own soldiers, Archibald . . ."

Isabela tuned out all the praise and commentary. She'd only wanted to show up Lofton and collect the recreation hours for herself. The beach called to her, classes did not. As they walked back to campus among their cheerful peers, Isabela hugged Taylor, and stroked the spot on Nigel's face where she'd punched him as Nine.

"Did I hurt you too bad, skinny boy?"

Nigel chuckled. "Don't flatter yourself, Izzy. I had to sell that punch like a professional wrestler, yeah? You got none of Nine's strength." He stroked his neck. "Those shock collars, though. Nasty bit of business."

"Yes. I did not enjoy those either," said Kopano. The

Nigerian's usual grin hadn't yet reappeared after his defeat by the Peacekeepers.

"There she is! The champion scammer!" Lofton swooped in and pulled Isabela into a hug, literally sweeping her off her feet. Her face remained expressionless while he spun her around. When, at last, he set her on the ground, Isabela put a hand on his face and shoved. Lofton stepped back, his features drawn in confusion.

"You mad at me, babe?" he asked.

"Bloke's good at picking out those subtle details, huh?" Nigel said in a loud aside to Ran, who nodded in agreement.

Isabela lifted her chin and rolled back her shoulders, her chest out, as she fixed Lofton with a withering stare. She had fully intended to let their relationship come to a painless close with his departure in a few days, but this morning's slight was too much to let slide.

"You boys, always mistaking boredom for anger," Isabela declared, her voice loud enough that the other students on their way back to campus couldn't help but overhear. "I am tired of your dumb face and soft brain. Good-bye forever, Lofton."

Isabela turned on her heel. Lofton, stunned, grabbed her arm.

"Whoa, wait! What about—?" He lowered his voice. "What about our plans for tonight?"

"Those plans are canceled," Isabela replied. She stuck her finger in his face. "You would be wise to forget they ever existed. Furthermore, I forbid you from thinking about me in that way during your many lonely nights to come. Now, get off me."

Lofton let her go and Isabela resumed her walk to the dorms. Nigel and Kopano were both holding in laughter. Taylor came up alongside Isabela and hooked her arm through her roommate's.

"You okay?" Taylor asked.

"Why would I not be okay?"

"You just broke up with your boyfriend."

"Pfft. I have already forgotten him. My only disappointment is that we cannot . . ." Isabela trailed off. She'd been looking forward to her evening plans with Lofton. Just because he was out of the picture didn't mean those plans had to change. "Come," she said excitedly to Taylor. "We must celebrate our victory!"

◇ ◇ ◇

Back in their suite, Isabela pulled clothes out of her closet, trying to decide what she would wear for the night.

"You're crazy," Taylor said, leaning in her doorway. "I'm not sneaking out."

"No, I am not and yes, we are," Isabela replied. "Come on, Taylor! You will love San Francisco. I found a bar where they don't ID."

"I don't really drink."

"Ha. Well, whatever, we can get you some new clothes, at least. Have dinner. Sit in a restaurant like normal people. Check out some boys who lack delusions of grandeur." Isabela turned to face Taylor. "Does that not appeal to you?"

"When you said you could help me escape, I didn't think you were serious." Taylor shook her head, slightly in awe of her roommate's secret life as a jail-breaker. "How long have you been doing this?"

"I went for the first time a few weeks after I got here. Just to see if I could. And I could."

"How many times since?"

"Like, every other week?" Isabela pressed her hands together in a steeple pointed at Taylor. "Please, roommate! You must come! I am getting over a breakup. I cannot stand to sit around this dormitory and do nothing."

Taylor snorted. "Oh, now you're broken up about Lofton, huh?"

"I feel a deep emptiness yawning open beneath me and will surely sink down into it if you do not come with me to San Francisco," Isabela said with a straight face.

"I will go," Ran said.

Neither Taylor nor Isabela was aware that Ran had been listening to their whole conversation. Taylor turned with a small smile to look at Ran. Isabela's eyebrows shot up and she dropped a dress onto her bed.

"Eavesdropper!" Isabela yelled.

"I apologize," Ran replied. "But you are a very loud talker."

"You want to go?" Taylor asked, unable to keep the surprise out of her voice.

"Yes," Ran said. "I have been stuck on this campus since before it officially opened. I would like a break."

"You know we aren't going down there to do meditation,

right?" Isabela asked with a sternly arched brow. "We're going to party."

"Yes," Ran replied. "Good."

"Well, if you're both going, I can't just sit here by myself," Taylor relented. "You sure we won't get in trouble?"

"We will never be caught!" Isabela declared.

Ran turned to her. "I would like to invite Nigel."

Isabela stuck out her tongue. "Why don't we just invite the whole school?"

"Well, he was on our team today," Taylor said. "He should get to partake in the victory party."

"He enjoys drinking, like you," Ran observed to Isabela. Then, she cocked her head. "Unless it will be too difficult for you to sneak that many people out."

Isabela tossed her hair over her shoulder. "Of course not. I already know how I will do it."

"In that case," Taylor said, unable to keep the blush out of her cheeks, "could I invite someone, too?"

◇ ◇ ◇

Shirtless, Kopano stood on the common room couch and punched the air. "What was the name of this band?" he yelled to be heard over the music blasting from Nigel's iPod.

"The Dead Kennedys, mate," Nigel replied, already thumbing through his collection to choose the next song.

"I cannot understand anything they're saying!" Kopano shouted.

"I know! Isn't it great?"

"Yes! It makes me want to throw this couch out the window!"

The door to their suite banged open. Isabela entered with a flourish, dramatically covering her ears. Taylor and Ran followed behind her.

"Ugh, turn those terrible sounds off," Isabela complained.

With a smirk, Nigel released his Legacy's hold on the music. The screaming of the Dead Kennedys was reduced to a tinny buzz, emanating as it was from a pair of simple headphones. He slouched down in his chair and eyed the three girls. Meanwhile, Kopano hopped down from the couch and began to search for his shirt.

"Are we interrupting something?" Taylor asked with a smile.

"Not at all, not at all." Nigel winked at Ran. "It's a rare occasion for us to be graced by all three of the lovely ladies of room 308. To what do we owe the pleasure?"

"Oh, stop flirting when you don't mean it," Isabela said with a dismissive wave. She put her hands on her hips, surveying the boys' messy living environment. "It is truly disgusting in here."

"I was just going to clean up," Kopano said, unreasonably intimidated by the fiery shape-shifter. He began to gather up some loose clothes. Isabela slapped them out of his hands.

"Stop that!" she said. "Chores later. Tonight, we are going out."

Nigel leaned forward, bony elbows on his knees. "What's this, then?"

Isabela explained the plan to sneak away from the Academy. Her tone made it clear that the boys joining them was something of a foregone conclusion.

"My, my, my," Nigel said. He shot Ran a baffled look. "You're into this, even?"

Ran folded her arms. "We have been cooped up here too long, have we not?"

"Gods yes, I could use a pint," Nigel said, his smile crooked. "When do we leave?"

"Dark," Isabela said. "Obviously."

"I always wanted to see America," Kopano said dreamily. He finally found a shirt that was clean enough and tugged it on. "I thought they would show us more when we came to the Academy. There should be field trips."

"Yeah. Instead they bring in military guys to beat us up," Taylor added. "We deserve a night off after that ordeal today."

Kopano smiled at her. He liked the rebellious glint that he saw in Taylor's eye. He spoke to her in a tone of faux virtue. "It is my duty to warn you, Taylor, that this activity does not sound very boring."

She smiled at him. "Nope. It does not."

Just then, they all heard a loud bang from Caleb's room, followed by a pair of identical voices agitatedly whispering to each other. Everyone slowly turned towards Caleb's closed door. Except for Isabela. She whipped around to glare at Nigel.

"Your freak roommate is here? The whole time?"

Nigel ran a hand over his spiky hair, exchanging a look

with Kopano. "We, ah . . . we didn't check."

Isabela stomped her foot and yelled at the closed door, "Spy! Come out of there!"

Slowly, the door to Caleb's room creaked open and Caleb poked his head out.

"I didn't hear anything," he said.

Isabela groaned and flailed her arms. "This one! He is the ultimate tattletale. We must tie him up and gag him until we return."

Kopano laughed until Isabela turned to glare at him. "Wait. You are serious?"

Taylor watched Caleb warily, their weird encounter the week before not forgotten. Ran and Nigel, meanwhile, exchanged a subtle look. For his part, Caleb seemed to regret stumbling into the whole plan. He held up his hands.

"I won't say anything. I promise," he said.

"No. He cannot be trusted," countered Isabela.

Suddenly, Caleb stumbled forward. A duplicate hidden behind him had pushed Caleb out of his room. "Tell them you want to go, pansy," the duplicate hissed.

Nigel sighed and stepped forward. "Caleb, mate, what did we say about the duplicates?"

Caleb glanced over his shoulder, then absorbed the duplicate back into himself. Isabela shuddered.

"Sorry," Caleb said.

"Our roommate, he's got difficulties expressing himself proper like," Nigel declared, turning to face the rest of the group. "Bit of a weirdo, innit he? He owes it to his rigid upbringing and troubled childhood or some such."

"Um, we don't need to get into all that, thanks, Nigel," Caleb said quietly.

"I don't suppose any of us have similar back stories?" Nigel continued. "Or have had some trouble fitting in around this bloody Academy?"

"I am not a weirdo," Isabela declared.

Taylor smirked. "You aren't?"

Isabela shot Taylor a look. "No."

Kopano shrugged happily, like he'd missed most of the discussion. "You should come with us, Caleb. We are going to San Francisco!"

"I . . ." Caleb looked uncertainly at Isabela. "I mean, I would go if . . ."

"Six is too many," Isabela said, stomping her foot. "I cannot sneak out a small army."

"Yes, you can," Ran said, breaking her long silence.

Isabela glared at Ran. The Japanese girl stared back impassively. After a few seconds, Isabela relented with a toss of her hair.

"Fine," she said. "Fine. I will do it because my heart is so big and full of charity."

The six of them waited until dark before they set out from the dorms. There were no rules about the students roaming the grounds at night—at least not before the midnight curfew—so they made their way towards the woods at a casual pace.

They hiked deep into the trees, until the fence that surrounded the Academy came into view. Isabela stopped them before they got too close.

"Do we climb over?" Kopano asked.

Isabela gave him a deadpan look. "I do not climb." She checked her watch. "We need to wait about seven more minutes."

"For what?" Caleb asked.

"Perimeter patrol."

Sure enough, seven minutes later, a Peacekeeper truck rumbled by on the dirt road that encircled the fence. As soon as the red taillights were out of sight, Isabela stepped out of hiding. The others followed, cautiously.

"First," she said, "we deal with the camera."

The others hadn't even noticed the little camera mounted on top of the fence. With a gentle nudge of her telekinesis, Isabela turned the device so it pointed in the other direction.

"Doesn't someone notice that?" Taylor asked.

"Of course they notice," Isabela replied. "But it is very windy out here. A technician will come out, turn the camera back around, tighten the screws. No big deal."

Next, Isabela stepped carefully back into the overgrown woods. She returned with a huge dead log, levitating the mossy debris with her telekinesis.

"It took me awhile to find one exactly the right size," she said. "I keep worrying that one night it will be gone, that the groundskeepers will clean it up."

Isabela propped the log up against the fence. She took off

her heels and gracefully scaled the improvised ramp. Lightly, she jumped down on the other side of the fence, dusted off the soles of her feet and put her shoes back on.

"Coming?" she asked the others through the fence.

One by one, they each ascended the ramp and jumped down. Kopano caught Taylor when she leaped down. Caleb watched them, biting his lip. When they were all on the other side, Isabela used her telekinesis to shove the log away from the fence.

"What happens now?" Nigel asked. "It's a long walk to San Francisco."

Isabela pointed across the dirt road. "Now, you wait here. There is a ditch over there. Hide in it until I return."

"Where are you going?" Taylor asked.

"You are all so nosy! Please. I know what I'm doing," Isabela complained. The others stared at her, so she threw up her hands resignedly. "Look, I am going to get us a car. Then, we drive off. Nothing to it. Get in your ditch so the patrols won't see you."

Isabela sauntered off into the darkness, leaving the others to hunker down in the grass on the side of the road. They stared up at the stars—blinking and visible out here in the middle of nowhere. They were nervous at first, but as the seconds turned into minutes, a peace settled over the five of them.

"This is kinda nice," Caleb said.

"Don't ruin the moment by talking about it," Nigel replied. Ran elbowed him.

They tensed up when another car rolled by, the headlight beams gliding right over their position. The patrol didn't even slow down.

"It'd be kind of funny if she just left us out here," Caleb said.

"She wouldn't do that," Taylor replied.

"I know . . . I'm just joking." Caleb shrugged. "We could camp out here. Worse comes to worst."

Kopano chuckled. "Sleeping outside on purpose. Something I will never understand about this wonderful country."

Another vehicle puttered up the dirt road. This time, it was a van. And this time, it slowed to a stop right above their ditch.

"Gotta be Isabela," Nigel said, standing up before Ran could stop him.

He was greeted by the face of the red-bearded soldier who he'd scared in the competition earlier, the man staring at him through his rolled-down window. "The hell are you doing out here, boy?"

Nigel tensed up. "Uh . . ."

In a blur of flesh that looked like melting clay, the soldier's face changed into Isabela's. She grinned at him. "Just kidding. Come on, get in!"

Laughing and excited, they scrambled out of the ditch and into the van. Taylor sat shotgun. There weren't any seats in the back—Isabela explained that the van was meant for doing supply runs, which was the pretense she used to sign it out from the vehicle pool, all under the identity of one of the many soldiers she'd memorized. The four others held on to leather cargo straps that dangled from the van's walls and ceiling.

"You're really something else," Taylor told Isabela.

"I know."

"In addition to something else, I hope you are also a good driver," Kopano said.

"Oh, I am," Isabela replied, setting off at a breakneck pace that jostled the four in the back. They were too amped up to complain, a game soon developing where they tried to keep their balance as Isabela zoomed through the curves of the patrol road. She slowed down when they reached a paved turnoff that led toward the Peacekeeper base proper and the final checkpoint before their exit.

"You should hide in the back. I need to put my face back on," Isabela told Taylor. The five of them all crouched in the shadows of the cargo area, holding in laughter, even Caleb giddy with the possibility of escape. "Are you ready?" Isabela asked. "Soon, there will be no turning back."

"We're ready," the others said in unison, not at all nervous as they approached the checkpoint. Isabela's confidence was contagious.

They were waved through without incident.

CHAPTER TWENTY-THREE

IN THE "FAMILY AREA" OF JIMBO'S MOTOR HOME, Einar ground his teeth until his jaw hurt. The room stunk—a mixture of body order and cigarette smoke. His legs ached from standing, but he refused to crowd in with the others around the faded dinette set. Not until Reverend Jimbo was done with his Bible study.

He hated Reverend Jimbo.

He hated his disgusting mobile home.

He hated the Americans.

In the background, Reverend Jimbo read a passage in his slow drawl. Einar watched the old man without listening—thick gray hair slicked halfway down the back of his neck, pockmarked face, the glistening eyes of a true believer. A group of Reverend Jimbo's followers crowded in around him, rapt, paying attention, although Einar figured the reverend could have read his flock anything—*The Lion, the Witch and the Wardrobe*, for instance, one of Einar's childhood favorites—and they would have taken it as gospel.

All of Jimbo's followers—bikers, ranchers, survivalists, burnouts—had the same stupid tattoo. A scythe slashing down on a serpent as it burst forth from a circle. The symbolism didn't require much unpacking.

Harvesters, they called themselves.

Einar glanced around the motor home. On the walls were pinned a jumble of newspaper stories about alien life, hand-drawn maps of UFO sightings and snatches of Scripture. Piled against one wall was a stack of rifles.

These people weren't professional. Compared to the research and resources of the Foundation, Jimbo's group was laughable.

Even though they often looked at him like a child, Einar missed the efficiency of Jarl and his Blackstone mercenaries. They were banned from operating on American soil, which made getting them into the United States for this operation too much of a risk. His employers had to use what resources were available. In this case, a grassroots cult that believed the Loric were devils made flesh and that any humans touched by them were irredeemably corrupted.

He and Rabiya were alone on this one. A calculated risk by the Foundation, Einar supposed. Even with the addition of the Italian Earth Garde healer, his employers still needed more healing power. Einar sensed the matter was becoming desperate.

If the Harvesters knew what Einar and Rabiya really were, they would certainly try to kill them. Einar sensed the way Jimbo and some of his brighter lights looked at him. They already had suspicions. But his presence had come with a generous contribution to the reverend's mobile church, both in money and weapons. Not to mention, Einar promised them violence, gave them a purpose. That kept the Harvesters from looking too hard at him and his partner. At least for now.

The weapons Einar provided were like nothing the Harvesters had seen before. They were designed specifically to fight the Garde and currently available only to select government agencies. Select government agencies and the Foundation. Einar and Rabiya were posing as representatives from Sydal Corp, the weapons manufacturer, spending time with the Harvesters so that they could field-test their anti-Garde technology. That made the Harvesters feel special.

"That's an honest-to-God multinational corporation, y'hear?" Reverend Jimbo had told his men when he introduced Einar. "We ain't just pissing in the wind out here. The powers-that-be, they're starting to take notice." That Einar and Rabiya were a little young to be representing a prominent weapons manufacturer like Sydal Corp didn't seem to

occur to the Harvesters. That they were both obviously foreigners didn't raise any red flags either. Jimbo had stressed
multinational, after all.

And what better place to test these weapons than out
here, on the coast of California? They just had to wait for a
suitable target to come along. A straggler. That's what Einar
had told Jimbo and the others, anyway.

They didn't need to know that he and Rabiya were waiting for someone in particular.

Einar brushed a spot of lint off the front of his black
button-down. The Harvesters favored what Einar considered
silly postapocalyptic costumes—leather, gas masks, outlaw
bandannas. He stuck out in their company by wearing a fine
gray suit and wingtip shoes. Despite the preponderance of
mildew in Reverend Jimbo's narrow motor home shower,
Einar managed to stay immaculately clean. He kept his light
brown hair rigidly parted from the side. There was not a
speck of dirt under his fingernails.

He and Rabiya had been out here for a week. Living among
the vermin. Waiting.

A walkie-talkie buzzed to life. "Got one coming your
way," said the scratchy voice of a Harvester. Aside from the
reverend, Einar hadn't bothered to learn any of their names.
"White van. Looks like another supply run."

Einar quickly picked up his attaché. He turned to the reverend and his disciples, who had paused in their reading.

"I'll look into it," Einar said. "Ready yourselves."

"With the Lord's guidance, we are always ready," the

reverend responded. He motioned for one of the Harvesters—
a muscular young man with slicked-back black hair—to join
Einar. The reverend always had someone watching him.

Einar stepped outside, the cool night air a relief after the
stuffy odors of the motor home. His escort followed him.
Outside were a dozen more Harvesters and their motorcycles. They had skipped Bible study to drink beers and
grill what were probably steaks but Einar imagined to be
squirrels.

Their encampment was on a ridge that overlooked the Mar
a Vista scenic roadway. In the decades before the Academy
took over this piece of California, Mar a Vista was popular
with tourists and surfers. Now, according to the Foundation's
source inside the Academy, it was the route the Peacekeepers used when they wanted to travel unobserved. Unlike the
nearby Shoreline Highway, this road was secluded. Usually
without traffic. Perfect for discreet travel, but also ripe for a
trap.

Thanks to their source, Einar knew exactly where the
Academy's security checkpoints were located. The Harvesters had a handful of vagabond-looking bikers posted nearby
there—far enough away to avoid detection but close enough to
observe any comings and goings. That's who had radioed in.

In addition, there was a small team farther south on the
highway, ready to spring a roadblock on Einar's command.
Rabiya was down there, supervising that piece of the operation. If they were discovered as Garde and the Harvesters
turned on them, it was better that Einar be with the bulk of

the group. He could handle them.

Einar's source had assured the Foundation that the target made frequent visits to San Francisco, where she honed her skills at a local hospital. She would come this way. In all likelihood, she would be escorted by Peacekeepers and some Academy personnel. All expendable.

Whenever a vehicle left the Academy via Mar a Vista, they checked it. So far, there had been no sign of their target.

The Peacekeepers would detect their presence eventually. They couldn't camp out here forever without attracting attention. Every day, much to Einar's chagrin, the number of Harvesters increased. Word was spreading, a small army amassing. The atmosphere around the reverend's camp got more and more like a party. But Einar could tell the Harvesters were growing restless. Soon, they'd want some action, whether approved by Einar or not. He'd already overheard the idiots pondering an assault on the Academy. A lot of bold talk.

The operation would have to fold up if the Harvesters became too unruly. He hadn't been sent here for a pointless attack on the Academy.

The whole mission was riskier than Einar would've liked. Riskier, even, than kidnapping the sniveling Italian boy in the Philippines. Acting so close to the Academy; there would be consequences. His employers surely knew that. They'd likely run dozens of cost-benefit analyses.

Acquiring the target was worth the exposure.

And, if all went well, the whole operation would simply

be blamed on the Harvesters.

Three days ago was Einar's eighteenth birthday. He'd spent it among these sweat-stinking cretins. He hadn't told anyone, not even Rabiya.

As a belated gift, he hoped to see some of these Harvesters die.

Einar speed-walked towards the ridge with his Harvester escort. Once there, he crouched down in the grass, careful not to get any dirt on his suit. He opened his attaché and took out his goggles. They were bulky things and Einar tsked in annoyance as one of the straps caught on his ear.

"Here, let me help," said the Harvester. He straightened the strap on the back of Einar's head before Einar could stop him.

Einar turned to regard the Harvester. His eyes looked bulbous and huge with the goggles on.

"Thank you," said Einar coldly.

"No problem," the guy said. "That accent. You Russian or something? Been meaning to ask."

"Icelandic," Einar replied.

He turned to watch the road, waiting for the van to come into view. The goggles were not night vision. They did not magnify Einar's vision. He stared into the darkness.

If his target came down that road, he would know.

"Never met anyone from Iceland before," the Harvester continued. "That's cool."

"What is your name?" Einar asked.

"Silas."

"You are talkative, Silas," Einar observed. "Does the dark make you nervous?"

Silas laughed. "Hell no, man. I'm just making conversation."

Einar concentrated on this young man. Silas's palms began to sweat. His stomach turned over, clenched in a knot. His heart was pounding now. Was that movement in the grass? What were those shadows? Einar smiled thinly when he sensed Silas creep a little closer to him, as if for protection.

"Actually, it is a little freaky out here," Silas said, his voice cracking. "Shit, man. I'm weirded out."

"Be calm," Einar said, and released his hold on the Harvester. It was so easy to put the fear in people when they didn't know what was happening.

Headlights appeared in the distance. Einar turned his attention to the road below. The van approached . . .

"What . . . ?" Einar mumbled.

He struck the side of his goggles with the heel of his hand. What he saw didn't seem possible. He checked the diagnostic in the bottom-left corner of the display. Everything appeared normal; the goggle's batteries were fully charged.

The reading had to be correct.

Einar's lips quirked in a bemused smile. Through his goggles, he watched six vivid blue energy signatures pass by on the road.

He pulled his walkie-talkie from his hip. "Rabiya?"

His partner came back a moment later, her voice soft as always. "Yes, Einar?"

"There are six coming your way. Confirm the target is among them before engaging."

"Yes, Einar."

Calmly, Einar returned the goggles to his attaché. He felt Silas's eyes upon him, his mouth agape.

"You say six, fella?" Silas asked. "Six of—of those things down there in that van?"

"Yes. Six of them without an escort," Einar replied. He turned on his heel and headed back for camp. "Your men must arm themselves and prepare to engage."

CHAPTER TWENTY-FOUR

TAYLOR COOK
MAR A VISTA—CALIFORNIA

TAYLOR GOT AN UNEASY FEELING IN THE PIT OF her stomach as soon as the taillights came into view.

They were on a back road headed south from the Academy. Probably gorgeous in daylight, but empty and ominous at night. Taylor couldn't understand where her anxiety was coming from. She'd grown up in big, empty expanses like this. She'd never been unnerved by stretches of lonely country.

That was before the attack on her farm. Before the nightmares.

Isabela had the radio on. Bright pop music that seemed at odds with the night. Nigel agreed.

"Turn that rubbish off," he complained again and again.

"I am the driver," Isabela replied. "This means I choose the music."

"Bloody hell, let me drive then."

"No. You would kill us all. Drive on the wrong side of the road or something. Or poison our characters with your terrible punk rock."

"Aw, your character's already poisoned enough, darling."

"You should broaden your horizons, Isabela," Kopano said. "Nigel's music is awesome." Isabela shot him a withering look and he held up his hands. "What you're playing is fine, too."

Taylor looked over her shoulder. Ran sat cross-legged in the back, the bumpy riding not at all disturbing her meditation. Caleb sat next to her, his hand holding one of the cargo straps so he didn't slide across the van whenever Isabela took a turn too fast. He was watching her. Taylor still didn't know what to make of him. He had a crush on her? He was mentally disturbed? He was a sort of dorky boy from the Midwest? She caught his eye and immediately worried such a look would be misinterpreted.

"Everything okay?" Caleb asked her. He must have read the unease on her face.

"Yeah," she replied, and forced a smile.

"America is much bigger than I thought," Kopano observed cheerily. He'd wedged himself in between Isabela and Taylor, his butt on Isabela's armrest, his arm across the back of Taylor's chair. "Do you know I used to think one could drive from New York to California in a day?"

Taylor chuckled as she glanced up at him, relaxing a little. "Maybe if you drove like Isabela."

Isabela nodded firmly. "Yes. I could do that."

"Are we there yet?" Kopano asked.

"God, you are like a child," Isabela snapped. "It was an hour when you asked five minutes ago. Do the math, big boy."

"Don't make her turn the car around," Taylor said with a smirk.

"Look!" Kopano said, pointing through the windshield. "An accident?"

The taillights.

Kopano was the first one to spot them. Up ahead, a beat-up station wagon was parked across the center lane. The hood was popped, the headlights on, two silhouettes visible as they peered down at the engine. A curl of steam or smoke emanated from the open hood.

Immediately, Isabela stepped on the brakes. As the van slowed to a crawl, Isabela turned down the music.

"Looks like a breakdown," Caleb said.

"We should help," Kopano put in.

"I actually know a few things about cars," Caleb added. "Used to hang around with the base mechanics—"

"Should we really be stopping?" Taylor asked, embarrassed by the quaking unease in her voice. "We don't know these people."

Kopano gave her a surprised look. "Seriously? We just drive by them?"

"Need I remind you, we aren't supposed to be away from the Academy?" Isabela said sharply. "In San Francisco, we will blend into the crowd. But out here? What if that is someone from the school?"

Caleb squinted into the headlights as the van creaked closer to the breakdown. "If they're from the Academy, they'll probably recognize us anyway."

Nigel glanced at Ran. She peered through the windshield with an arched eyebrow, her lips pursed. He turned to the others. "If they aren't from the Academy, then what are they doing out here?"

"Driving," Kopano said with a laugh. "Going to the beach? Hiking? You guys are being paranoid."

"I would think it best if we avoid being seen this close to the Academy," Ran said.

That settled matters for Isabela. She leaned over the wheel. "Everyone duck down and I will drive us on the shoulder."

Before Isabela could do that, one of the people standing by the station wagon jogged into their headlights and waved. Taylor relaxed a bit when she saw it was just a girl, no more than a few years older than herself. The girl's pretty face was framed by a hijab, the dark fabric gaudily bedazzled. She wore a dress that covered her from neck to ankle, obviously expensive and fashionable. Completely normal, thought Taylor.

"Hey! Can you help us?" the girl yelled, standing right in their way.

Kopano laughed. "A stranded girl! And you cruel people

wanted to flee the scene."

Isabela put the van in park and rolled down her window. The girl hustled over, smiling sweetly as she got on her tip-toes and looked into the van.

"Thank you, thank you," she said breathlessly. "My dad and I have been stuck out here for like an hour. We just need a jump."

"I do not know what that is," Isabela said.

While they talked, Taylor found herself not looking at the girl but at the burly shape of her father. She couldn't see much of him besides that he had a tangled mane of curly hair. As he fiddled with the engine, his arms briefly came into the light. Taylor spotted a strange smudge of grease on his fore-arm. She leaned forward, trying to get a better look . . .

"Do you have cables?" Caleb asked. He got up and opened the back of the van. "Hang on. Let me come take a look."

As Caleb brushed by him, Nigel pressed up against the window. His head tilted. Something moved out there. He was sure of it. He cupped his hands around his eyes, trying to see through the glass into the dark.

"Oi, Ran . . . ," he said quietly.

The Japanese girl perked up and came to his side.

"Someone's out there," Nigel whispered.

Meanwhile, as Caleb climbed out of the back of the van, the girl waved to her father. "These are the ones, Dad! They're going to help us out!"

These are the ones. What a strange way to say that. The girl's words set off Isabela's finely tuned bullshit detector.

She shot a glance in Taylor's direction, but Taylor was too busy staring wide-eyed at the girl's "father" to notice.

The man had straightened up from his hunched position over the station wagon. He waved to his daughter and his arm came fully into the light. Taylor immediately recognized the symbol tattooed on the inside of his forearm.

Circle. Snake. Scythe.

"Isabela! We have to go!" Taylor screamed.

But it was too late.

As Taylor turned to Isabela, panicked, the other girl smoothly pulled a pistol from within the folds of her dress and shot Isabela in the neck.

CHAPTER TWENTY-FIVE

EINAR
MAR A VISTA—CALIFORNIA

HIS ATTACHÉ IN HAND, EINAR WALKED SLOWLY down the dark road towards the sounds of chaos. Shouting, the roar of motorcycle engines, the electronic buzzing of the Inhibitor-2a's. Headlights from dozens of motorcycles flashed, creating a strobe-light effect in the otherwise peaceful night. Einar scratched his cheek thoughtfully.

Perhaps he should have waited for a more opportune moment to make his move.

The Academy Garde were trapped. They hunkered down around the van they'd been driving, fending off an assault from the first wave of Harvesters. Meanwhile, a dozen bikers rode in a circle around the area, fencing them in.

If he'd had the Blackstone Group out here instead of these half-witted trailer trash, this battle would already be over.

Reverend Jimbo had almost fifty men at his disposal. Einar had been worried about how their numbers had been growing.

Suddenly, they didn't seem like enough.

"I thought you said there were only six of them!" Reverend Jimbo yelled in his ear. The old man walked next to Einar, nervous but excited, brandishing a chrome-plated six-shooter. Silas stood on his other side, watching the fight with wide eyes.

Only. Einar sniffed. As if six Garde, even poorly trained ones, could ever be taken lightly. Oh well. It wouldn't be long now. One way or another, his mission to America was at an end. After tonight, he could wash his hands of the Harvesters and their ignorance.

"There are only six of them," Einar replied to the reverend.

"Then why do I see—?" The reverend squinted into the distance, trying to count. "A whole goddamn bunch?"

"One of them duplicates," Einar said.

"He does what?"

"He produces clones of himself."

"That's the unholiest thing I've heard yet."

Einar suppressed a sigh. He had read the file on Caleb Crane and found his Legacy to be an enviable one. According to his dossier, Caleb deferred to authority and followed instructions readily. Strange, then, to find him out here, apparently engaged in an attempt to escape from the Academy. Einar did recall some mention of instability with the boy. Possible multiple personality disorder. That would make sense, considering his Legacy.

"If your men can isolate the real duplicator and render him unconscious, the clones will disappear," Einar said.

"They'll do more than render that abomination unconscious," the reverend replied. He cocked his pistol.

Einar turned to glare at the reverend.

"I told you. No lethal weapons until I have what I'm after."

"Right, right. Your precious field test," Reverend Jimbo said with a snort. "Son, I'm grateful for the support and all, but I can't promise my boys won't get tired of batting these devils around with your little toys."

Einar took a step close to the reverend, focused his power and coaxed a feeling of fear out of the older man. Intimidation. If he pressed any harder, he could have the reverend on the ground praying to him. But there wasn't time for that.

With a shaky hand, Reverend Jimbo eased down the hammer on his pistol.

"I'll—I'll make sure my men don't fly off the handle," the reverend said meekly. He waved Silas and one of the other Harvesters towards the battle. "Sorry," he muttered to Einar, clearly unsure why he was apologizing.

"Mm," Einar replied noncommittally. He turned to watch a burly biker sneak up on a Caleb and fire an Inhibitor-2a leash at him.

The Inhibitor version 2a. One of Sydal Corp's finest creations. It then fired a collar made of a proprietary mercury-based alloy that snapped into place around the target's neck and self-welded shut. If knocked off course—say, by telekinesis—the weapon's sensors automatically recalibrated for the target's throat by homing in on the heat of the carotid artery. Once attached, the collar remained connected to the crossbow by high-strength tensile wire, delivering shocks on command to the target. The electric bursts were enough to disrupt any Legacies.

Einar would know; he had been on the receiving end many times during the weapon's testing. He remembered bitterly how an early version had nearly decapitated him.

The Inhibitor fired by the biker snapped around the Caleb's neck. He watched Caleb convulse from the shock. Then, the collar dropped uselessly to the ground; Caleb had disappeared. A clone, then. Not the real deal.

As the biker reeled his inhibitor back in, he was struck in the chest by a vicious punch to the sternum. The biker flew backwards, slammed into the van the Garde had been driving and lay still.

That was Kopano Okeke who threw the haymaker. Einar's intelligence on him was far from complete. The exact nature of the Nigerian's Legacies was unknown to the Academy, and thus unknown to Einar's employer. Einar didn't need reports to tell him that Kopano's strength was enhanced. He could see that for himself.

That would be useful.

Two more Harvesters armed with Sydal Corp tranquilizer guns fired at Kopano. The darts bounced harmlessly off him. A moment later, a glowing orb landed at the feet of the two Harvesters. They barely had a chance to register the projectile before it exploded, throwing the two bikers to the side of the road.

Ran Takeda. And if she was here, then it was likely Nigel Barnaby was as well. Skilled combatants, survivors of the massacre at Patience Creek. Einar might not have initiated this operation had he known they were present. The pair crouched for cover at the back of the van, using the doors for a shield. As Einar watched, Ran picked up a handful of gravel and charged it with her Legacy. She chucked the stones at another pack of Harvesters, the resulting concussive blast knocking them off their motorcycles. Word had reached the Foundation that Ran had sworn off using her Legacies. Apparently, she had chosen tonight to make an exception.

"My men are getting destroyed out there!" Reverend Jimbo screamed.

"Yes. They are very poorly trained," Einar replied as he continued to scan the battlefield.

There. Near the driver side door of the van, Einar could see a trio of three Calebs standing shoulder to shoulder. A human wall. They were protecting someone. Through their legs, Einar could see a body in the road, a second person crouching over it. An injured person and a healer.

"I see you, Taylor," Einar said to himself. He waited a moment for a Harvester on a motorcycle to pass, then darted through their snarling chopper perimeter and headed towards the battle.

"Where are you going?" Reverend Jimbo shouted.

"To finish this."

Time was of the essence. Already, the frustrated and frightened Harvesters were abandoning the nonlethal weapons he'd provided them with and were turning to more conventional, and deadlier, methods of assault. Although any injuries would surely be blamed on the Harvesters, a bunch of dead Garde would not be a welcome development. This mission would already bring too much attention.

A group of Harvesters armed with tire irons and baseball bats had descended upon Kopano. He blocked each of their attacks with a forearm or a shoulder or, in one case, his face. None of the blows hurt him. Einar watched as, one by one, Kopano knocked the Harvesters out with powerful uppercuts.

"Leave us alone!" the young man shouted, a note of fear in his voice despite his near invulnerability. "Leave us—!"

Kopano hesitated. He had spotted Einar walking towards him. A strange sight—a young man in a suit and tie, holding a briefcase, walking calmly through the fray.

Meanwhile, a Harvester advanced on Kopano from behind. He carried an old-fashioned sawed-off shotgun. Einar wondered if that would be enough to break Kopano's thick skin.

All of the Garde were occupied with other Harvesters. Einar sighed. He reached into his attaché, pulled out his blaster and fired a concentrated burst of energy. Kopano ducked as the red-tinged beam sizzled by his head and right into the Harvester's face.

Einar's weapon was far from nonlethal; the Harvester fell dead, his face a charred mess. The blaster was Mogadorian in origin, a little collector's item from the invasion. Einar relished any chance he got to use it.

"Who are—?" Kopano started to ask, his fists up.

"I'm your only friend," Einar said, getting closer. He reached out to Kopano with his Legacy and filled the boy with feelings of affection and trust.

"Right!" Kopano said. "Yes! Good to see you!"

"All these people want to hurt us. All of them," Einar said. "Hurt them before they can hurt us."

Anger. Einar made it flow through Kopano. It was a simple chemical reaction—lower the serotonin, pump up the adrenaline. Especially easy with males, actually. Kopano's eyes widened, his lips curled into a feral snarl, his fists clenched impossibly tight.

With a roar, Kopano whipped around and clotheslined the nearest Harvester. While that man gasped for breath in the dirt, Kopano lunged at a Caleb and punched the clone so hard that its head spun 180 degrees before it disappeared.

"Good boy," Einar said.

Emotional manipulation. It wasn't the flashiest Legacy, but it had its uses.

Kopano plowed through another pair of clones, then pummeled a fleeing Harvester. Everyone in the battle—Garde and Harvester—was now paying all their attention to the Nigerian.

Well, not everyone.

Einar took a moment too long admiring his handiwork. Something thudded at his feet. A glowing rock.

"Shit," he said.

He felt a yank on the back of his jacket and let his body go limp. Just as Ran's bomb exploded at his feet, Einar flew backwards on a telekinetic tether. He landed in the road, scraping his elbows. He'd been pulled backwards by Rabiya, who was hiding behind the tire of the broken-down station wagon they'd used as a roadblock. An unconscious Harvester was slumped next to her.

Einar cringed, fingering a tear in his jacket.

"I'm all dirty," he complained.

"Yes. But you aren't blown to pieces, so there's that," Rabiya scolded.

The two of them flinched as a motorcycle flew overhead, the bike obviously propelled by telekinesis and glowing with Ran's kinetic energy. It fell right in the midst of the Harvesters riding in circles around the fight and exploded, knocking a few of them off their bikes and driving others to retreat.

"This is going poorly," Rabiya observed. "We should have waited. It would've been easier to take her with the Peace-keepers than with these other Garde."

"Hindsight," Einar replied with a dismissive wave. "Besides, we don't know if she was planning to return to the Academy. They could have been running away."

Einar peeked out from behind the car. By the van, Kopano's berserk rampage was slowing down a bit. Normally, it took a few minutes for Einar's control to wear off, but the attack from Ran must have shaken his Legacy. He concentrated on Kopano and amped up his adrenaline, his rage, then smiled when the Nigerian smashed the heads of two Harvesters together with renewed ferocity.

"Kopano! Hey! What are you doing?"

That must be Caleb. The real Caleb. He stood in front of the larger boy, trying to calm him down. He couldn't have known what Einar had done to Kopano's mind, how it would take time for him to come down from the manipulations.

Kopano grabbed Caleb by the front of his shirt and flung him back-first into the windshield of the van. The glass crunched and spiderwebbed as Caleb bounced off it, tumbled over the hood and landed on the back of his head in the road. A moment later, the clones crowding the battlefield blinked out of existence.

"We make our move now," Einar told Rabiya. "Get our exit ready."

"Hurry, please," Rabiya said. She extended her hands. A blue glow started to emanate from her palms.

Einar slipped out from behind the car, blaster pointed ahead of him. With the clones gone, he could see Taylor leaning over one of her friends. Who was that? He couldn't tell and it didn't matter. She was unconscious or dead. Probably dead, based on the dark red scars that covered her face and neck. One of the damned Harvesters must have burned her up. Taylor was focused on pouring healing energy into her, but from Einar's perspective the effort seemed wasted.

As Einar scuttled towards Taylor, Nigel strode into the road and started to scream.

The decibel level was like nothing Einar had ever experienced. He doubled over and vomited, his head spinning. It felt like his eyes would bulge out of his head. The Harvesters who had remained standing during Kopano's assault now fell over, writhing and clutching their ears.

So did Kopano. In fact, he took the brunt of Nigel's scream. The attack seemed designed to bring him down.

Hand shaking, Einar managed to lift his blaster just high enough to shoot Nigel in the leg. The searing pain surprised him and cut off his scream. Nigel fell to his knees, but immediately started to get back up. Einar grabbed a rock with his telekinesis and flung it at Nigel's head. The blow wasn't enough to kill him, but it made certain that he wouldn't cause any more sonic disruptions for at least a few minutes.

Einar felt a tugging sensation across his knuckles. A second later, his blaster was ripped out of his hand. He glanced to his right and saw Ran Takeda. Unlike the Harvesters, she was still on her feet. Einar glanced around for Rabiya but didn't see her. She must have gone down when Nigel screamed. Einar struggled to his knees and watched as Ran stalked towards him.

Bang! Bang! Bang!

A bullet grazed Ran's shoulder. She dove for cover behind the van as Reverend Jimbo stepped onto the scene, his six-shooter blazing. He came with a small contingent of Harvesters. They seemed more concerned with gathering their injured than with pressing the fight against the Garde.

Thanks to the reverend's distraction, Einar was able to scramble to his feet. The way to Taylor was clear. She'd been affected by the scream, too, and was wiping her eyes, trying to gather herself so she could go back to unsuccessfully healing her dead friend.

Einar pulled a tranquilizer gun from his attaché and shot Taylor in the neck. She slumped over.

"Finally," Einar muttered.

Einar raised a hand, hoisting Taylor up with his telekinesis. Out of the corner of his eye, he saw Ran poke her head out from behind the van. He fired a dart in her direction, unsure whether it found its mark.

"Rabiya! Are you ready?" Einar yelled as he turned. He couldn't be sure she heard him. The ringing in his own ears was thunderous.

The girl was back on her feet at least. Her headscarves were a mess, blood dampening one side of them. She must have fallen and hit her head on the station wagon's bumper.

Rabiya extended her hands and focused. A stream of cobalt-blue energy flowed from her palms and struck the pavement. Slowly, the energy coalesced into a craggy pyramid of stone.

Loralite. Rabiya could produce the stuff at will. Now, all they had to do was envision the stone tucked away in Einar's backyard, touch the Loralite and they'd be out of this mess.

"Deceivers!" Reverend Jimbo shouted. Einar could hear his booming voice even through the intense ringing. "We have been infiltrated by the abominations!"

The reverend had seen Rabiya using her Legacy. He'd likely also surmised that Einar was the one floating Taylor through the air.

The reverend pointed his revolver at Einar. Quickly, Einar yanked Taylor to him so that he was carrying the girl over her shoulder.

The reverend squeezed off a shot. Einar brushed it aside with his telekinesis.

He started to fire again.

Einar gripped the man's arm with his telekinesis and twisted. The arm snapped at the elbow. Jimbo screamed. He still managed to pull the trigger.

But the gun was aimed under his own chin.

The leader of the Harvesters collapsed, his head blown apart. His men recoiled in terror.

Einar couldn't deny the satisfaction he felt at that.

He reached the stone just as Rabiya finished creating it. "Can we please get out of here?" she asked. She held out her hand to Einar. "Your place, right?"

The detached wheel of a motorcycle flung with telekinetic force struck Rabiya in the stomach. She doubled over and fell backwards. Einar glanced over his shoulder, saw Ran charging an object, saw Caleb stirring on the roadside, saw Nigel struggling back to his feet.

He looked down at Rabiya, catching her breath, now too far away from the stone. He started to reach out with his telekinesis.

A glowing rock floated in his direction.

One of the last Harvesters dove on top of Rabiya. He grabbed her and smashed her face into the pavement.

It was all happening too fast.

"I am sorry," Einar said to Rabiya, although he was sure she couldn't hear him. He touched the Loralite stone and, with Taylor, teleported himself to safety.

CHAPTER TWENTY-SIX

ISABELA SILVA
BIG BOX—STOCKTON, CALIFORNIA

ISABELA AWOKE SLOWLY, GROGGILY, LIKE SLIDING out from a pleasant dream. Her muscles were stiff, her back sore. It felt like she'd been sleeping for a long time. Where was she? In bed at the Academy? Back home? She smelled breakfast. Her mother must be cooking. She yawned luxuriously.

Someone gently shook her shoulders.

"Isabela. Isabela." Ran's voice. "Wake up, now. It is time to go."

Isabela snapped awake. This cold metal slab beneath her, it wasn't her bed. And she wasn't alone.

She sat up sharply, her back cracking, a rush of wooziness pumping through her head. Ran crouched in front of her. The Japanese girl's gaze was, as usual, completely inscrutable.

But Ran had seen her. Of that, Isabela could be certain.

"It is okay," Ran said. "You're safe."

Isabela touched her cheeks. She ran her fingers over leathery furrows, the patchwork border of skin grafts, puckered scar tissue. She brushed her hand over her scalp, the spiky bristles where her beautiful mane of hair once grew. Her eyes widened, locked on Ran, and she stifled a scream.

Then, she shape-shifted. Isabela put on her old face, the one from before the accident. The burn scars melted away, her skin smoothed out, her hair grew in. Ran watched with her head tilted, saying nothing. Isabela wondered if the other girl was capable of registering surprise.

"You saw me," Isabela said flatly.

"Yes."

"You weren't supposed to."

"The others, too," Ran said, glancing over her shoulder at the van's closed back door. "At first, we thought you had been injured . . ."

Isabela put her face in her hands. Months of keeping up appearances—literally and figuratively—wasted. They would talk and she would become an object of pity, undesirable, disgusting . . .

She peeked out through her fingers. Wait. There was something more happening here. They were in the back of the stolen Academy van, except it wasn't at all in the condition Isabela remembered. A warm wind blew in through the missing windshield. There were blood splatters on the floor.

She noticed that Ran's shoulder was wrapped in a fresh bandage.

"What . . . what happened?" Isabela asked.

"We were attacked," Ran said. "You were shot with a tranquilizer dart."

Isabela touched a sore spot on her neck. "Jesus Christ."

"A young man—we think he was Garde—took Taylor. Teleported her away somewhere using a Loralite stone."

Isabela's mouth dropped open. "No. That doesn't make any sense."

"We are trying to decide what to do now," Ran continued. "To begin with, we are getting rid of the van. That's why I woke you."

Isabela rubbed her eyes. "Where are we?"

"Stockton, California."

"Ugh. Why? If we were attacked, why don't we go back to the Academy?"

Ran reached past Isabela. From under the driver seat, she grabbed a broken weapon. A crossbow-looking rifle. The shock-collar thing. One of the guns the Peacekeepers had used against the Garde in the Wargames event.

"The people who attacked us had these," Ran said. "They could be working with the Peacekeepers. We don't know. Nigel and I do not feel safe going back there. And Caleb and Kopano . . . well. They want to go after Taylor."

Isabela brushed a hand through her hair. "Where are they?"

"Outside," Ran said. She nudged a plastic shopping bag in

Isabela's direction. "We got you a change of clothes."

Isabela looked down at the bright blue bag. The logo said Big Box—a huge chain of American stores that sold super-cheap versions of everything from underwear to guns. With great trepidation, she peered at the clothes within. A boring T-shirt and a terrible pair of mom jeans.

"These are awful."

"They were the best we could do."

Isabela sniffed. The cute and strappy dress she'd worn for their night out was ruined, smudged with grime and stained with blood. It was just one thing after another. She touched her wrist where, luckily, Simon's translator bracelet remained secure.

"Let me get changed," she said.

Ran nodded and turned to exit the van. She paused, half glancing over her shoulder.

"You are using your Legacy all the time," Ran said.

Isabela frowned. "I haven't figured out how to do it when I'm sleeping. Obviously."

"Don't you get tired?"

Isabela rubbed the scratchy fabric of her new T-shirt between her fingers. "Of course," she said. "My tolerance is getting better and better, though."

"It seems . . ." Ran paused. "I am sorry. It seems like it would be difficult."

"Walking around the way I am, the way I really am . . . that's harder than any amount of shape-shifting," Isabela said quietly.

Ran nodded once, opened the door and hopped out of the van.

Isabela exhaled slowly. She'd spent almost a year hiding her true self from her classmates, cultivating the image of the girl she was before the accident. Now, all her hard work had been unraveled.

Not to mention, Taylor, who Isabela begrudgingly had to admit was her closest friend, had been kidnapped by some psychopaths. This, too, was unacceptable. Taylor, who had seen her real face already—who had kept her secret and not judged. Taylor, who should be here now, who would know the right stupid positive thing to say to make Isabela feel better.

Dressed in her ugly Big Box clothes, Isabela emerged from the van. They were parked in a dingy alley behind a shopping center. Ran sat on the bumper of the van. Nigel stood a few feet away, a small bandage on his head and a larger one on his calf. It heartened Isabela to see that he'd been forced to abandon his punk rock attire for a pair of cargo shorts and a too-big Mickey Mouse T-shirt, which he had ripped the sleeves off of. Kopano stood at the end of the alley, keeping watch, his face as dour as she'd ever seen it. Isabela wrinkled her nose; the pungent aroma of warm trash emanated from a nearby Dumpster.

"Couldn't you have found a less disgusting place to hide out?" she asked.

"That's funny," Nigel said. He smiled at her in a way that she'd never seen before. Usually, his smiles were mocking or smug, but this one . . . it was as if he were smiling at a three-legged dog.

The pity. Already they were starting in with the pity. Kopano stared at her hard, like he was trying to see through her disguise, checking for seams. She snapped her fingers at him.

"Stop looking at me like that," Isabela snapped. "What do you think? That if you cross your eyes you will be able to see my real face? You already saw enough."

Kopano simply looked away. "Sorry."

Nigel cleared his throat. "Listen, love, you don't have to hide yourself from us, we're your fri—"

Isabela rounded on him. "Hide myself?" She gestured at her body. "You think this is for you? That I do this for your benefit? Pah." Isabela spit on the ground. "This is how I like to look. It's my choice."

Nigel held up his hands. "All right, all right."

"Did it happen during the invasion?" Ran asked.

Isabela threw her shoulders back and sighed. "This is the only time we will talk about this, okay? After this special bonding moment, you will never comment on my appearance again, unless it is to pay me a much-deserved compliment. Understand?"

They all nodded.

"It happened a month before the invasion," Isabela said. "I was at a warehouse party. Something caught fire. There were too many people. I was stuck and . . ." She shrugged. "When John Smith called us all to action, I was in a hospital bed, my body wrapped in bandages. I did not care about the invasion or what happened to the world. I only hoped that one of these aliens would come heal me. They did not. But I was given the next-best thing."

"Fate," Kopano said quietly. "You got exactly the Legacy you needed."

"Fate? Luck? Who cares?" Isabela tossed her hair. "Is that enough sharing? Do we not have more important things to worry about?"

"Yes," Kopano said. He looked down at his feet. It was strange to see the cheery Nigerian brooding. "We must find Taylor."

Isabela raised an eyebrow, turning to look at Ran. "You said she got kidnapped. Teleported?"

"Yes."

"They were Harvesters," Kopano said grimly. "Taylor must have told you about them coming to her farm."

Isabela nodded. "The whore who shot me didn't look like some religious nut."

"We think she came with the tosser who teleported away," Nigel said. "She created a Loralite stone. Her friend took Taylor, left her behind. Harvesters attacked her. Snatched her up while we was making our escape."

Isabela put her hands on her hips and looked at Ran. "Why didn't you just kill them all?"

Ran looked back at her, but said nothing. It was Kopano who grunted, shoving away from his spot on the wall. "We should go find Caleb. He's been gone too long."

"Where is he?" Isabela asked.

"Caleb is getting us a new car," Ran said.

"Him? Really?" Isabela asked.

"He knows cars," Nigel replied. "Figures he can get one started all telekinetically."

"Yes, but he is—what do the Americans call it? The little camper children."

"A Boy Scout," Nigel replied with a half smile.

"Not who I would put in charge of stealing a car," Isabela said with a shrug.

"Wasn't no Boy Scout last night. Lad fought like he was possessed. Might've turned those Harvesters away himself, if . . ."

Nigel trailed off, glancing gloomily in Kopano's direction. Kopano's frown deepened and he walked out of the alley. Isabela pursed her lips—she really had missed a lot.

"What's his problem?" she quietly asked Nigel as they walked, nodding in Kopano's direction.

"He bloody lost it last night," Nigel whispered. "We think the knob in the suit used some kind of mind control on him."

They made an odd-looking group as they emerged from the alley, but luckily the shopping center parking lot was uncrowded this early in the morning. Even so, Isabela felt exposed being out in the open. She'd been on numerous excursions since coming to the Academy, but none had ever spiraled out of control like this. At best, they were in deep trouble with the Academy. At worst, they were being hunted. For the first time since she'd come to the Academy, Isabela felt her confidence begin to waver.

"Shouldn't we at least call in to the Academy?" she asked. "Tell them that Taylor's been kidnapped."

"That lot's got to have noticed we're missing by now," Nigel said. "We give them a ring, they'll track us down."

"Would that . . . would that be so bad?"

"We don't know if we can trust them," Ran said. "I, for one, am not ready to go back yet."

"We can't go back without Taylor," Kopano said firmly. "I promised her . . . I promised I would protect her."

Isabela rolled her eyes at the macho posturing, but didn't say anything. Instead, she turned to Nigel and Ran.

"Taylor could be anywhere," she said. "Where would we even start?"

Nigel reached into one of his cargo pockets. "Took the liberty of searching a couple of bodies before we made our escape last night. One'a them wankers had this on him."

He handed Isabela a pamphlet. It looked like something hastily thrown together in Photoshop and then spit out from an ancient printer. Her eyes skimmed over the imagery—the Harvester logo, bulbous-headed green aliens, the devil, random Bible quotations. More importantly was the message, scrawled in Sharpie on the back. "Apache Jack's. 4866 Route 15. Gila. Outside Silver City. Ask for Jimbo."

"Where is this?" Isabela asked.

"Biker bar in bloody New Mexico," Nigel replied. "We think it's a spot where these Harvesters sharpen their pitch-forks and grope their cousins."

"How do you know all this?"

Nigel pulled a cell from his pocket. "Nicked this from one of the bikers. Battery's all dead now, though. Found a bit of cash, too. How we afforded our lovely new wardrobe."

"That reminds me," Isabela said. With a bit of concentration, she changed the appearance of her clothes—made the jeans more formfitting and turned the T-shirt into a silky tunic.

Nigel scowled at her. "Not fair."

Isabela smirked. "So the plan is to track down these maniacs who already tried to murder us once and hope they will tell us how to find Taylor?"

"About sums it up," Nigel said. He looked to Ran. "Right?"

"Yes," she said. "Either they tell us, or perhaps we find the girl who creates Loralite. The Harvesters who survived took her when they were escaping."

"How did we escape?" Isabela thought to ask.

"The baddies hightailed it when their leader all of a sudden decided to off himself. Think the wanker in the suit played a part in that. Otherwise, don't make any sense," Nigel said. He glanced at Ran. "The ones who had a mind to keep fighting got their asses exploded."

Isabela eyed Ran. "You . . ."

She flexed her fingers, knuckles cracking. "I am not a very good pacifist. Especially when men are trying to kill me and my friends. We will find them. And they will talk."

Nigel smiled at Isabela. She realized he was actually having fun with this. "Going off half-cocked without official approval is the way Garde get things done," he said. "Or hav-en't you heard the stories, love?"

"Oh, I have heard. But you are no John Smi— Oof!"

Kopano stopped directly in front of Isabela and she bumped into the large boy's back. He didn't seem to notice.

"Uh . . . ," Kopano said. "This looks like a problem."

In the back row of the parking lot, Caleb stood with his hands on the hood of a minivan, not moving. Three other Calebs swarmed around him, all of them speaking over one another.

"We shouldn't be doing this," said one Caleb, this one rocking back and forth on his heels and hugging himself. "We shouldn't be doing any of this. We need to go back to the Academy. We need to tell the administrators everything and hope we aren't in trouble."

"Imagine how hot she's going to be for you when you bust in and rescue her," another Caleb said, this one strutting back and forth. "This is gonna be awesome, bro. Don't listen to these other shitheads."

The third duplicate stood a bit away from the others. He stroked his chin ponderously. "Has anyone considered the implications of a terrorist organization having access to the same weaponry as our government? Or the fact that there are Garde being used for violent acts against other Garde? I'm beginning to think we don't know as much about our situation as we should."

"We know exactly enough," whined the first duplicate. He tugged at the silent Caleb's arm—that one, Isabela surmised, must be the real Caleb, since these duplicates were all trying to coax him to action. "Please! Please can we go back?"

The strutting Caleb slapped his nervous counterpart hard across the face. "Shut up, man! Goddamn. You are pathetic."

Meanwhile, a Big Box worker pushing a train of shopping carts paused to stare at the arguing quadruplets. Isabela spotted him first and nudged Ran. "We're attracting attention."

All at once, the clones went silent, although their many mouths were still moving. Nigel had lowered their volume. He jogged forward, shoving through the duplicates to get at the real Caleb.

"You all right, mate?"

Caleb looked up. "Huh?" He stretched, the movement seeming painful. "Sorry. I spaced."

Nigel looked around, drawing Caleb's attention to his squabbling copies.

"Oh," Caleb said. "I didn't . . ."

"Quit listening to the voices, yeah?" Nigel said quietly. "We got work to do."

Caleb closed his eyes. In a blur of ghostly movement, the duplicates became incorporeal and flowed back into Caleb. Isabela shuddered. The Big Box store employee screamed and ran in the other direction.

"Oops," Caleb said.

With a burping sound, the engine of the minivan came to life. Caleb used his telekinesis to unlock the doors.

"We should probably go," he said.

"You think?" Isabela replied.

Caleb looked at her, surprise registering on his face. "You look . . . better."

Isabela groaned. "I'll tell you in the car, weirdo."

With that, they piled into the minivan and headed for New Mexico, the Harvesters and whatever waited beyond.

CHAPTER TWENTY-SEVEN

TAYLOR COOK

A ROOM WITH A VIEW—HOFN, ICELAND

THE HARVESTERS HAD COME FOR HER. THEY WERE going to finish what they started back in South Dakota.

That strange girl they had with them. She killed Isabela. Shot her right in the neck with some kind of poison that melted her face.

No. No . . . she was panicking. *Get it together, Taylor.*

Isabela wasn't dead, just knocked out. The scars on her face weren't from the girl's weapon; they were the same as what Taylor had seen that night in the dorms. They were what Isabela was trying to hide.

All that seemed so obvious now, as Taylor dreamily recollected it. Yet, in the moment, she had desperately pumped healing energy into Isabela. It was all she could think to do as chaos unfolded around her.

"I'll protect you," Caleb said, a trio of his duplicates surrounding her.

And then Kopano, frothing at the mouth, mad with anger, like nothing Taylor had seen before—he tossed Caleb into the windshield of the van. He was out of control.

A powerful shriek that made Taylor woozy. A sharp pain in the back of her neck. Was that a dart?

She floated up. Carried by telekinesis. Hard to keep her eyes open. A glowing stone in the middle of the road . . .

Taylor woke up screaming. Her temples throbbed. Woozily, she sat up in a bed that wasn't her own, shoving silk sheets off her body.

Wait. Silk sheets?

Taylor caught her breath and looked around. She was in a king-size bed, the dark blue sheets incredibly soft, the mattress more comfortable than anything she'd ever slept on. The room looked like a posh hotel suite. Directly across from her, a flat-screen television hung over a decorative fireplace. A bookcase stocked with classics; a writing desk; an expansive window with the curtains drawn. A stick of chamomile incense burned on the nightstand.

"What?" Taylor said aloud. "What the hell?"

This room didn't jibe with her idea of the Harvesters. They were bikers or rednecks or both. They didn't invest in hardback copies of the works of Albert Camus.

Cautiously, Taylor swung her feet out of bed. She wore a

pair of flannel pajama pants and a cotton T-shirt. Someone had taken the liberty of changing her. She shivered at the thought.

Across the room was a thick wooden door. Taylor went for it. Only when she stood right in front of it did she realize that there wasn't any doorknob or handle on her side.

She shoved against the door with her telekinesis. It didn't even shake. Must be reinforced somehow.

Taylor ran to the window and threw open the curtains. She gasped.

The view outside was otherworldly. Taylor's window overlooked a lake of the bluest water she had ever seen. Chunks of ice bobbed on the surface, steam rising up from between them, bending the landscape. Beyond that was an ice-covered mountain—a glacier? an icecap?—run through with cerulean veins that glowed in the hazy sunlight.

This was definitely not California.

Taylor pressed her face close to the window, looking down. She was on the second floor. Below, smooth obsidian pebbles fought a battle with stubborn patches of grass for control of the ground. There wasn't another house in sight. However, she did notice a small rowboat beached on the frozen lakeshore.

Taylor didn't know why she had been brought here or where here was. She didn't intend to stick around and find out.

She could jump. Find some place safe. Get home.

Taylor looked for a latch on the window. Like the door,

there was no way to open it.

Well, subtly sneaking away was out of the question. Time for a more direct approach.

Without further hesitation, Taylor picked up the writing desk with her telekinesis and smashed it against the window.

Not even a crack.

Taylor's eyes filled up with angry tears. The window was solid. Probably bulletproof. That didn't stop her from trying again. And again.

She bludgeoned the window with the desk until there was a small pile of wood on the floor at her feet. She ran her fingers across the window. Smooth as the sheets.

Maybe something sharper would do the trick?

As Taylor looked around, she heard a series of beeps from the other side of the door.

Someone was coming in.

Quickly, she grabbed one of the legs from the broken desk and gripped it like a club. She advanced on the door, fully intending to clobber whoever stepped through. She heard a hydraulic wheeze and then a metallic clanking as the steel pylons that reinforced the door gave way. Taylor cocked her arm back. The door slid open . . .

The little girl yelped when Taylor lunged at her. Taylor was just barely able to hold back from striking her. The girl nearly dropped the metal tray she carried.

"Don't hurt me!" the girl shouted. She stumbled back a few steps. Taylor, her teeth bared, brandishing the table leg, realized she must look like a total psychopath.

The girl couldn't be more than ten. She wore a white blouse tucked into a long black skirt and dark clogs. She was pale, dark-haired, her eyes almond-shaped and wide with fear. Upon her tray was a tall glass of water, a couple of Advil and a meticulously folded set of clothes.

"Who are you?" Even though she made an effort to calm herself, Taylor's voice was sharp. She lowered the club. "Where am I?"

The child swallowed hard, then tiptoed by Taylor. She stared at the destroyed desk for a moment, then set the tray down on the bed.

"I am Freyja," the child said nervously, her English accented. "You are in Iceland."

"Iceland?" Taylor exclaimed. "You mean, like . . . ?" She tried to picture where Iceland was on a map, imagining a jagged block of land hovering over Europe. "Iceland?" she repeated.

"Yes," Freyja said. "If your head hurts, I brought you medicine."

Taylor stared at the girl. Her head did hurt, but she wasn't about to ingest anything from this strange child standing guard on her posh prison cell.

"I also brought you a change of clothes," Freyja continued.

Freyja seemed as skittish as Taylor felt. Taylor took a closer look at her. The girl wore a choker with a bulbous red gemstone over the throat. The jewel flashed in the sunlight—or at least that's what Taylor thought at first.

Upon closer examination, Taylor realized there was a steady pulse happening within the stone, like the lights on a computer.

"Freyja, what am I doing here?" Taylor asked, her tone now under control.

The child looked away. "The man downstairs will explain. Also, there is breakfast."

Taylor glanced at the open door. Then, she went to kneel in front of the frightened girl.

"Are you in trouble?" Taylor asked. "Did they take you, too?"

Freyja gave a tug at her choker, which, Taylor realized, did not appear to have a release clasp. She nodded slowly, her watery gaze now fixed on Taylor.

"If you're good," Freyja whispered, "nothing bad will happen to me."

"If . . . I'm good?" Taylor's throat tightened. She stood up. "Yeah, that doesn't sound sinister at all."

Again clutching the broken table leg, Taylor left the frightened child behind to go see this "man downstairs." Outside her room, her surroundings became clearer. She was in a modernized log cabin, the hallway chicly decorated with paintings and sculptures. There were a couple of bedrooms identical to hers, their reinforced doors open. Their beds hadn't been slept in. At the end of the hall, by the stairs, was a bathroom with gilded fixtures, obsidian floor tiles and a Jacuzzi. There was a closed door kitty-corner to that, presumably the master bedroom.

Whoever the pervert was who lived here, he had fancy taste.

Taylor crept downstairs. She heard music—some eighties-sounding synth band played at a respectful volume. Her stomach growled; she smelled bacon and pancakes. The stairs led to a living area that featured a couple of lush sectionals and a tastefully large flat-screen television mounted above another fireplace. The whole downstairs was open. She could see into the kitchen—all glittering stainless steel and polished countertops.

The so-called man downstairs sat at the kitchen counter, reading a book and sipping a cup of coffee. He didn't look like much of a man to Taylor; the guy looked like a teenager like herself. He had soft features only slightly offset by his sternly slicked-over brown hair. He wore a cashmere turtleneck and immaculately pressed slacks.

Taylor didn't wait for him to notice her. She chucked the table leg at him.

He held up a hand and the chunk of wood stopped in midair. Telekinesis.

He was Garde. But if he was also a Harvester . . . that didn't make any sense.

Taylor didn't waste time thinking about it.

"Why the hell have you brought me here, you creepy asshole?" she shouted. At the same time, from the kitchen, she grabbed a trio of cast-iron skillets and a butcher knife with her telekinesis. She flung these objects at the boy, who hadn't been able to speak at all.

He deflected each of them except the butcher knife. The blade arced through his mug, shattering it, and spraying his off-white sweater with coffee. He frowned.

Something hit Taylor in the back of the legs. A sofa. He'd pulled it into her. She fell backwards, landed softly.

"Stop," the guy commanded.

She didn't. Again with her telekinesis, she picked up the shards of his mug. Soon, they were buzzing around his face like a swarm of porcelain hornets. The guy was having a difficult time fending them off.

Taylor heard a shriek and a thud. She turned in time to see Freyja come tumbling down the stairs. The small girl's body rag-dolled to the floor, her forehead hitting the bottom step with a sickening crack.

"No!" Taylor yelled and tried to get up from the sofa. Blood was already pooling beneath Freyja's head.

But Taylor couldn't get up. Or . . . she didn't want to. A deep sense of calm settled over her body. Moments ago she'd been tense, on the attack. Now, her muscles were relaxing, her heart rate slowing. She felt the way she did after an especially hot shower, like she could just melt.

Her head heavy, she looked to the guy at the kitchen counter. He stared at her. Focused on her. There was a spot of blood on his cheek from where she managed to cut him.

"What . . . are you doing to me?" Taylor asked sleepily.

"I am making you calm," he said, his accent similar to Freyja's. "My name is Einar. I am not here to hurt you. In fact, no matter what you do here, you will not be harmed."

He pointed across the room, towards Freyja's slumped little body. "She will be hurt instead."

Taylor blinked. Analytically, the threat on a child's life disgusted her, but the dire situation didn't quite penetrate her dreamy sense of tranquility. She just wanted to chill out and float away.

"I guess . . ." Taylor shrugged. "I guess I should heal her or something, right?"

Einar studied her. "I will let you do that in a moment, but first you need to accept the reality of your situation."

Taylor put her feet up on the couch. "Sure. I accept it."

Einar rolled his eyes. "I've calmed you too much. Hold on."

The mellow vibes that had washed over Taylor like a gentle wave receded, like a shark was suddenly in the water. Her adrenaline kicked back in, her heart raced. She shot off the couch, gave Einar a horrified look and raced to Freyja's side. The fact that she hadn't done this immediately appalled Taylor—how could she just sit there on the couch?

It wasn't her. This Einar guy had done something to her.

"She's just a little girl," Taylor said as she knelt down next to Freyja.

"Yes. She's just an ordinary little girl taken from a small fishing village up the coast. Her parents love her. They would like her returned. If you behave, that might be possible," Einar intoned. The speech sounded practiced.

"You're—you're an animal," Taylor said over her shoulder.

She took Freyja's head in her hands and healed a gash at the base of her skull. The girl, still unconscious, let out a tiny moan. Taylor looked her over quickly; she was bruised from her tumble down the stairs, but none of her other injuries seemed life threatening.

Taylor stood up and rounded on Einar. He had returned to the kitchen and was pouring himself another cup of coffee.

She stalked towards him. "I don't know what sick, psycho cult thing this is—"

Einar laughed. "You think I'm one of those Harvester idiots? That's . . . actually, that's quite insulting."

Taylor picked up a broken piece of Einar's mug. She brandished the shard like a knife.

"I don't care who you are," Taylor said. She made an effort to keep her voice steady, even though her knees were shaking. "I'm leaving and I'm taking the kid with me. If you try to stop us, I swear to God, I'll cut your throat."

"God, you Americans, always like something out of an action movie," Einar said. He picked a piece of his broken mug off a plate of pancakes and bacon, flicked it aside and slid the plate towards Taylor. "I made this for you. Eat and we can talk."

He was so calm; that both frightened and angered Taylor. "You aren't listening—"

"No. You aren't listening."

Taylor felt a sharp pressure on her chin and then her head was being whipped around. He had grabbed her with his telekinesis. He was strong—stronger than she was. With Einar controlling her head, Taylor had no choice but to swing her body around to follow. He forced her gaze upwards, to a corner of the room.

A security camera.

"I am not the one who hurts the girl," Einar said. "They are watching us. This place is wired. If they lose connection, if you misbehave, if you refuse their requests—they will kill her. Then, they will bring in someone else. Another power-less innocent. One after the next, until you comply. If the fate of strangers fails to compel you, they'll move on to peo-ple you do know." Einar's voice cracked. He paused, clearing his throat. "You don't want that on your conscience, do you, Taylor?"

Einar released his hold over her. Taylor let out a breath and slumped against the counter, her neck aching. She glared at him.

"Who—who are they?"

"The Foundation for a Better World," Einar said. "They are a private company that recruits people like us—Garde—whose powers can have a positive impact on society."

"You kidnapped me," Taylor seethed. "That's not recruit-ment."

"The current political climate forces the Foundation to operate using somewhat unorthodox methods," Einar said, almost like he was reading from a press release.

Taylor continued to stare at him. He was unflappable, almost robotic. She wanted to run, but sensed that would be considered misbehavior.

Einar watched her back. He picked up a piece of bacon

from the plate he'd prepared for her. "Do you mind?" he asked, before biting into it.

"What . . . what do they want from me?" Taylor asked quietly.

"That is the good news, Taylor," Einar said with a smile. "They only want you to do what you do best. What comes naturally. They want you to heal people."

CHAPTER TWENTY-EIGHT

KOPANO OKEKE • CALEB CRANE
FRESNO, CALIFORNIA

THEY HELD ON TO THE MINIVAN FOR ONLY A FEW hours.

"Someone will have reported this stolen," Isabela explained. "The Academy people are probably already looking for us. We don't want to add local cops, too. Not to mention, that nerd at the grocery store might have reported your little scene with the clones."

"I can get us another car," Caleb offered. He drove without taking his eyes off the road, always minding the speed limit. "It's no problem."

"Not just any car," Isabela said. "We need the right car. A car that nobody will miss."

Kopano thought the Brazilian sounded a lot like his father. A gifted scammer. Those two would get along. Imagine the grifts Udo could have pulled if Isabela were his daughter. He pictured the two of them working together, the daydream ending with short-tempered Isabela berating his father. On a different day, the thought would have made Kopano smile.

He stared out the window, still thinking about last night.

The guy in the shirt and tie had done something to him, of that Kopano had no doubt. Kopano had thought he was a friend—he'd wanted to take a break in the middle of the fight to hug this well-dressed stranger!—but now felt only emptiness towards him.

And then the anger. Reflecting on what he had done, it was as if he'd had an out-of-body experience. He remembered the violence felt like pressure building up inside him. It felt so good to unleash. Pummeling those Harvesters, smashing their faces with his rock-solid fists. When they weren't enough to sate him, he had turned on Caleb and his duplicates.

Whoever got close, he threw all his strength against. They tried to fight back, but in his rage he was unbreakable.

Kopano bit his lip. He had never thought of himself as a violent person. What he'd done last night . . . that was not heroic. The devil with his briefcase had forced him to act that way.

But the very fact that his Legacies made him capable of such acts . . . he could now understand why Ran had sworn off her powers for a time. What if someone made him do that again?

His companions had been looking at him differently.

Warily. Kopano had noticed.

Had he killed any of those men? He wasn't in control of his actions and they were certainly trying to kill him, but that didn't make him forget the bodies he'd left broken on the highway. It was self-defense. It was mind control. It was . . .

Kopano rubbed his knuckles. Tried not to think about it.

"There!" Isabela shouted, pointing at a highway sign for Fresno Yosemite International Airport. "That will be perfect!"

Caleb guided their minivan towards the exit. Isabela turned around in her seat and held out her hand to Nigel.

"I will need some money," she declared.

Nigel dug into his pocket and produced the wad of bills he'd stolen from one of the Harvesters. Kopano's frown deepened; his brutality had made that possible, his roommate looting the gravely injured.

"Not exactly rolling in it," Nigel said, counting through the wadded bills. "Need to make sure we got money for petrol if we want to make it to New Mexico."

Nigel set some of the cash aside and handed Isabela the rest. She counted through it.

"It'll do," she said.

"Heartened to hear it," Nigel replied.

They drove into the airport, where Caleb and Isabela got out. Kopano took over driving duties. He hadn't been behind the wheel since his days running illicit errands in Lagos. He navigated back towards the gas station they had just passed—the last one before the airport—where they had agreed to meet back up once Caleb and Isabela had acquired a new vehicle.

"She's good to have around, innit she?" Nigel said, referring to Isabela.

"Yes," Ran agreed. "We are lucky to have someone so . . . ethically flexible."

"Speaking of which, what'd you make of those two last night?" Nigel asked. "Fancy boy in the suit and his sidekick the Loralite grower."

Kopano's hands tightened on the wheel at the mention of the mind controller.

"Not Earth Garde," Ran said simply.

"Yeah, bloody obvious, that," Nigel replied. He itched the bandage on his calf. "But who, then? Free agents? Reckon that was a Mog blaster he shot me with."

"Yes," Ran agreed. "That was strange."

"I thought the Academy had all of us Legacy types rounded up," Nigel continued thoughtfully. "I know some countries didn't join the party but I figured our people at least had tabs on 'em. Spies or what have you. So is there some other group out there? Some shadow Academy we don't know about? One fulla ne'er-do-wells in dress-up?"

The picture Nigel painted—a murky one, where Garde did not all work together for the betterment of mankind—greatly disturbed Kopano. He parked alongside the gas station, thrusting the shifter into place with more force than was necessary. He sensed both Nigel and Ran watching him.

"I'm going inside," Kopano announced. Without waiting

for a response, he got out of the van and slammed the door.

He thought of the bodies in the road, of Taylor being carried off by a strange Garde with malicious intentions. Anger bubbled up inside him. Not the violent rage the mind controller had burned into him, but a righteous fury that such awful things could happen. This world was not as he'd imagined.

"What's it like? Pretending to be someone you aren't?"

Isabela and Caleb wandered through Fresno International Airport's long-term parking lot. Just two travelers who had misplaced their car. Isabela had altered her features again. She appeared as a woman in her midthirties with tied-back black hair and glasses, wearing a professional if colorful pantsuit.

She shot him a glare when he asked his question, then quickened her pace so she could walk a few steps ahead of him.

"I already went over this with the others," she said, a note of exasperation in her voice. "I am not pretending to be anyone. That is me. At least, it is who I should be. Who I used to be."

"Oh, I don't mean that," Caleb explained hurriedly. "I mean like when you pretended to be Professor Nine or . . . or right now. How you're looking like, uh, an attractive Spanish teacher, I guess?"

Isabela smirked and raised an eyebrow at him. "Did you

have a crush on your Spanish teacher, Caleb?"

"I took German."

"Of course you did."

Caleb didn't know what that was supposed to mean, but he sensed it was an insult. Last night, he and his duplicates had stood over Isabela's prone body, protected her, while Taylor tried to heal her. But he didn't expect any special treatment from the Brazilian. What did his older brother used to call him? A magnet for mockery? That's just how it was.

"A middle-aged woman and her goofy son will draw less attention than two teenagers," Isabela said simply.

"Oh. Okay." Caleb frowned, but didn't dispute the goofy part.

They wandered down another row of cars. Isabela tapped her fingers on her chin, looking for the perfect vehicle. Caleb thought she was done talking, so was surprised when Isabela decided to elaborate.

"It is liberating, to be someone else," she said. "And it's enlightening. Seeing the world through different eyes. Seeing the way the world looks back at you, how it can be so different depending on which face you have on."

Caleb nodded, feeling a slight sense of jealousy. "Yeah. I imagine it'd be freeing."

She looked over her shoulder at him, an eyebrow raised. "What is it like to be able to physically confront the parts of yourself that you don't like, hmm?"

Caleb snorted. "What? I don't know."

"Of course you do. All those duplicates. Some of them mean, some of them geeky, some of them strange, some of them perverted." She smirked. "There are parts of me that I would like to slap across the face, if they would pop out of my brain for just a minute."

"Really?" Caleb smiled.

"No, I am perfect," Isabela replied sharply. She got up on her tiptoes and tapped Caleb on the forehead. "What is it like in there? Do they ever shut up?"

Caleb looked away. "No. Not really."

"Hmm. You know, I heard you before the Wargames started, telling Lofton your strategy ideas. He did not listen because he was stupid. But they were not bad ideas. Not as good as mine, of course, but not bad." She patted Caleb gently on the cheek. "I think you should practice being the loudest voice in the room. Or, at least, being the loudest voice in your own head. Yes?"

"Yeah," Caleb agreed. "Okay."

"Good," Isabela said, clapping her hands. She pointed out a shiny black Escalade. "Now, steal me that car."

Inside the gas station, Kopano sullenly spun a rack of postcards. Fresno, Death Valley, Salt Lake City, Las Vegas, Reno—all these colorful places flipped past. He wanted to pick a couple out to send to his little brothers. He'd written to them every week, telling them about his days at the Academy. With every postcard, the details about Kopano's training started to seem, to him, to be mundane and routine.

But his brothers always wrote back with enthusiasm, eager for more details.

His mother and father were less forthcoming in their letters. A few sentences here and there. A detail about some distant cousin who had struck it rich or fallen ill. A prayer. Earth Garde had provided them with a new apartment on Victoria Island, a secure place where they would be protected. His mother only wrote that it was "too big."

Finally, Kopano had something exciting to tell his relatives. A story of adventure scrawled on a colorful postcard. An ambush on the road, a great battle.

But adventure in the real world—the ugly real world—it no longer seemed so glamorous.

He remembered how it was after he and his father were attacked in Lagos. How he'd wanted to just go home and sleep. He wished he could do that now.

Kopano jumped as Nigel clapped him on the back. He hadn't heard his roommate approach, so lost was he in his gloomy thoughts.

"You all right, mate?"

"No. I don't think I am."

"You want to cuddle up in my lap, have a chat about it?"

Kopano looked down at the much smaller Nigel, his frown unwavering.

"This is serious," he said.

"I'm just taking the piss," Nigel replied. He glanced over his shoulder. The gas station attendant—a very tan man in his fifties wearing a sweat-stained tank top—watched them with narrowed eyes. The two of them certainly made an odd pair. Nigel elbowed Kopano. "Come on. Let's retire to the privacy of the snack aisle."

Kopano gave the postcard rack one last spin, then followed Nigel. They were surrounded on all sides by colorful packages, greasy chips and candies. Kopano's stomach growled. He ignored it.

"My mom never wanted me to eat stuff like this. She said it was how my father got his fat belly," Kopano said, wistfully dragging his fingers across a package featuring a cartoon cheetah bathing in cheese dust.

"My mum was a health nut, too. Also an actual nutter, come to think of it." Nigel put his hands on his hips and looked up at Kopano. "You want some crisps? That what this is about?"

Kopano went on as if he hadn't heard Nigel. "When I first got my powers, my family was proud. All except for my mother. The way she looked at me changed. She saw me as . . . as an abomination. Something against God. Taylor told me about those Harvester men, about the things they preached. I think, if she had been born an American, my mom might have been one of them."

Nigel leaned against the shelves, the better to look at Kopano. "Brother, I doubt that. Those Harvester wankers don't raise upstanding young lads like yourself."

"I am starting to think . . ." Kopano hesitated. "I am starting to think maybe my mom was right to look at me like that. I thought the Academy would be like one of those superhero movies, you know? But now I see what I am capable of. Now I see how the world works. For the rest of our lives, we'll have to fight like we did last night."

Nigel bit the inside of his cheek, gathering his thoughts. "I know the look you're talking about, brother. The hairy eyeball. My parentals used to hit me with that before I even got Legacies. They couldn't understand me or didn't want to. Shipped me off to a private school with a bunch of hateful rich assholes."

Kopano slowly turned to look at Nigel. "That sucks."

Nigel nodded. "It did indeed. Couldn't wait to get outta that place. John Smith gives me a telepathic ring and I bust out of Pepperpont faster than an eye blink. I felt like you did—like it was the start of some grand bloody adventure and I was the main character. All those years of suffering were leading up to this." Nigel looked down at the floor. "Got my rude awakening during the invasion. Mogs came to our hideout, killed some of my new friends and a whole lot of soldiers. Brutal stuff. Grown men screaming and crying, dragging themselves about with missing limbs. Not like in the comic books, you know?"

"No," Kopano said quietly. "It's not like that at all."

Nigel gripped Kopano's shoulder with enough force that Kopano felt his Legacy almost trigger. "But listen, I stuck it out after that, nightmares and all. So did Ran."

"She swore off her Legacies."

"Oh, so it was some other quiet Japanese girl blowing shit up last night?" Nigel asked. "She did what she had to do, when it mattered. To save lives. The world ain't pretty like we hoped, mate, it's not sequined leotards and capes."

Kopano made a face. "I didn't imagine sequins."

"Makes one of us, eh?" Nigel smirked. "Point is, we don't have to fight ugly with ugly. We can be the change we want to see in the world. You know that fuckin' cliché? The Loric didn't make us monsters and they didn't make us heroes. They just gave us bloody Legacies and said have at it. We choose what happens next."

Kopano nodded along for most of Nigel's speech, but still couldn't shake the memory of the broken bodies he'd left in the middle of the highway. "I couldn't choose last night," he said quietly and ran a hand over his face. "If I can be made to do that . . . maybe my mom is right. Maybe we shouldn't have such power, maybe—"

"I been meaning to tell you," Nigel interrupted. "Those blokes you roughed up, they were all alive when we left 'em. I should know. I was the one with the foresight to nick what they had in their pockets."

Kopano's eyebrows rose. "Really? I didn't . . . ?"

"Nah, mate. Some of 'em might not be walking right for a while, but they're all still wasting space on our unhappy planet. Even Hulked out, your heart's still big enough to pull punches, ya bloody softie."

Outside, a car horn honked. Kopano poked his head out of the snack aisle and spotted Isabela sitting shotgun in an enormous SUV. An Escalade. His father used to talk about buying a car like that when he struck it rich. Isabela dangled her arm out the window. She caught Kopano looking at her, wiggled her fingers and winked.

For the first time that day, Kopano smiled.

He turned back to Nigel.

"Yes," Kopano said. "I am ready. Let's go rescue Taylor." He paused, then put his hand on his friend's shoulder. "Thank you, Nigel."

"Wasn't nothing, mate."

Kopano left the aisle, walking out to the SUV. Nigel lingered for a moment. Ran, who had been listening from the next aisle over, appeared quietly at his side.

"You lied to him," Ran observed. "Many of those men were surely dead."

Nigel's frown deepened. "You want to tell the big guy that?"

Ran shook her head. "Such knowledge would do him no good."

CHAPTER TWENTY-NINE

TAYLOR COOK
HOFN, ICELAND

ALL SHE HAD TO DO WAS HEAL WHO THEY TOLD HER to. That was the deal.

"In exchange," Einar explained, "you will be taken care of. Once you've proven yourself to the Foundation, they will build you a place like this. You'll want for nothing."

Taylor stood at the far end of the marble kitchen counter. She still held one of the stainless steel kitchen knives. It made her feel more comfortable and Einar didn't seem to mind. He sat on a stool and picked at the plate of food he'd prepared for her. Behind them, Freyja lay on the couch, tentatively rubbing the spot on her head that had been cracked open.

The flat-screen TV, the record player and speakers, the shelves of books ranging from pretentious literary novels to pulp detective stories, the massive collection of Blu-rays. The more Taylor looked around, the more she began to see this place as an extension of Einar—a dream house for a studious young loner.

"So they built this place for you?" she asked. "Because you proved yourself?"

He nodded. "They've treated me well."

"I guess they didn't kidnap you, then?"

He raised an eyebrow. "My recruitment was not painless either."

"But you gave in, so they hooked you up."

Einar didn't respond. He cut off a corner of cold pancake and swirled it around in a skinned-over pool of syrup.

"So if I play nice, they'll build me and my dad a five-hundred-acre farm in South Dakota? Let us live out there in peace except for when I need to go off to heal someone?"

Einar set down his fork. "I'm sure a farm could be arranged. But you will have to live somewhere outside the jurisdiction of Earth Garde."

"That's what? Iceland, China, Russia . . . the Middle East?"

"Venezuela," Einar offered. "Many other nations."

"Oh, so many enticing options," Taylor said dryly.

"Better than being a prisoner who is forced to fight shadow wars for a corrupt government agency," Einar replied.

Taylor raised an eyebrow. "Oh, you aren't a prisoner?"

"No. Not like you were."

Since Taylor had gotten ahold of herself, she'd been able to better survey her surroundings. There were more cameras than the one Einar had forced her to look at. There was at least one in every room. From her current position, Taylor could see the camera hanging over Einar's refrigerator, the one positioned beneath his television and the one tucked into the corner aimed at the front door and staircase. She suspected that the glowing gem on Freyja's choker was a camera as well.

"They must really trust you," she said. "To let you live all by yourself out here without supervision."

Einar followed Taylor's gaze to the camera. He sneered. "Please. As if you aren't under constant surveillance at the Academy."

Taylor's stomach twisted into a knot. Waking up here had been so disorienting, her short confrontation with Einar so infuriating, she hadn't paused for a moment to wonder about the fate of her friends.

"What happened . . . ?" Her fingers tightened on the knife's handle. "What happened to the people I was with?"

Einar shrugged. "I don't know."

"That's it?" Taylor asked. "That's all you can say? They're my friends."

"If it helps, those Harvester fools were very poorly trained," Einar said. "I'd wager that at least some of your friends survived."

Taylor fought back the urge to stab him by looking in Freyja's direction. The little girl had curled into a ball on the couch, staring off into space.

Another detail popped into Taylor's mind. Isabela with

the dart sticking out of her neck, courtesy of a girl in a hijab.

"What about your friend?" Taylor asked. "Where's she?"

Einar's expression darkened. She had hit a nerve.

"I don't know," Einar said evenly.

"Did you leave her behind?"

"She knew the mission parameters."

A tense silence hung over him. Einar picked up his fork again, but didn't eat anything. Taylor watched him, wondering how far she could push him. Further, she decided.

"Must get pretty lonely out here by yourself. Why don't these Foundation people kidnap you some friends?"

"I have friends," Einar said somewhat defensively. "There are others. We . . . occasionally socialize."

"Until you ditch them."

"Shut up. You were unconscious. You don't know the situation."

Taylor tried to make her voice as tender and understanding as possible. "You know, I was pretty weirded out by the Academy. I didn't want to go there. There's still some stuff about it that bothers me, like all the army-type training. But this? Getting kidnapped by some . . . charity? Corporation . . . ?"

"Group of private investors," Einar said stiffly.

"Whatever. I mean, this is gross." She glanced at Freyja. "The Academy never threatened any children to get me to go there."

"They didn't have to," Einar replied. "They simply arrested and incarcerated you. Forced you to sign your rights away."

"What about her rights?" Taylor waved in Freyja's direction, realized she was still holding the knife and finally set it down. "The Academy's never killed anyone."

Einar chuckled. "They haven't? What do you think all that combat training is for? Who do you think Earth Garde fights?"

Taylor thought of Kopano—the good he talked about doing, the imagined enemies he would one day bring to justice.

"Bad guys," she said, realizing how dumb the words sounded only once they were out of her mouth.

"That's such a meaningless term," Einar replied with another infuriating chuckle. "We Human Garde, we're all still young. What do you think will happen when we're older? Wars between countries will be fought between our kind, decided by our kind. Earth Garde hopes to get a monopoly on that."

"And your precious Foundation doesn't?"

Einar stood up, took the plate of food and dumped it into a tall garbage can.

"The Foundation only invests in Garde with nonviolent Legacies," he said, his back to her. "The others are viewed as threats to the human race."

"Invests," Taylor repeated with a shake of her head. She waited for Einar to turn back her way so she could study him. "Seriously, you're acting like this isn't insane and illegal. Did they brainwash you or something?"

"No," he replied curtly. "Feel free to make use of my home.

You know what will happen if you do anything stupid. I'm going to take a nap."

"A nap. You're going to take a nap?"

Einar nodded and went around the counter—taking the long way so he wouldn't come into stabbing range—and headed for the stairs. "We have an appointment later. Well, you do. You'll want to be rested, too."

Taylor couldn't rest. Now that the effects of the tranquilizer had worn off, she felt too energetic. Instead, she explored Einar's Icelandic hideaway.

For all his movies and books and expensive gadgets, the first thing Taylor noticed was that the place lacked a computer. Maybe there was a laptop or something up in his bedroom, but Taylor suspected that wasn't the case. Just like the Academy regulated their internet use, so did this shadowy Foundation.

After a little poking around, Taylor went to the front door. Her hand hesitated over the handle. Was she allowed outside? She figured there would be a hydraulic lock like the one on her bedroom if the outdoors was off-limits. Taylor tested the knob. The door opened easily.

Cold air rushed in. After a few months in California, Taylor wasn't used to the chill. And she was still wearing the flannel pajamas she'd woken up in. She opened a nearby coat closet and found a pair of fur-lined moccasins and a heavy leather jacket. They were Einar's. She could smell his sandalwood cologne on the coat and it almost changed her mind about going outside. She took a breath, shrugged on the coat and stepped into the bracing air.

Oddly, the seclusion reminded Taylor of home. She looked around the rocky landscape as she stepped away from Einar's cabin—not another house in sight. There was a dark blue hatchback parked along the side of the house. She could make that her getaway vehicle if worse came to worst.

Taylor laughed bitterly. Wasn't this already the worst? When she developed her powers, she couldn't have imagined a more bizarre fate. She'd resented having to go to the Academy, but at least she was settling in there. The instructors were kind, she had friends, she was learning about herself. This . . . this Foundation situation, it was on a whole different level of strange and disturbing.

She heard footsteps crunch behind her. Little Freyja had followed her outside, snuggled up in a blanket.

A dark part of Taylor's mind reminded her that she hardly knew this girl. She could make a run for it. If she could live with Freyja on her conscience . . .

No. She couldn't. She would never be able to live with herself. Taylor glanced once more at the car. There wouldn't be any escape. Not if she couldn't figure out how to save the kid, too.

Taylor looked up at what she thought was Einar's window. She wondered how the Foundation had convinced him to join them. Did he have a Freyja, too? He was so cold, it seemed unlikely.

"Thank you," Freyja said quietly, arriving at her side. "For healing me."

"You're welcome," Taylor replied. "I'm sorry that you have to go through this."

"Me too," Freyja said. "Do you know when I'll get to go home?"

"No, I don't."

"When you give them what they want, right?"

"I guess so."

"Will that be soon?"

"I don't know."

The two lapsed into a melancholy silence. Taylor trudged towards the crystalline lake, Freyja following a few steps behind her. A chill wind swept in over the water, bobbing the chunks of vivid blue ice that floated on the surface. She could hear the ice crackling and shifting as the blocks bumped against each other.

"It's beautiful here, at least," Taylor said.

Freyja said nothing. Taylor looked over at her, saw that she was worming her index finger under the choker.

"It's cold on my skin," Freyja said with a sigh.

"Do you remember what happened before?" Taylor asked. "When you fell down the stairs?"

"This . . . this shocked me," Freyja said, dropping her hand away from the collar as if she were scared it would happen again. "I fainted."

"Jesus Christ," muttered Taylor. "This is demented."

Taylor turned away from the frozen lake and headed around the side of the house. She wanted to see the place from every angle.

"What're you doing?" Freyja asked, dutifully following behind her.

"Just looking around."

"For what?"

"I'm not sure yet."

On the back of the house, Taylor found a small wooden sunporch, the reddish timber coated in a thin layer of frost. The porch overlooked a rock garden. Polished stones were stacked atop of each other, some of them decorated with hardy vines. A small fountain stood in the middle of it all, although it was turned off at the moment.

At the back of the rock garden stood a high wooden fence. Taylor approached, walking the perimeter of the fence. It was a square, about twenty feet in each direction. On the side nearest the porch was a door with a keypad just like the one on Taylor's room.

"What's he got back there?" Taylor wondered aloud.

"I don't know," Freyja replied, her teeth chattering.

"If you're cold, you can go inside," Taylor said.

Freyja remained stubbornly nearby. Was she afraid that Taylor would try to escape if Freyja let her out of her sight? Taylor couldn't blame her.

With her telekinesis, Taylor knocked over one of the stone sculptures and floated a good-size block of granite over to the fence. Freyja jumped out of the way.

"What're you doing?" Freyja asked.

Taylor hopped up onto the stone. If she jumped from there, she could reach the top of the fence. "I want to see what's in there."

She leaped up, grasping the wooden barrier with both hands. She pulled herself the rest of the way, managed to swing one leg up so that she was straddling the fence.

Down below, inside the cube of fence, was just another rock.

But not just any rock. This one glittered cobalt blue, but in a shade different from the ice on the lake. The rock made something in Taylor vibrate. It called to her.

Loralite. That was Loralite.

Taylor knew the stories. All she had to do was hop down and touch the alien rock, visualize another stone's location and the Loralite would teleport her across the world. This must be how Einar brought her here.

Freyja let out a sharp cry. Taylor turned her head in time to see the wide-eyed girl clutch at her choker.

"It—it shocked me!" Freyja yelped.

With a frustrated grumble, Taylor climbed down from the fence. She landed next to Freyja and gently stroked the girl's shoulder.

"Sorry. Guess whoever's watching wanted to give me a warning."

Freyja said nothing. She rubbed her neck and stared sullenly at Taylor.

"Come on," Taylor said. "Let's go inside."

Halfway to the back porch, both of them stopped in their tracks. They heard the crackle of gravel and the purr of an engine.

Someone was driving up the solitary road.

Without stopping to think, Taylor ran around the side of the house, Freyja a few steps behind her. She wasn't sure what she was going to do, exactly. If this was some random Icelandic police officer or the mailman—she couldn't very well involve them without risking their life too. Still, she wanted to see who came to this remote location. Maybe it would give her an idea.

Taylor caught sight of the car coming down the road before she fully rounded the cabin's corner. Something about the vehicle gave her pause. It was a green Jeep, mud-splattered and dented from hard driving, with chains on the wheels. There were four men inside, but from her viewpoint Taylor could make out only the one sitting shotgun. He had reddish-brown hair, a thick beard and bulging neck muscles. Even at this distance, Taylor could see the fat scar that ran from his eye to the corner of his mouth.

These were not friendly neighbors.

The Jeep parked in front of the house. Taylor waited a few seconds, hidden around the corner, curious to see what they would do.

Nothing. The men just sat there. One of them rolled down a window to smoke a cigarette.

Freyja was at her side, one of her hands on Taylor's arm. "Who is it?" she whispered, then peeked around the corner to see for herself.

The girl nearly tripped over her own feet in her hurry to backpedal away. Freyja's face had gone ghostly white. She recognized them, Taylor realized. And she was terrified.

"Who are they?" Taylor asked.

"Those are the men," Freyja replied. "The men who took me."

CHAPTER THIRTY

ISABELA SILVA
OUTSIDE SILVER CITY, NEW MEXICO

IT WAS A FOURTEEN-HOUR DRIVE TO SILVER CITY.
They bought a map from the gas station to help navigate.

"We want to stick to back roads, yeah?" said Nigel. "Don't want to be spotted."

Isabela drew a random pattern on the Escalade's tinted window. "No one will spot us. And no one will be looking for this car."

Caleb traced his finger east across the map. "There aren't really any back roads, anyway. Or it's all back roads. I can't tell." He held up the map so Nigel, driving, could see. "All the way through the desert."

Nigel nodded. "Lovely." He checked the gas gauge. "Could've nicked us something with a bit more fuel efficiency, Izzy."

She snorted. "That's what you're worried about?"

"Limited funds," Nigel said. "And a long bloody drive."

Ran reached out with her telekinesis and plucked the wad of bills from Nigel's cargo pocket. She counted through them. "I think we have enough," she announced.

"Hope so," Caleb said.

Isabela groaned. "God, we'll be fine. If we run out of money, we get more. No big deal."

"You mean steal more," Kopano said.

"Uh, yeah," Isabela replied. "Obviously."

Kopano was quiet for a moment. "We must find Taylor. That is the most important thing. But when that is done, we should make sure the cars we stole are returned to their owners. And that anything else we take is returned." He looked out the window. "I do not want to be a thief."

"Sure, mate," Nigel said. "We'll send 'em nice thank-you notes, too."

Soon, they had left the city behind and were cutting across the desert. Scrubby plants and cactus whipped by, whorls of reddish sand blown across the hot pavement. They passed through Joshua Tree, the fuzzy branches of the yucca trees reaching up like twisted alien arms. As they drove out of California and into Arizona the land became flat and burned, the view dotted by bursts of emerald palms that stood in opposition to the sun. For stretches, they could see for miles, but then the horizon would rise up and become mountainous. They navigated through chasms, the highway itself cut through the jagged sandstone mountains.

"I just saw a cattle skull on the side of the road," Caleb said as he peered out the window. "You know, with like the horns all bleached by the sun?"

"So?" Nigel replied.

Caleb shrugged. "Dunno. Thought that was just a thing they put in movies to make it seem hot out." He paused thoughtfully. "There's this game we could play. Roadkill bingo?"

"No," Isabela said sharply.

They all took turns behind the wheel. Whoever sat shotgun tried to keep the driver company. The others took turn dozing off, either sitting upright in the middle row or stretched out across the backseat.

Isabela was grateful that they'd found a blanket in the trunk. When she felt herself getting tired from all the sitting around and endless desert, she draped herself across the backseat and pulled the blanket over her. She turned to face the trunk, leaving a small gap in the blanket for air. This way, no one would be able to see her when she dozed off. None of the others commented on her huddled form.

When Isabela woke up, they were driving on the outskirts of Phoenix. It was sunset. The city glittered orange in the distance, an oasis of glass and life after hours of mountains. She shifted around under her blanket to get a look at the others. Nigel and Ran were both asleep, too, Nigel with his head resting on the Japanese girl's shoulder. Isabela smirked at that. In front, Caleb drove while Kopano kept him company.

The two of them were quietly talking about Taylor, going

over the events of the night before for the hundredth time. The guy who had taken her didn't seem like a Harvester. Unlike the cult, whoever he was, he wanted Taylor alive. Both Kopano and Caleb agreed that was a good thing. Well, as much as kidnapping could be a good thing.

"If he has hurt her in any way," Kopano declared, "I will have vengeance."

"Yeah," Caleb agreed. "Me too."

Under her blanket, Isabela rolled her eyes.

"I am sorry, by the way," Kopano said. "For throwing you through the windshield of that car."

Caleb rubbed the back of his neck, which was covered in small cuts and bruised up. Isabela noticed he had been sitting rigidly, but she'd thought that was just Caleb's normal posture. He was hurt, she realized. Ribs probably broken, but hiding it.

"No worries," Caleb told Kopano. "It wasn't you. That prick took control somehow."

Did either of the two would-be heroes know they both had a crush on Taylor? They were both oblivious and going out of their way to be nice, but Isabela figured they had to see each other as competition. All that macho talk, battling over who could promise revenge with the most gravitas. Dense boys. She couldn't wait to tell Taylor about this.

Weeks ago, Isabela realized, she would've been jealous of Taylor getting all this attention. But now, she missed her friend. She even felt a tinge of sadness for the two love-struck meatheads in the front of the van, at least one of whom would surely be rejected.

Ugh. She was getting soft.

It took another couple of hours to reach New Mexico. By then, night had fallen and they were all awake.

They found Silver City and then Route 15. Caleb unfolded the map and studied it in the Escalade's yellowish dome light. Silver City's architecture was more modest than Phoenix, the buildings not as glittery and lower slung, man-made hunks of stone popping up from the desert.

"Did they want their town to look like a graveyard?" Isabela asked.

"The place we're looking for isn't really in town," Caleb said. "I think it's up north in the forest."

They passed along the edge of town and drove to Gila National Forest. According to the map, the area stretched over four thousand square miles. The rocky desert sloped upwards, gradually giving way to masses of thick, triangular pine trees. The grass grew taller here and didn't look as scorched; it appeared purple and wavy in the moonlight. They ascended via a series of switchbacks, the trees thickened and soon the dots of light from Silver City were swallowed up behind them.

For a while, there wasn't another car on the road. Nearby, a wolf howled.

"Bloody hell," Nigel said. "Of course they would set up in axe murderer country."

"I find it serene," Ran replied.

Nigel smirked at her. "See if you still think that when

312

some inbred bloke in a hockey mask is carving you up into little pieces."

Ran looked back at him. "I would like to see this bloke try."

Isabela chuckled, enjoying the banter. It helped ease the mood a bit. Kopano and Caleb were both wholly focused on the road ahead, ready for battle at any moment.

"Are we sure this is even the right way?" Isabela asked.

As if in answer, a pair of headlights appeared behind them. Kopano squinted into the rearview and slowed down a bit. The glowing headlamps behind them crisscrossed— not a car, but two motorcycles—the bikes soon careening by them up the road. They each carried the sort of leather-clad tough guy who had accosted the Garde last night.

"Want to bet those lads show us the way?" Nigel asked.

"Do not get too close to them," Ran warned.

Kopano let the motorcycles get out of sight, then continued up the winding road through the forest. Five minutes later, as they came around a bend, a wooden sign wreathed in Christmas lights came into view. Scrawled in chipped paint across the boards—*APACHE JACK'S*.

"My dad used to talk about places like this," Caleb said. "Dive bars off the beaten path. Used to brag about all the brawls he got into."

"Thanks for sharing," Isabela said.

A hundred years ago, Apache Jack's was probably a trading post. There was still a hitching rail outside the long brick building, but instead of horses there were now motorcycles parked in front. The gravel parking lot was also filled with trailers, pickup trucks and muscle cars, many of these decorated to look like postapocalyptic war machines. The whole scene was lit by neon beer signs in the bar windows and fire barrels in the parking lot. A couple dozen men milled around the vehicles or drank on the shaded porch. Half of them were armed with either shotguns or rifles.

Kopano slowed the Escalade, but Isabela snapped at him, "Keep going!"

"But . . . she could be in there."

"Does it look like we would belong in that parking lot?" Isabela asked. "I'm surprised they're not already shooting at us. Go, go, go!"

Kopano stepped on the gas and they zoomed by Apache Jack's. Some of the men in the parking lot tracked the Escalade with their eyes, but none of them made any move to follow. As they drove by, Isabela caught a glimpse of some kind of tall wooden structure behind the bar but couldn't make out any details.

They put a half mile of winding road between them and Apache Jack's to make sure they weren't followed. Eventually, Kopano pulled off to the side of the road and killed the engine.

"How are we going to do this?" he asked.

"We can hike in through the woods," Ran said. "Come at the place from the back."

"I should go in alone," Isabela said. "Do . . . what do you call it? Reconnaissance."

They turned around to look at Isabela and all of them jumped when they saw her new appearance.

She had taken on the look of a male midfifties biker. Hefty and hairy, with coarse salt-and-pepper hair tied in a sloppy ponytail. She wore an open leather vest that exposed her prodigious beer belly, a pair of scuffed-up jeans and cowboy boots.

"What do you think?" Isabela asked, her normal voice issuing from the biker's chapped lips.

"Your hottest look yet," Nigel said, staring at her.

"You want to make out with me?" Isabela asked, leering.

Ran reached back and poked Isabela's new belly. "Very good," she said.

Isabela grinned, the biker's teeth yellow and crooked. "Thank you."

"I could go in with you," Caleb offered. He looked around at the others. "No offense to you guys, but the rest of you wouldn't be able to pass for a Harvester."

"No offense taken, mate," Nigel said.

"But if there are any of them in there who were at the fight last night, they will definitely recognize you," Kopano said. "There were a bunch of you."

Caleb frowned. "I guess you're right."

"It'll be easy," Isabela said. "I'll sneak in there, find out if they've got Taylor or the little bitch who shot me and if not I'll ask a few questions. Find out what they know. You all watch from the woods. If I get in trouble, I'll send a signal."

"What kind of signal?" Ran asked.

Isabela shrugged. "I'll have to improvise. So, just keep an eye out."

"If you're gone too long, we'll come in looking for you," Caleb said.

Isabela stroked her blubbery man-belly in a way she hoped was disturbing. "Give me some time, cowboy. This is a slow-moving body I'm in."

Caleb chuckled and looked away.

"Ugh," Nigel added.

"We should try not to kill any of them," Kopano said suddenly. "These people should be brought to justice for what they've done . . ."

Ran and Nigel exchanged a look. Caleb said nothing, just stared out the window.

"Okay?" Kopano pressed.

"With any luck," Isabela said, "they will never know we're here."

The five of them left the Escalade behind and hiked downhill through the trees. They moved cautiously and Nigel used his Legacy to muffle the sounds of their approach. As the lights from Apache Jack's appeared, they realized their caution had been pointless. The Harvesters didn't have any guards posted. Most of them were too busy getting drunk. The Garde huddled in the shadowed cover of the trees and watched them.

"They must think this is a safe place for them," Ran observed.

"Well, the madmen don't lack for artillery," Nigel said,

pointing out a number of armed Harvesters milling around on the bar's back porch.

"These types of guys always carry guns with them," Caleb said. "It's their thing."

"What are they doing with that?" Kopano asked.

He pointed out the wooden structure that Isabela had noticed from the road. It was a twenty-foot-high snake in a ready-to-strike S shape, the thing made out of thin slats of clapboard and wicker. The snake sat atop a mound of sand. At its base—right at the snake's belly—there was a small door secured with a padlock. A few Harvesters milled around the snake, stuffing rags in between the wooden ribs. The wind picked up and carried the smell of gasoline to the Garde.

"That, my friends, is a good old-fashioned effigy," Nigel said. "The nutters are probably gonna light it up and dance around it naked before commencing the orgy." He glanced at Isabela. "Have fun with that."

Her biker's face contorted in a very uncharacteristic moue of disgust. "Nasty."

"That is a cell," Ran observed, pointing at the locked opening. "They are going to put someone in there."

"Our kind are the snakes in their stupid bloody metaphor," Nigel said.

"Taylor," Kopano whispered. "They would . . . they would burn her?"

"Still want to go easy on them, mate?" Nigel asked.

Kopano said nothing. The five of them remained still for a few more moments. Finally, Isabela stood up from her crouch, dramatically knuckling the broad back of her biker body.

"I'm going in," she announced, her voice now gruff enough to match her costume.

"Be careful," Caleb said.

Isabela strutted out of the woods. She walked the way she had seen some of the older men move around the Rio beaches; like her balls were too big for her pants and constantly getting in the way. Belly thrust forward, knees pointed out, shoulders back. When the first Harvester noticed her, she made a show of zipping up her fly as if she'd just returned from pissing in the woods.

Before leaving her friends, Isabela took the pamphlet that Nigel had swiped from one of the defeated Harvesters. If anyone questioned her slovenly alter ego, she planned to use that as her invitation. None of the Harvesters hanging around the back of Apache Jack's paid her any attention. Most of them were too busy putting the finishing touches on the effigy. A pair of scrawny college-age boys with matching sets of cauliflower ears nodded at her as she climbed the porch's rickety staircase.

"You ready for tonight, old-timer?" one of them asked.

"Hell yeah," Isabela replied.

"Can't wait until they light that bitch up," said the other, raising his beer bottle in Isabela's direction, then throwing back the contents.

Isabela grunted a response—that's how these types communicated—and made her way to the bar's back door.

A woman in her fifties sat on a stool next to the entrance, smoking a cigarette. She wore ill-fitting leather, her neck swimming in beads and charms.

"Haven't seen you before," the woman said as she tapped some ash off her cigarette.

"First time," Isabela said. She tried to move past the woman, but she wedged her foot against the screen door. Was this old hag flirting?

"Picked an interesting night to join the movement, honey."

Isabela paused. She sensed the two drunks behind her were now watching her exchange with the woman. She took the pamphlet out of her pocket and handed it over.

"Jimbo asked me to ride up here," she said in her scratchy voice. "Where's he at?"

Isabela detected something wrong immediately. An uneasy silence fell across the back patio. The older woman's face fell and she traded looks with the two men standing behind Isabela.

After a moment, the woman spoke. "You ain't heard?"

"Heard what?"

"Reverend Jimbo's dead," she said. "Killed by those abominations."

Oops, thought Isabela and stifled a smirk. Instead, she clenched her fists.

"When did that happen?" she growled. "How?"

"Last night," the woman replied. "Probably while you was making your way here." She shook her head. "We're going to pay them back, though. Promise you that."

Isabela nodded. "Who's in charge now?"

The woman jerked a thumb over her shoulder. "You want to talk to Darryl. Big guy. Skull tattoo."

Isabela grunted her thanks and was finally allowed to step inside. The smell of gasoline struck her immediately. The back hallway of Apache Jack's was cluttered with canisters of the stuff. Up ahead, she heard heavy metal blasting and men and women shouting at each other. She lumbered in the direction of the barroom.

She passed by a pair of bathrooms, the stink rolling out of them unacceptable. Isabela kept the disgust from registering on her face; she wasn't alone. Up ahead, two men with shotguns stood guard in front of a metal door. They were both thickly built, scarred up, with the Harvester symbol branded into their forearms. They weren't day-players like some of these people; they were real killers.

Isabela made note of them. Unusual to have a couple of badass dudes guarding the bar's freezer. She nodded as she walked by them. They nodded back.

She emerged into the bar proper. The screaming and thrashing music was worse than the garbage Nigel listened to. The room was crowded, nearly every seat filled. Mostly men, but a few women—an assortment of bikers and cowboy types, all of them with that same stupid tattoo. They guzzled beer and shouted at each other about conspiracy theories that Isabela couldn't make sense of—chem trails, sovereign citizens, Loric anal probes, blah blah blah.

A huge photo of a greasy old man sat on the bar

surrounded by wilted flowers and shell casings. The Harvesters kept coming over to dribble beer or liquor in front of it. She assumed that was the deceased reverend.

No one paid Isabela any undue attention. She bellied up to the bar and surveyed the crowd, looking for a skull tattoo. Finally, she noticed the bartender, the sleeves ripped off his flannel shirt, had a skull with a dagger plunged through the eyehole inked on his bicep. She waved him over.

"Everything's on the house," he said, "on account of the funeral."

"Get me a beer," she said.

The bartender went and came back with a frothy mug. Isabela resisted the urge to wrinkle her nose at the glass, which had smudges all over the rim.

"You Darryl?" she asked.

The bartender squinted at her. "Nah," he replied when Isabela simply stared back at him. He waved towards the guarded freezer. "If you want him, he's in with the creature."

The creature.

Isabela grunted her thanks and waited, not drinking any of the beer. Subterfuge was one thing, but she wasn't risking catching whatever contagious stupidity was circulating around this bar.

She sat on a stool and waited, keeping an eye on the cooler. After about five minutes, the door squealed open and a tall man wearing a black duster emerged. The man was bald, a complicated spiderweb tattooed across his skull. The woman outside had been being literal.

Darryl said something to the guards, then headed down the hall, into one of the smelly bathrooms. Casually, Isabela got up from her stool, walked past the two guards and followed him in.

Two stalls and two urinals, a sink with a cracked mirror, mold and mildew all over the broken floor tiles. Isabela paused just inside the doorway, observing it all. There was a Harvester at a urinal. Darryl stood at the sink, washing blood off his hands. Isabela checked the bathroom door. It had a dead bolt.

None of the men looked at each other. Isabela went to the other urinal and set her mug of beer on top of the cracked porcelain. She pretended to pee while waiting for the other Harvester to leave. He didn't wash his hands.

As soon as he walked out, she used her telekinesis to lock the bathroom's dead bolt. She turned around to look at Darryl.

"Heard you got one of those abominations," she said.

Darryl glanced over his shoulder and grunted. He continued scrubbing his hands. "Got the thing's blood on me. Don't want to catch some extraterrestrial plague."

"She still alive?"

"Of course. We going to burn the sin out of her proper, like Jimbo would've wanted." Darryl half turned, surprised to find Isabela standing right behind him. "Who are—?"

Isabela smashed her beer mug across his face.

Darryl reeled but didn't go down. Blood streamed down the side of his face, into one of his eyes. He took a swing at her, but Isabela ducked with agility that must have seemed supernatural for a fat biker. She thrust out with her telekinesis and slammed Darryl's face into the bathroom mirror.

He slumped over the sink, breathing heavily but not yet unconscious. Isabela leaped onto his back. She clenched her legs around his torso and looped her arm around his neck. Squeezed. She'd learned the chokehold at a self-defense class before she even came to the Academy.

Darryl's legs gave way. Isabela rode him to the floor, pleased with the sound his face made when it smacked against the tiles. He was out.

With her telekinesis, Isabela hoisted Darryl's body and shoved it into one of the empty stalls. She sat him on the toilet and studied his busted face.

Then, she shape-shifted into him.

Isabela stepped out of the stall and telekinetically locked it from the other side. She looked at her new appearance in the cracked bathroom mirror. Gross, but accurate.

Just then, someone tried to enter the bathroom, found it locked and pounded on the door.

Isabela as Darryl yanked the door open. She stared down at one of the boys from outside. He took an uneasy step back.

"What're . . . you looking at?" she asked, not meaning to pause so much. Isabela hesitated because she hadn't heard Darryl talk enough to perfectly mimic his voice. With the loud music, she hoped it wouldn't matter.

"Sorry, Darryl," the guy muttered.

Isabela shouldered by him.

She approached the freezer. The two guards stepped aside for her.

"Boys say the snake is ready," one of them said. "You want help bringing her outside?"

A fuzzy feeling came over Isabela as she tried to answer. For some reason, she was really struggling with Darryl's voice. This hadn't happened to her before. Nerves?

"I want . . . more minutes . . . ," Isabela grunted. "I'll bring her out . . . quick."

The guards eyed her, but they didn't make any move to stop her. They probably just assumed that Darryl had chugged some grain alcohol like all the other drunks in this freak show. Isabela unlatched the freezer, yanked open the door and stepped into the cold. She slammed the door behind her.

Isabela immediately had to swallow back a scream. A gutted deer carcass hung from a hook right in front of her. She carefully stepped around the animal, her breath misting in front of her.

The girl from the road, the one with the headscarves, hung by the arms behind the deer. Her headscarves were gone, her raven hair loose and greasy, blood clumping the curls together. The girl had been beaten savagely—her face was swollen, lips split, her clothes bloody tatters. Isabela's stomach turned over. Yes, this girl had made an enemy of her, but no one deserved this disgusting brutality.

At least they hadn't put her on a hook. Instead, the girl's hands were secured by a pair of the heavy-duty handcuffs the Peacekeepers had used against the Garde. The magnetized cuffs were attached to the corrugated-metal ceiling. Isabela also noticed a couple of strange objects attached to the girl's temples—triangular in shape, about the size of quarters, they looked like twin microchips. Some kind of Garde-fighting technology, surely, but not something she'd seen demonstrated back at the Academy.

Isabela approached the girl. Her breathing was ragged, her lips blue from spending so much time in the freezer. With a cautious glance over her shoulder, Isabela shape-shifted back into her normal form. She touched the girl gently on the chin, eliciting an exhausted moan.

"Please . . . ," the girl said, followed by words Isabela didn't understand.

"Stupid, open your eyes," Isabela snapped.

The girl did open her eyes at the sound of Isabela's voice. She gasped and strained against her bonds, babbling away in a language Isabela recognized but didn't understand. Isabela shook her.

"Stop talking," Isabela ordered, speaking quickly. "I will get you out of here, but only if you lead us to our friend who you kidnapped. Otherwise, you are useless and can stay here. They plan to set you on fire, so at least that will be a relief after this cold."

The girl stared at her. "English?" she asked. "English, please?"

Isabela stared back at her, brow furrowed. "I am speaking English, you stupid . . ."

She paused. The fuzzy feeling she'd felt before. The difficulty finding the right words for Darryl. It wasn't because she hadn't heard him speak enough . . .

Isabela looked down at her wrist. The bracelet. She tugged at it, looking for the one bead that should be emitting a faint glow. Brought her face close, cupped her hand against her wrist to see . . .

When was the last time she'd visited Simon for a recharge?

Slowly, it dawned on Isabela that she'd been speaking to this girl in Portuguese.

The bracelet was dark. Useless jewelry.

Her English was gone. Behind her, the door to the freezer clanked. Someone was coming in.

"Merda," Isabela said.

CHAPTER THIRTY-ONE

TAYLOR COOK
HOFN, ICELAND

AS TAYLOR CREPT BACK INTO THE HOUSE, SHE heard Einar's raised voice coming from upstairs. He was yelling at someone.

She took the stairs quickly, but as quietly as she could. Freyja stayed in the living room, furtively peeking through the curtains at the men in the Jeep.

At the end of the upstairs hallway, Einar's door was ajar. Taylor tiptoed forward. Through the crack, she saw Einar pacing back and forth, obviously agitated. The flat-screen TV on his wall was tuned to a video conference. Taylor could see only the lower-right corner of the screen—a woman, blond hair in a proper bob, a white dress shirt and pinstriped jacket, professional. Seeing only the woman's mouth and shoulders wouldn't be enough to identify her, if

Taylor was ever able to get out of here. She inched closer.

"Please explain to me why there's a team of Blackstone men parked outside my house," Einar growled.

"You know why," she replied with icy professionalism. Her accent was British. "There is concern your location is compromised."

"Nonsense."

"Rabiya knows how to get to you, does she not? You lost Rabiya. Therefore, your location is compromised. The Blackstone men are simply there as a precaution."

"If you'd let me take them on the mission instead of those moronic Harvesters, this never would've happened," Einar replied.

Taylor inched closer, trying to get a better look at the woman. A floorboard creaked under her foot.

"Now, Einar," the woman said, drowning out Taylor's misstep. "'Tis the poor craftsman who blames his tools. Rabiya is quite valuable to the Foundation. We've yet to catalog another Garde capable of producing Loralite."

"For weeks all you could talk about was acquiring another goddamn healer," Einar hissed. "I got her for you. If I hadn't—if I hadn't escaped when I did, all three of us would have been killed."

"So you said in your report," the woman replied dryly. "Nonetheless, it was sloppy work. Earth Garde is making inquiries. Thus, we are keeping the Blackstone men close by in the event we need to liquidate the Iceland side of our operation."

Taylor didn't like the sound of that. Creeping closer, she made out more details of the Foundation woman. A sharp blue eye, delicate wrinkles, maybe in her late forties or early fifties . . .

"Please, listen," Einar said beseechingly, obviously not liking the connotation of "liquidate" any more than Taylor. "You don't understand what it was like—"

"We've moved up your appointment. The others are tele-porting in," the woman interrupted crisply. "Get your house in order, Einar. She is eavesdropping."

The screen went abruptly blank. Taylor glanced up, saw the hallway camera pointed in her direction and cursed under her breath. So, that was the woman on the other side of all this surveillance. She wished she had gotten a better look.

Einar stood in his doorway, glaring at her, his face a cold mask. He had changed out of his coffee-stained sweater and into an immaculately tailored gray suit. Taylor felt suddenly underdressed in her pajamas and borrowed leather coat.

"Are we going to prom?" she asked.

"Get dressed," he said simply. "We're leaving."

"Who was that woman? Your mean British nanny?"

"You may get to meet her one day, if things go well. She's a visionary."

"Oh, wow, do you promise?" Taylor replied with a snort. She locked eyes with Einar, probing for weaknesses like Isa-bela would. "You're in trouble, aren't you?"

"No."

"You screwed up in California. I heard her. Made a big mess. They're going to liquidate you."

"Not me," Einar replied with a meaningful look.

"Yeah, right. I'm a healer. Sounds like I'm more valuable than you." She made a point of addressing the camera overhead. "You'd rather have me than this fussy screwup, right?"

Einar took a sharp step towards her. "Stop it."

"They don't care about you," Taylor said quietly. "Or me. But the Academy could protect us. They'll be looking for me . . ."

Einar laughed in her face. She'd been close to getting a reaction out of him, but had pushed too hard in the wrong direction.

"I told you. Get dressed," Einar said through his teeth.

Taylor's muscles tensed. Her heart beat faster, stomach rolling over. She was suddenly afraid. Taylor took a step backwards, towards her room. She better do what he said or else—

No. She noticed the way Einar looked at her. Concentrated on her. This was his Legacy again. He was manipulating her emotions. Knowing that didn't make the fear any easier to resist.

"Stop—stop it," she said.

"Go," he ordered.

Taylor's palms started to sweat and her knees almost buckled. She gritted her teeth, but couldn't keep her body from reacting. With a yelp, she ran for her room, slamming the door behind her as if there were a monster on her heels.

In a way, she thought, there was.

The fear didn't subside until she began changing into the clothes Freyja had brought for her that morning. An austere peach-colored blouse and a long black skirt. The outfit was stuffy and didn't fit her exactly right. She had to roll up the sleeves. There was also a long sash of dark silk that she didn't know what to do with.

She came back out of her room and found Einar still waiting outside. The fear was gone now, resentment in its place.

"You're an asshole," she said.

Einar frowned. He held out his hand and took the silk from her. Then, before Taylor could stop him, he stepped in close and began loosely wrapping the scarf around her head. Taylor had to resist the urge to punch him in the mouth. Once her head was properly covered, Einar stepped back to appreciate his work.

"There's a dress code where we're going," he said.

"And where is that?"

"Abu Dhabi."

"What? Seriously?"

Einar headed downstairs, forcing Taylor to chase after him. Freyja was still wrapped in the curtains, keeping a close eye on the men parked outside. Taylor glanced in her direction and grimaced. Einar ignored the young girl completely, marching towards the back deck.

"What about her?" Taylor asked.

"Who?"

"Freyja. You know, your other prisoner."

"She stays here," he replied. "If you have an idea that you might do something stupid, imagine her dying gruesomely."

Einar shoved open the back door and strode across his frost-covered deck. Taylor hurried after him, grateful that Freyja was out of earshot.

"Isn't that going to happen anyway?" she asked. "I heard that Foundation lady use the word 'liquidate.'"

Einar paused and turned to look at her. "That isn't going to happen."

"But if it does . . ." Taylor waved towards the front yard. "Those guys outside will kill her, right?"

Before he responded, Einar glanced over Taylor's head at the camera mounted over his back door. It seemed to Taylor he wasn't sure how much he should say.

"That won't happen," Einar repeated. "We're too valuable."

He didn't sound entirely convinced.

Einar crossed through the rock garden and approached the wooden enclosure that contained the Loralite stone. Taylor watched over his shoulder as he punched in the four-digit access code, making no effort to hide it.

"All right," Taylor said resignedly. "So, what are we doing in Abu Dhabi?"

"You and the others will be healing the prince of one of the royal families," Einar replied, pushing the wooden gate open.

Taylor blinked. So many questions. "What others?" she asked first.

"You make the fourth healer the Foundation has acquired."

"Four," Taylor repeated. She was the only healer enrolled at the Academy. "You've kidnapped four . . ."

As they approached the Loralite, the chunk of cobalt stone pulsed in greeting, the glow coming and going like a heartbeat.

"The prince has leukemia," Einar continued matter-of-factly. "The others have so far been unsuccessful in healing him. Hopefully, the addition of your power will be enough." He put his hand on the Loralite stone, then hesitated, biting the inside of his cheek. "It has to be enough," he said, "or this entire operation will be judged a failure."

Liquidate. The word echoed in Taylor's mind and a sense of nervousness fluttered in her belly. She thought of the cancer patient who she had failed to heal back in California. Would failure here mean punishment? Death for Freyja? Some other unimaginable consequence? Her mind worked feverishly—she needed to save Freyja and escape—but she saw no outs. All she could do was continue to play this game.

Einar held out his hand impatiently. "Coming?"

Taylor made a face, wanting to be sure Einar saw her look of revulsion, before taking his hand.

The world spun and reality bent. Taylor had been unconscious when they last teleported, so this was her first experience with the alien process. It felt like her body dissolved—not in an unpleasant way—but a gentle coming apart, as if in a dream. The only thing she could still feel was Einar's hand, like an anchor that dragged her towards their destination. She felt dizzy, a speck of dirt blown in the wind. For a moment, her vision was filled with darkness penetrated by thousands of pinpricks of bright blue lights. Other Loralite stones, other locations. The cobalt fireflies swirled by her and then—

The heat hit Taylor all at once. That might have been the most disorienting part—to have the chill of Iceland wiped away so quickly, replaced with a dry heat that made Taylor immediately sweaty. It felt like she was baking. She shielded her eyes from the sun. Unlike the clouded-over Iceland, here the sun hung red and blistering in the sky. Taylor found herself surprisingly grateful for the scarf wrapped around her head.

She and Einar stood in the courtyard of a genuine palace. All around her were statues of lions and women, these gilded with what she assumed was real gold. A trio of burbling fountains flanked by fastidiously groomed palm trees complemented the cobblestone path in front of them. Taylor gazed up, slightly in awe, at the four-story building—blowing silk curtains from thrown-open windows, cupolas and crenellations covered in ancient-looking oil paintings, balconies filled with men holding machine guns.

The guards gave Taylor pause. There were dozens of them, both up high and along the edge of the courtyard, all identically dressed in long-sleeved white thobes and mirrored sunglasses. A small army. Taylor swallowed; she'd been around too many armed groups of men recently.

"They don't entirely trust our kind here," Einar said quietly, following Taylor's gaze. "The prince's father—"

"The king?" Taylor asked.

"Sheikh, actually," Einar replied. "He is a generous supporter of the Foundation. But not all of his brothers and nephews see our . . . utility." Einar adjusted his tie. "Behave. Remember Freyja."

Taylor sighed, looking around at all the guns. She glanced back at the Loralite stone. Making a move here would probably get her killed. She followed Einar down the cobblestone path, towards the palace entrance.

"About time."

A rail-thin Asian girl who had been hanging out in the shade of one of the palm trees smoking a cigarette from a sleek gold-plated holder cut them off before they could enter the palace. The guards eyeballed this girl in the same uneasy way as they did Einar and Taylor, which meant she must be Garde. Like Taylor, she wore a hijab, although hers was decorated with frolicking seahorses. The new arrival wore high heels that made Taylor's feet ache in sympathy, a half blazer and a sleek pencil skirt. Her nails were painted red and black to match her outfit. Although she looked only a year or two her senior, Taylor immediately felt like this girl was much older.

"Jiao," Einar said by way of greeting. When he attempted to walk around her, the girl simply fell into step with him. She completely ignored Taylor.

"We need to talk."

"Do we?"

"You told me, you promised me, that the Foundation would get my family out of Shenzhen."

"It'll happen," Einar said with a sigh. "You need to be patient."

Taylor got the feeling this wasn't the first time they'd had this conversation.

They entered the palace, Jiao's heels echoing loudly against the marble floors. The air was much cooler in here. Taylor tried to keep track of her surroundings—paintings that probably belonged in museums, dozens of rooms, more and more guards—while also listening to Einar and Jiao.

"It's been months," Jiao said sharply.

"Extractions take time," Einar replied. "I promise. I'll look into it."

"You'd better," Jiao said. "Tell that British gao bizi this is the last assignment I'm taking until they keep their end of the bargain."

Einar nodded stiffly and said nothing. Jiao flicked a glance over her shoulder, sizing Taylor up in a split second.

"This is the new girl? She's supposed to put us over the top?"

"Yes," Einar replied.

"Hmpf." Jiao gave Taylor another look, then turned back to Einar. "Where's Rabiya?"

"Couldn't make it."

Jiao studied Einar for a moment, obviously hoping he would elaborate. Taylor volunteered no information. If she was looking for an ally to help her escape, it wouldn't be this girl. She almost seemed like more of a shark than Einar.

"Wonderful conversation as always, Einar," Jiao said bitterly, then sped up her walk down the palace's domed hallway. She knew where she was going and didn't want to arrive at the same time as them.

After a moment, Taylor chuckled. Einar looked in her direction, lips pursed.

"I finally get it," Taylor said.

"Get what?"

"There used to be this clique in my school, the mean girls from a couple grades above me. They all worked in the same store at the mall. This—well, you probably don't have it in Iceland. It's like a popular store where they sell distressed jeans and sweatshirts with big store logos stitched into them."

Up ahead, Jiao pushed open a set of hand-carved double doors and entered the room at the end of the hall. Einar slowed down and then stopped, turning to face Taylor. The guards following them—herding them, really—stopped a respectable distance back.

"Please get to the point," Einar said.

"Okay. These girls were real tight until one of them got promoted to supervisor and then she got all serious, bossing the other ones around, basically acting like a huge tool. A little power went right to her head." She pointed at Einar. "That's you, man. You're like . . . an assistant manager. How lame is that?"

Einar closed his eyes for a moment, then reopened them. "Are you finished?"

"Well, the moral of the story is that the store went out of business and they all had to find new summer jobs, but their friendships were already totally ruined," Taylor said with a bright smile. "So, take that for what it's worth."

Einar took Taylor by the arm and led her towards the room Jiao had gone into. "These attempts to get under my skin won't get you anywhere," he said. "I'm not some silly bitch from your high school."

"I'm not trying to get under your skin," Taylor insisted. "I'm trying to make you see how dumb your situation is."

"Shut up, now," Einar commanded.

Einar ushered her through the double doors. It took Taylor's eyes a moment to adjust—the rest of the palace had been soaked through with sunlight, but this room was kept purposefully dim, all the curtains drawn, candles flickering in wall sconces. The room was huge, with a domed ceiling that featured a chipped mosaic of birds soaring through trees. Incense burned in one corner where a group of women were gathered, all of them covered head to toe, on their knees, foreheads to the ground in prayer. Spread out around the room were more guards with more guns. Taylor swallowed.

An older man with a thick white beard sat at a small table, a goblet of dark wine not far from his hand. He wore a robe of gold and white and Taylor could tell immediately that he was in charge here, the mood of the room seeming to bend around him. This must be the sheikh. He gave both her and

Einar a stern look when they entered, his fingers drumming on the table, but said nothing. At his side was an Arabian woman, not wearing the head-to-toe coverings of the group in the corner, but dressed in a hijab and lab coat. A doctor of the traditional variety. She crouched next to the older man and showed him a chart, explaining something in Arabic.

"We're late," Einar said quietly to Taylor.

"I got that impression."

Taylor's attention soon turned to the king-size canopy bed that dominated the center of the room. Laid up there was the sick prince. He looked like a younger and handsomer version of the sheikh. His beard and hair were clipped meticulously. Unlike the healthy olive bronze of his father and bodyguards, the prince's skin was ashen, his cheeks hollow, his body pointy and emaciated beneath the sheets. He was hooked up to an array of medical equipment, the steady beeps and hums creating a strange chorus with the prayers from the back of the room. If not for the slow rise and fall of his chest, Taylor would have thought the prince to be dead.

Jiao already stood at the prince's bedside. "Hurry up, new girl," she said.

There were two other young people around the prince's bedside. The first was a heavyset boy with a mane of curly hair. His eyes were red-rimmed, the side of his face discolored by recent bruises. He glanced up at Taylor skittishly, then quickly looked away. Another prisoner of the Foundation. Taylor remembered Isabela mentioning a healer who had graduated to Earth Garde, an Italian guy . . . could this be him? Vincent, she thought his name was.

Across from Vincent was an even younger boy with dusky skin, a shock of bright white hair and no legs. He sat in a wheelchair and seemed completely out of it—his head lolled from side to side, his eyes unfocused. A pair of strange-looking microchips were stuck to his temples. A conservatively dressed older woman stood behind the wheelchair, her hand resting gently on the boy's shoulder. Taylor found herself staring at this poor soul, sympathy mixing with apprehension.

"The Foundation is generous," Einar said in her ear, startling Taylor. "But, as you see, they can also be cruel."

He pushed her towards the prince's bedside. Taylor ending up standing at the foot of the bed, Jiao at the head, the two boys on either side. Taylor glanced nervously at the two traumatized boys, at least until Jiao snapped her fingers.

"Focus up," she barked. "Follow my energy."

Taylor's brow furrowed. "Follow your . . . I'm sorry. I've never done this with a group before."

She sensed the sheikh shift impatiently behind her, but ignored him.

Jiao rolled her eyes. "You'll know what to do once we get started." She gestured in the crippled boy's direction. "Even a vegetable can do it."

Paying no attention to Jiao's remark, the woman handling the wheelchair bent down and whispered something in the legless boy's ear. Robotically, he reached out and clasped the wrist of the sleeping prince. Vincent, still avoiding Taylor's gaze, did the same with the prince's other arm.

"See?" Jiao said, and set her hands on either side of the prince's face. She closed her eyes and went to work.

Taylor could sense all of them using their Legacies. The rest of the people in the room might have been blind to it, but to Taylor, the healing energy gave off a warm aura.

Carefully, she moved the sheet aside, and readied her hands over the prince's feet.

She sensed movement. The prince had opened his eyes. He stared, blinking, at Taylor, and a small smile formed on his lips. He looked almost peaceful. There was a kindness in his expression, a gentleness.

"Are you a good person?"

The words popped out before Taylor could stop them. She sensed a restless shifting from the many guards in the room and felt Einar step up behind her. Meanwhile, the sheikh's fingers suddenly stopped their drumming on the table.

The prince struggled to work moisture into his mouth. ". . . What?"

"Are you a good person?" Taylor repeated. "Because, you know, all of us were basically kidnapped to heal you. Some of us probably tortured. So, I want to know if you're, like, worth the trouble . . ."

Vincent trembled, but pretended not to hear, his eyes closed. The legless boy remained slumped over the prince, pouring his healing energy out. His handler glared daggers at Taylor. Jiao slowly opened her eyes, her lips curled in disdain.

The prince peered around Taylor, searching for his father. He looked confused. Something wordless passed between him and his father. Finally, he looked back at her and slowly shook his head.

"I . . . I cannot answer that," the prince said.

"Well, think about it when you're better," Taylor said. "Because this Foundation thing is totally fucked and somebody needs to do something about it."

With that, Taylor closed her eyes and clasped the prince's feet. She sensed the sickness lurking within him, just as she sensed three pulsing beacons of light trying to burn it away. She added her healing energy, giving as much as she could, as if her life and not the prince's depended upon it.

CHAPTER THIRTY-TWO

CALEB CRANE

APACHE JACK'S, NEW MEXICO

HIDDEN IN THE WOODS, THEY WATCHED APACHE Jack's in uneasy silence. The Harvesters appeared to have finished preparations on their snake effigy; a handful of them were gathered around the wooden structure, some holding torches, eager for whatever came next. Even more were hanging around on the bar's back deck.

Caleb remembered a scene from when he was fourteen and was called by his oldest brother to pick him up from one of the bars nearby the base. He wasn't even old enough to drive, but he'd snuck away regardless under threat of catching a beating if he didn't. The atmosphere there—drunk people looking for trouble—reminded him a lot of the one at Apache Jack's.

Isabela had been gone twenty minutes.

We shouldn't have let her go in there alone.

We should bail now. Call the Academy.

We can take them. This hiding is moronic.

Kill everyone down there.

Prove yourself.

They don't even like us. Run in the other direction. Leave them.

SHUT UP, Caleb insisted.

In the darkness, Caleb saw Nigel looking in his direction. He realized he was clenching his teeth, veins in his neck bulging. He forced himself to relax.

The muffled sound of gunfire erupted from inside the bar. The Garde all jumped and so did the Harvesters outside. They looked unsettled—some of them moved towards the building, others away from it. Those who had guns raised them.

"You heard that?" Caleb asked the others.

"Yes," Ran replied.

Seconds later, a fireball exploded through the back door of Apache Jack's. The force knocked the screen door right off its hinges and blew out the bar's back windows. Several Harvesters were knocked clear over the deck's railing, the others outside rushing to their aid. Fire crackled along the door frame and black smoke billowed into the night. A biker ran out the back door and tossed himself to the ground in an effort to put out the flames on his back.

"Bloody hell," Nigel remarked. "Imagine that's a distress signal, yeah?"

"We have to go in," Kopano said firmly, starting forward.

Caleb put a hand on his arm, stopping him. "Hold on. Let me go first." He paused. "I mean, let them go first."

A dozen duplicates slid out from Caleb. His three friends stepped back, giving him room as their patch of trees became suddenly crowded. Caleb was grateful for the opportunity to let his duplicates out; it quieted the voices in his head. Mentally, he commanded them to spread out. Keeping low— even though there was little chance the Harvesters would see them with all their attention on the fire—the duplicates fanned out into the woods.

"I'll attack them from all angles," Caleb said. "Keep them busy."

Ran hadn't taken her eyes off the chaos at the bar. She turned a pinecone over in her hand, a small pile of the things collected at her feet.

"I don't see her down there," Ran said. "I don't think the explosion was a diversion. Isabela might be trapped in there."

"I'll get eyes on her," Caleb said.

Nigel put a hand on his shoulder. "You can handle that many clones?"

Caleb nodded, although he wasn't entirely sure. A dozen at once was as many as he'd managed during the fight last night and that had left him feeling ripped apart, like his body had been stretched too far.

Hell with it. They needed to find Taylor.

He urged the clones forward. Focusing, he divided his

attention among the duplicates, making them move cautiously.

The duplicates spread out through the trees so they wouldn't give away Caleb and the others' position. Some of them looped around farther, towards the sides of Apache Jack's. The goal here was to locate Isabela and she could be anywhere within that bar. Caleb's vision blurred. Each duplicate's view of Apache Jack's was like a still frame from a movie made transparent and laid over the next angle. If Caleb concentrated, he could isolate one view at a time, but that meant losing some control over the other duplicates.

"I'm sending them in," he said through his teeth. Throughout the woods, the duplicates whispered his words.

"We've got your back, mate," Nigel said, sticking close.

A dozen Calebs charged towards Apache Jack's. The Harvesters didn't see them coming. They were too focused on the fire and whatever else was happening inside the bar. He hit the stragglers first, the ones closest to the woods. Two of the duplicates tackled one overweight biker and pummeled him into unconsciousness.

One of the nearby Harvesters—this one dressed like a cowboy and holding a shotgun—heard the commotion and spun about. A third duplicate was there when he turned and ripped the gun right out of his hands. The duplicate gracefully whipped the gun into a firing position and took aim.

This duplicate wanted to kill, but Kopano had encouraged them to limit their bloodshed. So Caleb took control. He smashed the Harvester across the face with the gun's butt and then tossed the weapon into the woods.

His duplicates scrambled onwards. They were like a wave, catching the Harvesters from behind and smashing them into the ground. A woman who'd been working on the effigy heard a muffled shout and turned just before one of the clones would've pounced on her. She thrust her torch in the duplicate's direction, burning his face. The pain didn't register with Caleb, only the vague sense that that particular duplicate was no longer fully whole.

"We're under attack!" the woman screamed.

A shirtless man who was trying to put out the fire turned at the woman's warning. He pulled a pistol from the back of his jeans and shot the burned clone right between the eyes.

No more element of surprise. But at least the clones had taken out a handful of Harvesters before they were discovered.

Caleb felt a jolt pass through him as the duplicate disintegrated and returned to him. Immediately, he gritted his teeth and manifested the clone again, sent it sprinting through the woods to take a new angle on the bar.

"The abominations have followed us, brothers and sisters!" shouted a scrawny Harvester cowering on the back deck. "Strike them down for Reverend Jim—!"

One of the clones clamored over the deck's railing and punched him in the mouth. Seconds later, a long-haired Harvester who looked like he'd spent the last five years living in the woods emerged from the smoke-filled back exit. He coughed raggedly but carried an automatic rifle.

The Harvester began to spray bullets wildly. He gunned down three clones and possibly a few of his own allies. The bullets even reached the trees. Ran and Kopano lunged for cover, while Nigel dragged the focused Caleb down to the ground.

With a sharp intake of breath, Caleb felt the clones return to him. He immediately set them loose, forcing them to charge back into battle.

"How long can you keep this up?" Nigel asked.

"Not sure," Caleb replied, a migraine tearing through his brain. He'd been wondering who would run out of ammunition first—him or the man on the back deck.

The Harvesters on the back deck took cover behind the broken wooden slats of the railing. They were pinned between the fire and the clones, but they were starting to get organized. They were picking off Caleb's clones faster than he could make them. Some of his duplicates grabbed weapons from fallen Harvesters and returned fire. The situation was too desperate to handle gently. They needed to find Isabela and get out of here.

In the darkness of the woods, Caleb couldn't see if Kopano wore a look of disapproval. Caleb switched views, looking through the eyes of a clone that had looped around to the side of Apache Jack's. He peered through a dirt-smudged window. Inside, a group of panicked Harvesters were getting the fire under control—it appeared to be localized around the back door, where Caleb could see charred and twisted hunks of what used to be fuel canisters. Other Harvesters had popped open a trapdoor beneath the bar that contained a stockpile of weapons, the bartender handing out rifles to whoever wanted one. Soon, they'd be in real trouble.

That's when Caleb noticed the freezer. Towards the back of the bar, near where the explosion had been, was a heavy steel door. A trio of menacing bikers in gas masks were taking turns whacking the door with axes, trying to break in.

Just then, one of the newly armed Harvesters came around the corner from the front of the bar, heading for the back. He spotted Caleb's duplicate and, without hesitation, shot him in the head.

Caleb gasped. "She's locked in a freezer," he announced breathlessly. He pointed towards the singed back entrance. "Right in there."

"You're sure?" Ran asked.

"Has to be," he said. "The Harvesters are trying to hack their way in."

"I'll get her," Kopano said, cracking his knuckles. "Their bullets cannot hurt me."

"I'm going with you," Ran replied.

Nigel put a hand on Caleb's shoulder. "You going to be okay back here, mate?"

Caleb nodded. In truth, he was beginning to feel ragged, like his body was sliding apart. All the same, he pushed another clone into existence and sent him towards the fray. "I'll keep the decoys coming as long . . . as long as I can," he said.

Nigel nodded and turned to Kopano. "Big man, let me and

Ran create a wee distraction before you go all juggernaut on 'em, yeah?"

The three of them started forward, sticking close to the shadows and the trees to avoid any stray bullets. At the moment, the Harvesters were too preoccupied with the remaining clones to notice their approach. Caleb kept his most recent duplicate with his three classmates, wanting to make sure he could see and hear what happened with them.

One of the Harvesters had dropped a lit torch in the grass. It was still burning. Ran or Nigel—he couldn't be sure who— used their telekinesis to pick up the torch and float it right to the effigy.

The gas-soaked wooden snake sculpture went up in flames with a mighty *whoosh!* Even back in the woods, Caleb could feel the heat. That Harvesters stopped their shooting for a moment, confused by this latest development.

Confusion turned to outright terror as the burning snake effigy levitated right off the ground. It must have taken Kopano, Ran and Nigel working together to accomplish the telekinetic feat, but soon the snake hovered over Apache Jack's deck, fireflies of burning wood drifting down on the Harvesters. A few of them pointlessly shot at the effigy.

"YOUR BULLETS CANNOT HARM ME, MORTALS!"

The booming voice erupted from the vicinity of the snake. It was Nigel, using his Legacy to throw his voice and make it as loud as possible. Desperate as the situation was, Caleb couldn't help but smirk.

"YOU WANKERS HAVE TAKEN MY NAME IN VAIN

TOO MANY TIMES!" the flaming snake bellowed. "NOW I'M GOING TO BELLY FLOP YOUR DAFT ASSES!"

Many of the Harvesters on the deck had already begun to scatter and the rest soon followed as the burning effigy crashed down on the back of Apache Jack's. Embers flew up into the air, burning wood breaking apart, small fires starting everywhere. The Harvesters dove aside, many winding up in the dirt, where Caleb's remaining clones could charge in and disarm them.

The Harvesters who managed to stay standing soon found glowing pinecones at their feet. The concussive explosions knocked them backwards.

Suddenly, there was a lull in the action and a clear path into Apache Jack's—well, clear except for all the smoke and burning chunks of wood.

Kopano barreled into that gap, knocking aside debris with his telekinesis. Nigel and Ran came in behind him, with Caleb's clone bringing up the rear. They kept low to avoid the smoke that was now everywhere. The heat from small fires made them all—except the clone—immediately begin sweating.

The trio of Harvesters in their gas masks had stopped trying to hack into the freezer and now stood at the ready. They saw Kopano and one of them charged. His axe clanged against Kopano's forearm and the Nigerian took him down with a well-placed right hook. A glowing pinecone exploded against the chest of a second Harvester, sending him and his axe tumbling over a nearby table. Nigel used his telekinesis to turn the gas mask around on the third. While the man yanked the mask's straps away from his eyes, Kopano put him down with a push kick to the sternum.

"Easy-peasy," Nigel remarked, glancing back at the clone. He banged on the severely dented freezer door. "Oi, Isabela! You in there?"

They heard a grinding sound on the other side of the door—something being pried loose. A moment later, the freezer swung open. Isabela stood hunched before them, her face blackened with ash, her side dark with blood. She said something in Portuguese.

"Huh?" Nigel replied.

Isabela groaned. She held up the bracelet that Simon had charged for her, waved it in Nigel's face and tossed it away.

"Her English is gone," Ran observed.

"Bloody great timing, that," Nigel said sarcastically.

Ran put her hand on Isabela's shoulder, peering at what looked like a gunshot wound on her side. "How bad are you hurt?"

Isabela glanced down, then tilted her hand back and forth, as if to say *so-so*. She pointed behind her, speaking rapidly in Portuguese.

Crumpled on the floor of the freezer was the girl from the road. She'd been beaten badly, but was conscious. A piece of metal ceiling that looked to have been recently ripped loose was attached to her wrists, stuck there by a pair of those magnetized shackles the Peacekeepers had used. She struggled to sit up.

Nigel and Ran went to the girl. Caleb kept his clone in the doorway, holding up Isabela. Kopano stood guard outside, watching for Harvesters.

"My, my, love. They did a number on you," Nigel observed as he grabbed the girl's arm and, with Ran's help, pulled her to her feet. "What's your name?"

"Rabiya," the girl croaked. A trickle of blood dribbled down her chin.

As they dragged her out of the freezer and into the smoke-filled remains of Apache Jack's, Nigel noticed the odd triangular microchips affixed to Rabiya's temples. "What're those?" he asked, tweaking one of them.

Rabiya pulled her hands up to touch the microchips and nearly struck herself in the face with the ceiling plate. "They . . . neurotransmitters. They scramble my telekinesis."

Nigel raised an eyebrow and exchanged a look with Ran. "Bet you'd like us to take those off, eh?"

"Yes."

"You know who we are, then?"

She nodded forlornly.

"You took our friend," Nigel continued. "About got us killed. But here we are, coming to your bloody rescue."

"Thank . . . thank you," Rabiya said.

"Don't thank me yet. You can make Loralite, yeah? That's your thing?" He paused to let Rabiya nod. "You know where that smartly dressed chum of yours took Taylor? You can bring us there?"

Rabiya's mouth opened as she searched for words. "They

are dangerous people."

As they picked their way across the burning debris of Apache Jack's back deck, a Harvester with a knife lunged at them. Kopano slapped the blade down with an open hand, then knocked the Harvester off his feet with an uppercut.

"We are dangerous people," Ran said coldly.

Rabiya glanced at Ran, her expression slowly hardening. "He was . . . they were supposed to be my friends," Rabiya said quietly. "Instead, they left me to die. We were supposed to take your friend to a safe house in Iceland. I can bring you there. But you have to free my hands."

Nigel looked at Ran. The Japanese girl shook her head stoically. She let go of one of Rabiya's arms and the girl almost sank to the ruined deck.

"I don't believe her," Ran said. "Leave her here. Let these animals finish her off."

Even through the clone's ears, Caleb could tell that Ran was bluffing. It was a classic case of good-cop-bad-cop. He had the clone glance down at Isabela, who he was still holding up. If she could understand English, Caleb was sure the Brazilian would appreciate this bit of subterfuge.

Rabiya bought it. "Please!" she yelled, her voice hoarse. "I never even wanted to join the Foundation! They forced me—they—!"

Ran grabbed Rabiya by the manacles. "This is going to hurt," she warned.

With a touch, Ran charged the manacles securing Rabiya's wrists. She didn't put as much energy into the metal as she normally did when making a grenade, but the high-tech restraints still exploded with enough force to throw Rabiya onto her back. She sat back up, rubbing wrists that were already swelling up.

"I think you broke my hand," she said quietly.

"Too bad you stole our healer," Nigel replied as he helped her to her feet.

Rabiya reached up to pick the microchips off her temples. Nigel slapped her hands down. "Nuh-uh. No telekinesis until you prove you're on the up-and-up."

She didn't argue, instead gesturing into grass beside the smoky deck. "Over there. The Loralite only grows from the ground."

At that moment, a gunshot rang out from inside the bar. The bullet bounced off Kopano, who returned fire by telekinetically lobbing a pair of chairs into the hallway behind them. The Harvesters were beginning to regroup. They'd fled to the front of the bar when the effigy came crashing down, but they were still armed and stupid. They'd strike again soon.

Kopano nervously rubbed the spot on his shoulder where the bullet had hit him. "Let's go!"

Caleb quickly switched views to one of his duplicates that was posted up around the side of the bar. He could see the Harvesters massing out front, steeling themselves for another attack.

"Quickly, quickly," his clone said, helping Isabela down from the deck. Nigel and Ran followed with Rabiya sandwiched in between them. Kopano came last, using his telekinesis to barricade the back door with furniture and debris.

Just then, an icy feeling came over Caleb.

It wasn't necessarily an unpleasant feeling. It was like a numbness, spreading through his legs. At first, he thought it was a sensation that he'd picked up from one of the clones. But no—this was happening to his actual body.

Something was wrong.

Caleb attempted a lurching step forward and fell onto his hands. His legs were heavy.

They were stone. Literally.

With a groan, Caleb rolled over. He sensed movement in the trees behind him and a glint of silver-tinged energy.

"Oh, what up, Caleb?"

Daniela.

He hadn't seen the girl for more than a year, not since she was sent directly to Earth Garde instead of the Academy. Daniela looked much the same except for her gear—she wore an armor-plated black bodysuit that hugged her lean sprinter's body, and her usually unruly braids were collected into a thick ponytail. She stood over Caleb, a team of Peacekeepers with night-vision goggles picking through the woods behind her.

"How—how'd you find us?" Caleb stammered.

"We didn't find you, we found them," Daniela replied conversationally, waving in the direction of Apache Jack's and the Harvesters. "Everyone's looking for you guys, glad you're in one piece. The others okay?"

Caleb didn't answer right away. Instead, he looked through his clone's eyes, stopping the duplicate in his tracks as his friends dragged Rabiya across the field towards the woods.

"Stop!" he had the clone yell. "Earth Garde's here! They've got me."

In the distance, the *whup-whup-whup* of helicopters became audible.

"Hell," Nigel said. He elbowed Rabiya. "Hurry up. Make the Loralite now."

Rabiya glanced nervously over her shoulder, worried the Harvesters might be on them at any moment. "Here—?"

Daniela shook Caleb's shoulder and he focused back on her. She'd crouched down beside him as the Peacekeeper soldiers continued on towards Apache Jack's.

"Hey, man, where'd you go?"

"Why'd you stone me?" Caleb replied. "I can help."

"Yeah, sorry about that," she replied. "Earth Garde's running this operation and you aren't authorized for combat. Can't let you get hurt." She touched a radio mounted on her shoulder and spoke into it. "I've got Caleb Crane down here . . ." She listened to a response, then smirked at Caleb. "Oh man, Professor Meathead isn't happy."

"Nine? Nine's here?"

The helicopters came into view. Three of them, all circling. Their spotlights swept across the wooded hillside around Apache Jack's.

Caleb checked in with his duplicate hiding at the front of the bar. Many of the Harvesters were bailing, scrambling for motorcycles and trucks and tearing down the road. Some of them took potshots up at the helicopters. They were quickly cut down by sniper fire.

"Harvesters retreating, Earth Garde closing in," Caleb reported through his clone.

A funnel of cobalt-blue energy rippled out from Rabiya's outstretched palms and struck the ground. With a groan from the earth, a craggy pile of Loralite slowly began to rise up.

The blue light caught the attention of one of the helicopter pilots. They swung the spotlight around, illuminating the group of Garde, and soon the chopper was almost right overhead.

"How much do you need to make?" Kopano asked Rabiya.

"Almost . . . ," she said tiredly. "Almost there."

"Que porra é essa?" Isabela said, pointing up at the helicopter.

Something had fallen out of the chopper's open bay door.

THOOM! Nine hit the ground with an explosion of dirt and broken bits of wood. He landed right in front of his students. All their eyes widened at the shallow crater he made and Rabiya yelped, cutting off her creation of the Loralite stone. Nine smirked as he straightened up.

"It's way after curfew, guys."

Nigel was the first to recover his wits. "Fancy meeting you here, teach."

PITTACUS LORE

Nine gave them the once-over, checking for injuries. Perhaps satisfied none of them were gravely wounded, he put his hands on his hips. His eyes widened a fraction when he noticed Rabiya and the steady pile of glowing stone at her feet.

"That's Loralite," Nine said, and they could all tell their professor's mind was working. "We found some at the spot where you guys were ambushed, been trying to figure out where . . ." He took a step towards Rabiya. "What's your name? Where'd you come from?"

Ran put herself between Nine and Rabiya. He stopped short, an eyebrow raised.

"Keep going," Ran said to Rabiya over her shoulder.

"We're going to find Taylor," Kopano told Nine.

"No, we're going to find Taylor," Nine insisted, gesturing around at the Peacekeepers and Earth Garde. There were sounds of a small firefight from in front of Apache Jack's. Meanwhile, Daniela led stone-booted Caleb out of the woods, her team of Peacekeepers fanning out. Caleb and his clone exchanged a look.

"Been doing a bang-up job of that, haven't ya?" Nigel asked.

Nine raised an eyebrow. "We found you, didn't we?"

"You stumbled onto us," Caleb had his clone say.

Nine waved this away. "Same difference."

"We know where she is," Kopano said. "She's in Iceland. We're going to get her."

"No. You're not."

Nine took another step forward. Or, at least, he attempted to. As one, Nigel, Ran and Kopano extended their hands, gently pushing Nine back with their telekinesis. Isabela, still holding her wounded side with one hand, joined them a second later.

"Oh, give me a break with this shit," Nine said. He dug his heels in and powered forward. Caleb watched with a growing tightness in his chest. Nine was strong. He could probably break their telekinesis if he wanted to.

"Stop, Professor," Kopano appealed. "We'll bring Taylor back. I promise."

"Like your lot never ran off half-cocked to save someone's life," Nigel added.

"I can't let you go," Nine replied, the words sounding hollow. "What you're doing isn't safe. I'm sure it's in violation of one of those stupid Garde bylaws, too."

"Nowhere is safe for us," Ran said. "That was proven at Patience Creek."

"That was during the war," Nine replied. "It's different now."

"Doesn't feel so bloody different," Nigel said. He glanced in the direction of the approaching Peacekeepers, noting that some of them were armed with the nonlethal weaponry that had been used during the Wargames. "You want to tell us how these wackjob Harvesters got hooked into the same weapons as your mates in the army?"

"I don't know," Nine replied. "We're looking into that."

"Yeah. Right. So, you keep doing that, behind your desk,"

Nigel replied. "We'll handle the hero shit."

Nine sneered and started to say something more, but Ran cut him off.

"You knew," she said suddenly, as if the fact had just dawned on her. "That night on the beach. You were warning me. Telling me to keep an eye on Taylor. You knew someone might be after her."

"I . . ." Nine glanced up at the helicopter circling above. "There's a lot going on you guys don't know about."

Rabiya took a breath and sagged against Nigel. The Loralite stone was done, the blue stone reflecting the small fires still burning at the bar.

"Mate, you can fill us in when we get back," Nigel said. "Who do you trust to go get Taylor? Us or these Earth Garde blokes?"

Nine sighed. Through his clone's eyes, Caleb saw something like nostalgia on the Loric's face. He was relenting.

Caleb tried to drag his feet, which wasn't difficult considering they were encased in stone. He wanted to slow up Daniela and the Peacekeepers, give the others a chance to convince Nine and escape.

"We'll come back," Kopano said solemnly, reading the hesitation in Nine's face. "We'll be safe."

"Yeah," Nigel added. "Just gonna pop on over to Iceland for a bit. No biggie. Things get hinky, you come pick us up."

Nine lowered his voice as he came to a decision. "At least make it look good." He jerked his chin in Isabela's direction. "And leave her. She's too hurt."

"Estou bem. Eu quero ajudar!" Isabela stomped her foot in frustration when the others simply stared at her, then wobbled and sagged against Caleb's clone. "Talvez não. Va, va . . ."

Ran nodded once to Nine, then gave Rabiya a shove. "Take us."

Rabiya reached for the Loralite. Ran had a vise grip on her arm. Nigel held Ran's hand, his other hand on Kopano's shoulder.

Nine made a dramatic lunge forward.

The Caleb duplicate tackled him.

Isabela stood there looking puzzled, holding her bloody side.

In a flash of vivid blue light, the other four teleported away.

CHAPTER THIRTY-THREE

NIGEL BARNABY
HOFN, ICELAND

NIGEL REMEMBERED THE SENSATION OF TELEPORT-ing well. He was the bloody pioneer champion of teleportation, for God's sake. He'd been the first Human Garde to use a Loralite stone back during the invasion. That dizzying feeling of getting flung halfway across the world toward adventure—he'd missed it.

This was what he always wanted. To make a difference. To take action. To do.

Like he'd told Kopano at the gas station, it wasn't always glamorous. Nigel still had flashbacks to the massacre at Patience Creek. He still got a bitter taste in his mouth when he thought about the bodies.

But the reality of the fight—against Mogadorians, against Harvesters, against snotty-looking Garde from frozen wasteland countries—it didn't scare Nigel off or make him second-guess his Legacies. The ugliness only made him want to fight more and fight harder. He'd spent so many years as a nobody, ignored by his parents, relentlessly picked on at Pepperpont—and now finally, finally he was going to take his rightful place in the world.

That's why, when they arrived in Iceland, Nigel was grinning.

The change was jarring. First, it was cold here, and Nigel's T-shirt was soaked through with sweat from the battle with the Harvesters. His breath misted in front of him and steam curled up from his narrow shoulders. It was also early morning. Even though the skies were clouded over and gray, the brightness stung his eyes. All the same, Nigel grinned.

Maybe it was Nigel's half-mad smile that caused the large man in body armor to hesitate bringing down his sledgehammer. Nigel liked to think so. But it was probably the four teenagers who manifested right in front of him that momentarily stunned the intimidating chap.

That was their welcoming committee. A badass-looking dude poised to bring his hammer down on the stone they'd teleported in on. He hesitated only a moment, then continued his downwards swing, not appearing to care that Nigel's head was now in the way.

Kopano caught the hammer in the palm of his hand with a metallic clang. Then, his fist heavy and hard, Kopano punched the guy square in the cheek. He slumped to the ground, unconscious, his jaw broken.

"He didn't look friendly," Kopano said.

Nigel patted him on the back. "He most certainly did not."

They stood in a small wooden enclosure. The gate was open, footprints in the frost leading from the house to the now-unconscious brute. The house was quaint and cute, a log cabin, with a rock garden outside. It looked entirely too peaceful.

Ran put her forearm under Rabiya's chin and slammed her up against the wall. "Where is this? Where did you bring us?"

Rabiya gagged, her eyes bugging out. Nigel touched Ran's shoulder and she let up on the pressure.

"I told you! Iceland!" Rabiya said hoarsely. "This is Einar's house. He took your friend." Her gaze drifted to the man Kopano had knocked out and her eyes widened.

Nigel kicked the unconscious man. "Who's this, then? You recognize him?"

"Blackstone," Rabiya said. "Mercenaries. If they're here, this place is burned. Your friend is gone or already dead. We should leave or they will kill us, too."

Nigel looked down at the unconscious mercenary. "This wanker won't even be able to eat solid foods in a dream, much less kill anyone."

"There will be more."

Ran half turned to look at Nigel and Kopano. "How should we—?"

The second Ran turned her attention away, Rabiya made a dive for the Loralite stone.

If she hadn't been so badly injured by the Harvesters, she might have made it. Her body moved too slowly, though, and Ran brought her elbow down on the back of Rabiya's neck. The girl slumped to the ground, her fingertips inches away from the Loralite stone.

"Damn," Kopano said.

"Coulda let her go," Nigel said with a shrug. "Poor thing's been through the ringer."

"The Academy does not know enough about these people," Ran said. She dragged Rabiya's body to the back of the enclosure and set her gently against the wall. "I am sure they will have questions."

"That shit she said about Taylor—," Nigel started to say.

"We must check," Kopano replied.

As soon as he stepped out of the enclosure, Kopano was greeted by a burst of machine-gun fire. He grunted as the bullets struck him in the center of the chest. They didn't penetrate, but his Legacy was slow to kick in. He would have bruises. Bad ones.

A second mercenary crouched behind a pile of rocks. When he saw that his bullets hadn't harmed Kopano, he dropped his rifle and took a different weapon from his belt. An energy weapon. Mogadorian.

"Where is Taylor?" Kopano roared.

He charged across the backyard before the mercenary could get a shot off. Kopano picked the man up in both hands, headbutted him and kept running with the man held out in front of him. He smashed through the house's back door using the mercenary's body as a battering ram.

"Not a lot of teamwork in his approach, but it's efficient," Nigel commented.

Ran's lips quirked in her almost-smile. "Let's go," she said.

The two of them emerged from the cover of the enclosure with a little more caution than Kopano had shown. They weren't bulletproof. From inside the house, they could hear the sounds of objects breaking and Kopano repeatedly shouting Taylor's name.

"This what you were expecting?" Nigel asked, looking over the cabin.

"Absolutely not," Ran replied.

"Me neither." Nigel nodded up at the wall above the back door. "See that?"

"Camera," Ran said.

Nigel wiggled his fingers. "Wonder who's watching."

It was a lucky thing. If Nigel hadn't called her attention to the camera, Ran might not have looked up and seen the glint of reflected light in an open upstairs window.

A scope. A sniper rifle.

"Watch out!" Ran yelled and shoved Nigel hard to the side.

Ffft! Ffft! Ffft!

The shots came like puffs of air, fired through a high-powered rifle's silenced muzzle. Chunks of dirt and ice struck Nigel's legs, one of the bullets hitting where he'd just been standing. He and Ran scrambled in opposite directions.

Nigel got close to the house and around the corner, while Ran dove behind a pile of discus-shaped stones.

"Ran! You good?"

"Yes," she replied, but Nigel heard a hitch of pain in her voice.

Ffft! Another shot exploded a rock near Ran's head.

"I'm pinned down," Ran yelled.

"On it!" Nigel replied.

From inside the house, Nigel heard the crash of a table being overturned. He peeked through a nearby window. Kopano was locked up against a large man with a thick beard and a scarred face, smashing through a fancy kitchen. Kopano punched the mercenary in the ribs, but his body armor absorbed the blow.

The man swung a combat knife for Kopano's throat and connected. The slice merely made a grinding sound, though, not breaking Kopano's impenetrable skin.

"Hah!" Kopano shouted, swinging again.

The knife attack was only a feint, though. With his free hand, the mercenary pulled a manacle from his belt. As he ducked Kopano's punch, the mercenary snapped the shackle around his wrist. Immediately, the bracelet emitted a humming vibration and Kopano was jerked downwards, his arm stuck to the side of the stainless steel fridge.

Kopano roared, trying to pull his arm free, failing, then trying to lift the fridge entirely and finding it too heavy. Quickly, the man drew a pistol from the holster attached to his thigh.

"Let's see if your eyes are bulletproof," he growled.

"Boo."

Nigel threw his voice so it sounded as if he were right behind the mercenary. He spun around, found no one there. Nigel took the opportunity to yank the gun out of his hand. The man got off one shot that harmlessly thudded into a couch.

Kopano took the opening to seize him by the scruff of his neck using the arm that wasn't pinned to the fridge. He slammed the guy's head down against the countertop, then hefted him using his telekinesis, rammed his back against the ceiling and finally let him fall to the floor.

While that was happening, Nigel clambered in through the window. He glanced out the back door—Ran was still huddled behind some rocks. As he watched, she used her telekinesis to fling a glowing stone at the second level of the cabin, aiming blindly for the sniper.

A small explosion soon followed. The air was still for a moment. Ran started to peek her head out—*ffft!*—and yelped when another bullet nearly took her head off. The shot grazed her cheek, opening a deep cut there.

"Sniper upstairs!" Nigel yelled to Kopano as he ran for the stairs.

"I'm stuck!"

"One bloody thing at a time, mate!"

Nigel bounded up the steps, taking them two at a time. His telekinesis tingled on his fingertips—ready to disarm the sniper as soon as he came into view. He raced down the hall, counting doorways to match the windows outside.

He burst into the room where the sniper should be. The window was empty.

"Where—"

Behind him. The sniper spun Nigel around and clocked him in the bridge of the nose with the butt of his rifle.

Nigel fell on his back with a cry, blood streaming down his face. The sniper spun his gun back around, smiled and took aim—

Nigel screamed. The sound was piercing and high-pitched enough that the glass on the rifle's scope shattered. The mercenary flinched and grabbed at his ears.

That was all the space Nigel needed. He yanked the rifle away from the mercenary with his telekinesis, grabbed it out of the air and pulled the trigger.

He shot the sniper right in the chest. The bullet cracked into his body armor and sent him flying backwards into the hall, where he slumped against the wall. Nigel got up, still holding the rifle, and stood over the man as he gasped for breath.

"Shouldn't go shooting at everyone who teleports into your backyard, mate," Nigel said as he chambered another round. "Maybe we were just coming by for a cup of sugar, eh? Guess you'll never know."

Nigel might have killed the mercenary—the guy had shot Ran and certainly would've done the same to Nigel if given the chance. But movement in the corner of his eye distracted him.

A little girl stood at the end of the hallway. Frightened and pale, she watched Nigel with wide eyes. Around her neck was a strange choker that she kept nervously tugging at.

Instead of shooting the mercenary, Nigel sighed and brought the rifle around and down like he was swinging a golf club. A swift blow to the temple knocked the sniper unconscious. Nigel then used his telekinesis to bend the muzzle of his gun into an unusable pretzel, a trick he'd picked up from Nine.

Finally, he turned to the girl. "Are you some kind of tiny assassin?"

"No . . . ," the girl replied with a shake of her head.

"Didn't think so."

"Are you here to rescue me?"

Nigel looked around. "Sure, love."

The girl approached him cautiously, still tugging at that weird collar. Nigel noted more cameras mounted along the hallway and in the rooms. What kind of weird shit went on in this Nordic cabin?

"How many of these guys were here?" he asked, nudging the unconscious mercenary with his foot.

"Four," the girl said.

Nigel made a quick count. "Right, then. Got them all." He crouched down to better look the girl in her face. "What's your name?"

"Freyja."

"Freyja, is there another girl hiding hereabouts? My age, American, pretty if that's your thing."

"Taylor," Freyja said, then shook her head. "She was here, but he took—"

A scream from downstairs distracted Nigel from the rest of Freyja's sentence. That didn't sound like Ran or Kopano.

It sounded like Taylor.

Regardless, screaming was a bad sign. "Stay here," he snapped at Freyja, then bolted back downstairs.

The first thing Nigel saw when he came down the steps was Kopano, still pinned by the wrist to the side of the fridge by that magnetized manacle. An uneasy feeling came over Nigel. There was fear in Kopano's eyes—not an emotion he'd seen on the big man before.

"Nigel Barnaby," said a smooth, accented voice.

The guy from the highway—Einar, Rabiya had called him—stood in the back door. He wore gray slacks and a white dress shirt, the latter spattered with fresh blood. He smiled at Nigel in a way that made his skin crawl.

"You have no idea how happy I am to see you."

CHAPTER THIRTY-FOUR

TAYLOR COOK
ABU DHABI, UNITED ARAB EMIRATES • HOFN, ICELAND

"TAYLOR," EINAR SAID, HIS VOICE SOFT BUT commanding. "Get up."

Taylor opened her eyes slowly. Her muscles felt tired, her fingertips and palms still tingling from the protracted use of her healing Legacy. Her mouth was dry, as were her nasal passages. She coughed scratchily, sitting up on the divan where she had passed out.

Einar handed her a glass of water. "You've been sleeping for almost six hours," he said. "I think that's long enough."

Taylor worked some moisture into her mouth. "You didn't do any healing. How would you know?"

Einar didn't reply. He simply grabbed her by the arm and helped her stand. They were in one of the palace's hundred guest bedrooms. This one was decorated with pictures of

the sheikh—grim as he looked when Taylor first saw him—
standing next to a variety of expensive cars. Taylor rubbed
her eyes.

"What happens now?"

"We go home," Einar said.

Taylor gave him a look.

"Back to my home," Einar clarified.

"And then what? Wait around until this Foundation of
yours picks another rich prick to have me heal?"

Einar raised an eyebrow. "Did you not enjoy it? Using
your Legacy to save a life? To do the impossible?"

Taylor hesitated. She and the other healers—they had
cured the prince's leukemia. Cleaned it right out of his body.

The cancer was deep in the prince's cells. She could feel
it there. Alone, Taylor wouldn't have been able to produce
enough healing energy to cure the sickness—but with the
group, it was possible. Vincent had been of similar strength
to Taylor; Jiao's healing energy was the most focused and
precise; the crippled boy a font of raw power. After getting
over her initial reservations, Taylor had thrown herself into
the work, her energy commingling with the others, beating
back the corruption that infested the prince's body.

The process had taken four hours. After, all of them were
spent and ready to pass out. Oddly and despite the fact that
they were strangers to her, now that she'd broken away
from the other healers, she missed the warm feeling of their
energy.

Taylor didn't tell any of this to Einar. "You know, the

Academy had me healing people too," she said instead. "They didn't pick special cases. They let me heal whoever was in need."

"The prince is a valuable ally. His family helps keep this region of the world stable."

"Who told you that? The Foundation?"

Einar said nothing, which Taylor took as a yes. He walked out of the guest room, forcing Taylor to follow him.

"These people you're working for, they get to decide who gets healed? They get to control the healing? Is that it?" Taylor pressed him.

"I'm sure we could arrange for you to do some kind of charity, if that makes you feel better," Einar said.

"It would make me feel better to not have some shadowy organization controlling my life."

Einar stopped, looking around. The hallways of the palace were clearer now than when they'd arrived; there didn't seem to be a squadron of guards assigned to them. There also weren't cameras mounted over every doorway.

"I liked what you said to the prince. 'Are you a good person?'" Einar chuckled quietly. "It does these people well to be reminded, once in a while, who really holds the power."

Taylor started to say something, but realized that Einar was being genuine. Opening up, even. She closed her mouth and let him keep talking.

"The Foundation, Earth Garde, the Academy. They are all just ways to control us," Einar said. "We are young now and not strong enough to make our own way. One day, though, we will be. In the meantime, we're forced to choose who we allow to exploit us. The Foundation . . ." Einar met her gaze. "They provide a good life. To fight against them, at this point, would be futile."

Einar resumed his walk down the hallway. Taylor followed after him, mulling over his words. So, he wasn't blindly loyal to the Foundation. But they'd corrupted him to the point where he'd do their bidding. She didn't agree with what Einar said about the Academy—that felt like home to her, which surprised her. Taylor hadn't wanted to go there in the first place, but now badly wanted to go back. She needed to find a way out. A way to free herself, and Freyja, from the grasp of these Foundation creeps.

As they entered the courtyard with the Loralite stone, Taylor had begun to remove her headscarves; they'd become annoyingly tangled while she was passed out. She and Einar stopped short. A dozen of the white thobe–wearing guards stood in the courtyard, blocking their path to the Loralite stone. All of them were armed and, while their weapons weren't raised, they all seemed ready for action.

Taylor swallowed hard. Maybe the sheikh hadn't appreciated her insolence.

"What is this?" Einar asked, apparently as surprised as Taylor to find their way barred.

Jiao emerged from the crowd of guards. She looked fresh and awake—a sharp contrast to how Taylor felt after their marathon healing session. The smartly dressed Chinese girl smiled at Taylor like they were old pals, then fixed Einar with an icy look.

"You can't leave, Einar," she said simply.

"Excuse me?" he replied. "What are you still doing here, Jiao?"

"The Foundation asked me to stay in case you got out of hand. But you'll be a good boy, won't you?" She wiggled her fingers in Taylor's direction. "Come on, darling. You're coming home with me."

"Um, what?" Taylor replied.

"Einar will remain as a guest of the sheikh," Jiao said.

Einar took a step forward and put a hand across Taylor, preventing her from going to Jiao. Not that she made a move in that direction anyway.

"I don't understand," Einar said flatly.

Jiao snorted. "Really, man? You lost Rabiya. Probably got her killed."

"I made healing the prince possible," Einar retorted.

"Yeah, and I assume that's why the sheikh hasn't already beheaded you," Jiao replied. "Doesn't mean he's happy that you threw his niece to the wolves."

"She belonged to the Foundation," Einar said sharply. "That was the deal. We heal his beloved son and we gain the services of his niece."

Jiao shrugged blithely. "Guess you should tell the sheikh that."

Slowly, Taylor put the pieces together. The girl with the headscarves from the road was related to the sheikh. Einar had lost her in the process of kidnapping Taylor. Now, he

377

was in trouble. She remembered the conversation she'd eavesdropped on between Einar and the British woman.

Taylor ignored Jiao's outstretched hand, not making any effort to push by Einar. This was an opportunity to make a move, but whose side should she take? She was frozen.

"After everything I've done for the Foundation," Einar said bitterly. "One screwup and—"

"Oh, stop," Jiao said. "You know how it works."

Jiao made a gesture and two of the guards stepped forward. One of them carried a pair of manacles, the other held out two microchips like Taylor had seen attached to the crippled healer.

The two guards made it within five feet of Einar before they both began hysterically crying. They fell to their knees, clutching their faces, sobbing uncontrollably.

He was playing with their emotions.

"Einar—," Jiao started to say.

And then the shooting started.

It came from the two guards farthest at the back. Their weapons went off, shots firing into the dirt. Taylor noticed that they looked surprised. They hadn't pulled the triggers.

It was Einar.

The other guards spun around, startled, weapons coming up—and then Einar was telekinetically pulling all the triggers at once, a cross fire beginning, the sheikh's guards gunning each other down.

Jiao screamed. A bullet had struck her in the knee. She fell to the ground. Taylor remained rooted in place.

"I find this very disrespectful of my talents," Einar said. He lifted Jiao with his telekinesis and flung her through one of the second-story windows.

Then, he grabbed Taylor by the hair.

"Sorry," he said. "But you need to come with me."

Taylor was too stunned, staring at the bloody bodies of the murdered guards, to immediately react. Or maybe that was Einar, making her docile.

He dragged her to the Loralite stone and touched the cobalt surface.

The spinning sensation. Blinking blue lights. The sudden chill of Iceland.

Finally reacting, Taylor shoved away from Einar as soon as they were inside the wooden enclosure. He didn't seem to notice. Einar was too focused on the crumpled body propped up against the wall. She'd been so badly beaten, it took Taylor a moment to recognize Rabiya.

Einar laughed, looking down at the unconscious girl. "This is tremendously ironic."

"You asshole, what does this mean for—?" Taylor gasped. Outside the enclosure, Ran lay on her back, taking cover behind a pile of rocks. She was stunned to see her roommate there—and in rough shape. Ran had a gash along her cheek and a bullet wound in her thigh.

"Get down!" Ran shouted at her as Taylor made to run across the grass. "Sniper!"

Taylor ignored her friend's instructions, hopping over the unconscious body of one of those Blackstone mercenaries as she rushed to Ran's side. No bullets came from the upstairs window.

"You're hurt," Taylor said as she slid in next to Ran. "How did you . . . ?"

But then, it made sense. Rabiya. They'd gotten her to teleport them here.

"We came to rescue you," Ran said. She looked over Taylor's shoulder, tensing up when she saw Einar.

Einar edged out from the enclosure with more caution than Taylor, peering up at his cabin.

Quickly, Ran grabbed a stone, charged it with her explosive energy and sent it flying towards Einar.

He looked up just in time, swatting the rock away with his telekinesis. His lips curled in annoyance and he thrust a hand in Ran's direction.

Taylor recoiled as Ran's entire body began to vibrate. Veins in her neck bulged, all her muscles tight. Blood from her cheek flattened out against the side of her face. It looked like Ran was trying to sit up, but she couldn't. Her eyes were wide and bloodshot.

Einar was using his telekinesis to grind her into the ground.

"It's funny how the instinct is to use our telekinesis to throw things at our enemies," Einar said conversationally. "Even the Loric behave that way. You can see it in videos of them fighting during the invasion. They rip away guns, hurl around cars. But the body's an object, just like anything else.

My theory is, the Loric had an instinct bred into them, not to use their telekinesis on each other directly." Einar shrugged. "I've been trained a different way."

"Let her go!" Taylor shouted.

"How does that feel, Ran Takeda?" Einar asked. "Is it like Tokyo again? The feeling of being crushed?"

If Taylor thought there was some glimmer of humanity in Einar, she'd been woefully mistaken. He was insane. With her telekinesis, she grabbed a sledgehammer that lay near the Loralite stone and flung it at him.

The head of the hammer struck Einar right between the shoulder blades. He yelped and fell onto his hands, his grip on Ran broken. She grabbed her ribs, gasping for air.

Taylor plucked the sledgehammer out of the air. She stood over Einar and cocked her arms back.

"It's more satisfying to hit people with things," she said. "You'll see."

She almost brought the hammer down. But then a feeling of deep sympathy came over her. Who knows what the Foundation had done to this poor kid. He wasn't bad. He didn't want to hurt her. It was all just a misunderstanding.

No. That was Einar. Manipulating her.

By the time Taylor realized that, it was too late. Einar stood and ripped the sledgehammer out of her hands. He cracked Taylor across the face with the wooden handle, knocking her down.

"Hmm," Einar said. "You're right."

He raised the hammer and brought it down on Taylor's ankle. She screamed as the bones shattered, and nearly fainted.

"That should keep you busy," Einar said. He tossed the sledgehammer across the yard, stepped by Ran and walked into the house.

Tears stung Taylor's eyes. Warm blood trickled down the side of her face from a gash on her eyebrow. Her ankle felt as if there were broken glass under her skin.

"Tay . . . Taylor . . ."

That was Ran. She struggled to sit up, clutching at a nearby rock. Patches of mud and bits of ice clung to her shoulders where she'd been driven into the ground. She arched her back strangely and craned her head back, gulping air.

Or trying to, at least.

"I . . . can't . . . breathe . . . ," Ran said.

Einar must have broken one of her ribs or crushed a lung. Taylor looked at Ran dazedly, trying to focus through the immense pain and her spinning head.

"Hold on," Taylor said, her voice cracking.

As fast as she could manage, Taylor dragged herself across the yard towards Ran. Her lips were turning blue. Taylor needed to get there. Needed to heal her. Fight through it.

Meanwhile, from inside the house, Taylor became vaguely aware of Kopano shouting.

They'd come here to save her. All her friends.

And Einar was killing them.

CHAPTER THIRTY-FIVE

KOPANO OKEKKE
HOFN, ICELAND

KOPANO STOPPED TRYING TO YANK THE MAGNE-
tized handcuff loose from the side of the refrigerator when
he saw Einar enter. A feeling of dread washed over him as
the young man trained his beady eyes on Kopano. He was
relieved to be stuck.

If Kopano couldn't move, Einar couldn't make him hurt
his friends.

Einar sized Kopano up briefly, concluded he was trapped
and ignored him. He went into the living room and pulled
an attaché case out from underneath the couch. With his
case in hand, he started to leave out the back door.

That's when Nigel bounded down the steps from upstairs.

Einar paused. He smiled slowly.

"Nigel Barnaby. You have no idea how happy I am to see you."

Nigel took a deep breath, filling his lungs with air, ready to unleash one of his sonic screams.

His mouth snapped shut, teeth clacking together hard. Einar had forced it closed with his telekinesis. Nigel's eyes were wide with surprise. Kopano could tell Nigel was struggling, but he couldn't break Einar's telepathic grip.

Kopano shoved Einar with his own telekinesis. Einar stumbled for a moment, but quickly regained his balance. A powerful telekinetic force overwhelmed his own and Kopano bounced back against the refrigerator.

"They need to teach better telekinetic control at that school of yours," Einar said.

Helplessly, Kopano watched as his index finger bent all the way back to his wrist. The bone popped. Kopano shouted in pain.

"Unbreakable skin, yes? But not unbreakable bones." Einar glared at Kopano. "Stay still or I'll rip you apart."

Fear clutched at Kopano's stomach. He held his injured hand close to his belly. His lip quivered as he watched Einar, unable to do anything else.

The anger had been bad. The fear was worse.

Einar glanced up at one of the room's cameras. "I hope you're watching," he said to whoever was on the other side. Then, he looped an arm around Nigel's shoulders.

The British boy, always so confident, possessed of so much swagger—his face crumpled into a mask of utter sadness.

His entire posture changed—shoulders slumped and turned inwards, chin to chest, eyes downcast and watery. To see his friend like this made no sense to Kopano.

"I want you to think about Pepperpont," Einar said softly. "All those years, without a single friend. Abandoned by your parents. A worthless piece of forgotten shit. Something the better-looking boys passed around like a toy, hmm? Do you remember those days, Nigel?"

Nigel shuddered, said nothing. Kopano stared. How did Einar know so much about Nigel?

"Will they hold you down in bed tonight and beat you? Will they lock you in a closet? Will they force you to take a shower with the water boiling hot?" Einar's lips were nearly against Nigel's ear. He led Nigel towards the door. "Better to end it, isn't it? Better to give up than endure another day?"

"No . . . ," Kopano croaked, the words hard to get out against the terror gripping him. He wanted to shrink back into himself, to get small . . . but he couldn't let this evil bastard get into Nigel's head. "Don't listen to him, Nigel! Don't listen!"

But Nigel didn't hear. Or, if he did, Kopano's shouts didn't penetrate the crushing depression that Einar was forcing Nigel to feel.

"It will be over quickly," Einar said. "Just walk out and let the cold take you."

He led Nigel out the front door. Kopano could hear their feet crunching across gravel.

There was an iced-over lake out there.

"Nigel!" Kopano shouted. "Ran! Someone!"

No answer. The backyard was quiet.

The fear disappeared. It turned off all at once, giving Kopano a nauseous feeling as the muscles in his abdomen unclenched. Einar must have gotten too far away from him. The effects of his control wore off.

The fear was replaced by desperation.

He had to save his friends.

With a bellow, Kopano used his telekinesis to lift the refrigerator. Food spilled out of it as the doors swung open—a glass bottle of milk shattered on the floor. Kopano crunched through the broken glass, carrying the appliance like an albatross, his wrist aching from the manacle still attached to the fridge's side.

Kopano charged across the living room. The refrigerator crashed against a chair, knocked it over. He smashed the base into a TV, shattering the screen and knocking it off the wall. Didn't matter. He maneuvered as best he could towards the front door.

He could see Nigel. Walking out on the ice. Like a zombie. Einar watched him from the edge of the lake with his arms crossed.

One second Nigel was there, the next second he was gone.

The ice cracked beneath Nigel's feet and the water sucked him down.

Kopano shouted. He tried to run through the front door, but the refrigerator became wedged in the doorway. He pulled against it, using both the strength left in his handcuffed arm and all the power he could muster from his telekinesis. The metal of the appliance squealed and bent; the wooden door chipped and broke.

But he was stuck. In the end, all Kopano's tugging did was get the refrigerator jammed worse. His wrist was a raw and bloody mess from where he'd pulled against the manacle.

Nigel had been under the water for thirty seconds.

He glanced warily around the lake's edge. Einar was gone. Out of sight.

Kopano had to get his arm free. Brute strength wasn't doing it. He tried to slip loose of the cuff, but it was fastened tight.

He pulled and pulled. The bracelet had to give. Or else, let it slice right through his arm. Take his hand right off. He could get to Nigel, save his friend, and worry about that later. Kopano snarled, bracing one of his feet against the fridge, ignoring the pain as he wrenched against the handcuff with all his might.

Kopano fell onto his back with a thud.

It gave. He was free.

His wrist was whole. The cuff was unbroken. It didn't make sense.

He didn't pause to think about it.

Nigel had been underwater for a minute. More, maybe.

Kopano sprinted towards the crystalline lake. During training, Dr. Goode had told Kopano to think of himself as heavy. That seemed to help him control his power—he often focused on that feeling, making his skin impenetrable and his hands hard as bricks. But he didn't want to be heavy now. He needed to be light. Nimble.

He hit the icy lake at a full sprint, the frigid water filling up his sneakers. The surface was already cracked where Nigel had walked on it. Kopano's long strides, his large body—he should've plummeted straight into the water.

He didn't. Somehow, Kopano's feet were light as feathers. He practically floated across the ice. Was he moving so fast that the ice didn't have a chance to break? Was it luck? Something else?

Kopano didn't care. He saw the dark and jagged hole where Nigel had fallen through. That was his goal.

He sucked in as deep a breath as he could and dove.

The water was so cold that it stunned Kopano and he nearly gasped. He steeled himself against the pinpricks and numbness, plunging deeper. He was never a strong swimmer and the water was dark. He couldn't see Nigel. He looked for bubbles but didn't see any.

Kopano needed to go deeper. He let himself get heavier, like Dr. Goode had taught him. He sunk farther down, his chest tightening.

Spinning, Kopano began to pull with his telekinesis. He didn't grab for anything in particular, he just made the water churn around him. He created a whirlpool with himself at the center.

Two minutes? Three minutes? How long had Nigel been down here? Kopano's lungs were beginning to burn.

A broken chunk of an old rowboat was pulled into

Kopano's whirlpool. A school of fish spun past him. Smooth black stones from the lakebed began to blur his vision.

There! It looked like a blond jellyfish waving back and forth, almost glowing in the dark water. Nigel's bleached mohawk.

Kopano reached down. The other boy wasn't moving, unconscious, his mouth open to the water. Kopano grabbed him by the back of the shirt.

Lighter, thought Kopano. *Be lighter. Up, up, up.*

Dragging Nigel with him, Kopano kicked his feet and sped towards the surface. He was surprised by how buoyant he was; it felt like the water itself was trying to shove him towards the surface.

A sheet of ice became visible above him. Kopano's heart beat harder, his lungs screaming for air. As a boy, he'd read adventure stories about a young man traveling the globe; always, when he was in cold climes, someone ended up trapped beneath some ice. His stinging eyes couldn't find the break in the ice that he'd jumped through.

Kopano reached out towards the ice with his free hand— his injured hand, the broken finger hanging loose, forgotten about in his rush to rescue Nigel. He prepared to thrust out with his telekinesis, ready to break the ice apart.

He didn't need to. Kopano's hand passed right through the ice, like he was a ghost. His eyes widened, uncertain what was happening. His whole body floated upwards, transparent, sliding through the frozen barrier. He could feel something happening within him—an opening sensation, like his body's cells were spreading apart to allow the ice to pass through. He glanced down and saw that Nigel had gone transparent too.

And then Kopano stood atop the ice again, his feet feeling light on the fragile surface. His Legacy—he'd unlocked something, figured something out in his desperation.

Kopano didn't have time to relish the milestone. Nigel wasn't breathing. His face was blue, his body limp and freezing.

Gulping in air, Kopano gathered the British boy in his arms and ran towards the shore.

"Kopano!"

The Nigerian let out a groan of relief when he saw Taylor and Ran running towards him from the house. Neither of them looked well—Ran's clothes were dark with fresh blood, Taylor was hobbling and bleeding from a head wound—but they were alive. They were alive and they would know what to do about Nigel.

Kopano set Nigel down on the rocky shore of the lake. His clothes were cold and heavy on his thick frame and he felt suddenly, unbearably heavy.

"He's—he's not breathing!" Kopano said. "That bastard made him . . . made him . . ."

Kopano couldn't bring himself to finish. He looked around wildly for Einar, his fists clenched.

Taylor went to her knees next to Nigel, immediately pressing her hands to his narrow chest. Ran caught Kopano's crazed look and put a weak hand on his arm.

"Einar's gone," she said. "He teleported away with Rabiya while Taylor was healing me."

Ran looked shaken and rough. She crouched next to Nigel and held his hand, rubbing it between her own. Kopano leaned in over her shoulder, staring between Nigel and Taylor.

"Can you . . . ?" He tried to catch his breath. "Can you heal him?"

Taylor didn't respond. She was concentrating on Nigel. There were dark bags forming under her eyes, her skin pale. She'd been overtaxed in the short time since her kidnapping. Kopano wondered how much healing she could manage.

A bubble formed on Nigel's lips. The water he'd swallowed slowly trickled out of his mouth, pushed out of his lungs by Taylor's healing Legacy. Kopano let out a sigh of relief.

But Taylor didn't look happy. She put her ear against Nigel's chest.

"He's not breathing," she said, her voice cracking. "His heart's not . . . I don't know how to heal this. It's not wounded, it's just . . . stopped."

Tears streaked down Taylor's cheeks. Nigel was still, no color returning to his cheeks.

"Step back," said Ran.

Taylor did as she was told. She stumbled to Kopano and he instinctively wrapped his arms around her, grateful for the warmth of her small body in his arms. His teeth were chattering.

"I didn't get to him quickly enough," Kopano said quietly.

"It's not your fault," Taylor replied.

Ran touched Nigel's cold cheek. Her shoulders shook. She bowed her head for a moment, whispering a prayer.

Then, she ripped open Nigel's shirt.

"Ran—?" Taylor said, startled.

Ran put her hand on Nigel's chest. She charged his sternum with her Legacy. He glowed. His body vibrated.

"Ran!" Taylor yelled, alarmed. "What are you doing?"

"Waking up . . . his body," Ran replied, her eyes flashing with energy. "Making . . . breakfast."

Kopano took a step back, bringing Taylor with him. Nigel's body pulsed with crimson energy. Kopano could see where Ran's energy surged out of Nigel's pores, out of his nostrils, his eyes.

And then, she pulled it all back into herself.

The force of yanking that much energy out of Nigel blew Ran backwards. Acting quickly, Kopano caught her with his telekinesis.

Nigel's whole body convulsed with the concussive force, bouncing against the rocks.

And then he screamed.

Coughing raggedly and holding his chest, Nigel rolled onto his side. Taylor clapped a hand over her mouth and Kopano let loose with a cheer. Color slowly blossomed in Nigel's cheeks. He shuddered, peering around at his friends with bleary eyes.

Ran grabbed him in a hug, squeezing him close. Her hands and forearms were already dark purple with bruises from where she'd pulled back the energy, but the pain didn't seem to bother her.

"I found a nonviolent use for my Legacy," she said.

"Fuckin' hell, Ran," Nigel said. "Tell me about it later, yeah?"

Then, he fainted.

CHAPTER THIRTY-SIX

FROM ICELAND, THEY TELEPORTED BACK TO NEW Mexico, where Isabela, Caleb and Professor Nine were still waiting. There was a lot of commotion over the amount of blood on their clothes, but Taylor had healed most of their injuries. She'd done a bad job mending her own broken ankle—had put only enough healing energy into the shattered bones to allow her to walk on it—so she needed to lean on Kopano for support.

He didn't mind.

They brought Freyja with them. Strangely, they found that the choker had simply fallen off her neck. The little girl claimed it "just happened." Taylor wondered what that meant. It seemed as if the Foundation had let them off the hook.

Freyja was turned over to the UN Peacekeepers. She'd have a long flight home, but they would reunite her with her family. She thanked Taylor and Nigel before the Peacekeepers took her away, but Taylor was disappointed to see fear in her eyes. The child was afraid of Garde. It was hard to blame her; the girl had seen firsthand what the worst of their kind could do.

Kopano offered to teleport the Peacekeepers and Earth Garde back to Iceland so they could apprehend the mercenaries and investigate Einar's house. It took them thirty minutes to get clearance for such an operation, but eventually they took him up on the offer.

But when they were ready, Kopano found he was unable. The Loralite stone in Einar's backyard was gone. Someone must have smashed it.

The six of them returned to the Academy. They were allowed two days of rest and recovery. Then, the punishment kicked in. They were assigned training sessions at dawn five days a week, immediately followed with a shift serving breakfast in the dining hall, not to mention weekly sessions with Dr. Linda to deal with any psychological fallout.

Rumors about the six of them swirled around campus. They didn't talk about their adventure. Even Isabela refrained from bragging.

People started calling them the Fugitive Six.

As the weeks went by and things ostensibly returned to normal, the six of them had a hard time hanging out with other students around the Academy. The others—they hadn't seen what was out there. They hadn't really fought yet. They had Legacies, but they weren't yet Garde.

After one of their early-morning training sessions on Nine's brutal obstacle course, Caleb turned to the others as he toweled off.

"Do you guys ever get the feeling that this isn't exactly punishment?" he asked.

"No," Isabela groaned, rubbing her sore neck. "It is worse than punishment. It's torture."

"No, I mean . . ." Caleb shrugged. "I don't know. These team workouts, it's like . . ."

"We are being groomed," Ran said.

They all looked up at the catwalk that crossed over the training center.

Nine watched them from above.

✧ ✧ ✧

She might have hated the arduous physical training, but Isabela threw herself into her studies like never before. One subject in particular interested her. Almost every night, she would knock on Taylor or Ran's door.

"Flash cards?" Isabela would ask with a nervous smile.

They practiced her English for hours every night. Soon, she wouldn't need Simon's Legacy at all.

✧ ✧ ✧

"Can I show you something?" Caleb asked Nigel, about a month after they'd returned from Iceland.

"That question makes me nervous, mate," Nigel replied

with a smirk. "What is it?"

"It's upstairs."

Nigel followed Caleb up three floors to one of the unoc-cupied sections of the dorms. Technically, they weren't allowed up here, but even with the stricter security proto-cols that had been implemented since their little excursion, the dorms remained largely a free-for-all. The abandoned floors were a popular hookup spot if you had a prudish roommate.

"Caleb, man, you're a good lad and all, but I don't feel that way about you."

"What? No!" Caleb glanced over his shoulder at Nigel and blushed. "I'm not—I mean—it's okay that you are but I'm—um . . ."

"Relax, mate. I'm messing with you."

"I know," Caleb said, relaxing.

He stopped in front of a door at the end of the hall. Nigel noticed soundproofing pads had been stapled to the surface.

"Ready?" Caleb asked.

"I'm not sure that I am, brother."

Caleb swung the door open.

Inside was a garage band setup that warmed Nigel's heart. A five-piece drum kit, a bass guitar, a banged-up elec-tric guitar and a keyboard. Each of the instruments and the soundboard that managed the volume were manned by one of Caleb's clones.

"Seriously?" Nigel said. "Clone band?"

"Hardly anyone ever uses the music room, so I liberated

some stuff and brought it here," Caleb explained. "It's our practice space."

"You can play all these instruments?"

Caleb shrugged. "I mean, not well. But we're learning. It helps that I can have each clone practice on their own."

Nigel raised an eyebrow at that. "Seriously?"

"Yeah." He walked farther into the room and grabbed the microphone stand. He tilted it in Nigel's direction. "Thing is, we need a front man."

Nigel grinned.

"I'm afraid we've been going about your training all wrong," Dr. Goode told Kopano apologetically. He had the Nigerian young man hooked up to an array of machines that produced a variety of readings, all of them gibberish to Kopano.

"I don't know," Kopano said cheerily. "I think you've been doing a solid job."

Dr. Goode smiled. "Yes, well, you see, we believed your Legacy was a variation of Fortem that was tied to your skin. That you were somehow creating an impenetrable subdermal layer."

"But I'm not," Kopano replied. "Right?"

"No, it's much more amazing than that," Dr. Goode said. "Your Legacy is in your every cell, Kopano. In the atoms, in fact, that make up your cells. To put it simply, based on my preliminary findings, you can separate or contract your cells on a subatomic level. You can alter your density. You can become very heavy and hard or weightless to the point of transparency. Now, it's just a matter of learning how to control it."

Kopano looked down at his hands. "I haven't been able to do what I did since . . . since the ice."

"Oh, we're going to change that, big boy," Professor Nine said, striding into the room. In front of him, he floated a cube wrapped completely in barbed wire. He let the strange object bob in the air before Kopano.

"What's this?" Kopano asked.

"That's a box with a cupcake inside it," Nine said. "I wrapped it in razor wire. You want the cupcake, you gotta reach through the razors and into the box. Break apart your atoms and feast on deliciousness. Or slice your hand up. Come on. Try it."

Kopano eyed the box warily. "What kind of cupcake?"

It took Kopano weeks to finally master Nine's game with the barbed-wire box. When he finally did, he wrote home to his parents, describing the function of his Legacy.

He had yet to hear back.

✧ ✧ ✧

They weren't supposed to talk about what happened in New Mexico and Iceland, but that didn't extend to their weekly therapy sessions with Dr. Linda.

"Do you have those feelings often, Nigel?" Dr. Linda asked in her usual lilting way, Nigel spread out on the couch across from her. "The feelings that you felt when you walked out on the ice?"

"No."

"Are you being truthful?"

Nigel's lips curled. He scratched the back of his neck.

"Maybe I used to feel like that sometimes. Like a hopeless bloody case. But I haven't had that darkness in my life for a while. Not since I came here." His look turned dark as he thought about what happened in Iceland. "It was that wanker, the one I told you about. He put those feelings in me."

"I'd very much like to meet that young man," Dr. Linda replied. "His Legacy . . . it's quite interesting."

"Yeah. Quite," Nigel said dryly. "I'd like to see him again, too. Get some things off my chest."

"Now, Nigel, these thoughts of vengeance aren't healthy."

Nigel grinned crookedly. "I feel just fine, Doc. But you're right. They ain't healthy. For him."

"It's very unlikely you will ever get to act on these revenge fantasies," Dr. Linda said. "If you let them fester inside you . . ."

Nigel didn't reply. His cavalier smile gave nothing away.

But there was something Dr. Linda didn't know.

Dr. Goode and Nine had personally driven their wayward students back from New Mexico to the Academy. They were all exhausted and injured, traumatized to varying degrees, but Taylor remembered how happy they were to be together. How close she felt to them all.

She told them everything. Einar, Iceland, the Foundation, Jiao, the sheikh, the healers, the strange British woman. Everything.

When she was done, Nine and Malcolm exchanged a look. Dr. Goode pulled over the car. Nine turned around to address his students. Behind them, the sun was just starting to rise.

"Listen, this might sound weird, but I think it's best if you keep most of the details of what happened between us," he said.

Taylor's brow had furrowed. "What? Why?"

"We think there are people within the Academy . . ." Dr. Goode hesitated. "We believe we've been compromised."

"A mole," Nigel said quietly.

"Like a spy movie," Kopano added.

"We've known about these Foundation assholes for a while, but we haven't had a name for them," Nine continued. "We just know that they're constantly trying to hack our system." Nine exchanged a look with Malcolm. "But we've got some brainy computer people of our own. We've been able to head them off, most of the time . . ."

"They knew things about me," Nigel said. "Things they shouldn't have known."

"Me too," Ran said.

Malcolm nodded. "Indeed. With their efforts to access our systems blocked, we think they've resulted to planting agents. Perhaps faculty. Perhaps students."

"Falta muito para chegar?" Isabela asked in Portuguese, looking around confusedly, not understanding the discussion.

"We're going to root these people out," Nine said evenly,

looking at each one of them in turn. "We're going to expose them. And you can help us."

"How?" Caleb asked.

"To start with, by keeping your mouths shut," Nine said.

Taylor thought about that conversation often in the weeks after their return to the Academy. She thought about all the things that she'd seen since becoming a Garde. The kindness and heroism of her friends; the ugliness of the Harvesters; the cruelty of the Foundation. The other Garde, both here at the Academy and spread around the world, all of them with desires and agendas, with the potential to shape the future.

When she first got her powers, she'd wanted to hide them. But now, Taylor knew that wasn't an option. She couldn't settle for a boring life. She needed to be here. She needed to be where she could make a difference.

A package arrived for her, filled with letters from the students at her old school. At least the ones who didn't think she was a freak. They were sweet—wishing her well, asking for details and gossip, wondering what John Smith was like in person. Taylor read each one of them, even if she felt like she didn't know these people anymore and, more important, like they couldn't possibly know her.

Slipped in among the letters from high schoolers was a piece of expensive stationery, thick and cream-colored, covered in a delicate cursive. Immediately, Taylor knew this letter didn't belong with the others.

Dear Taylor,

I hope this letter finds you well. Thank you for your assistance in Abu Dhabi and Iceland. I am truly sorry for the unpleasantness that transpired with your host. I fear that his bad example has created a poor impression for our organization. I hope, in the future, you will give us a second chance.

The world is a better place for your efforts. The prince sends his fond regards. A number of sizable donations have been made in your name to a variety of low-income hospitals in the region. By saving one life, you have saved thousands more.

I look forward to working with you again in the future, should you desire such an opportunity.

Sincerely yours,
B
The Foundation

The British woman she'd caught a glimpse of on Einar's screen. It had to be.

Taylor's teeth clenched. She nearly crumpled the letter in her hands.

Then, she marched straight to Professor Nine's office. He stood at his window, gazing out at the students walking from the dorms to the student center. Taylor tossed the letter onto his desk.

"They want me back," she said. The hardness and resolve Taylor heard in her own voice surprised her.

Nine picked up the letter, scanning it quickly.

"They've got moles here," Taylor said. "Maybe we should get some there."